Rosie Fiore was born and raised in Johannesburg, South Africa, and has worked as a writer for theatre, television, magazines, advertising, comedy and the corporate market. She lives in north London with her husband and two children.

D1140048

Also by Rosie Fiore

Babies in Waiting

Wonder Women

Rosie Fiore

Quercus

For Tom.

First published in Great Britain in 2013 by

Quercus
55 Baker Street
7th Floor, South Block
London W1U 8EW

Copyright © 2013 Rosie Fiore

The moral right of Rosie Fiore to be
identified as the author of this work has been
asserted in accordance with the Copyright,
Designs and Patents Act, 1988.

All rights reserved. No part of this publication
may be reproduced or transmitted in any form
or by any means, electronic or mechanical,
including photocopy, recording, or any
information storage and retrieval system,
without permission in writing from the publisher.

A CIP catalogue record for this book is available
from the British Library

PB ISBN 978 0 85738 960 2
ISBN 978 0 85738 961 9 (EBOOK)

This book is a work of fiction. Names, characters,
businesses, organizations, places and events are
either the product of the authors' imagination
or are used fictitiously. Any resemblance to
actual persons, living or dead, events or
locales is entirely coincidental.

10 9 8 7 6 5 4 3 2 1

Printed and bound in Great Britain by Clays Ltd, St Ives plc

Typeset by Ellipsis Books Limited, Glasgow

PART ONE

1

JO AND LEE NOW

In the darkest hours, at around 2 a.m., the idea came to Jo in a dream. She had often had dream ideas that woke her with their brilliance, but inevitably, in the cold light of the morning, they were both insane and unworkable. But this . . . this was different. She lay awake for hours thinking about it, and whether it could work. She wanted to get up to write it all down, but Lee was sleeping peacefully beside her, his hand in the curve of her waist, and she didn't want to disturb him. Eventually, as the sky turned grey outside, she fell deeply asleep again.

In the morning, she was distracted and clumsy. Her toast popped and was too pale so she pushed it in again and forgot about it until the smoke detector went off. Zach came in and asked for help with his jumper and she absent-mindedly handed him a dish towel. Then, as she reached up to put the battery back in the alarm once the kitchen was cleared of smoke, she knocked over the warm milk for Imogene's cereal. Lee came into the kitchen buttoning his cuffs to find her cursing and using Zach's jumper to mop up, while Zach kneeled on a chair, feeding jelly beans to

Imogene, who was smearing yoghurt across the tray of her high chair and in Zach's hair.

Lee scooped Zach up under one arm while he grabbed a handful of baby wipes and cursorily rubbed the worst of the mess off both children and the high chair. He handed Zach a bagel to chew on while he warmed more milk and made Imogene's cereal. He fed her with one hand while he switched on the kettle and flung teabags into mugs. By the time Jo had cleaned up the milk and tossed the jumper and sundry dish towels into the machine, he had a cup of tea ready for her and a fresh piece of buttered toast. Neither of them had spoken a word. Jo dropped a kiss on the top of his head and thanked the Lord, not for the first time, that Lee was as even-tempered as he was.

'Bad night?' he asked.

'Not really, just a weird dream. No, not weird exactly. Possibly a brilliant dream.'

'Was it the one with Hugh Jackman paragliding in through the bathroom window again?'

'Sadly not. No . . . I had a dream about a shop.'

'A shop where you could buy Hugh Jackman dipped in chocolate and rolled in diamonds?'

'No, a clothes shop. A clothes shop for kids. I dreamed I was out shopping with Zach. You know what it's like, trying to hang on to his hand and push the pushchair at the same time.'

Lee nodded. Zach hated shopping and never stopped looking for opportunities to escape. They'd been barred from several shops in their area because of his scorched-earth policy where clothing racks were concerned.

Jo continued. 'Anyway, he was screaming and wriggling

and trying to get his hand free, and then he made a dash for it – but he was flummoxed, because in this shop all the clothes rails were at adult head-height, and from the waist down, it was a kids' soft-play area, with things to climb and rock on, and big puzzles built into the walls with pieces that he could spin and bash. But nothing he could break.'

Again Lee said nothing. She wasn't sure if he'd really got it. 'So I could look at the kids' clothes in peace – stuff for him and Imogene, and he could play at my feet without destroying anything. Imi was happy because there was stuff for her to look at . . .' Lee had his preoccupied frown on now. She was sure he had stopped listening to her and was thinking about work. She finished triumphantly – 'And the best bit was that he couldn't get out because the door was guarded by a seven-foot bouncer with a walkie-talkie and a pit bull.'

'That's ridiculous.' Lee smiled. 'It couldn't be a pit bull. They're banned as dangerous dogs. A Rottweiler or a Dobermann, maybe.'

'Okay, so maybe that last bit isn't entirely practical,' Jo said insistently. 'But the idea of a kids' clothes shop that's fun for kids, child-proof and stress-free for mums, well, that's bloody genius, isn't it?'

Lee nodded but didn't answer. He shovelled the last mouthful of gloop into Imogene. Then he glanced at his watch, rinsed his hands at the sink, grabbed an apple from the fruit bowl, kissed Jo and the kids and left. As she launched into the morning flurry of teeth brushing, filling Zach's book bag, wrestling Imogene into her coat and strapping her into the pushchair, Jo realised with disappointment that Lee hadn't actually responded to the idea at all. Maybe it was just a silly, irrational dream.

But later, once Zach was at nursery and Imogene had gone down for her nap, she found herself sitting at the computer and writing notes. It would obviously have to meet all kinds of safety standards, and it shouldn't be one of those chi-chi children's boutiques that mums like her would never walk into, where a miniature leather jacket costs more than a pair of adult winter boots. The stuff would have to be cool, hard-wearing, different, but affordable. Come to think of it, she would quite like to redress the imbalance most shops had between boys' and girls' clothing. There always seemed to be heaps of cute and funky outfits for girls, but toddler boy clothing came in blue, stripes, cartoon characters/monsters or was of the tiresome 'I'm a cheeky monkey'-slogan variety. So maybe it would be a shop for boys, or mainly boys. Sorry, Imogene. Her wardrobe was way better than Jo's anyway. She realised her thinking had somehow passed from 'should be' to 'would be', as if the shop was in some way a reality.

She spent some time trawling the Net for websites for children's boutiques, looking for pictures of their interiors, and then ran a search for children's clothing shops within the immediate area. Without planning to, she started shaping the rough notes she was making into a formal proposal. By the time Imogene woke up, she had a three-page document, complete with web links and images. She had no idea who she would ever show it to, but now she knew for certain that there was something there.

That afternoon, she took the kids to the park. She put

Imogene into one of the baby swings and stood beside her, gently rocking her to and fro while Zach ran through his standard playground routine . . . swinging from the monkey bars, then climbing up the slide and down the stairs, finding a stick to drag along the railings, then climbing on to the little metal rocking horse and singing 'Horsey, horsey' at the top of his voice as he flung himself back and forth. He always did the same things in the same order. Jo knew that within a few minutes he'd come over and demand to go for a walk to the kiosk to get an ice lolly. It didn't matter how cold the weather was, he always wanted one. Then they'd walk a slow circuit of the park, with Imogene chewing on a biscuit in the pushchair while Zach skipped ahead or dawdled behind, keeping up an endless rambling mono-logue, usually an extended fantasy about one or other cartoon character smashing something. Jo sighed as she swung Imogene. It wasn't that she didn't love spending the time with the kids . . . and who wouldn't love being in the park on a sunshiny spring day? It was just, a little variety would be nice, a little . . . oh dear God. Here comes that woman.

Jo didn't know the woman's name. She should know it, because her daughter was at nursery with Zach and they had been introduced by the mother of one of Zach's friends at the beginning of the school year, but Jo had promptly forgotten it, and now it was way too late to ask. She often saw the woman in the park with her little girl and a fat, bald baby who was a month or so younger than Imogene. The woman always came over and talked and talked at her in a breathy voice about child development and baby-led weaning and babywearing and sleep training, and never, ever about any topic that was not directly linked to child-rearing in some way. Once or twice Jo had mentioned a current news story or ventured a comment about a book she'd read or a film, only to be met with a blank stare.

'Hiya!' said the woman, her face shining as she barrelled over. 'How ARE you?' Without waiting for an answer, she launched straight into an account of the nit outbreak at the nursery, and her views on which children had brought the lice in. Then the woman started telling her how she'd spent hours combing conditioner through her daughter's hair and how the nit shampoos didn't work any more because the creatures had mutated, and Jo had to fight an almost irresistible urge to scratch her head all over. She wanted to kiss Zach when he came running over to say he wanted his ice lolly now.

At the kiosk, she treated Zach to a choc-ice and got one herself. They strolled around the park, and Zach hopped on and off the little retaining wall along the flower beds, holding on to Jo's shoulder as she pushed the pushchair alongside him.

'Zachy,' she said, 'you know when we go to buy clothes for you?'

'Yucky. I don't need clothes. Are we going today? Let's not.'

'Why not?'

'It's boring. And you always say, "Don't touch!" and then I have to try on horrible scratchy new things and not get them dirty.'

'What if—'

'And then you want to go and get a coffee and Imogene and me have to sit all still and be good.'

'You get cake though.'

'I like the cake part. But not the shopping. Yuck.'

'What if shopping was fun?'

'How could it be fun?'

She explained her ideas for the shop to him.

'So I could play and jump around and not get into trouble?'

'Exactly.'

'What would it look like?'

'Not sure yet. What do you think would be cool?'

'Tigers,' said Zach firmly. 'It needs tigers. And a giant Tyrannosaurus-rex. And vines to swing on, like Tarzan.'

'That does sound cool,' said Jo, laughing, and wishing she had a pen to write this all down. 'Sounds like a jungle.'

'It would be,' said Zach. 'Just like a jungle, but in town. Jungle town.'

Jungle town, thought Jo. Jungletown. Yes. She wanted to hug Zach and kiss him for his brilliance, but he had got bored of the conversation and had run off to hit a tree with a stick.

That evening, after the kids were in bed, she sat at the kitchen counter with a glass of wine as Lee concocted his famous chilli, the only dish he knew how to cook. 'I've been thinking about my shop idea all day,' she said. Lee frowned and nodded as he scooped up a big spoonful of cocoa to add to the bubbling saucepan. It was one of the secret ingredients that he said made all the difference to the bottled sauce mixture. Jo took a sip of her wine. He clearly wasn't going to say anything, so she told him about her conversation with Zach, and Zach's 'Jungletown' comment. Lee laughed at that, but still didn't pick up her conversational ball. She took an even bigger sip of wine. She was starting to feel quite narked at him.

'So you think it's a stupid idea?' she said persistently. 'I mean, I know I don't know the first thing about owning or running a shop or the fashion business, but I do still think that there's something there.'

'Are you serious about it?' Lee asked. 'I mean, would you actually think about starting it? Really?' He looked up at her, and to Jo his expression seemed full of scepticism and doubt.

'Jesus!' Jo exploded. 'Could you be any more unsupportive? I might have been at home with the kids for a few years, but I'm not a moron. I've got PR and marketing experience; I know how to research, to network . . . Why couldn't I do it? Bloody hell, Lee, of all the people in the world I thought would back me up . . .' She felt tears prick behind her eyes, and she grabbed her glass and stalked out of the kitchen.

She flung open the French windows and flopped down on the bench on the patio. There was a cold breeze. The spring days might be warmer but the nights were still cool, and she wished she'd grabbed a jumper before she'd stropped off out. Still, nothing would convince her to go back inside. She'd have to stupefy herself with wine and ignore the cold. But as she sat there, she became uncomfortably aware that the bench was slightly damp as well. And her wine glass was empty. And the chilli was nearly ready and she was very hungry. Maybe she'd go in, ignore Lee in a frosty manner, fetch a jumper and a fresh glass of wine and a cushion before bringing her chilli out to the patio. She knew she was being irrational, and she couldn't quite pinpoint why she was so angry. She and Lee seldom argued, and she wasn't sure why this idea mattered enough to her to have picked a fight about it.

She walked back into the living room, and found Lee sitting at the dining table. He had his markers out and the table was covered in large sheets of cartridge paper. He was obviously using the time while the chilli cooked to do some work. Typical. She stomped into the kitchen to refill her wine glass and sneak a taste of the chilli. Her cardigan was draped over the back of the chair Lee was sitting in. She couldn't get at it without talking to him and asking him to move. Sod it. She'd go upstairs and get another jumper. She crossed behind him, and was about to head for the stairs when he said, 'Right. Now you can see.'

'See what?' she said grudgingly. He shuffled the pages on the table and laid them out in a rough order. The first one looked like an architect's drawing for an empty space . . . a gallery maybe, or some kind of shop. The next had rails and display racks sketched in, and a brightly coloured jungle design around the lower half of the walls. The third and fourth were full of vibrant colour, with rocking horses (or rocking giraffes, Jo noted) on the floor, along with big soft toy snakes, toucans and other exotic animals. The rails were crammed with brightly coloured children's clothes. The last drawing showed the exterior of the shop, with a big glass window. Lee's ink had barely dried on this one. He had just added the name of the shop in funky curly script: 'Jungletown'.

2

JO AND LEE THEN

Jo first saw Lee at a party at university. She was a few weeks into her first year at Goldsmith's, and her roommate in halls, Helen, had brought her to this party in a dingy student house a little way from the campus. Other than Helen, she didn't know anybody to speak to, but the room was full of familiar faces: other students from the arts courses that she'd seen in the corridors and social areas, some she recognised from lectures. She got herself a beer from the kitchen and looked around for Helen, but Helen's principal interest in attending the party was a guy called Frank who was rumoured to have a limitless supply of recreational pharmaceuticals. She had disappeared into a bathroom with him within minutes of their arrival. Jo knew she was unlikely to see her again, or if she did, Helen would be in no fit state for conversation. She didn't mind; the party was mainly filled with second- and third-years and she was keen to meet some of the older students and get to know more about the campus and the course. Somehow, however, she ended up wedged in a corner trying to make halting conversation with two geeky girls from the music course. Jo had seen them perform during

Freshers' Week and knew one was a harpist and the other a pianist. They both looked terrified, as if they had spent so much time in the practice room that a party was an alien landscape. One of them, the pianist, was clutching a four-pack and was gulping down the beers one by one with grim determination, as if they were medicine.

'I'm Harriet, and this is Amelia. We're not usually big party animals,' she said, rather unnecessarily, and then giggled. 'We're here because Amelia's got the hots for Renaissance Man and we've been stalking him across town.'

'Ah, of course,' said Jo knowingly, as if she knew who they meant. Renaissance Man? Who could that be? A lecturer in the arts department who specialised in da Vinci? A superhero she'd never heard of, who buzzed about in a cape dispensing a Golden Age of Enlightenment?

'Do you know him?' said Amelia, the light of fanaticism in her eye.

'Well, I don't *know* him exactly,' said Jo, desperately playing for time, 'but his work, well . . . it precedes him, doesn't it?'

'What exactly do you mean?' said Amelia, standing too close and staring searchingly into Jo's face through her thick glasses. 'You've slept with him, haven't you?'

'Oh no, I . . . er . . . I . . .' Jo found herself wishing that she hadn't ended up with the musical fruitcakes, or that at the very least she'd led with, 'I loved your rendition of the "Trout" Quintet.'

At that moment, music started to blare, and Amelia swung her speccy gaze desperately towards the door. 'That's him!' she said excitedly. She pushed past them and ran towards the living room. Harriet and Jo followed rather more slowly, and by the time they got there the dance floor was so packed they couldn't even get into the room. They edged around the door frame and stood pressed up against the wall. It took a while for Jo to spot Amelia, who was dancing wildly just in front of the table where the music was coming from. For a highly competent musician, she didn't seem to have much rhythm or coordination.

Jo leaned over to yell in Harriet's ear. 'So, this Renaissance Man . . . ?' she asked.

'DJ'ing.' Harriet yelled back. 'Everyone is desperate to get him to do the music for their parties.'

The crowd parted for a second, and Jo caught a glimpse of a tall, gangly, mixed-race guy with a great cloud of hair, pressing his headphones to the side of his head as he deftly flipped a disc off one deck and replaced it with another, using just one hand. Renaissance Man? He looked more Lenny Kravitz than Shakespeare, but who was she to judge? He definitely knew how to keep a party going though. He played banging tune after banging tune, mixing dance tracks with eighties cheese and then raising the tempo with some great rock classics. Jo wasn't much of a dancer, but she found herself on the floor jumping around with Harriet and Amelia, until they were all sweaty and red-faced. After about an hour, Renaissance Man took a break and someone took over whose taste ran to thrash metal played at full volume. The dance floor emptied like a stampede, and Jo and the others headed for the kitchen to grab a drink.

She was standing by the open door, holding her hair off her neck and drinking a beer while Amelia chattered on about Renaissance Man and his brilliance, when she saw him come into the kitchen and fight his way through the crowd, straight towards them. Amelia saw Jo staring and turned to see what she was looking at. She went red, then white, whipped off her glasses and tried in vain to fix her hair. Jo was sure Renaissance Man was just heading for the door to get some air, but he stopped and said to her, 'Do you sing?'

'What?' Jo said stupidly.

'Do you sing?' he said impatiently. 'I know you're not a music student, but do you sing?' She opened her mouth to answer him but then she felt a claw-like grip on her arm.

'I can't *believe* you know him and you didn't say,' hissed Amelia venomously, her breath hot on Jo's ear.

'I don't!' she said involuntarily.

'Oh,' said Renaissance Man. 'Pity.' He began to turn away.

'No!' said Jo sharply. 'I mean, I do sing. But I don't know you. Him.' She turned to Amelia to offer clarification, but Amelia had turned away, her jaw set and her arms folded. Well, there was nothing Jo could do to rescue that particular situation. She turned back to Renaissance Man and smiled. 'I sing, insofar as I was in a choir and can read music and sing in tune. I'm not trained or anything.'

'Perfect,' he said.

'Why?'

'I'm doing a performance art project. You look right. If you could sing, it would be perfect. Can we meet at the Union for lunch on Monday to talk about it? Say . . . one?'

'Um, okay,' said Jo uncertainly. He gave her a big grin and walked off.

She turned to Amelia. 'See? I don't know him. I've never spoken to him in my life before. And I don't fancy him. It's a work thing, okay?'

'Oh, you don't fancy him?' said Amelia, her eyes filled with tears. 'What are you? Blind? Or gay?'

'Neither! He's just not my type. Honest.'

But Amelia was not to be appeased. Any possibility of a friendship between her and Jo died right there, in a grubby kitchen in New Cross. Luckily Amelia soon got over her entirely unrequited passion for Renaissance Man, when she met and fell in love with a conducting student called Henry, who enthusiastically reciprocated her feelings. She performed outstandingly in her studies and went on to win loads of prestigious music competitions and have a highly successful international career. Jo never spoke to her again after that night, but whenever she caught a glimpse on television of Amelia's long white hands stroking the strings of her harp, she was reminded of the awfulness of their one encounter.

On the Monday, she got to the Union early as she had no class just before lunch. She sat at a table organising her lecture notes and wondering whether Renaissance Man would show up at all. She felt ridiculous sitting there, and she was increasingly certain that he wasn't coming, when he flopped down in the chair opposite her and handed her a sticky bun in a paper bag. It was in that moment that she realised she didn't know his name.

He seemed to sense her discomfort, and held out his hand formally. 'Lee Hockley,' he said.

'Jo. Jo Morris. So what's this performance-art project?'

'Well, I saw you dancing at the party on Saturday, and I thought you looked American.'

'American? I'm from Stevenage.'

'Yeah, well, you look like one of those corn-fed American girls who roam the prairies.'

'Roam the prairies! What? And corn-fed? Do you mean I'm fat? Or yellow?'

Jo's sole experience of anything corn-fed was the suspiciously saffron-coloured and overpriced chickens in the supermarket.

'It's a figure of speech,' Lee said impatiently. 'Anyway, you're a drama student, right? You can do an American accent.'

'Sure can!' said Jo, in her best peppy, ponytail-swinging *Grease* imitation. Lee looked dubious.

'We can work on that. The point is, I've worked out that you can sing pretty much any Emily Dickinson poem to "The Yellow Rose of Texas".' Helpfully he hummed a few bars. Jo continued to stare at him, flabbergasted into silence. In a raspy tenor voice with a Southern twang, he sang:

'A door just opened on a street –
I, lost, was passing by –
An instant's width of warmth disclosed
And wealth, and company.'

He nodded as if everything now made perfect sense.

After a moment, Jo found her voice. 'So – Emily Dickinson, famous, reclusive, morbid poet, and you're going to set her poems to some little country and western ditty? Doesn't that trivialise her work completely?'

'Except that it isn't a little country and western ditty! It's a song with a rich history, the story of a mulatto woman who helped win the battle of San Jacinto, the decisive battle in the Texas Revolution!'

'Okay . . .' said Jo hesitantly. But Lee was on a roll.

'It says something profound about American history, about our expectations of women and people of colour, about our European reading of what looks like a trivialisation of culture.' He was clearly happy to go on about it pretty much ad infinitum so Jo jumped in to try to understand what exactly he expected from her.

'So I sing Emily Dickinson poems to "The Yellow Rose of Texas" . . . ?'

'While I draw interpretations of political cartoons from the time,' he said, as if that was self-evident.

'And we do this – where?'

'In the quadrangle. I've got permission from the college. I've found two music students – one who plays steel-string guitar and one who can play a snare drum. It'll be awesome!' He continued to enthuse about the project and describe how they would incorporate the singing with his real-time drawing. Jo stared at him. He was okay-looking, she supposed, a little skinny and tall, and his huge cloud of hair made her want to laugh. As she'd assured Amelia, not her type, but his crazy, creative grasshopper brain was so exciting, she knew she wanted to get to know him a lot better.

The Emily Dickinson project was met with mass indifference by the student body and the staff of the university. Jo wore a red-checked gingham dress and sang her heart out, accompanied by the musicians, while Lee, his mad hair bobbing, drew furiously in charcoal on big sheets of paper spread on the ground. People strolling past mostly ignored them, or glanced at the pictures and shrugged. A few of the music students stood listening to Jo sing for a moment, then sniffed as if she smelled bad before walking away. But Lee was completely undeterred.

Later, in the pub, he enthused about the 'slow drip-drip of impinging on people's consciousness', and how their next project would move things on another tiny step. Jo didn't understand everything he said, but she guessed what he was getting at was that people were affected and changed by what they had seen, even if they didn't know it. She didn't really believe it, but she was willing to go along with it and be involved in whatever came next. Lee was a nice guy. And besides that, she was developing a serious crush on Adrian, the guy who played the guitar. He was shortish, muscular and moody with unruly blond hair, pronounced cheekbones and a long sweep of dark eyelashes that made Jo, a little tipsy after two pints of cider, want to kiss him and feel them flutter against her face.

It was a Friday night and the cider was cheap and plentiful, so it was no big surprise that Jo found herself in Adrian's bed that night, and for a lot of nights after that. It wasn't every night though – Adrian was fanatical about his 'space'. It took Jo until halfway through her second year to work out that the space he reserved away from her was regularly shared with at least three other women. At around the same time, Lee started going out with a petite dancer called Jean, who spelled her name Jeanne and annoyed Jo with her sulky demeanour and utter refusal to eat or talk to anyone who wasn't Lee. After Adrian, Jo dated a drummer called Pete (it took her a few goes to get over her musician phase) and after Jeanne moved to Paris, Lee decided to embrace celibacy, a plan he stuck to for about four months. Then he was seduced by his thirty-five-year-old painting lecturer, causing a university-wide scandal and a disciplinary hearing.

Through all these romantic shenanigans, Jo and Lee stayed friends. They did a number of performance-art pieces together and helped each other with other artistic projects. Lee designed and painted the set for Jo's third-year directing assignment. She modelled for a series of charcoal drawings he did. They wrote a (terrible) play together.

They were part of a large, ever-shifting group of friends. Sometimes they would do things alone together, and sometimes they would do them as part of a crowd. They could go weeks without speaking, and then spend a fortnight together every day. But however they interacted, Jo valued her friendship with Lee enormously. He was the cleverest, most widely read and multi-talented person she had ever met. The nickname Renaissance Man was totally apt: he craved knowledge and loved to enlighten and challenge people through whatever he did. He could draw and paint, play musical instruments, sing, act, DJ and dance. He could quote more poetry and Shakespeare from memory than anyone Jo had ever known, and he wrote prolifically and cleverly.

Jo, in her time at university, surprised herself. She started her studies determined to be an actress, but as time went on, she found that just focusing on one character wasn't enough for her. She was fascinated by all aspects of the process, from set design to lighting, and she worried about every detail of any play she was in. At the end of her second year, one of her lecturers gently suggested that her strength might lie more in direction than acting. Jo pondered the idea over the summer, and at the beginning of the new academic year, she put together a production of an absurdist play she liked: Ionesco's *The Bald Prima Donna*. It was only a tiny show, with no budget at all, to be staged in a poky little venue over three midweek lunchtimes. She worked every hour of the day that she wasn't actually in lectures on every aspect of it. She stayed awake at night poring over the text, spent early mornings painting set pieces and went out late in the evening to spend what little money she had on clothes for costumes from charity shops. Like the Emily Dickinson project in her first year, it was seen by few people and ignored by most of them. But it lit a fire in her, and she decided then and there that she was going to be a theatre director when she left university.

However, like most arts graduates, the unsympathetic reality of life outside the halls of learning hit Jo hard. Trying to survive in London was almost impossible. Without a student grant, she had to take a succession of waitressing jobs to pay her meagre rent, and she found herself working fifty-hour weeks just to cover bills and a diet of Pot Noodles and almost-past-their-sell-by-date vegetables. There was no time to make theatre, and definitely no money. Then a friend of her dad's offered her a job as a receptionist in the offices of a small but influential theatrical PR firm. Jo reasoned that it was in her chosen field, or thereabouts, and the hourly rate was twice what waitressing paid. The job was perfect. It gave her money to move to a slightly better flat, eat better and occasionally visit the launderette. As she worked conventional office hours, it also gave her time to direct a few staged readings with friends, although she still didn't have an agent, or any way of graduating to bigger productions. Her day job just kept getting better though. She was a graduate, dynamic and hard-working, able to speak well and write clearly, and it was only a matter of months before she was doing a PR assistant's job. That meant more money, but also more responsibility and longer hours. One day, Jo realised it had been six months since she had done any theatre. It brought about a small crisis of confidence. She felt she had lost her way, and the next day she went into the office and poured her heart out to Susie, her boss. Susie had had many an out-of-work actress working in her office, so she offered Jo a sabbatical and said she would keep a job open for her if and when she wanted to return.

Jo knew she wouldn't be able to afford rent and bills without her salary, so she moved back to Stevenage with her parents and booked a slot to do a play in a well-respected small venue in North London. She put out a call for scripts, and astonishingly her party-girl roommate from her first year, Helen, contacted her to say she had recently written a play. Rather hesitantly Jo asked to see the script. It was a tense thriller, with just two characters, set entirely in a bedsit, and it was really good. It was perfect.

She contacted a list of people she knew and respected from university and asked them if they wanted to be involved. A few people were already doing well and were committed to theatre or television projects, and one or two were even in long runs in the West End. But she managed to gather a cast she could be proud of, and get Lee, who was working in a small design studio, to commit to doing the set.

It was a hard, hard slog to get it all together. Jo sank every penny of her meagre savings into the show and her parents even invested a little. She used her experience at the PR company to drum up as much publicity as she could, and they received more press coverage than was usual for a small show at a fringe venue. The production was tight and professional, the set and music were good and the few reviews they got were very complimentary. One of the two actors in the piece invited an agent to see it, and got taken on as a result. But at the end of the run, Jo was left with a handful of good reviews, a set too big to store in her dad's garage and a sizeable hole in her bank account. While she was immensely proud of what she had achieved, it hadn't changed her life or brought any great career offers. She knew in the cold light of day that she would have to ring Susie on Monday and ask her for her job back. She prayed Susie would come through as promised and there would still be something for her there. With £140 between her and destitution, it was that or waitressing at the Harvester in Stevenage.

Susie was as good as her word and took Jo back on, and the next time Jo wanted to do a show she worked around her daytime work commitments and then took a week's holiday for the production week. It felt a little bit as if she was compromising some higher artistic principle, as if her job was her real life and theatre had become her hobby, but it was a compromise that meant she didn't have to live with her parents and she could eat. She said as much to Lee when they met for dinner one night.

'Life is about finding balance,' he said.

'That's very profound, O Guru.'

'You know what I mean. You have to live, and you have to find a way to make art. It so happens we live in one of the most expensive cities in the world, and now we're in our late twenties a squat in Bethnal Green is not so attractive. But maybe we should give it all up and go and live in a converted warehouse in Berlin. I've heard it's the most amazing city in the world. Cheap, vibrant cultural scene, amazing people . . .'

Jo laughed, but she knew he wasn't serious. Firstly because Lee had just put all his savings and a large chunk of the bank's money into a tiny flat in North London, and was thrilled to be on the first rung of the property ladder, and secondly because the reason they were having dinner was because Lee wanted to tell her all about Hannah.

Hannah was an account manager at a big advertising agency. She had subcontracted some typographical work to Lee's small design firm, and Lee said that the minute she had walked into the room, he had lost his heart. She was tall and slim, with sleek, dark, almost black hair and a calm, beautiful face. She seemed mysterious, composed, enigmatic. He went on and on about her, until Jo felt the urge to meet the amazing Hannah and punch her right in her enigmatic face. As a perfectly normal woman who'd never been even vaguely mysterious, she had an instinctive distrust of women who had that indefinable quality. She and Helen had decided one drunken evening that women of mystery were all either breathtakingly stupid or constipated.

Still, Hannah was important enough for Lee to have requested a dinner just to talk about her, and like a good friend, Jo listened. Lee had asked Hannah out and they'd had one dinner where he had found her fascinating, well read and insightful (so maybe not stupid, thought Jo, it must be constipation after all). So far she had declined a second invitation, but Lee was keeping his hopes up. He quoted chunks of her last email to him from memory, and asked Jo what she thought about the hidden meaning behind the words – words that sounded to Jo both bland and totally devoid of subtext.

'Oh my word!' she teased. 'You're being such a girl! Listen to yourself!'

'I know,' said Lee ruefully, 'but the way I feel about her is serious. This is huge, Jo.'

He was right. It was. Hannah did eventually grant him a second date, and a third, and then suddenly they were completely in love and Lee disappeared off everyone's radar for about four months. He resurfaced just before Christmas and begged Jo and all their uni friends to join him and Hannah for a big dinner in a restaurant, a combination apology-for-being-so-absent/Christmas/meet-Hannah celebration. Everyone was curious to see the woman who had got Lee so smitten, and they all gathered at the restaurant in Islington for pre-dinner drinks.

Jo enjoyed seeing everyone: she'd been busy with work and with looking for a new script to direct, so she had also been a little out of circulation. They were all seated at a long table, with Lee at the head and Hannah to his right. Because Jo had arrived late, she was right down the other end, and waved and blew a kiss to Lee when she sat down. She'd have to wait for people to shift around once they'd eaten so she could get a chance to talk to him. Her position did give her a good view of the famous Hannah though, who was, as Lee had described, a serene, dark beauty. She sat very still, listening to people talk and nodding, but didn't seem to say much herself. She was wearing what looked like an elegant fawn jersey dress (it was hard to tell, she was sitting down), and her hair was immaculate. Jo wished she could say that her face was hard or unkind, but every time Hannah looked at Lee, her expression softened and she seemed to glow. She was clearly as smitten with him and he was with her.

Jo turned to Helen, who was sitting beside her. 'So this Hannah – have you talked to her? What's she like?'

'I haven't had a chance, but I spoke to Adrian and a couple of the other guys and they all said she's lovely.'

'Well, they would. I mean, look at her!'

'Lee loves her. She can't be all bad, can she?' said Helen sensibly. 'Anyway, anyone has to be an improvement on the awful French girlfriend.'

'Oh, Jeannnne?' said Jo. 'She wasn't even French. She was from Chelmsford. Well, how Hannah turns out remains to be seen.' She sat back and folded her arms.

Helen looked at her. 'You look like you're determined to hate her.'

'I'm not! I'm just always suspicious of someone who swoops in and wins the heart of someone I care about. Especially when they look like that.'

As it happened, she didn't get a chance to talk to Lee all evening. Everyone seemed to grab a chance to slip into the chair next to his for a chat, and every time Jo made a move to get close to him, someone else got in ahead of her. Hannah stayed in her chair, so there was no hope of getting in on the other side either. After everyone had had dessert and coffee, Jo got up to go to the loo. She was standing at the sinks tidying her hair and putting on some lipstick when Hannah came into the bathroom.

'You must be Jo,' she said. Her voice was low and quiet.

'Yes, and you're Hannah, of course. Nice to meet you properly.'

'And you. I've heard all about you.' Somehow, the way Hannah said this seemed quite loaded. There was no way to ask what she meant without sounding aggressive though, so Jo smiled and said, 'I hope you're having a nice time.'

'I am. All Lee's friends seem lovely.'

Hannah was standing behind Jo to her left, and when Jo looked in the mirror, she could see that Hannah was staring at her pointedly. Jo smiled again, now a little uncomfortable.

'Well, we all do go back a long way,' she said.

'I know,' said Hannah, and kept standing there, looking at her. Jo turned around to return the look. She wasn't quite sure what to say, but Hannah filled the silence. 'I'm sorry if I'm staring,' she said, 'but when your new boyfriend tells you about his old, old female friend and describes her by saying, "She looks like a *Sports Illustrated* model, but she's also funny and creative and clever, and when she smiles, the room lights up," well, that's a woman you're going to want to take a look at.'

'Wow,' said Jo. 'I can't believe he said that.'

'*Sports Illustrated* might be taking it a bit far, but you are working that tall blonde look.'

'Thank you,' said Jo faintly. Her mum had always told her to be polite if someone paid her a compliment.

'I love him, you know.'

'I can see that. I saw the way you look at him. And the way he looks at you. It seems pretty mutual.'

'I hope so,' said Hannah, her beautiful face impassive. 'This relationship means a lot to me, and without trying to sound like a country and western song, I would absolutely fight to keep him.'

'Fight who?' said Jo, and then, realising, 'Oh. Oh God, no, Hannah. There's absolutely never been anything like that between Lee and me. I just don't see him like that at all!'

'Really? How could you not? I mean, have you looked at him?'

Hannah opened the door to the restaurant, and Jo looked out at Lee, sitting at the head of the table, laughing at something Helen was saying. It was funny. When you knew someone as well as she knew Lee, you stopped really seeing them. In a way, the picture you carried in your head was a sort of faded picture of who they were when you first met, not a clear vision of who they had become. In her head, Lee was still the tall, gangly just-out-of-his-teens boy with crazy hair who wore baggy, multicoloured jumpers his nanna knitted, not because they were cool but because it would hurt his nanna's feelings if he didn't.

But nearly ten years later, she looked at him with new eyes. With Hannah's eyes. Lee now had his mad hair cropped

stylishly short. He had filled out, so that his broad-shoul-
dered, athletic body matched his height. He was anything
but gawky and skinny nowadays. He was wearing a fitted
charcoal shirt that looked well made and expensive. He was
undeniably sexy and handsome. How had that happened?
And how had she missed it? With a start, she realised she'd
been standing there staring for too long without saying
anything, and when she turned back, Hannah's beautiful
face had gone a little paler.

'He's all right, I suppose,' said Jo nonchalantly. 'But he's
never been my type.'

She wasn't sure whether Hannah believed her. And much
more worryingly, she wasn't sure whether she believed
herself.

She didn't have to worry though, because after the big
introduction dinner, Lee quite simply disappeared. None of
their crowd saw him. He let out his flat and moved into
Hannah's bigger place in Stoke Newington. He stopped
ringing and texting, and seemed to be busy whenever
anyone invited him to do something. Jo got her hands on
a brilliant debut script by a young Pakistani writer, living
in East London, and she asked Lee if he wanted to do the
set, but he cried off, saying things at work were too busy.
He had never been too busy for an exciting creative project
before, and Jo felt very sad.

Time passed, and Jo did two more productions, each in
a slightly bigger venue. They got good reviews, and on the
last one she even broke even, but she was nowhere near
being able to give up her day job. She didn't mind though.
She had more responsibility at Susie's PR company, and

surprisingly, she really began to enjoy her job. She felt less and less that it was a way to fill in time and earn money, and more that it challenged her and asked things of her creatively. Susie was a wonderful boss and sent her on a number of useful training courses in marketing and PR writing. Jo was busy . . . too busy for any kind of romantic relationship, and, truth be told, too busy to see her friends much. But that seemed to be the case with everyone. A few of her uni friends had got married and settled down, a few more had gone travelling and one or two had emigrated. The days of weekly get-togethers and impromptu breaks away together were over. It wasn't surprising . . . as they all headed into their thirties, it was the way things were likely to go.

So it was quite a surprise when, one day, Lee's name popped up in her email inbox. Before she even read the message, she tried to recall when they had last been in contact. She thought there had been an email exchange around her birthday ('Happy birthday'/'Thanks, can you come to my birthday dinner?'/'Sorry too busy.'), but other than that, they hadn't been in touch for about eighteen months. Intrigued, she opened the email.

Hey stranger,

This is the crappest friend of all time making contact, and for the most clichéd reason of all time. Yes, I'm single, although feeling far from footloose and fancy-free, and back in my old flat in Islington. Things between Hannah and me didn't work out, and it all ended rather badly, I'm sad to say. I have a new job, working for a design studio in Hoxton Square, so not a million miles from you if you fancy an after-work drink, or, if I don't make the grade for that, maybe a swift bite of lunch?

Grovellingly yours,

Lee x

She didn't hesitate for a moment, and fired off a reply offering drinks plus dinner, and telling him grovelling was totally unnecessary. As she sent it, she realised how much she'd missed him. She was sorry things hadn't worked out with Hannah, really she was, but it would be brilliant to have Lee to kick around with again.

They met in a quiet wine bar near his offices in Hoxton. He looked the same, but quieter somehow, more subdued. As if he'd grown up. When Jo came in, he jumped up and kissed and hugged her, then drew her to sit down. He'd already ordered a bottle of wine and he filled her glass. She'd expected it to be slightly awkward, but it was anything but, and after the third glass Jo decided she had been wrong, and that to her relief Lee hadn't grown up at all. He told her all about his new job. 'You know where I worked before I got into typography. I'd heard about this company . . . it's a font foundry, so I applied, and I'm incredibly lucky they took me on. We actually make our own fonts. Design them from scratch, letter by letter.'

'Foundry? Wow . . . that sounds cool. Do you all stand around furnaces in leather aprons banging anvils?'

'Not really . . . we have a large studio with a bunch of geeky people sitting at Macs, moving the middle bar on an *e* up a millimetre and then back down again for hours at a time.'

'Sounds gripping.'

'I'm talking it down, I love it. It's the coolest job I've ever had. And you? What have you been up to?'

They did a speedy catch-up on the missing months, and then launched straight into gossip about all their mutual friends, talking over one another and laughing. Before they knew it, they were halfway through the second bottle of wine. Realising they were both quite drunk, Lee waved at a waiter and ordered them a load of tapas – far too much, it seemed, but they munched their way greedily through the whole lot. Jo spilled something oily and tomatoey on her top, which for some reason was hugely funny, and they giggled about that. For the rest of the evening, either one of them just had to say 'tomato' for them to fall about like a pair of thirteen-year-old girls.

In a fruitless attempt to sober them both up (it was a school night, after all), Jo ordered them both wickedly dark Mexican hot chocolates, only to discover they were spiked with a whopping great tot of tequila. The bar was beginning to empty and their mood was slightly quieter.

'So can I ask about Hannah?'

'Ask what?'

'Well, what happened? It seemed so serious between you.'

'It was . . . but, well, it just didn't work out.'

'Didn't work out? What does that mean? That's a euphemism that means nothing, Hockley, and you know it.

Relationships don't just "not work out". What happened? Did you shag around? Did she?'

'No one shagged around. It's just one of those things, okay?'

'Ah . . . "one of those things" – another meaning-laden euphemism.'

'Indeed, and it means . . .'

'"Shut up, Jo, and leave the subject alone, for the love of God"?' Jo said, smiling.

'Very accurately read, my dear. Now, are we going to want another of these quite excellent hot chocolates?'

'I'm not sure whether it's the alcohol or the sugar that will kill me . . .'

'But there's enough caffeine in there to revive a dodo.'

'There is.'

'So that's a yes then?'

In spite of the heinous hangover the next morning, Jo was certain that it was the best evening out she'd had in months. Years, maybe. She emailed Lee to that effect and he concurred heartily. A few days later they got together rather more sedately for a weekend afternoon film, and the following week Jo invited him to the opening of a play she'd done the publicity for. The very next night they went to a private gallery view for someone they'd known at uni. Very quickly, they got into the habit of hanging out or attending functions together once or twice a week.

Jo told herself that it was fabulous to have a personable, intelligent old friend she could take to events. They had shared history, they were comfortable together, they knew a lot of the same people and they were interested in the same things. And besides, Lee was always a laugh. She kept telling herself all this, but deep down, when she got home after another evening out with him, there was something else. Something she couldn't admit to anyone, not even to herself. Something had changed the night she had met Hannah, the night Hannah had asked her to really look at Lee. It was, she was sure, the exact opposite of Hannah's intention, but she had awakened Jo's attention and she had seen Lee for what he was . . . a desirable, sexy man. Now, when they met and he hugged and kissed her as he always did, she found herself sniffing his neck, smelling the heady combination of cologne and warm skin. When he asked her to be his date at a cousin's wedding and they danced, she feared she would embarrass herself because it was so delicious to be held in his arms. She started to get a small thrill when she saw his name come up on her phone, or when an email arrived from him.

She knew she was being ridiculous. You couldn't just start fancying someone you'd been friends with for more than ten years. It was a one-way street to ruining a precious and long-standing friendship. She wished she could talk to someone about it, but who do you discuss a crush with? Your best mate. And as Lee had become her best mate, that was out. If she told any of her other friends, they either wouldn't understand, or, if it was someone like Helen who knew them both, would understand how totally hopeless the whole thing was. She wasn't ready to be told that, so she didn't discuss it with anyone. It was just a crush. She'd been single a long time, that was all. She'd get over it.

Nevertheless, when the big dance show, the biggest project

she'd ever run publicity for on her own, was due to open, she invited Lee to the opening night at Sadler's Wells. It was early summer, and the night was warm and clear. She had caught a little sun and her skin had a golden honey glow, so she'd chosen a simple white shift dress, and silver sandals. She wore her hair loose and a fine silver chain around her neck.

She was talking to a dance journalist in the foyer when, out of the corner of her eye, she saw Lee arrive. She kept her attention on the journalist, nodding and smiling, but she was acutely aware of Lee's tall frame edging his way through the crowd towards her. Then, with a miracle of timing, the journalist saw someone she needed to speak to, and as Lee got there, made her excuses to Jo and went off. Jo turned to Lee. He was staring at her, at her dress, her hair, her face. She waited for a standard Lee quip about her being all gussied up or corn-fed or something, but he said simply, 'You look beautiful.'

She didn't know what to say. He'd never said anything like that to her before. She stammered an awkward thank-you. Then another journalist swooped in with a tedious question about the lighting design, and dragged Jo away.

She was busy right until the curtain rose and she slipped into her seat beside Lee as the lights went down. Although she'd been looking forward to it for weeks, she barely saw the show . . . she was too busy concentrating on the heat of his arm next to hers. She really had to get a grip. She was acting like she was nineteen, not twenty-nine. So he'd said she looked beautiful. So what? It was Lee. He was always nice.

After the show, there was a drinks reception, and Jo was kept busy chatting to various patrons and journalists. Lee hung on the fringes of the group, not talking to anyone. Every time Jo looked up, he seemed to be watching her. She was a grown woman and she knew that look. She knew that if she walked up to him and said, 'Do you want to come back to mine?' they would go back to her flat, take off their clothes and have sex. But then what? An awful, awkward morning, waking up together, realising they'd chucked ten great years of friendship for a heady summer's evening shag? Was it worth it? Could she bear to lose him? No. No, she couldn't. This had been a terrible, terrible idea.

As the last elderly dance patron finished her lengthy goodbye, Jo looked up one more time, and caught Lee's eye. She had never seen him look so intense, and as she walked up to him, his beautiful dark brown eyes were almost black with desire. 'Listen, sweetie,' she said as casually as she could, 'sorry I've been such a poor hostess this evening, but I'm shattered. Sore head, sore feet, sore face from all the smiling. I'm going to hop in a cab and go home. Is that okay? Catch up tomorrow.' She couldn't bring herself to kiss him, so she patted his arm awkwardly and left.

She woke the next morning, kicking herself. Kicking herself for chickening out when it looked as if he might reciprocate her feelings, kicking herself for thinking it had ever been a good idea to try to change their relationship into something else and quite possibly ruining everything. Just kicking herself. Over the next week, she avoided his calls and texts, and answered emails with a terse 'V. busy, will get back to you.' She knew she couldn't avoid him forever though.

At the end of the week, the dance show transferred to the Theatre Royal in Newcastle. The whole way up north on the train, she stared out of the window, thinking about Lee, about their last meeting, about their friendship. In a funny way, she realised, it was too late already. Even if she had misread Lee's expression that night at the theatre, her feelings for him were irrevocably different. He wasn't Lee her mate any more. He was Lee the man she . . . what? Fancied? Had a crush on? Loved? Oh my God . . . was she in love with Lee?

She got through the set-up, the opening night and all the schmoozing in a kind of daze. Later that night, she walked back to her hotel. She was tired, but she knew she wouldn't sleep. She had to tell him. She couldn't just let this poison their relationship. She had to tell him, take the risk, see if he felt the same way. And if it meant she lost him, well, that was going to have to be okay. She didn't have him anyway, not as a friend the way she used to, and not as a lover, which was what she now wanted.

She sat on the bed in her impersonal business hotel room, her mobile in her hand. It was late, nearly midnight. Was it too late to ring him? What if he was asleep? Or not asleep, but with someone? That would be awful. She'd text first. Tentatively she typed 'Awake?' and sent it. No going back now. Her phone rang immediately.

'I am now.' His voice sounded soft and warm, as if he was in bed.

'Sorry, I didn't mean to wake you.'

'I'm teasing. You didn't. I was reading. Everything okay?'

'Yeah, yeah. I'm in Newcastle with the show.'

'Oh,' he said, and waited. There was a long pause.

Jo took a deep breath. 'So, Lee . . .'

'Yeah?'

'I didn't just ring to chat. I wanted to talk to you about the other night.'

'At Sadler's Wells?'

'Yeah.'

Damn. Why had she not written down what she wanted to say? How was she to do this? She was afraid. But Lee gave her the perfect cue.

'You looked very, very lovely that night. Breathtaking.'

'Thank you. The thing is . . . I didn't look like that by accident.'

'What do you mean?' His voice was quiet. This was it, the moment where she changed their relationship forever. But from his serious tone, she was pretty sure he knew what she was going to say.

'I wanted to look good . . . not because it was a work do. I wanted to look beautiful . . . for you. You see, Lee, I think—'

'Jo, can I stop you?'

Oh God. He didn't want to hear it. This was awful. She drew her knees up to her chest and hugged them, clutching her mobile to her ear.

But he went on. 'If you're about to say what I think you're going to say, will you do me a favour?'

'Yes,' she whispered hoarsely.

'Will you let me say it first? I think I've been waiting to say it for longer than you.'

The pause this time was delicious. Lee's voice cracked as he spoke. 'The thing is, Joanna Lesley Morris, I've loved you since the first moment I saw you at that party in New Cross.'

'I love you too, Lee.' Jo found herself laughing, although she was also inexplicably crying, great tears rolling down her face.

'I'm so, so glad,' said Lee, and he laughed too, a delighted, loud, happy laugh. 'I can't believe we finally got there. It seemed to me that somehow it's just never been our time. First you went off with that Adrian wanker . . .'

'Wanker? He's your mate!'

'And a wanker. Come on, we all know it – we can admit it after all these years. Anyway, I don't want to talk about Adrian. I want to say that you've always been the most beautiful, challenging, clever, creative, exciting and damned sexy woman I've ever known. But once we'd moved into the friend zone, there just didn't seem a way out.'

'I know. That's what's been killing me. I was so scared that if I said something, I would lose you.'

'Let me tell you something, my love,' said Lee firmly, and she let out an involuntary sob hearing him say 'my love', 'you are never going to lose me. Never ever, for the rest of our lives – not if I have anything to do with it.'

They talked for four straight hours. It seemed the easiest thing in the world to use words of love with Lee, as if they had always talked to each other that way. He shared memory after memory of times he had wanted to tell her how he felt, times he had wanted to make a move but had been too afraid. She told him about the night with Hannah, when she'd seen him differently for the first time.

'Ah, Hannah,' said Lee, his voice troubled.

'That was serious, wasn't it?' Jo said. 'Much more serious than any relationship I ever had.'

'Hannah is an amazing woman, and I tried, I did. But . . .'

'But?'

'If I say this, you're not allowed to freak out, okay?'

'It's three a.m., I haven't slept for twenty-one hours and I've just declared my love for my best friend. I'm way beyond freaking out.'

'I never told you why Hannah and I broke up.'

'Okay, why?'

'It was a classic late-twenties thing. She came to me and said she wanted to have a baby, and I told her I didn't want to. She asked me if I wanted to wait, and if so for how long, and I had to tell her I didn't want to have a baby at all. She was a year or so older, and she said if we weren't going to have kids, she needed time to meet someone who did want them. So we split up.'

'Oh,' said Jo, not sure what to do with this information. So Lee didn't want kids. She hadn't really thought about children, but it seemed quite extreme to rule them out altogether before they'd even begun their relationship.

'The thing is . . .' said Lee, 'and here's the freak-out part: the truth is, I didn't want kids with Hannah, because deep down, I knew I wasn't going to spend the rest of my life with her. But, Jo, I would love to have a baby with you.'

They sat in silence for a while after that statement, listening to each other's breathing. And suddenly Jo laughed. 'Oh my God . . . we're talking about making babies, and we've never even kissed.'

'I know.'

'Is it going to be weird? I mean, when I next see you, I suppose we'll kiss, and then we'll . . .'

'Oh, I hope so.'

'Me too . . . but it's going to be strange. I've known you for ten years, and I've never seen you naked.'

'If it helps, I've imagined you naked, a lot.'

Jo looked out of the window. 'The sun's coming up. It must be about four . . . I'll be home in twelve hours. I've got a few meetings here in the morning, and then I'm catching a train at noon.'

'You'd better get some sleep.'

'I don't think I can sleep.'

'If I have anything to do with it, you're not going to be doing any sleeping tonight at all. So you'd better get all the rest you can between now and then, okay?'

The next afternoon, when Jo stepped off the train at King's Cross, Lee was standing on the platform. She walked up to him, her heart thumping. They didn't say anything. He drew her into his arms slowly, gently, as if she was the most precious thing he had ever held and, for the very first time, they kissed.

3

JO AND LEE NOW

It was a very romantic beginning, and being with Lee was everything Jo had dreamed it could be. Of course in the beginning it was heady and thrilling and they had seemingly non-stop sex, but through all of that and beyond, it was just . . . right. It felt right to be with him, to wake up with him, to reintroduce him to her family as her boyfriend. And one of the things she liked best was that no one was surprised. Jo and Lee had agonised over telling their friends and families, but when they did, people generally just said, 'Ah, well, about time. We always knew you'd end up together.'

It felt right when Lee let out his flat and moved in with her, right when they both sold their flats and bought a three-bedroomed semi in Hendon, right when Lee quietly proposed at their kitchen table one Wednesday evening while they were eating spaghetti bolognaise. They got married in the local church and had a raucous reception in the pub next door. Their honeymoon consisted of five glorious days in Barcelona. When they got home, Lee designed a script font which he called Barcelona, based on the curves of Gaudi's art nouveau architecture. It was a bestseller for his firm and he got a bonus and a promotion to senior designer. Zach was born two years after they got married, and Imogene two years after that. The cost of childcare was iniquitous, and Lee was doing very well and could just about pay all the bills, so it made sense for Jo to take the time off to stay at home with the kids, at least until they were both in school. She'd never imagined herself as a stay-at-home mum, but she found she enjoyed it, most of the time at least.

So six-and-a-half years after their first kiss on the platform at King's Cross, Jo and Lee had turned a love story into a marriage, complete with two children, a mortgage, bills, piles of laundry and a niggling leak under the bath. Maybe it was no longer a fairy-tale romance, but Jo still felt as if she had totally won the jackpot when she got Lee.

She wasn't a fan of the twee names people gave to their partners: 'ball and chain', 'hubby' or whatever, but secretly, to herself, she did call Lee her 'other half'. Because he was. He complemented her in every way. He supported her, loved and admired her and told her so all the time. He was an amazing father and a great mate, he still made her laugh, and when they could grab the time when both kids were asleep and they weren't dizzy with exhaustion, still absolutely dynamite in bed.

Jo loved Lee's drawings of her dream shop. Just as he had designed sets for her theatrical productions in years gone by, he'd taken her ideas and made them visual. In doing so, he'd brought new dimensions to the concept and given Jo inspiration. As soon as she got Imogene down for a nap the next morning, she sat at her computer and wrote another three pages of ideas. But once she had done that, she sat staring at the screen for ages, her tea going cold. She had a degree in drama, a career in theatrical PR and three years as a stay-at-home parent. None of these qualified her to own or run a shop. She'd never worked in retail. The closest she'd got was working behind the bar in the Rosie, the student pub in New Cross, and even then all she'd done was pull pints and wash glasses. She didn't even know how to cash up a till, let alone order stock, run the finances or manage staff. It was a ridiculous idea.

She said as much when Lee came home from work that evening. 'I haven't a clue,' she said. 'I wouldn't even know where to start. It was a mad idea, and anyway, I have two children under four. I don't know what I was thinking.'

'Firstly, it's a bloody brilliant idea,' said Lee. 'I knew that the moment you first mentioned it. I've spoken to a couple of people at work about it too, and they all think it's inspired. And secondly, if you don't know how to do something, you can learn. Go on a small-business course. Chat to someone at the bank. Get a life coach or whatever.'

'A life coach?'

'I read about them in the *Metro*. Probably not your thing, but you know what I mean. There are probably a million sites on the Net you could look at. The information is out there. If you really want to do this, then start looking into it. You've got the creative flair, there's no doubt about that, and some relevant experience. Also, you're a parent. You know what works for kids. That's a whole body of knowledge too. Just go looking for help with the other stuff.'

'You make it sound so simple . . .' said Jo doubtfully.

'The most important question is – do you really want to

do this?' said Lee. 'Is this something you could see yourself doing for years to come? It's miles away from PR, and it seems a long way from your dreams of acting and directing.'

'I don't know,' said Jo, and she sat back and thought for a moment. 'Jo Hockley, shop owner. Hmm. It's odd, isn't it? When you're young, everything is so clear, so black and white. When I went to university, I knew without a shadow of a doubt that I was an Actress with a capital A. Then after a year or so, I realised it wasn't quite that simple and I wanted to direct, and that's what I was for a long, long time. A director. Even when I started working in PR, I was a director who did PR work to make money so I could direct. Then after a while, I suppose I became a PR person who did occasional directing, and then I jacked it all in to be a stay-at-home mother who might at some time go back to being in PR but will not be in a position to direct theatre any time in the foreseeable future.'

'Wow.' Lee smiled. 'You're going to struggle to fit that on a business card.'

'I used to know what I was, but now I don't. The path isn't as simple and clear as it was when I was eighteen. Stuff changes. Children come along, and financial necessity, and limited time.'

'So what are you saying?'

'What I'm saying is that ten years ago I wouldn't have dreamed of owning or running a children's clothes shop. But now . . . Who knows? Maybe it's time for something different in my life. It's a whole new industry . . . but I think it could be amazing. And it might be something I could fit in around the kids, once it was off the ground. It's not like

I'm going to be staging Chekhov at the National any time soon, or pulling on my power suit and heading for a meeting in Soho.'

'Well then,' said Lee, leaning back in his chair, 'go for it. Do the research, and I'll help any way I can. If you need to go and meet with people, I can take time off to look after the kids, or my mum could help.'

She started small. In the afternoons, when she had both kids, she went on a few excursions, visiting high streets in the local area, looking for possible premises. She wanted to go more upmarket than Hendon, but not as exclusive as Hampstead. Golders Green looked possible, or the Broadway in Mill Hill. Or maybe Finchley or Muswell Hill. She found herself peering through the windows of vacant shops, trying to imagine them transformed. So far she hadn't found anything that blew her away, but she knew the space was out there somewhere.

In the mornings, when Imogene napped, she started trawling through websites with information about starting a small business. There were hundreds. Many of them were dense and badly written, some of them just offered motivational claptrap – 'you can acheive any thing you want to, think of your dream and you can make it a Reality'-type nonsense. But she found a few that offered useful checklists and pieces of advice. She learned about SWOT analysis and PEST analysis, and she started to draw up a spreadsheet of possible start-up costs. There were lots of gaps and many things she couldn't begin to put numbers to, but it was a beginning.

She particularly liked a blog by a woman entrepreneur called Louise Holmes-Harper, who wrote in an easy, witty style, and whose ideas seemed simple and practical. Best of all, Louise H-H wrote quite a lot about balancing work and childcare. There was one particularly funny post about how much a busy mum starting a business could achieve during the average toddler nap time. It struck a chord with Jo, so she commented on it, and Louise H-H sent her a warm personal message in return.

That gave Jo courage, so she drafted an email and, after much hesitation, sent it off to the address on Louise Holmes-Harper's website.

Dear Louise,

Without wanting to sound too gushy, I just wanted to say I'm a big fan of your blog and I'm finding all your advice very practical and useful. I've got a background in PR and marketing in the performing arts, but I've been out of the world of work for a few years with small children, and now I'm thinking of starting a business in a completely new field. I'm sure everyone says this, but I have an idea which my research tells me is unique and might actually succeed. I have so much to learn, and many of my questions are quite specific. For obvious reasons, I'm not all that keen to blab my ideas all over the web, so I wonder if you ever offer individual coaching or give advice?

Best wishes,

Jo Hockley

She didn't expect to hear back from Louise any time soon, but a reply came within the hour.

Dear Jo,

Thanks for the compliment. When you stick something up in the blogosphere, you have no idea who, if anybody, is reading it, so any feedback is encouraging (except for the spam comments I get telling me my penis needs enlarging, those are not so useful!). To be honest, I've never done any one-to-one coaching: I used to work as a manager in the printing industry until my son Peter was born three years ago. Then I did some ad hoc lecturing in business practices at a local college, but I'm currently pregnant with my second baby, which means my time is soon going to be even more limited. I host weekend seminars on starting a business from scratch, and there's one coming up this weekend. I've just had a cancellation, so if you're interested you can take the place. There's a link with all the information on the blog. It's at a venue near where I'm based in Surrey . . . is that any good to you? Maybe then we could talk about individual coaching, if you still feel you need it.

Warmest wishes,

Louise

She had added a link to the page on her website which advertised the seminar. It wasn't expensive, and it was to be held at a hotel in Kingston, easily accessible by train or road.

The sessions were during the day on the Saturday and Sunday . . . Totally doable if Lee was happy to have the kids on his own for the whole weekend.

She forwarded her email and Louise's response to Lee's work address, adding a question mark at the top. She knew he'd understand what she was asking, and sure enough, within half an hour he fired back a message saying:

Sounds perfect, love. Go for it. Book it today. Zach, Imi and me will put you on a train and go off for adventures on the Saturday and lunch with my folks on the Sunday xx

It was all the encouragement Jo needed, and she filled in the online form and paid for the course there and then. Once she had done so, and had looked at the programme in more detail, she started to get quite excited, and began typing up a list of questions related to each of the sessions. When she looked at the three A4 sheets she had filled, she had to laugh at herself. She was going to be that annoying swot, sitting right in the front with her hand in the air, constantly interrupting to ask more questions. Still, it was wonderful to feel stimulated again.

On Saturday, Lee drove her to the Tube station, and she kissed him goodbye. Imogene and Zach waved cheerily to her from their car seats in the back. They looked perfectly happy to be spending the day without her.

She couldn't remember the last time she'd caught a Tube without a pushchair, an excited toddler and at least two enormous bags, so it felt very odd to get on to the train with just a satchel. She took out her notes and questions and her copy of the day's agenda, and by the time she got to Waterloo, she'd been through them ten times over. At Waterloo, she treated herself to a coffee and a magazine, and found her train to Surrey. She rang Lee, who answered his phone in a whisper.

'Everything okay?'

'Fine. You?'

'Fine here too. I'm sat on the sofa watching *Monsters Inc.* with Zach, and Imi's asleep on my chest.'

Jo let out a sigh she hadn't known she was holding on to. 'That's great. Well, I'm on the train, on my way. I'll give you a shout at the first tea break.'

'Have fun, love,' said Lee.

The train pulled out of Waterloo and Jo sipped her coffee, stared out of the window and leafed through her magazine. She felt as if she was going on holiday.

The hotel where the seminar was being held was close to Kingston station and she got there just after nine thirty, half an hour early. She found a chair in the foyer of the hotel where she could see the door of the conference suite and sat down. She felt unaccountably nervous. This was the first proper work-related event she'd been to in more than three years. She felt very out of practice and conspicuous. She jumped up and went to the loo to check her hair and make-up and make sure she had no baby porridge or snot anywhere about her person.

When she came back, there was a tall woman with dark red hair laying out conference packs on the table outside the meeting room. She must be Louise Holmes-Harper's assistant. Jo hung back a bit and looked around. There didn't seem to be anyone else who looked like a conference attendee in the foyer yet, but then what would they look like? It was a seminar for people seeking to start a small business, and that could be anyone. She plucked up her courage and edged over to the table where the woman was painstakingly lining up name badges. There were quite a lot of name badges, Jo noted with relief – at least twenty. She had had an irrational fear that there would only be about five of them sitting around a table, embarrassed, trying to fill gaps and pauses with questions.

'Hi,' Jo ventured. 'I'm here for the small-business seminar.'

'Hi!' said the woman. She looked about forty, and she had a wide, friendly smile. 'Let me guess. You must be Jo Hockley.'

'Wow. Good guess.' Jo smiled. 'Sorry, I'm really nervous.'

'Ah, I remember from your email you said you'd been at home with your kids for a while. I know how you feel; it can knock your confidence.'

The woman unbuttoned her jacket and took it off, and Jo realised that she was pregnant – not very far along, maybe fifteen or sixteen weeks.

'You're Louise Holmes-Harper,' said Jo, rather unnecessarily, because the woman was busy pinning on a name badge that made that clear.

'Sorry, yes, of course I am. I thought you knew.'

'I thought you might be Louise's glamorous assistant.'

'Sadly I don't have one of those,' laughed Louise. 'I try to keep costs down when I do these things . . . I know people are spending their own money to come on this seminar, so I want to give them as much as I can for a good price. I do the setting up, the photocopying – all the housekeeping tasks. I also pour a mean cup of tea!'

She seemed so warm and easy-going that Jo already felt more at ease. 'Well, as I seem to be the first here, I can be the teacher's pet and help you, if you like.'

'Thanks, that would be fab,' said Louise. 'Could you pop these notes into each folder, and make sure each person gets a pen and a notepad too? I'll go and double-check the laptop and projector are working; I have a morbid fear of being let down by the technology. I like to be sure that things will just do what I need them to do, when I need.'

She left Jo packing folders and went through the doors into the other room. Jo sneaked a look at the delegate list, but it was just a list of names. There were roughly equal numbers of men and women, but no indication what areas of business anyone might be interested in.

Once she had finished organising the notes, she looked around the hotel foyer. There were a few people standing around uncertainly: a middle-aged woman in a tweed skirt and sturdy shoes clutching a battered old briefcase, two teenage boys, looking uncomfortable in shirts and ties, an elderly chap who was sitting at a table looking at an iPad, and three or four men between the ages of twenty-five and thirty-five. She backed away from the table before anyone could approach and ask her questions. Just then, Louise came back out of the conference room and stood behind the table with a bright smile. She winked at Jo. 'Could you come over and get the ball rolling?'

Jo went up and signed in, gathering her delegate pack and name badge. The other people straggled after her and formed a queue. Louise indicated that she could go through, so she walked into the conference room, where chairs were set in a single row, forming a neat semicircle facing a screen. She dithered, then put her folder and bag on a seat slightly to the left of centre and fetched herself a cup of tea. One by one, the other people came into the room. Nobody seemed to want to make small talk, at least not yet, and they all sat rather awkwardly, folders on laps and balancing their teacups, until Louise came in.

She checked her watch. 'Hi, everyone. So glad you all made it. Everyone who should be here seems to be here, and we're all set to start on time. Miracles will never cease! Let's begin with some introductions. As you've probably guessed, I'm Louise Holmes-Harper, and I'll be running the seminar. I know that for each of you, your business idea is the most precious and valuable thing you have, so the one rule I'm going to insist on is that you don't tell everyone exactly what your idea is. Today, we're going to be focusing on general skills that will be useful whatever your business, and in the one-on-one sessions tomorrow with the various experts you can talk more specifically about any help or information you need that is particular to your field. Still, it's important to get to know each other, so I'm going to ask each of you to tell everyone your name, and one little-known fact about yourself. So, let me start by saying that my name is Louise, and I've never been able to spell the word "occasion". One *c*, two *s*'s? Two *c*'s, one *s*? And the last part: *i*, *o*, *n* – *i*, *o*, *u*, n? It gets me every time!'

She laughed warmly and it made everyone else laugh too. 'You see?' Louise said. 'Confessions are easy. Let's start with you, Eric,' she said, indicating the elderly man sitting on the far left of the semicircle.

'My name is Eric Pocket, and for years I've told everyone I don't have a middle name, but I do, and it's Hillary.'

This got a good laugh too. Next in line was one of the teenage boys.

'I'm Daniel, and there's this one Coldplay song I secretly like.'

His friend next to him looked utterly horrified. 'You WHAT? I can't believe you! Coldplay? Wow.'

Louise pointed to the friend. 'Now, now! It's your turn.'

'Hi, I'm Chris, and I totally judge people by their taste in music.'

Daniel looked unimpressed. 'It's supposed to be a little-known fact about you. Everyone knows that about you. Even people who've just met you.'

'Okay,' said Chris, leaning back and stretching his legs. 'I used to sing treble in the church choir.'

Daniel was so astonished at this he was speechless.

'Well, clearly that one WAS a surprise!' said Louise. 'Next . . .'

It was Jo's turn. She'd been enjoying everyone else's confession so much, she hadn't thought about her own. 'Er . . . um . . . I'm Jo, and I once dressed up as a pineapple and gave out leaflets for a travel company?'

She got a smattering of applause for that one, but nothing like the one for the middle-aged tweedy woman, who announced baldly, 'I'm Maureen, and I've been doing yoga

for thirty-five years. I can put both feet behind my head.'
She got a standing ovation. By the time they'd gone around
the circle, the ice was well and truly broken, and before
they knew it they were into the first session, where Louise
talked them through limited companies, partnerships and
sole trading.

In Hendon, Lee was enjoying every minute of his solo-daddy
day. He'd loved sitting quietly with the kids to watch a film,
and when Imogene woke from her nap, she was lively and
playful and kept pulling herself up on the furniture and
Lee's legs. Zach was playing on his sand table in the garden,
but he kept running in to tell Lee about some adventure
his dinosaurs were having in the sand. When he saw
Imogene was up and playing, he wanted to kiss her and
carry her around, but Imogene was having none of that.
She crawled determinedly under the kitchen table and sat
there, giggling to herself.

Lee remembered a game he'd loved as a child, so he
dashed upstairs to get a blanket from the linen cupboard.
He arranged four dining chairs into a square in the middle
of the living room, and showed Zach how to drape the
blanket over the chairs. They weighted it with books and
put cushions into their little house. It was darker than Lee
had expected, so he went to get a torch from the kitchen
drawer, scooping up Imogene as he went. He and both children crawled into their secret house under the blanket. Zach
thought it was fabulous, and kept dashing out to bring in
more and more toys, and Imogene saw it as the perfect
opportunity to crawl all over her daddy and bounce on his

tummy. They played in the house so long that it took Lee a while to work out that he was hungry and that the kids must be too. Jo had left a lunch of cold chicken and some salady bits in the fridge, and he fetched it, along with some cartons of juice and a few bread rolls, and they had a fabulous torch-lit picnic in their blanket house.

They crawled out after lunch, and Lee realised that the living room was in a state of advanced chaos. Even though the kids howled in protest, he dismantled the blanket house and hoovered up the crumbs and all the sand Zach had tracked into the house. He washed up and packed snacks, toys and a football for a trip to the park. It wasn't until two thirty that he thought to check his phone and saw he'd missed a call from Jo at lunchtime. She'd left a message raving about the course, and her voice sounded vibrant and excited. He felt a little bad that he'd been having so much fun he'd forgotten to miss her. He knew she'd already be in the afternoon sessions, so he fired off a quick text saying they were all fine and were off to the park.

It took him a while to get the kids organised: Zach needed a wee, Imi needed a nappy change and a clean top as she'd spat tomato pips all down what she had been wearing. He had to wrestle them both into their car seats and gather the necessary bags and equipment. As he drove to the park, he realised that it was the first time he'd done this all on his own with both kids. They tended to do stuff as a family at weekends, or he would sometimes do dad-and-son stuff with Zach, leaving Imogene with Jo. He felt quite proud of himself for managing as well as he had. So far so good: neither child had sustained an injury, there was no permanent damage to the house, and nobody was screaming or crying. Zach kept up a non-stop monologue all the way to the park, telling him what they had to do and in what order. Jo had warned him not to mess with the system and he didn't, although he did put Imi on the little roundabout and whizz her round, making her shriek with absolute delight. Zach told him off for that. 'Mummy doesn't do that,' he said prissily. 'I know,' said Lee, winking at him. 'It's a dad thing. Do you want a go?'

'No, thanks,' said Zach. 'I tried it before and it made me feel all sick and then I had my ice cream and I threw up. I'm not wasting my ice cream, especially if you're buying the proper kind in the cone with the flake in.'

'I'm definitely buying the proper kind in the cone,' said Lee seriously. 'But not if anyone's going to throw up.'

He took Imogene out of her seat on the roundabout. She seemed perfectly fine, not dizzy at all. He was loading her back in the pushchair, ready to head to the kiosk for ice creams when a plumpish woman with curly dark hair came hurrying over with a baby in a sling on her front, dragging a small girl by the hand. 'You must be Zachy's daddy!' she said excitedly. 'I'm Martha's mummy!'

Ah, this must be Jo's legendary tiresome and nameless park woman, Lee thought. Maybe he could find out her name and end the mystery once and for all.

'Hi, I'm Lee,' he said, offering his hand to shake.

'Of course you are! I've heard all about you!' gushed Martha's mummy. 'Zachy and Martha are BEST friends, aren't you, darlings?'

'No,' said Zach matter-of-factly. The woman ignored him.

Martha clearly didn't have anything to say for herself. She stood holding her mum's hand and looked at her shoes. Maybe she didn't talk, thought Lee, or maybe she'd just given up trying to get a word in. Martha's mummy was off again, asking breathily where Jo was, on such a lovely, sunny day.

'She's on a course,' said Lee.

'A course? How lovely! I was thinking of doing a course to become a doula, or maybe to do baby massage. What course is it?'

'An entrepreneur's course – how to start your own business.'

'Goodness me!' This was clearly outside her frame of reference, so she asked no more questions, and instead went on about how important baby massage was for sensory development. Zach pulled on Lee's hand. 'Da-ad . . .'

'Do excuse me,' Lee said smoothly. 'I promised Zach an ice cream.' As soon as the words were out of his mouth, he realised he'd made a rookie error.

'Oooh, ice cream! What do you think, Martha? Shall we have a little treatie too?'

There would be no escape. They walked together to the kiosk, and the woman talked non-stop. Jo was absolutely right. She had no topics of conversation outside babies and children. Zach skipped ahead and ran back, jumped and did roly-polies on the grass. Martha walked sedately, holding her mother's hand. At one point, Zach came rushing back and said, 'I'm having a whole day with my dad today. Where's your dad, Martha?'

Martha didn't get a chance to answer. Her mum giggled and said to Zach, 'Martha's daddy's playing golf today. He likes to play golf when the weather is nice.' She smiled at Lee. 'You know what men are like – boys and their toys . . .'

Wow, Lee thought, she really did love to trot out meaningless clichés.

They got to the kiosk and got ice creams for the kids and coffees for themselves. The woman ordered a chocolate brownie. 'They're the best brownies I've ever had!' she said, offering Lee a piece. 'I've tried to work out what's in them and copy the recipe but mine are never quite as good. I wish I knew what the secret ingredient was!'

Lee began to realise that she prattled on much as Zach sometimes did. It wasn't like him to tune people out, but he guessed that she kept up the non-stop chatter and the clichés to mask her shyness and awkwardness, and he only had to listen to about one sentence in ten and nod if she ended a sentence with an upward inflection that suggested a question.

It was a beautiful day, and even though the company was not who he would have chosen, he was enjoying his time in the park with the kids. He looked down at Imogene, sitting forward in her pushchair and chewing on a rusk. The sun glistened on her abundant curls. When she had been born, he'd imagined that she'd be just like Zach, in a female version, but now she was nearly a year old it was apparent that she was very much her own person. Zach had always been an unrelenting, noisy bundle of energy who required constant interaction and a lot of affirmation. Imogene was much more self-contained. She could keep herself occupied alone for a remarkably long time for such a small child, and she kept up a low mutter of baby noise, as if she was talking to herself.

She was very dextrous for her age and loved to sit and play with a textured toy, or, as she was doing now, gum and crumble a piece of food. Unlike Zach, she was a good sleeper too; from the age of four months or so, she'd done a solid twelve hours a night, seven till seven. Lee felt a little tug – because of the hours he worked, he often saw her for just a few minutes a day, and in a funny way, he felt he didn't know her. She was really cool too. He unstrapped her and lifted her on to his lap. She leaned back against him and continued to gum her rusk happily, smearing some on to his sleeve.

His phone rang, and to his surprise he saw it was Jo. 'So sorry,' he said to his companion, who had barely paused for breath. 'Hi, love,' he said. 'Are you done?'

'Yes, we finished at four today because we have so much homework for tomorrow. Oh, Lee, it was amazing! I learned so much. And Louise is really incredible. She's definitely our kind of person.'

'That's great, I can't wait to hear all about it.'

'Listen, I'm walking to the station now. I'll text you from Waterloo, just before I get on the Tube. I forgot to get anything in for dinner for us. Can we stop at the supermarket once you've picked me up?'

'I'll sort dinner, don't worry. You've got your homework to do.' Lee smiled. 'See you soon. Love you.'

It wasn't till he put his phone away that he realised the woman had stopped talking at last and was staring at him. 'You're going to get dinner? Gosh,' she said, and then, in a slightly wistful tone, 'You speak to her so sweetly. Like you're newly-weds.'

Lee smiled. 'Married five years, loved her for closer to fifteen. Look, lovely to chat to you, but since I've promised dinner, I'd better deliver.'

He called Zach, slipped Imogene back in her pushchair and headed off, leaving Martha's mum staring after him.

Lee knew his limits, so when Jo texted from Waterloo, he rang the local Italian and arranged to collect pizzas forty minutes later. He pulled up outside the station and Jo slipped into the passenger seat. She leaned over and kissed him on the corner of his mouth then twisted in her seat to blow kisses to both kids.

'Hello, lovelies! I missed you! Did you have a lovely day?' Then she sniffed rapturously.' 'Is that garlic bread I smell?'

'Garlic bread, that salad you like and two pizzas to share.'

'Ah, nobody orders takeaway like you do, sweetie.'

'Who needs that *Masterchef*? Masterdial, that's me.'

'I'm starving. I was too excited to eat much lunch.'

'So it was good?'

'Amazing. I've just got so much to do tonight. Today was all presentations: lectures on various aspects of business. Tax, set-up costs and so on, but it was all general, not specific to each person's business plan or anything. Tomorrow, there'll be all sorts of experts on hand and we all get one-to-ones with each of them, so I need to prepare all my questions so I can get the best out of each session.'

'Sounds like this course was real value for money.'

'When you think what I might have ended up with . . . Louise is amazing. And she has small kids of her own, so I know she understands what it takes to juggle a family and work. And she's funny. I think you'd like her.'

'I haven't heard you talk like that about someone for ages.'

'It's ages since I met someone I liked so much. You know what it's like . . . I hardly see the old lot because none of them have kids, and the people I meet at toddler groups and at the nursery gates . . . well, I don't think having children the same age is necessarily the basis for a meaningful relationship.'

'Speaking of which, I met nameless mumsy woman – Martha's mum – in the park. We had coffee.'

'Oh, my poor darling. Are you all right? Bored almost to death, I suppose.'

'She's not scintillating company, is she? But I couldn't shake the feeling that she seems . . . I don't know . . . sad.'

'Sad? She's always very "bubbly" with me. She's exactly the kind of woman who would describe herself as bubbly.'

'Maybe you're right,' said Lee as he pulled up outside the house. 'Anyway, I don't want to talk about her. I want to hear all about your day.'

'I'll tell you everything,' said Jo, jumping out and unstrapping Imogene from her car seat to give her a hug. But first . . . pizza!'

In the end, Lee went off to bed alone. Jo had started scribbling notes before she'd even finished eating. She took a brief break to bath the kids and get them into bed, and then sat straight down at the computer. He brought her a cup of tea, and then another, but by eleven, he was yawning.

'You go up,' Jo said, absently patting him on the leg as he stood beside her chair. 'I won't be long.'

He glanced at the clock when she finally slipped into bed beside him. It was after one. He could feel her lying very still beside him, but she seemed almost to vibrate, her brain was working so rapidly. He knew she was lying on her back, staring at the ceiling in the dark, and the ideas were tumbling fast. He put a tentative hand on her shoulder, and in one rapid movement, she turned into his arms and kissed him hard, running her hands up under his T-shirt. He was surprised at her passion, but more than happy to respond.

Afterwards, they lay side by side holding hands. 'Well, if this is what business does for you, I approve,' said Lee.

'Sorry I woke you.'

'Don't be sorry. You can wake me for that any time. But seriously, it's great to see you so fired up.'

'I think it could work, you know. I do. There are a million things I have to sort out, and a million obstacles. But if we can get past all those things . . . find the right premises, the right stock . . . I think it could be amazing.'

'I think so too.'

'Do you? Do you really?' She turned on her side and looked at him. It was dark, but he could see her eyes shining. 'Because it's going to be a hell of a thing, Lee. Balancing the shop and the kids, setting everything up. I'm going to need a lot of help.'

'And I'm here to help you. I'll do anything for you, my love. You know that.'

'You know, from anyone else, that would be a line. But I believe you. Now turn over.'

Lee turned on his side and Jo spooned around his back, holding him close, and they fell asleep breathing in unison.

The next morning, Jo wanted to leave early, so she walked down to the Tube station, leaving Lee and the kids lounging in pyjamas, eating Sunday-treat sugary cereal and watching a Disney film. It was a misty grey day, not raining yet, but looking like it might. Lee felt wonderfully decadent and lazy, sprawled on the sofa with Zach curled in the crook of his arm, and Imogene sat at his feet chewing on a giant jigsaw piece. They weren't due at his parents' till twelve, so he had plenty of time.

It would be nice, he thought idly, if Jo came home tonight and there wasn't a stack of laundry and an intimidating amount of housework for her to tackle. He wriggled out from under Zach, who grumbled for a second and then settled back into the sofa, his eyes glued to the screen. Lee bounded upstairs and grabbed the laundry baskets from their bedroom and the kids' rooms. He stuck on a dark load, making sure to exclude Jo's cashmere jumper. He noticed the kitchen looked a bit grim, so he loaded the dishwasher and, popping his head round the door periodically to check on the kids, set about cleaning all the surfaces and mopping the floor. The film had finished by then so he put both kids on the sofa, told them it was a ship and made a game of hoovering around them. Then he took them both upstairs to play and get dressed, and gave the bathroom a quick once-over too. Once he had both kids ready, he did a quick sweep, tidying the bedrooms, putting toys away downstairs, moving the washing into the dryer and putting on another load. Satisfied, he loaded both kids into their car seats and headed for his parents' house.

Lee's parents lived in Pinner, a few miles away. They were both retired. When Lee and his sister had moved out, they sold the family home and bought a comfortable bungalow. Lee's dad had worked for BT as an engineer for his whole working life. He was methodical and quiet, a son of Jamaican immigrants. Lee's mum was a brisk, slim blonde Yorkshire-woman who had come down to London in her early twenties to pursue a career in teaching. She joined a book club, where she met and fell in love with softly spoken Austin Hockley, and the rest, as she was fond of saying, was family history. She had risen through the ranks to become the head teacher of an all-girls' school, and when she wanted something done, her voice still had the authoritative ring of a head-mistress. It took a brave person to stand up to Betty Hockley. Imogene and Zach, naturally, had no such issues with her. She was a besotted grandmother, and she was much more indulgent with them than she had ever been with Lee and his sister.

She met them at the door, kissed Lee and immediately scooped Imogene out of his arms. 'Come through!' she said happily. 'Grandma has the table in the conservatory set up for painting.' Sure enough, the big table was covered with a plastic tablecloth, and there was a great sheet of news-print, as big as the table. There were pots of finger paint, and home-made stamps cut out of potatoes, and she had bought two all-over plastic bibs to protect the kids' clothing. She popped Imogene into the high chair she kept for the grandchildren's visits and set about getting the kids smearing and printing. Austin wandered in and smiled at the scene. Lee gave his dad a hug and they stood watching as Zach worked his way around the table with a dinosaur stamp, printing bright green dinosaurs all over the paper, and Imogene smeared paint on the tray of her high chair and gummed a chunk of raw potato.

'I wish I could play too,' said Lee. 'It looks amazing!'

'You can, as long as you don't get paint on your shirt,' said Betty with mock sternness.

'No dinosaur for Daddy!' said Zach possessively. 'Mine!'

'Any more potatoes, Mum? Can I make my own stamps?'

'Of course!' Betty brought him a few spuds and a sharp knife. Austin showed Imogene how to dip her fingers in the paint and draw on the paper, and tried to stop her eating too much of it, and Lee sat carving an intricate abstract pattern into his potato. Wonderful smells wafted out of the kitchen, and his mum emerged to bring drinks out for everyone.

'Beer? Wine?' she asked Lee.

'No, thanks, Mum – I'm driving and in sole charge of two small children. Better not.'

Betty nodded approvingly and passed him a glass of juice. 'How've you managed? Has it been hectic?'

'It's been great. Jo's loving her course, and I've just had a brilliant time with the kids. I've missed her, of course, but it's been kind of nice to have Zach and Imi all to myself.'

'How's the house? Bomb-struck?'

'No! I'll have you know I did all the housework before I came here today.'

Betty raised an eyebrow. 'Well, Jo's a lucky woman then, isn't she?'

Lunch was delicious, and afterwards both kids fell asleep on the sofa with their grandpa. Lee gently lifted Imogene and laid her in her pushchair. She snuffled and put a finger on her mouth. He looked at her long eyelashes and perfect little apple cheeks for a long time. Zach looked perfectly happy, sprawled halfway across Grandpa's belly, his mouth slightly open and a smear of gravy on his chin. Lee tiptoed into the kitchen to offer to help, but Betty had already loaded the dishwasher and put the coffee on.

He wandered back out to the conservatory, where the detritus of the painting was still spread all over the table. He tidied up and then idly picked up a potato and a sharp knife. With the tip of the knife, he scored a curve in the potato, and then carefully marked out the shape of a sleeping woman. He cut away the bits around his outline, dipped it in royal-blue paint and tried it out. It was a little uneven, so he dried the stamp, corrected the shape with the knife and tried again. Then he took another potato and carved a lithe and slippery fish and made a number of prints with the bright yellow paint. He was on a roll, and he started carving lots of different shapes, human and animal. Some didn't work at all – the octopus was too intricate and made a huge, messy blob, but some were interesting and primitive. Tired of the bright primary colours, he started to mix more subtle shades. Once he'd covered a large area of the paper with stamps, he hunted around for a brush and started to paint a vibrant sky with clouds and a crimson sunset, and bits of landscape between the printed animals. He'd been going for about an hour before he was aware of Betty sitting quietly near the kitchen door and watching him. He smiled, a little embarrassed. 'Just playing, Mum. I'll clear up after, promise.'

'It's lovely to see you paint again. Knock yourself out.'

'Zach's going to be furious when he sees what I've done to his dinosaurs.'

'You haven't painted over them. You've incorporated them. It's wonderful, darling.'

Betty wasn't one for fake or unearned praise, and Lee stepped back to look; it was kind of wonderful, a mad, colourful Garden of Eden craziness, with sea creatures in the mountains and elephants frolicking in the waves. Amazing what you could do with finger paints and a few potatoes.

'Can I keep it, Mum? Jo might like to see it for ideas for her shop.'

'Now, tell me about this shop,' said Betty. 'I know she's gone on this business course, but you've both been pretty cagey about what sort of shop it is.'

Lee described it, with the rails of kids' clothing high on the walls and the play area down below. Betty listened seriously without interrupting.

'It would need to be tremendously safe, that goes without saying.'

'I'm sure Jo will be getting advice on that.'

'And there might be potential to extend it . . . perhaps add a little coffee-and-cake area where mums could sit down for a cuppa after shopping? Maybe a bookshop corner?'

'Great ideas, Mum. Maybe for stage two, but great ideas.'

'But if anyone can make it happen, Jo can. She's a go-getter, that girl.'

Jo, sitting opposite a health-and-safety expert in the hotel in Kingston, was inclined to feel that her get-up-and-go had got up and left. Between them, the experts she had met with had sucked all the joy out of her idea. The financial expert had been gloomy at best, saying that considering the current financial crisis, it was a terrible time to start a luxury store. Jo protested and said that she wasn't planning on selling premium-priced goods, but he raised his eyebrows as if he didn't believe her and kept punching numbers into his calculator and shaking his head. The insurance woman told her she would end up paying a king's ransom in public-liability insurance, and the health-and-safety man's endless list of problems and potential hitches was making her lose the will to live. Did it have to be this hard? she wondered, but then she glanced around the room, and every one of the potential business owners had a face full of doom and gloom. At least she wasn't alone.

At the coffee break, she found herself next to Daniel and Chris, the two teenage guys. 'Maybe we should just go home,' Daniel was saying. 'This is bloody useless.'

'My mum paid for us to come,' said Chris. 'We can't bail out now. And anyway, what do these guys know about starting an online business? They're all like a hundred and three.'

'What kind of business?' Jo found herself saying. Damn. Louise had told them not to discuss their actual intended business. She didn't want the boys to think she was trying to poach their ideas.

They didn't seem bothered though. 'T-shirts,' said Daniel. 'I design them; Chris screen-prints them. We've built a pretty good following through friends, but it's time to take it to the next level.'

Jo didn't know what to say. She was probably as old as

both of them put together, and they already had a successful small business.

'Here's our card,' said Chris. 'My dad made us get cards, even though they're archaic. Still, Dan did a pretty good job on the design, and they're fun to give out.'

The card was bright orange and cut in the shape of a old-fashioned TV screen with rounded corners, and there was a brilliantly wobbly cartoon face peering in from the edge, pointing impishly at their company name: 'Outtake'. Their names were on the back of the card, with their email address, website, Skype details and Facebook page. Now Jo felt doubly depressed. They were so far ahead of her she didn't even know where to begin. She'd been naive, thinking she could do this. Her after-coffee session was with a PR expert, and she, like the boys, was tempted to cut and run. However, she reasoned, she may know next to nothing about insurance or finance, but she really knew PR. Maybe the meeting would offer a little confidence boost.

The PR expert was a bright young thing in her late twenties, with smooth blond hair and a way of using jargon that sounded as if she was beginning each term with a capital letter.

Jo outlined her business idea to the woman, who listened intently.

'You're going to want to Leverage Regional Capital,' she announced seriously.

'I'm going to . . . what ?'

'You'll need to build a degree of Neighbourhood Traction, so you can Generate Word-of-Mouth Momentum.'

'So, get local people talking about it?'

'Exactly!' said the blonde woman enthusiastically. 'It's what we call School-Gate Collateral. It's worth its weight in gold.'

'I'm so glad there's an industry term for chatting to my mates,' said Jo, smiling, but the Blonde seemed to have had her sense of humour removed at marketing college.

'If you Grease your Local Customer Funnel, there's a good chance you can generate a Meaningful Hook to entice Local Press or Influential Mummy Bloggers . . . that way you have more of a chance of Landing the Big Fish.'

'The Big Fish?'

'National Press,' breathed the Blonde reverently.

'Well, as it's only going to be a small local shop, I don't think national press interest is terribly likely. It would be wonderful of course, but very unlikely.'

'We should *always* aim for National Press Coverage,' stated the Blonde, as if this was a universal truth. And with that, the interview was over. She was the only dud in the panel of experts, and Jo made a note to mention it gently to Louise. It had been a laugh though, and made her feel a bit better.

She already had a raft of ideas to publicise the shop. That was, of course, if she ever found the money to fund it, the premises to house it, someone to insure the whole bloody thing and the stock to fill it. This last was her biggest concern. There was no point in a clothing store without clothes. Most people launched a clothing business by designing the garments and then worried about how to sell them. She had the greatest how, but no actual clothes to sell. The more she thought about it, the more certain she was that she didn't want to sell one-of-a-kind couture items that most parents wouldn't be able to afford and kids would only wear once or twice. The market for that would be tiny, and anyway, she wanted the shop to appeal to ordinary stressed and busy mums like herself. She wanted someone who could produce reasonably priced, hard-wearing and attractive kids' clothes, with a few extra fun and funky items. But where to find such a person? And how was she even to start looking?

At lunch, she found herself sitting on her own, glumly eating a sandwich without tasting it, and glancing through the notes she'd made in her meeting with Mr Health and Safety. She was going to have to learn about non-toxic materials and paints, it seemed. And then there was the issue of finding Criminal Records Bureau-checked staff, not to mention investigating stock-control software and till systems. She let out a big sigh, just as Louise slipped into the seat opposite her.

'I know that sigh. That's the "I can't do this, it's too hard" sigh.'

'You've seen people sigh that sigh before?'

'Every time we do this course. I know it looks like there are more problems than solutions, and it is going to be hard, but, Jo, I do think you have what it takes.'

Jo smiled weakly. 'I bet you say that to all the girls. And boys.'

'I don't. I think you have the drive and the organisation, and the courage. And you're a mum, so you know how to multitask and make the most of every little fragment of time. I don't even know what your idea is, but I still think you can make it as an entrepreneur.'

'Do you want to know my idea?'

'Do you want to tell me?'

'Only if you lie and tell me it's brilliant. Kidding. Only if you're honest and you tell me if you think it could work.'

Louise leant back in her chair, folded her arms over her little pregnancy bump and said, 'Okay, tell me.'

Jo was practised now that she'd run through her pitch for each of the experts that morning, so she rattled through the description of her shop and then opened her folder to show Louise Lee's initial sketches. Louise looked at them for a long time in silence.

'Old H&S Gerald is right: there are mountains of things you're going to have to get right to get this one past the authorities.'

Jo sank lower in her seat. Her fears were correct. It was too hard. But Louise was still going through the sketches, one by one. Finally, she pushed them back across the table and said, 'Having said that, this is the single most original and exciting idea I've seen since I started running these seminars. And as the mother of a small boy, I'd travel a long way to visit your shop. This is brilliant, Jo. You're on to a winner here.'

Jo floated through the afternoon sessions, through the farewell drinks and on to the train. She felt so fired up and full of positive energy, she could have burst. Lee picked her up at the station and took her home, but she held back on talking about it. It wasn't a conversation she wanted to rush through while they handled the kids' dinner, bath and bedtime and juggled the needs of two demanding toddlers. She wanted to discuss it seriously. Anyway, there'd be a million things to do in the house when they got in.

Except – there weren't. As they walked through the door, she could smell furniture polish. The living room was clean and freshly hoovered and there was a stack of clean, folded laundry on the kitchen table.

'Wow!' said Jo. 'The house looks amazing.'

'I thought I'd get some stuff done before we went to my parents, so it wouldn't be too bad when we got home.'

'Thanks, love. It looks great. Well, all I have to do is make dinner.'

'You don't even need to do that. My mum has as much faith in my cooking as you do, so she gave me a chicken casserole to bring home. It's warming in the oven right now. I'll just put some rice on, if that's okay.'

'That's more than okay.'

'I stopped on the way back from Pinner to get bread and milk for the morning, and I got us a bottle of Pinot, so, if you like, just sit down in the living room, play with the kids or whatever, and I'll bring you a glass.'

Jo didn't need to be asked twice. She kicked off her shoes and sat down on the floor with the kids. She had Imogene cuddled into her lap, and she and Zach set about building a fort out of wooden bricks. Progress was slow because every time they got any height to it, Zach would push it over, or Imogene would pull out a vital supporting brick to chew on. It was lovely to hear her kids laugh though, and she cuddled Imi's solid little body close. Zach suddenly flung himself on her, his bony little arms tight around her neck, and kissed her wetly on the ear.

'Did you miss me, Zachy? I missed you.'

'Nah. We had the best time at Gran and Grandpa's, and Dad's been cool. Can I have some juice?'

'Course you can. Go and ask Dad in the kitchen.'

He bounded off and she looked around her tidy living room. She felt a small sad knot in her stomach, and she berated herself for being the meanest, most ungrateful, small-minded person in the world. Because while she had said all the right things to Lee, and while she'd had an amazing day and was beside herself with excitement at the prospects for the shop, she felt nastily, jealously cross that Lee and the kids had managed so well without her. She felt, irrationally, that Lee's doing all the housework was a comment on the fact that she hadn't done it before rushing off for the weekend, and that Betty sending a casserole was a silent reproach for her absence. Knowing and loving her husband and mother-in-law as she did, she knew that these thoughts were hers and not theirs at all. But she couldn't shake the feeling that it was all too easy to replace her in her primary role as mother and carer. Lee came through with her glass of wine and dropped a kiss on the top of her head, which made her hate herself even more. He was the best bloke in the world, and she was incredibly lucky to have him. She'd heard story after story of women who'd left their husbands in charge of the kids and come home to a house that looked like a hurricane had been through it. Lee was thoughtful, practical and competent, and even though he had extremely limited cooking skills, his ability to hunter-gather (or get his mum to do it) was admirable. Imogene had crawled off her lap and was heading determinedly for the kitchen. Jo shook the negative thoughts away, put her wine glass down and crawled after her daughter for some cuddles and tickles.

Once the kids were in bed, she and Lee sat down to talk about what she had learned on the course and their next steps. 'A lot of what I need to do is just red tape and time,' said Jo. 'But there are two big problems that I don't know how to solve. The first is how we fund this project without bankrupting ourselves, and the second is finding the right clothes to stock the shop.'

'How much do you think you'll need to get this thing off the ground?'

'I need to firm up the numbers, and of course stock, which is an unknown, will be a big part of the set-up cost, but I think we're looking at about £50,000. That should cover premises, stock, set-up and salaries, for a few months anyway, depending on where we find premises.'

'Ouch.'

'I know.'

'What did you learn about funding on the course?'

'Well, there are quite a lot of business loan schemes, and grants for start-ups I can apply for. I just . . . well . . . it doesn't seem fair for me to get us into more debt while I'm not actually bringing anything in.'

'But you will be.'

'We hope.'

'I know. I have such faith in you, Jo. And from what you told me about what the woman running the course said, well, that sounds like it is a unique idea. And a good one. It would be wrong not to go for it.'

'Enough about me though,' said Jo. 'How did you find the weekend? Was it a nightmare being all on your own?'

'Anything but. I loved it. I loved having time with the kids and taking them to see my folks. I don't want to go to work tomorrow – I want to stay home and play again.'

Jo's laugh was strained. 'Well, it sounds like you had an easy time of it. If you'd ended up with a two-day stretch where Zach was throwing hourly tantrums, the washing machine packed up and Imi had one of her clingy fits, you might have had less fun.'

Lee, as always, got the subtext. 'I know what you do every day is hard. I know I got a lucky break this weekend and the kids were easy. But I really did have fun. I just want you to know that if you need time and space to work on your business in the evenings and at weekends, at least you don't need to worry about the kids being looked after.'

'I'll drink to that,' said Jo, refilling their wine glasses.

4

HOLLY NOW

She didn't care what anybody else said, London was just bloody freezing. Holly was cold all the time, even though people kept telling her it was summertime – the best summer they'd had in years. She wasn't sure if it was the weather that made her feel like that, or the constant, icy knot in her stomach. Everything was so strange, such a wrench. It was ten years since she'd last lived here. So much had changed, both in the neighbourhood around her mother's house, and in her. A crowd of teenage boys stood on the corner of the road, talking and laughing, and, as far as Holly could see, spitting incessantly. The old-fashioned corner shop she used to go to on her way home from school had been replaced by a Tesco Metro, and the pub up the road had closed down, to be replaced by a giant betting shop that was open till eleven every night. And what about Holly herself? The Holly who had climbed on the plane to South Africa, twenty years old, full of ideals and energy, couldn't be more different from the thirty-year-old woman hunched by the radiator, staring out of her mother's window at the suburban street. She'd been back to London in the intervening years, but only as a tourist, coming home for the odd Christmas or for family weddings or occasions. She always knew then that at the end of the week, or two weeks, she would be getting on a plane back to Jo'burg, to her large, sunny workshop, and the sprawling house she shared with Damon.

But now she was back. Back for good? She didn't know. All she knew was that she couldn't be in Johannesburg right now. Not with all the memories, not with the constant possibility of bumping into one of Damon's friends, or his mother. Not a chance. So she'd packed up her stuff, put most of it in storage in a friend's garage and got on a plane. And here she was, back in Ealing, with nothing to show for the decade she'd been away.

She'd kind of lost contact with the friends she'd had in London, and she didn't feel like explaining to anyone why she was back, what she was going to do or how long she'd be staying, especially as she didn't know the answers to the last two questions herself. As a result, she hadn't seen anyone or gone anywhere in the week since she'd been home. Her sister had rung her every day and kept offering to come and see her. Until now, Holly had managed to put her off. She'd done some grocery shopping for her mum, finding the aisles of an English supermarket strange and confusing after so many years away, and she'd sat shivering on a bench in the park for an hour each day, mainly to avoid her mum's constant offers of tea and overly sympathetic expression. She couldn't do another day of it though. She had to get out and do something, so she decided she'd get on a bus and head for North London to see Miranda.

Holly's sister was four years older than her, but the age

gap might as well have been three times that, their lives were so far apart. Miranda was married with two children, and keen to add at least two more to her brood. Her husband Paul did something with hedge funds in the City, and as a result they had a lovely big house and no shortage of money. Miranda didn't need to work, didn't want to work, and devoted every fibre of her being to her children.

Holly sat upstairs on a number-83 bus, looking out of the window at the endless rows of houses and shops that made up suburban London. Everyone behind each of those doors had something to do: a job, a family, a purpose. She had sod all, right now. First of all, she was going to need to get a job . . . she'd brought what little money she had back with her, but the exchange rate was not kind to her savings at all. She knew it wouldn't be hard to find work of some sort – she had transferable skills – but she needed to think about what she wanted to do. She needed to set some life goals. She'd had some, pretty clearly marked out ones, but then Damon had decided to change everything.

Maybe going to see Miranda was a mistake. Her mum's sympathy was bad enough, but in Miranda's eyes Holly would be a real failure – no man, no prospect of a family. Miranda wouldn't even care that Holly's career plans had gone down the pan. She'd never understood Holly's rather unconventional career path anyway. Like some kind of terrifying 1950s throwback, Miranda thought work was something women did until they had children. Holly seriously considered texting to say she was ill, getting off the bus, crossing the road and getting on another one going in the opposite direction. But when she thought about the silent house and her mother's face arranged in an expression of perpetual pity, she decided Miranda was the lesser evil.

When she got there, she expected to find Miranda calmly engaged in some perfect maternal pursuit – making cupcakes or reading an educational book to the kids. But instead she opened the door holding a screaming baby Oscar and smelling distinctly of vomit.

'Oh, thank God you're here. It's lovely to see you, but please forgive me if I don't kiss you.'

'Lovely to see you too, Randa, and no worries, I really don't need a kiss.'

'Oscar's come down with the twenty-four-hour bug. He's vomited up everything I've given him so far today. Most of it in my hair.'

'Delightful.'

I think he's empty right now. Could you hold him for five minutes while I dash through the shower?'

Without waiting for an answer, Miranda handed the fat, bald baby to Holly, who held him rather gingerly away from her. Miranda dashed off up the stairs, pulling her stained shirt over her head. 'Martha's in the living room!' she yelled over her shoulder.

Holly carried Oscar into the perfectly tidy living room. Martha was sitting in the middle of the enormous sofa, her legs stretched out in front of her, watching a Barbie film on DVD.

'Hey,' Holly said, and perched on the edge of a chair, still holding Oscar as far away from her body as she could. He was very sweet, she was sure, but he smelled decidedly iffy. Martha looked over at her.

'Who are you?'

'I'm your aunt Holly. The one who lives . . . lived in South Africa? We've talked on Skype, remember?'

'You look different.'

'That's because I'm not trapped inside a computer screen.'

Martha, a serious little girl, nodded her head and turned back to her film.

Holly bounced Oscar lightly on her knee and watched the screen too. Then it occurred to her that bouncing a nauseous baby might not be such a good idea, especially over Miranda's immaculate golden carpets, so she stopped. He didn't look happy, poor little chap. He was very round, but his little face looked drawn and pale. Even though he still smelled pretty gross, she drew him closer to her and he rested his head against her chest. It was the first time she'd ever seen him: the last time she'd been in the UK, Martha had been about eighteen months old and Miranda was pregnant with Oscar. Now Martha was three, and this sturdy little chap must be about nine months old.

Miranda came back down the stairs, dressed in fresh clothes, her wet hair combed back from her face.

'That's better!' she said cheerfully. 'Now, can I get you a cup of tea? Something to eat?'

'I'm fine.' Holly handed Oscar over to his mum, and Miranda settled herself on the sofa opposite.

'I know that you must be sad to be back, but honestly, Holls, it's such a treat to see you. I've been dying for you to get to know the children. Oscar's starting to crawl, and Martha can count up to thirty, can't you, darling?'

'One, two, three . . .' began Martha dutifully.

'You don't need to do it now, sweetie,' said Miranda. 'But I'm sure Auntie Holly would love to see some of your drawings.'

Martha trotted off dutifully and came back with a stack of paper, which she put on the table in front of Holly. She lifted each page one by one. Every picture was pretty much identical . . . a round face with stick legs and arms coming out of it, in shades of pink and purple. Holly made what she hoped were encouraging auntly noises.

'Why don't you draw some more?' said Miranda, and Martha went to fetch a pink princess pencil case, and knelt on the floor by the coffee table. Oscar, who looked wrung out, cuddled close to Miranda and chewed on his little fist.

'So how is it being back?'

'Awful? Freezing? Don't know. I've really just hidden in Mum's house; I haven't rung anyone. You're the first people I've been to see.'

'Well, we're flattered,' said Miranda. 'Sorry you've come to the house of puke though.'

'Ah, from the house of sighs, to the house of puke,' Holly grimaced.

'What do you mean?'

'Well, you know what Mum's like . . . she keeps creeping around me, offering me cups of tea in this sympathetic whisper, like I might die or something if she speaks in a normal voice. I must be such a disappointment to her.'

'Really?' said Miranda, surprised. 'I mean, I know she's sad that you're sad, about . . . you know . . . Damon and everything, but she was so excited about you coming back. She's been boasting about you to her church ladies for years, you know – her exotic, creative daughter, living in the wilds of Africa.'

Holly snorted. That hardly seemed likely. At that moment, Oscar sat up bolt upright and began to retch, his pale little face suddenly bright red.

'Oh dear, here we go again,' said Miranda, jumping up and racing for the downstairs bathroom. She just made it and held the poor little thing over the toilet bowl.

'Martha's okay so far,' she yelled out at Holly. 'I'm trying to keep everything spotless so she doesn't get it too. I'll have to scrub this bathroom again now.'

'Would it help if I took her out for a while?' called Holly.

'Oh, would you?' said Miranda coming out of the bathroom. She'd washed Oscar's little face, and within seconds he fell asleep, exhausted, on her shoulder.

'Where can we go?'

'Oh, the park is at the end of the road. Martha will show you where. Just let her have a go on the swings and the slide and have a run around for half an hour. Oh, and make sure you take some baby wipes. I like to give the swings and things a clean before she uses them.'

Holly nodded and accepted Miranda's Cath Kidston nappy bag, although she had no intention of being the crackpot in the park wiping playground equipment down with baby wipes. She helped Martha to put on a pink cardigan, which matched her pink tights and white and pink spotted skirt, and, taking her hand, set off for the park. They walked in silence. Holly didn't know a lot about small children, and she didn't know Martha at all, and Martha didn't seem inclined to chat like some little kids would.

The entrance to the park was around the corner at the end of Miranda's quiet little road. If you didn't know it was there, you'd be unlikely to happen upon it. It was a beautiful park, Holly noted with surprise, with plenty of unusual trees, green lawns and beautifully cared-for flower beds. Close to the entrance, there was a well-equipped children's play area, with sturdy, brightly coloured equipment and a soft rubbery surface. It was far from the grim tarmacked playgrounds she remembered from growing up, which were always full of scary teenagers smoking. Even though the park was well hidden, there were plenty of people in the play area on this weekday afternoon: lots of mums with their children, but also a fair smattering of grandparents, and some young women who looked too young to be mums and Holly guessed were au pairs.

They stood at the entrance to the park. Holly had expected Martha to run off and play immediately, but she stood quietly, still holding Holly's hand. 'What do you want to do?' Holly asked tentatively. Martha said something so softly that Holly had to get down on her knees and ask her to repeat it several times. Eventually she worked out that Martha was saying, 'I like to swing.'

She walked her over to the swings and carefully lifted her in. Martha sat very straight, her hands in the air as if she was being held at gunpoint. 'Mamma always wipes the bar before I touch it,' she said, clearly distressed, so, against her will, Holly was forced to dig the pack of baby wipes out of the nappy bag and wipe down the swing after all. Once she'd done it (and disposed of the wipe in the bin, on Martha's instruction), she was allowed to push the swing, very gently. If she got too vigorous, Martha wailed in distress and she had to slow the swing down and resume the slow back-and-forth pace. She asked a few times if Martha would like to go on the slide or the roundabout, but Martha shook her head and continued to sit like a little statue in the swing. It was very dull.

Holly looked around and saw a lot of the mums (and most of the au pairs) were looking at their mobile phones or chatting to each other, rather than watching their children. She wasn't surprised. Doing this every day would bore her rigid. As she was babysitting her niece for the very first time, she thought hauling out her phone for a Facebook session or a game of Angry Birds would probably look bad, so she contented herself with people-watching. It was definitely a rather well-off area: all the mums looked very well groomed and nicely dressed, and the pushchairs lined up along the fence of the play area were all new and expensive-looking. She felt scruffy in her old jeans and sandals, and the brightly coloured shirt she had made herself.

After a while, she got the feeling that someone was watching her. She looked around and saw a tall blonde woman looking at her. The woman was holding a baby girl who had a wild halo of fairish curls, and there was a little boy with a similar cloud of hair, jumping up and down in front of her, talking nineteen-to-the-dozen. The little boy saw his mum was distracted and turned to look at what she was looking at. When he caught sight of Martha on the swing he came running over. He stood squarely in front of Holly and said, 'You're not Martha's mum.'

'No, I'm not. I'm her aunt.'

'Where's her mum?'

'At home. Baby Oscar is sick.'

'Snot sick or throw-up sick? Or bottom sick?'

'Throw-up sick. And maybe bottom sick. I'm not sure.'

'I was bottom sick. I pooed on the kitchen floor,' said the little boy with great satisfaction. Holly wasn't quite sure how to respond to that, but at that moment his mum came over.

'Hi,' she said, smiling. 'Zach saw Martha and wanted to say hello. I'm Jo. Oh . . . and this is Zach, and Imogene.' She indicated the baby in her arms. 'Zach and Martha are nursery friends.' She was a strikingly attractive woman, tall and strong-boned, with a wide mouth and very blue eyes. 'Statuesque' was the word people used to describe women like that, Holly thought.

'Nice to meet you. I'm Holly, Miranda's sister.'

'Miranda!' said Jo, smiling widely, as if Holly had somehow given her the answer to a riddle. 'Miranda, of course! How is she?'

'Home with a sick baby. Zach and I have just been discussing whether it was throw-up sick or snot sick.'

'Oh dear, did he share the kitchen-floor incident with you? He's very proud of that. It's a worry.'

Jo laughed, and Holly found herself laughing too, for the first time since she'd stepped off the plane from South Africa.

'Miranda never mentioned she had a sister,' Jo said. 'It's nice to meet you.'

'Well, for the last ten years, I've been the sister who lived on the other side of the world. South Africa. I've only just got back.'

'Back to stay?'

'I think so. Not sure yet. Everything's a bit up in the air at the moment.' Holly tried to keep her voice as steady as she could, but she found herself pushing Martha's swing a little harder than she should, and it wasn't until Martha let rip with a wail that she realised what she was doing. She caught the chain of the swing and stopped it.

'Why don't you hop out and have a go at something else?' she said sweetly.

'I want to go on the roundabout with Zach,' whispered Martha.

'Zach,' said Jo to her little boy who was running around and around, pretending to be a very noisy aeroplane, 'will you take Martha on the roundabout?'

'Naaaah!' shouted Zach. 'I hate the roundabout. And she's a smelly girl!'

'Sorry,' Jo said, smiling ruefully. 'He's in that sexist phase. All boys are brilliant and all girls are smelly or boring. I'll beat it out of him eventually.'

'I think nature will probably do your work for you . . . In a little while, he might start to see girls differently.'

'No hurry for that!' said Jo.

Martha whispered something, and Holly had to lean over the swing and ask her to repeat it three times before she worked out that the little girl was saying, 'I want to go home, please.'

'Of course,' she said, and lifted her out of the swing. She turned to Jo. 'I'd better take her home and see how Miranda's coping in the sea of baby sick.'

'Oh, what a pity,' said Jo. 'I was just about to ask if you wanted to get a coffee. Another time, maybe.'

'Another time,' said Holly, and smiled. She couldn't imagine when she'd next be in North London in a park full of small children and mummies, but Jo seemed a nice woman. She took Martha's hand and they walked slowly home. Martha didn't speak the whole time, and Holly was aware of how small Martha's hand was in hers. The little girl seemed permanently slightly bewildered, as if the world was too loud, too busy and rather frightening, and she wasn't entirely sure she wanted to join in. And Holly certainly knew how she felt.

5

HOLLY THEN

Holly was born with the show-off gene that is often granted to the youngest child in largish families. Her siblings, David and Miranda, were close in age to each other, and five and four years older than her respectively. Theirs was a family where roles were assigned early and did not change. David was the clever one, who did well academically, got a scholarship to a very exclusive boys' school and then a place at Cambridge, followed by a distinguished career researching and lecturing in economics. Miranda was the good one, the average student who never gave her parents a moment's worry, loved to bake and sew and babysit the neighbours' children, had a series of unchallenging jobs and then sank with relief into marriage and life as a stay-at-home mum.

And Holly was the maverick, the funny one, the creative one. When she was little, everyone had adored her because she was pretty and sassy and outgoing. As she got older, her mother seemed to spend most of her time sighing and saying, 'Oh, *Holly*.' Holly's dad died of a heart attack when she was ten and Miranda and David were fourteen and fifteen. It was a profound shock to the whole family, and Holly found herself assuming the role of family clown in a desperate attempt to lighten the mood at the silent dinner table or on family outings. Between the ages of fifteen and nineteen, she dated a few unsuitable boys, learned to play bass (badly) and joined an all-girl metal band, got her lip and eyebrow pierced and dyed her hair some unfortunate colours. At sixteen, she started sewing her own clothes, and horrified her mother with her outlandish and experimental outfits. It wasn't as if she was properly crazy or even very wild . . . she was just a rather exotic bloom in her very domestic family bouquet. A tiger lily among the carnations. She was tall, with dark auburn curly hair and loads of freckles, and even as a teenager, she had an indefinable but very real sex appeal.

She was profoundly uninterested in school. She just didn't see the point, and when she could be bothered to participate in class, asked difficult and unanswerable questions. After Miranda's quiet path through the school, Holly was something of a shock to the teachers, and they didn't know what to make of her. She got average GCSEs and even more average A levels, certainly not good enough to get her into university.

She wasn't sure what she wanted to do when she finished school, so she did a foundation course in dressmaking. Once she'd finished that, she still didn't have a career path in mind, so she decided to go travelling. Her plan was to start in South Africa and get a job and earn some money so she could travel up through the African continent. Instead, she ended up flying into Johannesburg and staying a decade.

Johannesburg was a vibrant, exciting city, fast-moving and brash and full of opportunity, if you were brave and ready to work hard. Holly had no real skills other than her dressmaking and no work permit, but she managed to get a job in a small independent evening-wear shop in one of the big shopping malls, where the manager was prepared to turn a blind eye to her lack of paperwork because she had a nice English accent and was pretty and personable. There she sold ridiculously overpriced evening gowns to society ladies with more money than sense.

One day a glamorous but tiny woman swept into the shop, announcing she had a gala to attend that evening and she had nothing to wear. Holly gathered up an armful of dresses in the right size, but the woman swept them all aside and fell on a sheer tangerine floor-length dress with an asymmetrical neckline that left one shoulder bare.

'That's it.'

'I'm worried it'll be too long for you,' Holly said tentatively. 'Even with very high shoes . . .'

'Let me try it on,' said the woman. Sure enough, Holly was right. The grown trailed on the floor, and it was a little loose over her breasts. The colour was great against her chocolate skin, but the dress just didn't fit.

'Shall we look for something else, maybe?' Holly ventured.

'I don't like anything else,' said the woman, like a petulant child. 'I like this dress. Can't you fix it?'

'Before tonight?' said Holly disbelievingly, but the woman just looked at her, as if the request was not at all unreasonable. They sent their alterations out to a woman who worked nearby, and the turnaround time was usually about a week. However, the dress was one of the most expensive in the shop, and Holly knew if she sold it, the commission would make a sizeable difference in her pay-cheque at the end of the month.

The manager was out, and luckily things were quiet, so Holly ducked behind the counter and collected a box of pins and some tailor's chalk. She pinned up the hem and made two tiny darts in the bust. The asymmetrical neckline made this even trickier, but she did it well. Carefully, she helped the woman to slip out of it and sent her off to finish her shopping and get a coffee.

There was no sewing machine in the shop, and Holly wouldn't have trusted a machine anyway, as the fabric was so sheer and had a slight stretch to it. There was a haberdashery shop two doors down, so she put a 'Back in five minutes' note on the door and dashed along the mall to grab some thread. She was lucky to find a pretty close match to the tangerine of the dress, and she sprinted back to the shop and set about taking up the hem with tiny, neat invisible stitches. She was just stitching the second dart when the woman came back.

'Are you finished?' she said shortly, as if she expected nothing less.

'One more stitch,' said Holly, and the woman sighed rather impatiently. But when Holly lifted the dress and slid it over her head and it fitted as if it had been made for her, she smiled radiantly.

As luck would have it, the manager, Susanna, came back just as the woman was admiring herself in the mirror. Susanna went into full-scale obsequious mode and fussed over the customer extravagantly.

'Oh, madam!' she said smoothly. 'It's such a privilege to

have you in my shop. You look absolutely stunning! That dress is perfect on you.'

'Well, that's thanks to this girl here,' said the woman, waving her hand in Holly's direction, although without taking her eyes off her own reflection. 'Very good alterations.'

'Alterations?' said Susanna faintly. 'But Holly can't do . . .' She caught herself and looked over at Holly, who mouthed that she would explain later.

The woman drew a black credit card from her tiny, expensive handbag, and Susanna didn't ask any more questions. As she put through the transaction, Holly went into the changing room and helped the woman out of the garment. She folded it carefully in tissue and packed it into a box. When she carried it out and put it on the counter, Susanna, pretending that the dress needed refolding, took it out of the box and cast an eagle eye over the alterations Holly had done, before repacking it and handing it over to the woman with more fawning smiles and compliments.

'I'll be back,' said the woman. 'And I'll let some people know about you.' And she swept off in a cloud of expensive perfume.

'Do you know who that was?' breathed Susanna. 'Oh my God, Holly, do you have any idea at all who that was in our shop?'

Holly couldn't help noticing that Susanna had called it 'our shop', not something she'd ever said before. 'No, who was she?'

'That's Zini Kekana. She's a TV presenter. She's a HUGE star. What did you do?'

'She wanted the dress for an event tonight but it was too

long. I went and got some thread and took the hem up by hand and took in the top a tiny bit.'

'But it looked perfect.'

'I did study dressmaking,' said Holly defensively.

'Oh . . . I think I remember that from your CV,' said Susanna, her eyes gleaming. 'Well, well done! What a great sale! And if we can offer alterations while people wait, we'll have something totally unique here!'

Holly was rather taken aback, and not at all sure she wanted to spend her days doing rapid alterations under pressure without the proper equipment, but she needed the job and didn't want to say no. Zini was as good as her word, and one by one the great and the good of the South African entertainment industry started to come through the doors of their little boutique. Susanna grudgingly bought a sewing machine for Holly to use. She worked her fingers raw pinning and stitching, often with Susanna standing tensely over her, telling her to hurry up. It was no fun at all, and as Holly hadn't thought to charge Zini extra for the first set of alterations, word got around that she would do alterations for free, so she wasn't even making more money doing them.

She was a bit miffed, to be honest, but she couldn't afford to leave the job. She'd dug into the small amount of money she'd saved for travelling to pay the deposit and rent on a room in a rather nice shared house with a pool and a big garden, and she needed to earn some more before she could begin her great big African adventure.

One long weekend, she'd taken the shop's sewing machine home to alter some white linen trousers for a customer. It was a Friday afternoon, and by two o'clock, she found she had finished and had nothing to do. There was only sport (and that was mainly rugby) on TV. She hadn't a book to read. The weather wasn't great, so even sitting by the pool was out. Her housemate, Pierre, was a sweet Afrikaans boy, very camp and fey, who worked in advertising. He found Holly sitting at the counter in the kitchen grumpily swinging her legs and staring out of the window at the rain.

'Shame, *skattie*,' he said, patting her shoulder. 'You look so sad.'

'Not sad. Just bored. Nothing to do, not much money, hating the job. You know, the usual.'

'Well, come with me, I'm going to the Plaza. I want a new hat.'

'The Plaza? Is that a hotel?'

'No, man, the Oriental Plaza. Clothes, fabrics, cool stuff. All very cheap. And fantastic curry. I'll treat you.'

It sounded like a good offer, so she got into Pierre's bright blue Mini and they headed for Fordsburg. The Plaza was just amazing . . . packed with tiny fabric shops run by Indian traders who encouraged you to haggle for their wares. For a very small amount of money she got a few metres of gorgeous cherry-red satin and some gold tulle. Then she and Pierre shared a fabulously hot and fragrant lamb curry. It was the most fun she'd had since she'd got to Jo'burg.

They headed home in the late afternoon, and Pierre went to his room for a nap. Holly found an old newspaper in the kitchen, taped a few sheets together and began sketching out a pattern. She cut out the pattern pieces and pinned them together, then set about cutting and stitching the pretty fabrics she had bought. She worked until late that night, snatched a few hours' sleep and then carried on early in the morning. By the time Pierre emerged from his room at about ten, she was standing in the living room, admiring her new dress in the full-length mirror. It was a cheeky take on a 1950s cocktail dress, with a fitted bodice and flared skirt. She'd lined the skirt with layers and layers of the tulle, and then hooked up the hem on one side so you could see the gold froth beneath.

'Oh my heavens!' said Pierre. 'It's stunning! Totally, totally stunning! I can't believe you made that!'

'You like?'

'I love it. I LOVE it! It needs a hat though, and shoes. The perfect shoes. Black patent leather stilettos, I think. Or gold! And the hat needs to be a little pillbox number with a veil. Let's go shopping.'

'Stop!' laughed Holly. I haven't got any more money. And I've got shoes.'

'Well, at the very least, that dress needs to go out on the town. My friend Tertius is doing a drag show in Norwood tonight. You have to come.'

Holly agreed happily. She was proud of the dress and keen to show it off. However, she was not at all prepared for the response she got. The dress caused a stir from the moment she walked through the door, when a friend of Pierre's came rushing up. He had a cloud of curly blond hair and thick glasses. 'Oh, darling!' he breathed reverently. 'You look like Jane Russell and Marilyn and Cyd Charisse all rolled into one!' he fingered the fabric of the skirt. 'Where did you get this? It's DIVINE!'

'She made it,' Pierre said proudly, as if he'd made her. 'This is Holly, my housemate. She comes from London. Holly, this is my friend Wouter.'

'I lived in London for a few years,' said Wouter. 'Willesden Green. Where are you from?' He took her hand and drew her into the restaurant towards the bar. Pierre followed.

'Ealing.'

'Oh, I LOVE Ealing!' Wouter waved a hand at the barman, who put three cocktails on the bar in front of them. Two tall blond guys floated over. They looked so similar they might have been twins, but Holly noticed they were holding hands. 'This is Holly!' said Wouter proudly, as if they'd known each other forever. 'Look at her dress!'

The twins admired it and made her stand up and twirl so they could scrutinise every detail. Then Wouter's boyfriend Andile joined them and soon Holly was in the middle of an admiring crowd of handsome men. Admittedly, none of these handsome men was ever going to fancy her, but it was still fun. The cocktails flowed, and soon the club was full of women too. Some older and clearly very moneyed, some very young and glamorous, and Holly, four cocktails down, had made ten new best friends. The drag show was hilarious, and at 3 a.m. she found herself sitting on the bar with her legs elegantly crossed, singing 'Happy birthday, Mr President' to the assembled company. She felt like the most popular girl in the world.

One of the younger women sidled over and sat on the bar stool beside her. 'So would you make me a dress like that? A blue one. Like a peacock blue?' Her friend, a buxom and glamorous redhead, elbowed her aside. 'I want one too. But longer, I think, and maybe strapless? Could you do it? I've got a work party next month and I want something stunning to wear.'

'I could, I suppose . . .' said Holly doubtfully. Where would she find the time to make two dresses from scratch?

'I'm happy to pay . . .' said the first girl, and named a figure that made Holly gasp. It was a week's wages in the shop.

Wouter had been listening in, and he said firmly, 'You're going to have to go into business, Holly, my treasure. You need a stall at the Rosebank Market, and you'll make a fortune!'

'The Rosebank Market?'

'We'll take you tomorrow.' He looked at his watch. 'Today.'

What with the late night and the hangover, Holly, Pierre and Wouter didn't get going until lunchtime. The market was a large, busy affair held on the rooftop of a shopping centre. There were stalls selling African crafts and gourmet foods, but also many selling handmade clothes of all types: kids' and babies' outfits, T-shirts and funky summer frocks. Holly didn't see a stall selling evening wear, but she could see people weren't shy to spend.

They went for a cappuccino when they left the market, and as Wouter and Pierre chatted, Holly stared wistfully into the middle distance. Her own clothing line . . . It could work. It really could. If only she had the money and time to get the whole thing going. Then Pierre reached over and touched her hand. 'So here's our offer.'

'What offer?'

'Wouter and me have been talking. If you think you could make enough clothes to get a stall going, we'll lend you the money to get material and stuff. And Wouter knows the manager of the market, so he can probably get you a stand when you're ready.'

It was so crazy, so generous and so sweet Holly didn't know what to say. If the boys had faith in her, she'd just have to find the time. Evenings, weekends, early mornings . . . she'd make it happen.

'We also have a name for the clothing line, if you like,' said Wouter proudly. 'Doradolla.'

'What?'

'It means "fag hag" in Afrikaans.'

'Perfect,' said Holly. 'Doradolla – high-camp fashion.'

She spent evenings and late into the night that week sketching dresses, blouses and skirts, and drawing up patterns. Early on Saturday morning, she and Pierre headed for the Oriental Plaza and trawled through every fabric shop. Upstairs, down an obscure little alleyway, they found a tiny shop full of satins, velvets and brocades, and Holly chose six or seven fabrics that seemed right for her designs. As luck would have it, they found a Shantung faux silk in a gorgeous peacock blue, perfect for her first two commissions.

It took her six weeks of sewing every night and all weekend to make enough stock so that her stall wouldn't be look too sad and empty. She found a shop-fitting warehouse in an industrial area and bought two clothing rails cheap, and hunting around a junk yard was thrilled to find a pair of 1950s shop mannequins. One evening, Pierre excitedly presented her with a box of labels that he had had made, with the Doradolla logo sewn on to them and space to add the size of the garment in permanent ink. She stitched them in, steamed and pressed each item and hung them up. Her room looked like some kind of mad rainbow and sequin explosion, but Holly had to admit she was rather proud of what she'd created.

Early the next morning, Pierre drove her to Rosebank, his car piled high with her stock and the rails. The two mannequins sat in the back seat like a pair of sentinels. It didn't take her long to set up, but once she was done, Holly felt a lot less confident. There were so many clothing stalls, and what had looked like a lot of clothing in her room looked pitifully sparse in this enormous space. Pierre brought her a cup of coffee, and she stood shivering in the unseasonably cold morning. She wanted to go home and crawl into her bed. This was a crazy idea. It would never work. She'd sewn her fingers raw, and now she owed Pierre and Wouter thousands of rand.

Her gloom was justified. She didn't sell a thing all morning. People walked past her stall and glanced in, and a few people came in and fingered the dresses, asked the prices and moved on. Holly was glad Pierre had had to leave to go to lunch with his parents . . . she wouldn't have wanted him to stand there, hour after hour, and see her fail. She would have packed up and gone home if she could, but she had no car; she'd have to wait for her lift when Pierre came back.

But then, after lunch, something changed. The crowds seemed more relaxed, more inclined to spend longer browsing, happier to part with money. Two teenage girls came and tried on a few dresses, giggling and taking pictures of each other with their phones. It attracted more people to the stall, and suddenly Holly had four or five people leafing through her stock. Then one of the teenagers reached into her purse and brought out some crumpled notes to buy a pretty red and white spotted blouse with a pussy-bow neckline, and Holly had made her first sale. She fought hard to be nonchalant and resisted the urge to kiss and hug the girl. It didn't start a flood, but there was a determined little trickle. By the end of the day, she had sold one dress, three blouses and a skirt. She'd covered the cost of the stall for the day and made a little more. She'd learned that she needed a bigger changing-room facility than the flimsy screens she'd set up, and that the retro office wear sold better than the evening dresses. If someone asked her to define her mood, she would have said, 'Cautiously optimistic.'

That was, of course, until she went to work the next day, when Susanna met her at the door with pursed lips. 'What's this I hear about you opening a stall at the flea market?'

'Er . . . yes,' Holly said tentatively. 'I made a few things to sell.'

'Evening wear?'

'Some of it.'

'So you've set up in direct competition with this shop?'

'No!' said Holly, outraged. 'This stuff is all couture. I just made a few frocks . . .'

'On our sewing machine, I suppose.'

Holly had no answer for that.

'Pack up anything you have in the back. You can work today as you're here, and I'll pay you till the end of this week.'

It took Holly a full minute to work out that she had just been fired. She was outraged, but in the same moment knew she had no recourse, as she'd been working illegally anyway. She stood tall, walked into the back of the shop and collected the few belongings she'd left there. As she came back into the front of the shop, a customer was pleading with Susanna to get a dress altered in time for a function in two days' time. Susanna turned smoothly to Holly and said, 'Holly, dear, do you have time to take up the hem on Mrs Pienaar's gown today?'

'No, I'm afraid I don't,' said Holly, 'because I've just been fired. But, Mrs Pienaar, if you'd like a bespoke dress made in time for your event, please call me.' She handed the woman one of the cards Pierre had printed for her, picked up her bag and walked out. It was a small victory, and she got no comfort from it at all when she got back to the quiet, empty house and lay on her bed sobbing. No job, next to no money, and now no sewing machine. Things were not good.

After a good cry, a nap, a hot bath and a peanut-butter sandwich, however, Holly felt a little better, and ready to fight back. Her mum had given her a credit card when she left to go travelling. 'It's for emergencies,' she had said over and over again, 'real emergencies.' Well, as far as Holly could tell, owing two new friends a lot of money and having no way to pay it back except sewing was an emergency. She got online and looked at the price of second-hand sewing machines. On the Gumtree local website she found one similar to the one she'd been using, and rang the seller. He was happy to hold the machine for her for a few hours. She went to the bank, drew out the necessary cash and took a taxi to the seller's house. As soon as she got home, she set about making a few more blouses in a wider range of sizes and altering a couple of the dresses that hadn't sold at the market.

She carried on throughout the week, buying a little more fabric on her mum's credit card and making carefully chosen items. She gathered names from Pierre and the few other friends she had made, and sent out a mass email encouraging people to visit her stall at the market that Sunday and offering a ten-per-cent discount. She didn't give herself time to think about the enormity of the gamble she was taking. She just worked.

Sunday dawned, and her fear and trepidation increased a thousand-fold. The stall looked better than it had the week before, that was for sure, but the stakes were so much higher. She was less concerned that the morning was quiet, remembering the last time, but she began to get antsy as soon as lunchtime came. Just as she was about to panic, a girl she vaguely remembered from the night of the drag show came over. 'I'm looking for something for a hot date tonight,' she said. 'Pierre said you could sort me out with something glamorous.'

She was small and slim with white-blonde hair, and Holly knew just the thing. She had made a strapless, knee-length dress in a bright emerald green that would be a perfect fit. The girl looked dubious when Holly brought it out, but she tried it on. When she saw her reflection in the mirror, she stared at herself for ages. 'It's amazing!' she breathed. 'I'd never have chosen this colour, but it really works!'

The dress wasn't cheap, and Holly prayed silently that the girl would take it. She did, and a flirty miniskirt in neon pink. After that, the floodgates opened. Holly was kept running around for the rest of the day, and even when the market was closing up, she was still selling. She'd brought needle and thread so she could make minor adjustments to clothes if they needed it, and that proved a big draw too. She also took a few orders for items in different sizes, and those people had been perfectly happy to pay a deposit. As the afternoon flew by, she was too busy to keep track of the money she tucked into her money belt, so it wasn't until she and Pierre were sitting in a bar, sipping cold beers, that she dared count it.

It wasn't a fortune, but it was enough. She could pay her mum back the money she'd spent on the credit card, give Pierre an instalment of the money he'd invested and put aside enough for her rent, which was due the next week. It was a start.

She needed to be more self-sufficient, so she took driving lessons, got her licence and bought a second-hand estate car, which the South Africans called a 'station wagon', like the Americans do. It made her more independent and meant she could travel to suppliers and to the market without Pierre's help. It wasn't an easy life: she worked long, long hours and her income was very erratic, but somehow, month after month, she met her expenses. She wasn't saving anything, so her travel plans seemed, for the moment, to have been shelved. With Pierre's encouragement, she sought permission to stay legally in South Africa, and set up a bank account and a legal business entity.

Once she was mobile she became a little more adventurous. She found a couple of other flea markets around Johannesburg where she could get a stall on other days of the week. As demand increased, she needed someone to help with the sewing. She spoke to Portia, the domestic worker who looked after their house, and she recommended a friend of hers who was a talented seamstress. Phumi was a broad, sturdy woman with quick, capable hands, who could assemble and press a garment in half the time it took Holly. She also knew some very reasonable fabric suppliers, and business began, if not to boom, at least to rattle along.

One morning, Holly woke up and realised she had been in Johannesburg for three years. It was home. She hadn't consciously admitted it up till now, but she definitely wouldn't be heading off to travel up Africa any time soon. She was twenty-three, doing work she liked and she had a great crowd of friends. She loved the sunshine and the lifestyle, so different from grim, grey, rainy London. She loved the big airy house she lived in. She couldn't imagine wanting to live anywhere else.

Some of her clients suggested that she might want to set up a shop, but she quite liked the itinerant life of the flea-market stallholder. She did, however, approach a few trendy boutiques to see if they would like to stock some of her stuff, and a couple said yes. It gave another arm to her business and she enjoyed making things she didn't actually have to sell herself. She also hired a couple of well-spoken, willing young students to sell at the market on days she couldn't or didn't want to attend, and allowed herself the odd weekend off or night out.

She was so busy that there was little time in her life for romance. She met a lot of people at the markets, and she'd had a few short-lived flings with other stallholders and once with a busking musician, but she hadn't met anyone that rocked her world. Until Damon.

She had gone out for the evening with a crowd of mates to a trendy jazz bar in Melville. A Brazilian band was playing and the vibe was steamy and exciting. She was wearing a sexy little ice-blue dress she'd made herself: close-fitting and shimmery. She had a great tan and her short, curly hair was shiny and unruly. She knew she looked like a million dollars. The guy standing at the bar, however, looked like a million and a half. He was taller than her despite her heels, blond and handsome, and he had that easy confidence that comes either from being very, very rich, very successful or extremely well endowed. As it turned out, it was all three. She had muscled her way up to the bar to get a drink and he turned and looked at her, smiled lazily and gestured to the barman. He was one of those guys who got served instantly. He leaned over the bar and spoke quietly to the barman, who produced a bottle of champagne and an ice bucket from nowhere, which he handed to him along with two glasses. No money changed hands. The handsome man took Holly's hand and led her to a small table towards the back of the bar. They had not spoken, and she didn't even know his name. He hadn't bothered to find out her name or who she was with. At the time, she had found his arrogance quite thrilling.

Oblivious to the noise of the band, they talked intensely for three straight hours. He was a property developer, of

Afrikaans descent. He was successful, articulate and well read. He told her he had gone to university in Edinburgh and had spent two years travelling the world. He'd hitchhiked through South America, and had backpacked through Southeast Asia. He was fascinated by the story of her clothing line and how she had started it from nothing, and asked lots of probing questions about her plans to expand. She wasn't all that interested in talking about it, to be fair, especially once they had finished the bottle of champagne and another had appeared, and he was somehow holding her hand across the table. She kept staring at his unbelievably handsome face in the candlelight. She had forgotten all about her friends at the next table, and she was vaguely aware that she was way too drunk to drive home. She thanked the heavens that she'd arranged for her student helpers to run the stall the next day. There was no way she was going to be ready for a 7 a.m. start and heaving boxes of clothes.

The bar gradually emptied around them. Holly's friends came over to say goodbye and left. She had stopped drinking, but she felt drunk on desire. She didn't want to get up from the table and break the spell of this amazing evening, but Damon abruptly stood and took her hand. 'You'll come back to my place,' he said. It was a statement, not a question. Holly nodded, and they headed for the door. She stopped suddenly. 'The bill! We didn't pay the bill!'

'I own the bar,' said Damon shortly. 'I've paid for that champagne once. I'm not paying for it again.'

Damon's house was quite insanely luxurious; in fact it could only be called a mansion. It was short drive from the bar, on the crest of nearby Northcliff Hill. Holly gazed around, intimidated, at the great marble staircase and the atrium, which seemed the size of a football pitch and opened out on to a pool that looked roughly Olympic size. She didn't get much time to sightsee though, as Damon matter-of-factly unzipped her dress and let it fall to the floor.

They didn't sleep that night. Holly saw the sun rise as Damon did delightful things to her as she reclined on a lounger by the pool. He'd already ravished her halfway up the stairs, on his king-size bed and in the shower, before announcing it was time for an early-morning swim. Swimming was not what he had in mind though, or at least not yet, as he lay Holly down on a lounger the size of a double bed, spread her legs gently and began to pleasure her with his mouth and fingers. She gazed dreamily out over the view of the city, her body tingling and aching delightfully. It didn't get better than this, surely. This was as fabulous as life got.

But things were set to get a lot better, she discovered. Damon literally swept her into his life. She didn't go back to sleep in the house she shared with Pierre again. She worked there during the day, and made occasional trips to collect clothing, until after a few weeks, Damon sent a van to move all her stuff to his house. He paid off the remainder of her rent for the year, so Pierre got to keep the house to himself. He set her up to work in a big airy room at the back of his house, with room for clothing rails, cutting tables and the machines she and Phumi used.

Suddenly, she was living a very different life. Damon had plenty of money, and he was very generous. He refused her offer to pay rent, and he was happy to splash the cash whenever they went out. They ate in the best restaurants, entertained at his house all the time, partied in the trendiest nightspots and whenever Holly could take time off from the markets at the weekend, went off for luxury weekends in Cape Town or on exclusive game reserves. It was like living in a dream. But that wasn't true, thought Holly. Because sometimes dreams went all weird, and you almost always woke up just as the good bit started. No, it was like living in a film. She was head-over-heels in love with him. He was handsome, attentive and clever, he adored her, he made every aspect of her life easier and happier and the sex was just fantastic.

She wasn't at all used to being a kept woman, and at first it made her uncomfortable, but he was always happy for her to treat him, even if her offerings were more modest than his. He also never discouraged her from working. On the contrary, he was always on at her to work cleverly and more efficiently. He suggested she narrow her range down to the ten most popular designs, and that she should work hard to develop the side of the business selling to stores and retail outlets. Through his connections, he set up a meeting with an exclusive department-store chain, and she got a small concession in their flagship Sandton shop.

For their first-year anniversary, Damon took her to Venice for thirty-six straight hours and made love to her in a four-poster bed in a palazzo on the Grand Canal. Then they went to London, and he charmed her family and friends completely.

'What a catch!' giggled Miranda, then heavily pregnant with Martha. 'I can't believe how lucky you are!'

Holly didn't think she was lucky: she thought she'd been brave and bold. She'd gone to live on the other side of the world, started a business, and as a result had met this amazing man who lit up her life. Miranda's most dangerous life choice to date was wearing ivory instead of white for her wedding. Nothing ventured . . . Holly thought to herself as she and Damon sank into their first-class seats for the flight back to Johannesburg.

While their personal life was insanely happy, Holly was beginning to feel the strain from four years of sewing, early-morning trips to the markets and working long hours to meet the orders from shops and the department store.

'You need to grow,' said Damon, one evening as they sat by the pool eating their dinner. 'At the moment, your business is you. Your designs, most of the time it's you on the stall at the market, you source the materials . . . you need to diversify, so your business is making you money even when you're not actually doing the hard graft.'

'I can't grow,' said Holly reasonably. 'Even with the new work we have, Phumi and I can only sew as many clothes as we can sew in any given week, and I can't afford to employ someone else or buy more machines.'

'What if you could afford to?'

'What do you mean?'

'Well, what if you let me buy shares in Doradolla?'

'Shares? There are no shares,' said Holly, confused.

'Well, there could be if you decided to make them available,' said Damon patiently. 'We'll do a valuation of the company, work out what it's all worth, and you can decide how much of it you want to sell.'

'Sell?' Holly was suddenly unsure.

'It's just an investment,' he said soothingly. 'It's still your baby, you're still CEO and you get to make all the decisions, I'll be totally non-executive.'

'I don't know . . .' said Holly.

'Let me get my guys to do the paperwork and see what you think. You don't need to do anything you don't want to. Now, that's more than enough business talk,' he said, pushing his plate away. 'Come here and play with me.'

They didn't discuss it again for some time, but a month or so later, Holly had to pull an all-nighter to fulfil an order for ten bridesmaids' dresses. In the morning, Damon came down to the workshop and found her asleep with her head in a pile of taffeta. When he woke her up, she started to cry because the dresses weren't finished, and Phumi wasn't due for another two hours. Holly started shakily pinning up a hem, but her fingers were cracked and bleeding, and she kept getting spots of blood on the pink fabric. Damon gently took the dress out of her hands and said, 'Let me get you some help.'

He got Holly, through the tears, to give him the name of a seamstress who had helped her in the past when the workload got heavy. He rang the woman and had a taxi sent to her house to collect her. He managed to persuade Holly into a shower and got her to eat some breakfast. The seamstress arrived about half an hour before Phumi and, under Holly's guidance, they finished all the dresses with fifteen minutes to spare before the crowd of bridesmaids arrived for their fitting.

The fitting went like a dream, and once the last bridesmaid

had headed off down Northcliff Hill, her dress in one of the trademark shocking-pink Doradolla garment bags, Damon led Holly to the living room and sat her down.

'I can't sit down,' she said in a wavering voice. 'I have to tidy up. Joyce needs to be paid. And Phumi . . .'

'I gave Joyce cash,' he said, and named a figure that made Holly gasp.

'I also gave Phumi a bonus,' he said.

'But . . . you've blown my whole budget for the job!' Holly said, desperately. 'The margins were small anyway. It was a favour for a friend of a friend.'

'Okay, firstly, this one's on me, so don't worry about it. Secondly, if you're a premium brand, you can't be doing favours for friends of friends. Not even favours for friends. And lastly, work should not be doing this to you! Look at you! You're on the verge of a breakdown, and for what? The few hundred rand you could have squeezed out of this job? Let me help you, Holls. Let me invest, so you can get the people you need, and let your business work for you, not the other way around.'

Within a week, Damon had a couple of serious speccy blokes crawling all over Holly's business. They scrutinised her accounts, counted stock, crunched numbers, asked questions, visited outlets, asked more questions, and finally sat Holly and Damon down to talk. She was flummoxed by the spreadsheets and rows of numbers, and the projections they made, based on various scenarios, and finally Damon held up a hand to stop them.

'Basically, Holls, here's my offer. I put this in your account.' He wrote a figure with several zeros at the end of it on the notepad on the table between them. 'And for that, I own twenty-five per cent of Doradolla. The contract we have drawn up shows that I will have no executive input in the running of the business, although I will have the right to examine the figures. That money means you can hire another four seamstresses, as well as someone to manage the money side of things, and the business can grow. What do you say?'

It seemed an unbelievably generous offer, but Holly still felt uncomfortable taking his money, and losing a chunk of her little empire.

'Let me think about it, okay?' she said carefully. She didn't want to hurt his feelings.

'Of course,' said Damon. 'It's a hard decision to make.'

They didn't talk about it for a couple of days, but that Friday evening, he said to her, 'Who's running the stalls this weekend?'

'I've got students on for both Saturday and Sunday. I need to do some fabric buying, but I thought I'd have a slightly easier weekend.'

'Maybe we should try somewhere new to buy fabric,' he said, smiling.

'Like where?' Holly knew every fabric supplier within an hour's drive of Johannesburg.

'It's a surprise. Will you trust me? Just go outside and get in the car.'

'What, now? Nothing will be open!'

'Holly . . .'

'I'm going, I'm going!'

They got into his Porsche, and he drove straight to the airport.

'What are you doing, you loon?' said Holly, turning to him, once she realised where they were. 'We can't fly anywhere. I haven't got a bag! And what about getting the students off tomorrow morning? I have to pack stock!'

'I've asked Phumi to come in and organise the students. And I packed you a bag, it's in the boot. I also have your passport.'

'My *passport*? But I have to be back by Monday!'

'You will be,' said Damon soothingly. 'I also need to be back.'

He got their bags from the boot of the car, and they went into the airport, where they were ushered straight to the front of the first-class queue in departures. Damon made Holly stand back a little when he checked them in so she wouldn't see their destination, but she nagged so relentlessly that when they got to the first-class lounge, he handed her her boarding pass.

'You'd find out in a minute anyway, when we go to board,' he said.

She looked at the card in her hand and gasped. 'Mauritius?'

'Only the best for you, my love.'

They landed in the early hours of the morning, and there was a car waiting to whisk them to a exclusive hotel. They were both exhausted and fell into bed. When Holly woke up the next morning, however, Damon was not beside her. She stumbled sleepily out on to the balcony, and found him staring out over the snow-white beach and turquoise water. She slipped an arm around his waist, and they looked at the view without speaking.

Eventually Holly said softly, 'You're a total crazy, you know. This must have cost you a fortune, but thank you. I've never been to such a beautiful place.'

Damon didn't say anything for a long while and then he said, 'Holls, I brought you here with a plan. I wanted to do a whole elaborate thing tonight, with dinner on the beach, and you in a stunning dress. I've even got a string quartet booked and fireworks planned. We can still do all of that, but . . . well, now the time is nearly here, I've changed my mind. I want this to be a moment between the two of us. Just us, as we are.'

He was wearing a pair of pyjama bottoms, and Holly was wrapped in one of the hotel's white towelling bathrobes. She hadn't brushed her hair, and she had mascara panda eyes. Despite the gorgeous location, she had never felt less glamorous. But as Damon slowly went down on one knee, she couldn't have cared less. She realised that he'd been holding a ring box in his hand the whole time they had been out on the balcony, and he opened it now. The early-morning sun glinted off an enormous diamond.

'Holly, will you be my wife?'

She started to cry, happy, gulping sobs, and sank to the ground so she could put her arms around his neck. He gently disengaged them and said, 'Hang on, you haven't answered me!'

'Yes! Yes, you big crazy man! Yes, of course!'

He slipped the ring (perfectly sized, of course, she would have expected no less from him) on to her finger, and drew her to her feet. Then he gently pulled her back into the room and on to the big white bed.

Later, when Holly told people Damon had taken her to Mauritius to propose to her, they'd all asked how she'd liked the island, and she'd had to admit that from Saturday morning till Sunday night when they flew out, she'd only seen the inside of their suite and briefly, the view from the balcony. He promised her that they would go back there on their honeymoon. 'By then, of course, we'll be sick of each other, and we can do all the sightseeing you like!' he joked.

They were in no hurry to set a date for the wedding. Damon was in the middle of setting up the biggest property deal of his career: a multi-multimillion-rand hotel and retail development. And Holly, now she was going to be married to Damon, felt that accepting his offer to buy into Doradolla was the right thing to do. She signed the paperwork, and within a few days, the first of several large payments arrived in her business account. Damon told her to make free use of his advisors, and they recommended she hire a young, newly qualified accountant called Jonathan September to manage the money side of the business. She agreed readily, and she and Jonathan worked out the budget for hiring seamstresses and permanent market staff. She spent a busy six weeks interviewing and hiring, and overnight, Doradolla went from Holly and Phumi to a real company, employing ten people. The set-up period and training took the better part of four months, but after that, Holly slowly began to realise that Doradolla was a machine with its own momentum. She could take a day off, or spend a solid week in her office designing, and the work would keep happening. It was a revelation. She'd once read that you could never have a great job, a great relationship and a great place to live all at the same time, but it seemed to her at that moment that she was triply blessed, and did indeed have all three.

One morning, it dawned on her that she and Damon had not had sex for a week. That was the first inkling that all was not perfect in her world. They both had high sex drives, and it had always been a vital and consuming part of their relationship. They usually did it every day, often more than once a day. They rarely missed a day, and never missed two unless Damon was out of town. A week was unheard of. Holly had a moment of concern, and then smiled to herself and thought that maybe they were settling into a comfortable long-term relationship. By the time they got married, she thought, they might well be a once-a-week under-the-duvet lights-off kind of couple. It didn't worry her at the time: they'd both been working hard and she was sure they'd soon be back on track. But when, over dinner, she jokingly mentioned it to Damon, he snapped at her. 'God, Holly. I've got more on my mind than sex, you know. Give me a break.'

She was surprised. They'd always been light-hearted about their sex life, and she'd been expecting him to make a joke, or to sling her over his shoulder and carry her upstairs.

But he didn't. He picked up his plate and went into his study, shutting the door behind him.

She sat in the kitchen staring at her food, unsure what had just happened, but certain that it was something new and unwelcome in their relationship. It made her feel cold inside. She knew him well, and she knew going in to talk to him now would be the wrong thing to do, so she finished her own meal and then went and watched some television. At eleven, she showered and got into bed. She still felt upset and hurt, and she was sure she would never be able to sleep, but she did doze off eventually. Much later, in the early hours, Damon slipped into bed with her. It woke her, but she kept her back turned and her eyes closed. He immediately curled himself around her. 'I'm sorry,' he whispered in her ear as he cupped her breast with one hand. 'I'm so, so sorry, my precious Holly. Sorry I snapped, sorry I've been so busy. I want you so much. I do.' She relented and pressed back against him slightly, and that was all the encouragement he needed. He was feverish, almost desperate, and very demanding and quite rough with her. Holly would normally have found his ardour exciting, but somehow the small icy chip in her middle that had formed when he yelled at her just wouldn't melt.

It was the beginning of a very unsettling pattern. Damon was distant, very distracted and often away from home for long hours and more frequently overnight. Then he would suddenly overwhelm Holly with passionate declarations of love, intense sexual demands and extravagant gestures. She never knew which Damon was going to come through the door, and she found herself almost dreading his return. She began to wonder if he was quite sane, or whether he was exhibiting signs of some kind of personality disorder. It crossed her mind that it might be drugs, but Damon, a health freak and fitness fanatic, had zero tolerance for any kind of mind-altering substance beyond the occasional drink. But that was another change she noticed in him: he was exercising less and drinking more, both very out of character. Every time she tried to raise any part of this with him, he would either yell at her or be apologetic and tearful, assuring her that it was just work stress. There was no talk of planning a wedding, and they became more and more distant and estranged from one another. Holly found herself beginning to wonder how she might extricate herself from the relationship. She knew she could move out – in fact she knew Pierre would welcome her back at their old house. But given Damon's involvement in her business, the work side of things was a lot more complicated. She tried to tell herself things would get better, even though she didn't really believe they would. And then, suddenly, they did.

Damon announced he had been working too hard and was taking a week off. He was around the house every day, and was sweetly and patiently interested in the goings-on in her sewing room. He drove her to the suppliers, carrying her bags and waiting patiently while she agonised over fabrics, buttons and trimmings. He also spent a long time chatting to Jonathan, Holly's business manager, and looking at the financial side of Doradolla. In the evenings, he cooked for Holly or took her out for dinner. He was calm, even-tempered and in fact very much his old, sweet, romantic self. He talked about holidays, and even suggested that they pick a date for the wedding, so her family could begin to plan or book flights. That weekend, they went to a chalet in the Drakensberg. It was winter, and they spent a picture-perfect weekend, walking, drinking red wine and watching films, and making love in the big old wooden bed and in the living room in front of the fire.

On the Monday morning, back in Jo'burg, Damon was up and dressed long before Holly. She stirred and gazed at him in his crisp shirt and beautifully cut suit. He was looking at

ROSIE FIORE | 121

himself in the mirror, his face expressionless and, as always, beautiful. He saw her watching him sleepily from her nest of pillows and he came to kiss her on the top of her head. 'Go back to sleep, lovely,' he said softly. 'I'm off to the office. A million emails to catch up on.'

She smiled and drifted back to sleep. Later that morning, she supervised the seamstresses finishing a set of skirts that were going to a boutique in Pretoria, but they didn't have enough of the gold braid that was a feature on the pocket. Holly jumped into her car and went to her haberdashery supplier to get more. She also collected some pretty buttons for a new design she was working on, as well as an assortment of reels of cotton and some lovely cream-coloured lace trim. She took her selection to the till and handed over her business debit card. The shop assistant, who knew Holly well, chattered about the weekend as she put all the items through the till. Then she frowned, surprised. 'Your card's been declined,' she said, embarrassed.

'That's crazy!' said Holly. 'There's plenty of money in the account. Could the card have got damaged?'

'I suppose so,' said the assistant, but she didn't look convinced. 'Maybe you just had a big payment go out and you forgot about it.'

'Don't worry,' said Holly, and paid with her personal card. 'I'll sort it when I get back to work.'

On the way back to her car, she glanced at her mobile and saw that she had four missed calls from Jonathan. She rang him straight away. 'Hi, Jon,' she said cheerily. 'Such a weird thing just happened. My card got declined at the button shop. Any idea what's going on?'

'You need to get back here. Now,' he said, and his voice sounded raw and strangled.

'What do you mean? What's going on? Jon, you're scaring me.'

'Look, Holly, they won't let me explain. Just come back, okay?'

'Who? Who's "they"? Jon, are you being held up? Do I need to ring the cops?'

'No. Just come. Okay? Please.'

Holly drove well above the speed limit all the way back to the house. It took her about ten minutes and she felt sick with fear all the way. There were four or five cars in the driveway, and somehow she knew that it was the police. She leapt out of her car and ran up to the open front door. There were people all over the house, walking around with clipboards. A tall, burly man walked up to her. 'You are . . . ?'

'Holly . . . Holly Evans. I live here. And you are . . . ?'

'Detective Tshabalala. Are you the owner or part-owner of this property?'

'No . . . It belongs to my fiancé.'

'Damon Vermaak.'

'Yes,' Holly said faintly. 'Is he okay? Has something happened to him?'

'To the best of our knowledge, he is all right. But you might be able to tell us more. Where is Mr Vermaak?'

'He went to the office early this morning. I can give you the number . . .' She reached for her phone.

'Mr Vermaak is not in his office. His staff have all been dismissed, and the lease on the office was terminated some time ago.'

'What?'

'I am sure you'll be able to tell us more, Miss Evans,' he said insistently. 'Where is he?'

'I don't know! He left this morning, as normal, and I was expecting him back tonight.'

'Did he take a bag with him?'

'No . . . well, I don't think so. I was asleep when he left.'

'Could you check his personal effects for me and tell me if anything is missing?'

They went up the stairs to the bedroom. There were more police officers in there, cataloguing everything. Damon's wardrobe door stood open, and at a glance, Holly could see most of his clothes were gone. She started to cry, big tearing sobs, and she turned on Detective Tshabalala. 'What's happened? What is going on? Who are you? And where's Damon?'

'We're from the fraud squad, and if anyone is going to tell us where he is, it's you.' There was no gentleness in Tshabalala's voice. He clearly thought that Holly's fear and heartbreak was an act.

'You won't be able to stay here tonight,' he said briskly. 'Do you have somewhere you can go?'

'Yes, I . . . I can stay with friends. Can I take some of my stuff?'

'An officer will write down what you take.'

Holly suffered the humiliation of a junior officer painstakingly listing her bras, pants and toiletries as she packed them. Then she went to pick up her watch and engagement ring from the bedside table where she had left them the night before. She glanced up and saw Detective Tshabalala watching her with dark, suspicious eyes, and she left them where they were.

The shocks were far from over. She went downstairs to her work area, and found the officers had taken the details of her seamstresses and sent them home. They were busy pawing through her stock and materials and listing everything, making a dreadful mess. She went through into the office. An officer was pulling files and books off the shelves in a disorderly and destructive way, and Jonathan was sitting at his desk like a statue, his eyes red and swollen. She wanted to hug him.

'I'm so sorry, Jon,' she said. 'I don't know what's going on. But when this is all over, we'll put everything back and things can get back to normal.'

'It's all gone,' he said in a whisper.

'What do you mean? Nothing is gone. They're just making lists. It's a mess, but everything is still here.'

'No, the money. It's gone. The business accounts have been stripped. There isn't a cent left.'

'Our business accounts?' Holly said, her voice surprisingly calm, even to her own ears. 'But no one has access to them except you and me.'

'He . . .' Jonathan couldn't bring himself to say Damon's name. 'He watched me doing the online banking. He must have remembered all the passwords. It's all gone.'

There followed several weeks of intensive and painful questioning by the police. They gave her very little information, but bit by bit she pieced together the story. The multimillion-rand deal Damon had been working on had turned sour. He'd tried to shore it up by borrowing even more money, and then he'd mortgaged the house and taken out further loans against his car and other assets. It seemed that when he had run out of options, he had decided to take all the cash out of Doradolla, the only liquid and profitable business he had access to. The police knew he had left the country, crossing the border by road into Botswana, but from there he had disappeared. Detective Tshabalala was relentless. He was convinced Holly knew where Damon was and was in on it, but she kept telling the same story and what she said was always consistent. Once the detective understood the arrangement she had made with Damon over Doradolla and had grasped that she too had been robbed, he began to be a little gentler with her. Finally, reluctantly, when it was clear that Damon was not going to be found and could not be put on trial, he gave her leave to go.

She didn't want to stay in Johannesburg. The house now belonged to the bank. She had moved back in with Pierre, and she could have stayed there and started again, but she just didn't have the strength. She had no capital to get the company back on its feet, so she spent almost the last money she had paying off Jonathan and the seamstresses as fairly as she could. Then she packed up her few personal belongings, booked a flight to London and went home to her mother.

6

HOLLY NOW

A mother-and-child relationship is a funny thing, Holly thought. Although she wasn't one herself, she knew a lot of mothers and had observed them. Mothers grow their children inside their bodies, make every cell of them, nurture them, give birth to them and feed them. Many mothers will always feel that bond, no matter how old the child becomes. The phrase 'You'll always be my baby' has an element of truth to it. But for the child, the bond is not the same. They don't remember the gestation, the birth, the unceasing and intimate care. Once children are conscious beings, they believe they invented themselves, and they don't feel that constant physical bond with the mother. In fact, they might look at their mother and wish they could deny being of her body at all. She is so strange, so other, so foreign to them, they cannot possibly be related.

Or maybe it's only me who feels that way, thought Holly, as she sat at the kitchen table and watched her mother iron dish towels. Judith Evans was a small woman, slight of build, and she had been a petite size eight all her adult life. Holly had grown taller than her mother when she was twelve. If Holly was to choose three words to define her relationship with her mother, they would have to be, 'Oh, Holly, don't . . .' Sometimes it seemed that everything she had ever done, her mother had found too bold, too colourful, too adventurous. Whatever the situation, Judith would always counsel caution. She was forever saying, 'Well, maybe we should wait and see,' whether Holly was talking about travelling through Africa or buying a new kettle. She made these pronouncements in a wavering, tentative and almost girlish voice, and every time, it set Holly's teeth on edge.

Judith had grown up in west London, and the house she lived in now was less than a mile from the house where she had been born, and round the corner from the school she had attended. She had held the same job as the secretary for a small local medical practice for thirty-five years, until her retirement two years before. She had a small circle of friends, people she had met at school or church and had known for forty years or more. Now she was retired, her life revolved around the church: she did the flowers, helped to clean it once a fortnight, sang in the choir and attended coffee mornings and the bridge club.

She was only sixty-two, no age at all, Holly thought, but she had embraced life as a pensioner, and seemed happy to sink into old-lady activities without a fight. It was ridiculous. Her health was sound and she had a reasonable income. She could do anything she chose, but instead she inhabited a tiny world bounded by the North Circular and the Uxbridge Road, and it was very difficult to get her to go beyond those boundaries. When Holly had first returned home, she had tried to get Judith out and about. She'd suggested a trip into town to see an art exhibition or to watch a show. She'd even proposed they go away for a weekend to the Cotswolds or the Lake District. She'd been away so long that the prospect of being a tourist in her own country had seemed quite appealing, and she thought Judith would welcome the chance to do something new. 'Oh no, dear,' Judith responded to each offer of an outing. She always had an excuse: either there was a church event on the same date, or she didn't like to drive at night (or be driven), or the Tube into town got so crowded. After a while, Holly gave up. At a push, Judith could be convinced to get into her little Nissan Micra and creep around the North Circular to visit Miranda and her family, but that would only be on a Sunday, after church. David lived in Oxfordshire, and he knew perfectly well his mother would never come to visit him, so he and his wife and children made a duty visit once a month.

Holly tried hard not to get annoyed at her mother. It seemed unfair to be angry with someone so determinedly inoffensive, like being infuriated by mashed potato. In the end, she decided to accept that they were just completely different people, who could coexist peacefully, like different species in the same enclosure at the zoo. She stood up from the kitchen table, and her mum looked up from her ironing.

'Cup of tea, dear?'

What Holly really fancied was a gin and tonic. She was sick to her back teeth of tea.

'No, thanks, Mum. I thought I might . . .' Might what? Go for a walk? It was raining. Go out for a drink? With whom? She was low, but not low enough to go and nurse a drink alone in a bar. '. . . go to my room,' she finished, aware she sounded like a sulky teenager.

'All right, dear,' said her mum, sounding disappointed and, as usual, faintly martyred. 'Can I do any ironing for you, dear?'

Holly tried not to bristle. From anyone else, that might sound like an innocent offer, even a generous one, but from her mum, there was an implied criticism, as if Holly, who did take great care over her appearance, was somehow rumpled. 'I can do my own ironing, Mother,' she said, aware that she sounded petulant.

'I know you can, dear . . . and I suppose you wouldn't want me ironing some of your . . . special things.'

'What do you mean, "special"?' said Holly, unable to keep the tension out of her voice.

'Those outfits you've made – the fancy ones,' said Judith, aligning the edges of a dish towel perfectly and ironing the folded square. 'I've never ironed things like that.' She sighed, and with a touch of wistfulness said, 'So glamorous . . . like a bird of paradise.'

Holly raised her eyebrows. The idea of pale, wispy Judith coveting one of Holly's jewel-coloured silk-and-taffeta creations was too bizarre for words. She had to squeeze past her mum to get out of the kitchen, and as she went, touched her briefly on the shoulder. Judith quickly put her own small, soft hand over Holly's, just for an instant, and then let her go. Funny old fish, thought Holly, as she bounded up the stairs.

Her mother was the least of her problems, however. She had almost run out of money, and she had to find some work. She had never looked for a job in the UK, and except for her short tenure at the dress shop in Johannesburg, had never really been employed. She'd considered starting up a dressmaking business in London, but it would have meant looking for clients, advertising, maybe getting a market stall, and to be honest, she just didn't have the energy to start that all over again. Besides, taking the cover off her sewing machine and pulling out the well-used Doradolla patterns just reminded her of what she had lost. It was all too painful, and she quite simply couldn't do it. Eventually she walked down to Ealing Broadway and went from clothes shop to clothes shop, asking if they were looking for staff. Her CV was far from average, but she had little conventional retail experience, and many of the shops were reluctant, but eventually she struck lucky, and a small branch of one of the chain women's stores took her on.

Her life seemed better almost instantly. Just the day-to-day routine of getting up, going to work, getting a coffee on the way and chatting to customers lifted her black mood. She was naturally sociable and she enjoyed the work, even though she thought the clothes were uniformly dull and often badly made. She was at least six or seven years older than the other sales assistants, but they didn't seem to mind and dragged her on nights out to clubs in London, and to karaoke evenings at a local pub. She wasn't earning a lot, but then she didn't need a lot. Her mother would only accept a token rent, and she didn't have commuting to pay for. She felt like a thirty-year-old school-leaver, earning a starting salary, living at home, spending her money on drinks and partying. It was far from the life she had had, and light years from any life she might want in the long term, but it was a good transition and quite healing, after the appalling conclusion of her time in South Africa.

But what did she want to do? There was a question she couldn't answer. As far as men were concerned, she couldn't have been less interested. She got plenty of offers on her nights out, but Damon had broken something in her, and she knew it would take her a long time to heal. Damon himself had, quite simply, disappeared. Holly knew that through his business he had connections across Africa, as well as in the Middle East and China. His mother rang her about once a fortnight and wept over the phone, begging Holly to tell her if she knew anything at all about his whereabouts. It was awful and heartbreaking, and she dreaded the calls because she never had anything new to tell Mrs Vermaak. It gave her another reason to hate him, and made her more determined to avoid any romantic entanglements for a very, very long time.

Besides, she didn't feel she was much of a prospect at the moment. In terms of her career, she'd lost all the progress she'd made in her twenties and she was starting again. She thought about it every day as she walked to and from work, and resolved that she would plan a career path that involved all the things she'd loved about running Doradolla and exclude the parts of the business she hadn't enjoyed. She decided to write things down as they occurred to her. She had loved the designing, and enjoyed the sewing, to a certain extent, but she didn't want to be responsible for all of it. While she didn't mind her retail job now, she had no real enthusiasm for the selling part of the job, both pimping her clothes to stores and boutiques and the physical grind of standing at a market and interacting with customers. As for the business side: hiring people, managing the money, carrying the burden of debt, well, she could do it, but she wasn't sure she ever wanted to again. Damon had broken that part of her too.

One sunny autumn Sunday, she and her mum made the interminable trek from Ealing to Finchley to have lunch with Miranda and Paul and the kids. It should have been a twenty-five-minute journey, even in heavy Sunday traffic, but Judith, who insisted on driving, crawled along at exactly twenty-eight miles an hour for the entire journey, even when Holly, sweating with stress and jittery from the honking drivers behind them, pointed out that the speed limit on that stretch of the dual carriageway was fifty. 'I can't be remembering every time the speed limit changes, dear,' said Judith mildly, oblivious to the man in the four-by-four screaming obscenities and flipping her the finger as he roared past. 'I like to drive at this speed, because then I know I'll never be caught speeding.'

A pensioner on a mobility scooter would be more likely to be caught speeding, thought Holly, as she slid down in her seat and resigned herself to a long journey.

Judith spent an age carefully parallel parking in Miranda's pretty cul de sac, edging back and forth seven or eight times until she was satisfied she was a perfect six inches from the kerb. Then she spent another few minutes gathering her things, pulling in her wing mirror, painstakingly folding her coat over her arm and checking several times that all the windows were closed and the car was locked and that Holly had not left any valuables in sight in the vehicle. Even after all the faff, they still weren't late: wary of possible disasters, Judith had insisted they leave Ealing a full hour before they were expected for lunch, so they walked up the path to the front door bang on time. Holly wondered if the sun was over the yardarm and she could demand a drink as soon as she walked through the door.

Thankfully, Miranda had decided they were barbecuing, to make the most of the last of the sunshine, and there was already a jug of Pimm's on the table on the patio.

'Oh dear,' said Judith. 'Are you sure it's warm enough to be outdoors, Miranda? Won't the children catch a chill?'

Miranda looked instantly horrified, as if she might have failed her children in some way. But Oscar, sitting in his pushchair on the patio, was wrapped in a padded suit so bulky it made his little arms stick out at right angles to his body, and his little cheeks were red with heat. Martha, also in a bulky coat, was riding her tricycle on the lawn in precise circles. 'I think they'll be fine, Mum,' said Holly. 'Let them get some fresh air while they can. Why don't you go inside and help Miranda in the kitchen? I'll watch the kids.'

It was a bit mean of her, as she knew Miranda would already have organised everything that needed doing, and that Judith would now wander around the kitchen and then the house, quietly asking questions that, however innocent they might sound, would undermine everything Miranda had done. 'Oh dear,' she'd say. 'Did you mix the mayonnaise into the potato salad while the potatoes were still warm? I always worry about salmonella, don't you?' or 'Goodness me, Miranda, isn't it wonderful how you young people don't feel the need to scrub off limescale any more. You're so much more relaxed than we were.'

But after the drive from Ealing, Holly desperately needed a break from her mum, and most of all she wanted to drink a couple of glasses of Pimm's very quickly without her mother commenting how young women now felt free to drink so much more than in her time – and in the middle of the day! Actually, make that three glasses, Holly amended. She wandered over to the barbecue, a monstrous gas contraption, where her brother-in-law, Paul, was expertly flipping burgers. 'Those look good,' she said conversationally.

'Organic beef. Miranda made them herself.'

'Ah, and the sausages?'

'Organic, free-range pork.'

'I always feel so much better knowing I'm eating a happy dead animal,' Holly said sardonically, but she might as well not have bothered. Paul didn't have much of a sense of humour. He was a man who dealt in facts, so he just ignored her comment and kept minutely adjusting the knobs on his gigantic barbecue. Holly was convinced that if he got the right combination of buttons and switches, the thing would just take off. He was a big Arsenal supporter, so she went for football as a safe topic of conversation. A few well-chosen questions and he was off, droning about formations, players being kept on the bench and the reasons for their recent humiliating defeat by Man United. Holly nodded at appropriate intervals while she chewed on Pimm's-soaked chunks of cucumber.

In the end, Judith prevailed and they ate lunch inside.

The food was delicious, and Holly ate ravenously. She'd had enough Pimm's to be able to ignore her mother's barbs about her unladylike appetite, and Paul had served a quite simply lovely Chardonnay to complement the meal. Holly, pleasantly full of good food and booze, started to feel almost benevolent towards her dysfunctional family. She was sitting next to little Oscar in his high chair, who was gumming on a piece of bread roll and thumping his beaker of water up and down, loudly. He bashed his beaker close to Holly, and she reached over and banged the tray of his high chair with the flat of her hand. He jumped, a little startled, and then chortled delightedly, showing his two peg teeth at the bottom. He bashed again and Holly banged back. He let loose with an almighty belly laugh, a most delicious sound in the restrained atmosphere. 'Holly, dear, don't overexcite the baby,' said Judith. 'You'll make him ill.'

'Oh, for heaven's sake,' said Holly shortly, forgetting to be polite. 'I'm making him laugh, not bouncing him off the ceiling.'

She banged again, and Oscar laughed so hard that he inhaled a chunk of bread, went purple in the face and started coughing and choking. Miranda leapt to her feet and whacked him sharply on the back. The nugget of soggy bread flew out. Both Miranda and Judith looked at Holly with absolute horror as if she had choked the baby herself, but Oscar immediately turned to Holly. 'Again!' he demanded.

Miranda gasped. 'He's never said that before!' She squeezed Oscar and kissed him all over his red little face. 'Clever pickle! Do it again, Holly.'

Holly banged the high-chair tray, Oscar bashed back and

chuckled, then yelled, 'Again!' to the delight of his captive audience. They repeated the sequence over and over. It never seemed to get old. He was a dear little chap, Holly thought. She'd not paid much attention to him before: she'd always thought babies were rather dull, but she liked his round little face and his raspy chortle. He seemed simpler and less self-conscious than Martha. If she had kids (and in her present situation, she couldn't imagine when that would ever be), she would like boys better than girls, she decided. Sturdy, fat-cheeked little boys like Oscar.

Even Judith's mood seemed to have lightened with Oscar's mirth, and for once, conversation seemed to flow in a slightly less stilted way. Paul asked Holly about her work, and she told him a little about the shop.

'It's not a long-term plan, though, is it?' said Paul bluntly. 'Is there an opportunity for you to climb the ladder? Maybe do some management training? You're not getting any younger, Holly.'

'Paul!' admonished Miranda. 'Don't be so rude!'

'No, no, he's absolutely right,' said Holly. 'I took this job as a stop-gap, just to give me time to think about what I want to do. I have to start again from scratch, but I might as well really think about what makes me happy.'

'And what does make you happy?' asked Paul. Holly was glad of his abrupt, businesslike manner. It made her articulate her thoughts, think in a more focused way. It was better than the rather woolly wanderings she'd been having on her walk to work.

'I want to design clothes . . .' she began slowly, 'but I'm not entirely sure I want to run my own business. There were aspects of the business side of things I didn't enjoy, and I wouldn't mind not having to do them myself. I'd quite like to work with someone else, and I definitely don't want to do evening wear again. Not for a long time.'

'No evening wear?' said Judith. 'Oh, Holly, that's such a pity! You're so talented.'

Holly gritted her teeth. She really couldn't bloody win with her mother.

'Well, I'm talented in lots of ways,' she said tightly. 'I can design other things, you know.'

'I know,' said Judith. 'I know you're very talented.' She stared at her plate. 'I just meant . . .' but she let her sentence fade away.

Paul ignored his mother-in-law's interruption and kept his attention focused on Holly.

'Knowing what you don't want to do is a start,' he said. 'Now, how are you going to go about getting to do the things you do want to do?'

'I . . . I don't know yet. I suppose I'll work up a portfolio, gather some of the designs I've done before, and then I'll start digging around on the net for personnel agencies in the field.'

'Set yourself a time limit for each step of your plan. That would be my advice,' said Paul. 'Don't let your goals slip, or you'll find yourself six months down the line and no closer to your goal.'

A few days later, Miranda was outside the nursery waiting for Martha when Jo came running up to the gate, breathless, her arms full of a big folder of papers.

'Hello!' trilled Miranda. 'Such a long time since I last saw you! You haven't been in the park much lately.'

'No,' said Jo, still panting, and checking her watch in relief. 'I didn't think I'd make it. I was in a meeting at the bank and it ran over.'

'You can always give me a shout,' Miranda said, 'if you're held up. Martha would love Zachy to come and play.'

'Really?' said Jo. 'That might be a big help. Imogene's going to a childminder a couple of times a week now, but I have another meeting on Thursday and I wasn't sure I'd make it back in time to get Zach.'

'No worries,' said Miranda, and they swapped telephone numbers. 'So, I'm curious. 'All these meetings . . . what are they? Are you going back to work?'

'Kind of . . .' said Jo, a little reluctantly, but then she seemed to make up her mind. 'I'm starting a business. A kids' clothing shop. It's all in the early stages now, but it looks as if I'm going to get start-up finance from the bank. I've seen some premises in East Finchley that might be perfect if I can get the lease. If it all comes together, I'll be marketing like mad to all of you here at the school gate.'

'That sounds so exciting! You'll be a mumpreneur!' said Miranda enthusiastically.

'A what?'

'It's the new buzzword. "Mumpreneurs" are mums starting businesses that fit in with their families.'

'Ah,' said Jo, smiling, 'I love a good buzzword. Well, I have a long way to go. Lots of problems to solve before we open the doors. My biggest worry is that at the moment it's going to be a kids' clothing shop with no clothes in it. You wouldn't happen to know an amazingly talented fashion designer, would you?

JO, HOLLY AND MEL NOW

'These are . . . wow!' said Jo, paging through Holly's portfolio as they sat opposite each other at her kitchen table. 'They're just incredible. The detail! And the finish on them! Oh, I love this one.' She paused, looking at a floor-length silver evening dress, high at the front and cut low at the back, with a slim train like a mermaid's tail.

'It was one of my favourites,' Holly said, leaning forward. 'It was snapped up by a friend who's a drag queen. He certainly had the legs to work it.'

'A drag queen?'

'That kind of retro styling always appealed to the queens . . . Doradolla was started in the spirit of high camp.'

'I meant to ask you about that . . . Doradolla?'

'Afrikaans for "fag hag".'

'I don't know what to say,' said Jo, closing the portfolio and leaning back. 'I mean, you're an amazing designer, and you clearly know your way around a sewing machine, but this couldn't be further from the kind of stuff I need for the shop. Our main focus would be clothes for little boys, you see . . . and not fancy wear-for-best stuff. Hardwearing, fun play clothes that don't cost the earth.'

'I know,' said Holly, 'Miranda told me about that, so I had a bit of a go . . . I made these for my nephew Oscar.'

She reached into her bag and pulled out a pair of tiny denim jeans, baggy in the bum so they would fit over a nappy, with a soft, elasticated waistband. She'd embroidered them with stick figures and simple shapes: circles, triangles and squares, in primary colours. There were sturdy double-thickness pads over the knees. They were funky and adorable, and they looked like they'd withstand even the most determined toddler.

'I shoved them in the washing machine on hot half a dozen times,' explained Holly. 'Obviously they need to be able to take some knocks. It took a few goes to find embroidery thread that didn't lose its colour. And I also made these.' She had two little cowboy shirts in brightly coloured plaid, roomily cut to allow for plenty of movement and with press-studs rather than buttons.

'I took some pictures of Oscar in them.' She passed her iPad over to Jo, who flicked through the pictures of a laughing Oscar among the autumn leaves in the park. He wasn't necessarily a model baby, but he did look adorable in Holly's simple, well-made clothes.

'I've been thinking a lot about what kind of stock you might need,' she continued. 'I can take care of stuff like shirts and trousers, but you'd need more than that . . . coats for winter, and knitwear, and from the little boys I've been observing, you'll need a good-quality, hard-wearing range of T-shirts too. And maybe also baby wear, and I wouldn't know a lot about that. The challenge will be to get things made here in the UK at low cost. I'm pretty fast, but I'm not sure

I can sew a whole shop full of stock by myself, and getting material costs down is key. You also need to think about how fast you can respond . . .'

'Respond?'

'Well, you won't know what's going to sell and what might be a dud. It's difficult to predict, especially when you're first starting out. You might get a run on a particular line and need to get some more in fast, and some things might just not sell at all, and you'll have pre-ordered more. It's one advantage of being your own supplier. It's easier to be flexible.'

Jo passed the iPad back thoughtfully. 'Look, there's no question I want to work with you. The question is how?'

'Well, what are the options?'

'I don't know. I haven't got that far. I suppose initially I just imagined you'd be a supplier for some or all of the clothing. But listening to you talk . . . well, I want to lock you in my spare room and never let you go! You know such a lot. And you must know so many people.'

Holly laughed. 'Well, your spare room may be preferable to the one at my mum's house, which is where I'm currently living, and I'm afraid I know no one in the business here in the UK. All my contacts are in South Africa. It's a pity, because I do know an amazing baby-wear company in Johannesburg . . . they used to have a stall next to me at one of the markets. Oh, and if you decided to do something funky, there was a guy I knew who did the most stunning Hawaiian-style fabrics, which would make such sweet little shirts . . . And as for knitwear, there's a collective of *goggos* – grandmas – in one of the townships who knit the most beautiful things. They've all lost children to HIV, and they're raising their grand-children, so it's how they earn money.'

'Wow! Well, couldn't we make some of those connections work? I'd love to buy jumpers from the grannies, especially as we'd be supporting such a good cause.'

'We'd have to look at shipping costs, and what the situation might be with customs, and we'd need to see what the lead times would be . . .'

'Stop!' Jo laughed. 'Let's go back a step. Holly, I would love to work with you. My business plan allows me two full-time members of staff, as well as a budget for design and manufacture of clothes, so I think I could pay you fairly. If you'd consider being my design and stock expert, I'd be thrilled.'

'Not as thrilled as I would be,' said Holly. 'You have a deal.'

'So, if you don't mind me asking, what happened to make you leave your business in South Africa? It looks as if you had something great going.'

'Ah, now that's a long and rather gruesome story,' said Holly, her smile fading. 'We might need to save that one for a long evening and a large bottle of wine.'

Jo glanced up at the clock. 'Well, it's past four o'clock, and anyway, it's definitely evening somewhere in the world. Lee's got the kids in the park, and our new working relationship is the perfect excuse to celebrate. And as it happens, I have an average-sized but very nice bottle of something in the fridge.'

'Sounds good to me,' said Holly. 'But be warned, more than two glasses and I'm liable to start sobbing into my Chardonnay. Very unprofessional and unattractive, I think.'

'I'll reverse-medicate with chocolate if the need arises,' said Jo, getting up to fetch glasses and the bottle.

Holly stayed in her job at the shop in Ealing for the time being, but she spent her evenings with Jo in planning meetings, or at home sewing prototype garments. Her co-workers from the shop grumbled that she wasn't available for evenings out clubbing any more, and Judith gave a martyred sigh every time Holly bolted her dinner down and headed for the bus stop, or went back to her room to sew. She didn't care what anyone else thought though; she was happy. It felt like the early days of Doradolla, but without the crushing stress. She was having all the fun with very little of the responsibility, and it was fabulous.

Once the finance was in place, things started to move a lot faster. After months of wrangling, Jo got the premises in East Finchley she had long had her eye on. The area was perfect, with a great mix of well-off parents and more-average-income families, and within easy reach of many of the surrounding suburbs like Hampstead and Highgate, where there was plenty of disposable cash. The place Jo had found was on the high street and next door to a chain coffee shop. It was a double unit: a large, square space shop with a light airy feel and a big plate-glass window so that the exciting interior would be visible to passers-by.

Lee had done the initial designs and Jo had gone to a Swedish playground-equipment firm to build all the fittings. They were used to meeting very high safety standards, and what they built was built to last, but it was bright and colourful, although it did make a significant hole in the money

Jo had been lent by the bank. Holly supervised the design and ordering of the fittings to hang the clothes. Zach and Oscar served as reluctant but frequent models as she created her designs. Oscar would grumble or chuckle when she shoved him into something new, depending on whether or not she had a biscuit to bribe him with, but Zach was much more critical. If he thought something was fussy or uncomfortable, he would say so immediately. He also took the brief that these were supposed to be play clothes to heart, and as soon as Holly gave him something to try on, he would jump around, waving his arms, turn roly-polies and wrestle anyone who'd engage.

Holly also set about finding reputable clothing wholesalers to fill the gaps in their range. With winter setting in, she knew they needed coats, and until she could make contact with the collective in Johannesburg and arrange an order and shipping, she needed to source knitwear, especially hats and scarves. A search on the Internet alerted her to a wholesalers' trade show, which featured all sorts of children's products but especially clothing, and she and Jo booked to go. It was in an exhibition venue near Angel, and they decided to make a day of it. Lee's parents took Imogene and arranged to collect Zach from nursery, so Jo had no time pressure. She met Holly at Angel station and they went to a coffee shop for a leisurely breakfast.

'The luxury!' Jo laughed. 'I can't remember the last time I got to drink a whole cappuccino while it was still hot, or eat a whole pastry without sharing with two small people.'

'Have two pastries,' advised Holly. 'You'll need the carbs to sustain you through this.' She pushed the catalogue and a piece of paper across the table to Jo. She wasn't kidding about needing sustenance. There were hundreds of stalls listed, and Jo wouldn't have known where to begin, but luckily Holly had done her online research and chosen fifteen companies for them to look at, which she had put into a list.

'Fifteen?' said Jo, aghast.

'You want a good selection, don't you? And I'll be able to tell within ten seconds at any stall if the stuff is poor quality and we're wasting our time.'

Holly put Jo in charge of the map, and Jo cross-referenced it with Holly's typed list, plotting a route around the fair.

They got there as the doors opened, but it seemed lots of other people had had the same idea. Within an hour they had to push their way through crowds. Holly was relentless, going from stall to stall, picking up samples and immediately turning them inside out to look at the seams, more often than not then telling Jo they would be moving on. On the occasions where she found workmanship that was acceptable to her, she had a detailed list of questions about styles, prices, delivery times and so on. Jo kept up with her, taking detailed notes. They grabbed a sandwich standing up at the catering stand and carried on their quest. By three o'clock, they had seen all the suppliers on Holly's list. They hobbled back towards the coffee shop where they had had breakfast, but then Jo took Holly's elbow and steered her next door into the pub. With a big glass of wine each and their shoes kicked off under the table, they were ready to regroup. Holly had found a knitwear supplier whose work she liked, and they were confident they could get the prices down to something within their budget. They had both loved the crazy-patterned quilted jackets made by a supplier based in Devon. 'They're expensive though,' said Jo. 'We couldn't sell them for less than forty quid each or we wouldn't make anything.'

'Well, they could be our top-of-the-range items,' reasoned Holly. 'Those little body warmers and anoraks were also nicely made, the ones sold by the nice Asian couple, and they were much cheaper. We could take a load of those too.'

'Not the twee little corduroy waistcoats though,' said Jo.

'Oh Lord, no. Zach would have a thing or two to say about those.'

Once they had gone through all the brochures and notes, they had filled all the gaps in the range except T-shirts.

'There just wasn't anything that grabbed me,' said Jo, signalling a waiter to bring them two more glasses of wine.

'Me neither,' said Holly. 'Either they cost the earth or the quality was poor.'

'Or the designs were twee and dull,' observed Jo. 'Lee could do so much better.'

'So why doesn't he?'

'Well, where do we get shirts to print? And how do we do it? I know Lee knows how to silkscreen, but I'm sure he doesn't want to . . . Hang on a minute!' Jo interrupted herself excitedly and grabbed her handbag. She scrabbled in her purse and came out with the oddly shaped orange business card. 'When I did my Introduction to Business course, I met two teenage guys who'd started their own T-shirt printing business. I haven't seen their shirts, but I was impressed by the boys. They might be worth a look.' She gave the card to Holly.

Holly looked at the card, and the funky cartoon on it. 'Outtake,' she read. 'This is cool.'

'One of them designs them and the other does the printing, I think. But maybe they'd let us do our own designs and then just do the printing.'

'To be honest, I like this cartoon,' Holly said. 'I'll check out their website. Maybe they could do some kids' designs for us too. Something completely original. Tie in with Lee's designs for the shop.'

After they had finished their second glass of wine, they took a stroll around the trendy shops nearby. They happened upon a children's boutique with an antique rocking horse in the window and a display of little smocked dresses in pretty floral prints.

'Care to check out the competition?' Holly asked Jo.

'They're not the competition,' Jo said. 'Totally different area, different clientele, mostly girls' stuff, but yeah, totally. Let's go and spy.'

They walked nonchalantly into the shop. It was beautifully and expensively fitted out, with a solid wooden floor and all the clothes hung on padded white-satin hangers. There were glass shelves with baby gifts and christening robes, and racks of delicate jewellery. Jo thought about what chaos Zach would be capable of in a place like this, and gave an involuntary shiver. She looked over to Holly and thought she must be thinking something similar, because she was staring at something with open-mouthed disbelief. She walked over and saw Holly was looking at a little girl's dress. It was an old fashioned smock-style dress with two pockets, in a butterfly print fabric. It looked like something out of an Enid Blyton book: simple but pretty. Jo thought she wouldn't mind buying it for Imogene. But it was the price tag Holly was staring at. Jo glanced at it cursorily. Twenty pounds. That didn't seem unreasonable – about right for a dress like that. Then she looked again. She had missed a zero. The dress was two hundred pounds. Other than her wedding, she couldn't think of an occasion where she'd spend that on a dress for herself, let alone Imogene, who would dribble and spill on it, and have occasion to wear it three or four times before she grew out of it. Jo grabbed Holly's elbow and they backed out of the shop.

'You were right,' laughed Holly. 'Soooo not the competition. I don't think we're aiming at the same market at all!'

Later that week, after checking out their website and social-media presence, Holly set up a meeting with Chris and Daniel, the T-shirt guys. Jo had told her they were teenagers and she was expecting a pair of spotty fifteen-year-olds, so she was pleasantly surprised when two tall, well-turned-out young men in jeans and collared shirts walked into the West End restaurant where they'd arranged to meet. Chris was slightly shorter and rounder, with thick black hair that he'd obviously spent time arranging in an artful bed-head way. Daniel was tall and lean with sharper features and cropped light brown hair. They looked like what Judith would call 'Nice, well-brought-up young men'.

'Good to meet you,' Holly said, standing up to shake hands. When they'd exchanged greetings and sat down she ordered a coffee, and they both asked for Earl Grey tea, which she found rather endearing. They made small talk for a while and she discovered they had been friends since junior school and were now entering their A2 year, the end of A levels. Daniel had just turned eighteen and Chris was a few months younger.

They were clearly nervous, and Holly could see that this meeting was a big deal for them. She tried to put them at their ease. 'Let me just start by saying we really like your stuff, and we definitely want to work with you, if we can agree the right designs and the right terms.'

Daniel tried to look serious and businesslike, but his face broke into a wide grin. He had a lovely smile and very white teeth. A bit like a boy-band member, Holly thought. 'Well, as soon as we got your call, I started thinking about kids' T-shirts, and I did a few sketches. Would you like to see?'

He opened the folder he had brought with him. 'I came up with an idea ages ago for a kids' action hero, a little guy called Monkeyman,' he explained. 'My dad used to call me that when I was little. Monkeyman's sort of like Calvin, from *Calvin and Hobbes*, you know. A kid who's always in trouble but thinks he's saving the world. So we see him jumping off the sofa on to the cat, or battling an evil alien with his mum's spatula, and he always wears a cape made out of a towel. This is him.'

He pushed a drawing across at Holly, with an ink cartoon of an impish little guy with a towel knotted around his shoulders, and spiky hair like Chris's. His little face was full of mischief. He reminded Holly instantly of Zach. 'Aah! He's great!' she said, laughing.

'So we wondered about a range of Monkeyman T-shirts, and then we started thinking about the jungle theme of your shop, so we did some animal designs too . . .'

Daniel was so excited his words tripped over each other as he handed drawing after drawing to Holly. Most of them were perfect, though a few were too avant-garde or adult for the audience, and those she put to one side.

Chris, who had not said much up until that point, then reached into his bag. 'I got a few T-shirts from our regular supplier and printed some up for you,' he said shyly. He brought them out and handed them to Holly. They were neatly ironed and folded. He clocked her noticing and smiled. 'My mum was so excited about this meeting; she stayed up till midnight last night ironing these for us. And she made us wear shirts.'

'I would have worn a shirt anyway,' said Daniel seriously.

Holly unfolded the T-shirts. They were reasonable quality, and she liked the way they were printed in unusual colours and unusual places. Monkeyman ran along the hem of one T-shirt and peered out from under the wearer's arm on another. 'These are great,' she said. 'Let's talk wholesale price.'

Chris brought out a carefully typed list with their prices per size and quantity on it. Holly scanned it. 'That's a great start. Now go away and recost it with an even better quality T-shirt. I want something that won't fade or shrink and can withstand multiple washes, okay?'

'Okay.' Chris looked downcast.

'Don't get me wrong, these are pretty good,' said Holly. 'But we're talking about dressing a real-life Monkeyman. We're making clothes for kids that are going to get up to all sorts, and parents will expect the clothes to keep up. But let me just say we have a deal, and you guys are going to be very busy in the next few months. Now would you like something to eat?'

Chris and Daniel nodded enthusiastically and began studying the menu. Holly had grown up with an older brother, and she suddenly remembered how much teenage boys could eat. She almost regretted her generous offer, but what the hell. They were sweet kids, and their T-shirts were going to be fabulous.

They set an opening date of 1 November, reasoning that it gave them time to iron out any kinks in the running of the shop before the Christmas rush. With four weeks to go before the launch, there were a million things to do. Both Jo and Holly kept enormous lists, which seemed to get longer, never shorter. Holly worked out her notice at the shop in Ealing and breathed a sigh of relief. She'd been juggling two full-time jobs for so long, she'd forgotten what a good night's sleep felt like.

Jo was run absolutely ragged. She had to fit everything for the shop around the kids, who had pretty full-on schedules themselves. She found herself sitting by the pool while Zach had his swimming lesson, working on a spreadsheet on her laptop with one hand while feeding chunks of apple to Imi with the other. Then, in the week that all the clothes started to arrive, first Zach and then Imi came down with horrible colds and she was up all night with feverish, coughing children.

She was exhausted all the time, but there was no way to stop. If the kids were asleep, she had to grab the hours to do some work, so even after they got rid of their colds, she was managing on about four hours a night. Then, one day, she was so befuddled that she managed to reverse the car into her own gatepost. It wasn't a major accident, just a scratch on the bumper, but she knew it would never have happened if she was her usual competent self. She sat in the car, sobbing, while Zach patted her arm, full of concern, and then she took out her phone and rang Lee. 'I really need your help,' she said. Lee hesitated for a second, and that was all it took for her to start sobbing again.

'Don't cry, love,' he said, horrified. Jo was always so tough, so calm under pressure . . . she almost never cried. 'Let me see what I can do.'

He rang back ten minutes later. He had spoken to his boss, and she had allowed him to take a couple of weeks' leave from work to look after the kids so Jo could put in all the hours she needed. Things were a bit easier after that, and on Lee's orders, she made sure she got at least six or seven hours' sleep every night.

One of the most crucial concerns was finding a third staff member. Holly had made it clear that she didn't want to be stuck behind the counter. She'd done her time in retail, and while she was happy to give advice or fill in, she didn't want to work regular shifts. Jo wanted to be there day-to-day, but her family commitments meant her hours were limited. They needed someone full-time and utterly reliable. They wrote an ad and ran it on a few retail job sites.

Holly came into the half-fitted shop one day to find Jo sitting, her head in her hands, at the dusty counter, looking at a great stack of pages.

'What's the problem?'

'What makes you think there's a problem?'

'When you bury your fingers in your hair like that, it's because you're wrestling with something. What's up?'

'Have you been talking to Lee? He always says to me, "Are you trying to hold your head together, or pull it apart?"'

'Well, which is it?'

'This hiring thing. It's like the worst kind of blind dating.' Holly pointed to the pile of papers. 'Are those CVs?'

'So many CVs. More than sixty. How do I begin to choose? We don't have time to interview sixty people.'

'Okay,' said Holly in her best businesslike tone, 'let's split the pile in half, and be brutal. We have to go by feel. We need to choose a shortlist of not more than ten, I say. We can interview ten, surely.'

'Can we?' said Jo faintly. 'When?'

'We'll clear a day. Somehow. Look, we have to do this. We need this person.' Holly took the pile of CVs and split it roughly in the middle. Be brutal. Be judgemental. And go totally with your gut.'

On their first pass, they managed to lose thirty-five of the sixty. Jo felt dreadful. Most of those purged were excluded for the most minor reasons: they lived too far away, they didn't actively mention children in their application letter . . . Holly eliminated one girl because she'd inserted a photo into her CV. 'Nothing against her face – just think it's weird to include a picture if you weren't asked for one.'

'Now what?' said Jo. 'We can't interview twenty-five people. Not in a day. And we don't have more than a day. We don't even have a day! We have a fictional day, which you have invented, which doesn't exist in my diary. The thirty-second of something.'

'Okay,' said Holly. 'We need a method. But first, we need coffee. I'll get some from next door.'

'We might need cake as well. This decision needs cake. In fact, here's a better idea. Let's go next door. It's a new environment. Fresh energy. Clear thoughts.'

'Genius!' said Holly, hopping up and grabbing her bag and the pile of CVs.

They went over to the coffee shop, where they ordered lattes and slices of lemon cake and sat at a corner table.

'I think we're going about this the wrong way,' Jo said. 'We're looking for something wrong, a way to exclude people. We should be looking for something right. Something exceptional. A yes, not a no.'

'And that's why you're the boss,' said Holly, grinning. 'Let's read them all again, looking for a yes. For whatever reason. Let's each write down the people we think have something special, even if it isn't something we can define.'

They each read every one of the twenty-five CVs, passing them over as they completed them and making notes on their pads. They didn't speak for over an hour, except to order more coffee. When they had finished they each had a list of names.

'How many do you have?' asked Jo.

'Seven. You?'

'Nine. Let's swap and look.'

They exchanged pads. They both had five of the same names. 'Well, those are definites,' said Jo happily. Then they each went through the others they had chosen and explained why. They decided to lose two of Jo's and one of Holly's, leaving a total of eight.

'Job done!' said Holly, leaning back in her chair, satisfied. 'Now I need to get out of here. I'm on a total caffeine and sugar buzz. I'm shaking.'

They went back to the half-completed shop without speaking. But as Jo unlocked the door, she turned to Holly and said hesitantly, 'Any obvious favourites?'

'Oh, totally. You?'

'Yes,' said Jo, pushing the door open. They hesitated, and then said simultaneously, 'Mel Grey.'

'So . . . Mel,' Holly said.

'I know. She's the one, isn't she?'

'We need to do the interviews, but she is. I feel it in my waters.'

According to Mel Grey's CV, she had trained at Goldsmith's as a performer (Jo was thrilled – 'My alma mater!'), then worked with a children's theatre company, touring schools with a variety of educational programmes, before retraining as a nursery nurse.

'I bet she had a baby then and didn't want to tour any more,' said Jo.

'She did,' said Holly. 'She mentions it under "personal" at the end. Serena. Aged fifteen.'

After the nursery-nurse section, Mel's CV was all clothing retail – and mainly children's clothing. She'd worked in big department stores and boutiques, and she was currently the office manager for a clothing import firm in Finchley. She had experience of every aspect from stock control to service and fitting. Her covering letter was appropriately formal, but still warm and funny. It seemed like a small thing but she'd begun it 'Dear Jo and Holly, Re: Staff position at Jungletown'. Holly, ever the perfectionist, noticed that she had researched their first names, even though they weren't in the job ad, and she had got the shop name absolutely correct, noting that it was one word, not two. She was one of only three candidates who did.

They found a day to conduct their interviews among all the mayhem. Of their eight shortlisted candidates, two had already found other positions and one was away on holiday and couldn't make the interview date, so in the end they saw five people.

As a test, they decided to hold the interviews at Jo's house and have Zach and Imogene in the room with them. Mel burst into the interview with sparky energy, humour and warmth. She was short – just five feet tall – and wiry, with the compact, athletic build of a gymnast. She wore her sandy hair cropped short, and looked younger than her age, which Jo and Holly knew from her CV was forty-one. She greeted them formally and correctly and answered their introductory questions well, and when Zach bounded over to show her his new pride and joy, a Doctor Who Sonic Screwdriver, she politely excused herself to Jo and Holly and turned her full attention to Zach. She appeared to know a terrifying amount of detail about the gadget, and about Doctor Who in general, and she pitched her chatter just right for an enthusiastic but not very well-informed three-and-a-half year old. After a minute or so, she asked Zach's pardon, explaining that she had to speak to his mum, and turned her attention back to Jo and Holly. She answered all sorts of technical questions about running a shop, and when Imogene, who was teething, began to fuss, asked if she might hold her, and stood bouncing her on a hip while she talked. She was perfect, but most of all, they both really liked her. As Holly said, once she was gone, 'I don't know how to put it into words, but . . . she's our tribe.'

'I know what you mean,' said Jo. 'I feel about her the way I felt about you when we first met.'

Holly laughed. 'You soppy thing.'

'I'm not soppy. But sometimes you just have to go with your gut. When I met you, I knew you were the right person. And I was right. And I'm right about Mel too. We have our team.'

They planned a launch party for 5 November, which was a Saturday. Holly reasoned that they needed a few days to run the shop without pressure before they invited press and interested parties, and Jo agreed.

Jo had found the setting up of the shop endlessly challenging – exciting, but throwing up a series of obstacles and headaches for which it sometimes seemed she was ill-equipped. But when it came to PR and publicity for the launch, she was in her element. She called in every contact she had ever had who might be any use at all: she canvassed every local toddler group, posted on every online parenting forum, wooed mummy bloggers, set up Facebook and Twitter profiles, badgered the local press and invited everyone she had ever met within a twenty-mile radius who had a child or knew a child. She was confident that their opening event would be full to bursting and that there would be column inches about it.

The day the signwriter came, Lee came to t... supervise the typography. The chap they had hir... hand-lettering expert, but Lee stood over him to scr... ...se every swirl and swash. When he had finally finished, packed his tools into his van and driven away, shaking his head, Jo and Lee stood on the pavement outside the shop, their arms around each other, and stared. 'Jungletown' was emblazoned in bright tiger stripes across the window, in a glorious frame of monkey faces and vibrant palm leaves. Inside, the fitting of the bottom half of the shop was complete. It was a dramatic jungle scene with animals prowling the walls. There were giant jigsaws of parrots and tigers and thick ropes covered in fabric to look like jungle vines. The floor, which was covered in brightly coloured soft wipe-clean tiles, was scattered with giant toy animals to climb on and ride. There were things to bash and spin, to throw and build, but crucially, it was all safe, all cleanable and all pretty much unbreakable. Above this bright and vivid scene were Holly's meandering rails and hooks. Holly herself was busy hanging out the first of the stock. She was scrutinising every piece to see that it had been properly pressed and hung on a hanger with the correct size clearly marked. It was still a few days before the doors were to open, but Holly's attention to detail meant she would need that time to complete the job. Mel stood behind the counter, which was painted to look like a rough-hewn ship. She was busy programming the till, which had been delivered that morning. For Jo, it was the strangest feeling: the image she had seen in her dream all those months ago had become a reality. It hadn't happened by magic or accident; it had taken immense hard work and tenacity (and an eye-watering amount of debt), but it was real. Really, really real. She hugged Lee tightly.

'Thank you, my love,' she said. 'None of this would have happened without your support. I love you.' He smiled at her and hugged her back.

'Nonsense. This is all you. The launch is only a week away, babe, and then the sky's the limit.'

PART TWO

8

MEL THEN

It was dusk, and the traffic along Ballards Lane was crawling. Mel stood at the window of her dingy office on the seventh floor of Central House in Finchley and looked down at the cars inching along. Someone who had parked outside Tesco decided to pull out into the traffic and perform a three-point turn, thereby gridlocking the whole of the narrow high street. Even seven floors up, Mel could hear the hooting, and she could sense the swearing that would accompany it. It had turned chilly outside; she could see a woman hurrying along the pavement, hugging her coat around her and hunching down into her collar. The neon signs in the shops and takeaways were coming on, throwing bands of coloured light on to the people as they passed.

Mel was alone in the office. Her bosses, Mr Shapiro and Mr Seberini, had gone to a meeting with their lawyer. She had completed the Excel spreadsheet inventory they had asked for, collated all their messages and prepared the letters to be dropped into the post when she left. She had nothing to do but stay in the office until five thirty, in case the phone rang. It was the quietest, least challenging job she had ever had and she was going slightly mad in the long hours alone in the silent office. Shapiro and Seberini wanted their office run in the old-fashioned way. With reluctance they had given Mel a computer, but if she ever asked for software updates or more memory, they were deeply suspicious. Neither of them used email or the Internet, and they would have been horrified at anything as newfangled and informal as Mel forwarding the office phone to her mobile and going home.

She'd taken the job because it was so local, and because the hours were regular – nine to five thirty, Monday to Friday, and never any overtime or variation. She did it for Serena, so they could spend weekends and evenings together, so she could be available to chat and to help with homework. But she might as well not have bothered. As often as not, when Mel got home from work, Serena would be in her bedroom with the door closed. Mel would knock and say hello, and receive a monosyllabic grunt in return. She would make dinner and call Serena, who would sometimes just yell 'I'm not hungry', or might deign to emerge long enough to look at the food, wrinkle up her nose and proclaim some part of it 'disgusting', and then take her plate into her room and shut the door again. If Mel insisted, Serena would roll her eyes and sit at the table. Mel had no idea how they had got to this point. It had happened so gradually, so insidiously, and now they were in a terrible place, and she had no idea how to reverse it.

She had never been married to Serena's dad, Bruce. They'd had a relatively casual relationship, and when she fell pregnant, he'd been open about the fact that he wasn't particularly interested in being a father. For Mel, an abortion was not an option, so she decided to make a go of it alone, and Bruce agreed. He was a musician and spent a lot of time touring working men's clubs up north. He dropped in whenever he was in town, bringing Serena obscure band T-shirts and handfuls of crumpled cash. He had faithfully paid a small amount of money into Mel's account every month, and she counted herself lucky to have an uncomplicated and amicable relationship with him.

So for pretty much all Serena's life, it had just been the two of them. They'd been close, maybe too close, sharing private jokes from whenever Serena was old enough to understand them, and reading books together. First Mel read to Serena; then once she could read, Serena would read to her mum every evening. Serena showed an interest in music when she was just four or five, and Mel had sunk all her savings into buying her a piano, and then had scrimped and saved for lessons. She'd made sure Serena practised every day, and she was there at every exam grading and concert Serena played in.

They liked hanging out together, and Serena's junior-school friends all loved coming back to their flat after school for tea and DVDs or games. It was the perfect mother–daughter relationship, or so Mel thought.

On the night before Serena's thirteenth birthday, they had gone for pizza and to see a film. It was a Friday night, so when they got home, they sat up till midnight with cups of hot chocolate. Serena giggled and talked excitedly and non-stop about the film they'd seen, the party she was having the next day and what she had been doing at school.

At five to twelve, Mel said jokingly, 'You're going to be a teenager now. I suppose this is our last conversation. After midnight you'll have to start hating me and all I stand for.'

'Oh, Mum!' groaned Serena dramatically. 'You don't understand me! I have to go now. I have to paint the walls in my room black and listen to some metal music.'

'Really? I can lend you some . . . early Metallica, maybe? Or Slayer? What about Megadeth?'

'Mum . . . !' Serena giggled. 'It's not cool for mums to like kids' music. You know that. Sooo not cool.'

'It's not kids' music, it's ours. We're just letting you borrow it. And anyway, now you're going to be a teenager, you'll need the music. I'm going to lock you in your room until you're at least thirty-five to keep the boys away.'

'Thirty-five?'

'You're right – that's a bit young. I meant forty-five.'

'I'll grow my hair long and dangle it out of the window for a prince to climb up. It won't take long . . . we live on the ground floor.' Serena laughed.

'Seriously, though . . .' Mel began, 'just because you're older and you'll have a bit more freedom . . .'

'The world is a dangerous place, don't trust anyone, stranger danger, don't trust anyone, yadda-yadda-yadda. You've been drumming it into me since I was a baby, Mum. I know.'

'I know you know,' said Mel. 'Now get into the kitchen and see if there are any marshmallows left. I need a sugar rush to get me to midnight.'

It was, Mel reflected, the last evening they had together. It had seemed to start as a joke, as if Serena was pretending to be a teenager. Mel was into music and had a broad and eclectic collection, ranging from classical to electronica, from the eighties to contemporary stuff, and Serena had dipped in and out of bits of it throughout her life. She'd been able to play Simon and Garfunkel's 'Bridge over Troubled Water' and the opening riff to Guns N' Roses' 'Patience' on the piano by the time she was seven. All of a sudden she started listening to different music, music she had heard kids talking about at school – dubstep, grime and house. When Mel tried to show an interest, Serena got angry and took the music into her room to listen to. Mel thought it was quite sweet, this assertion of musical independence.

Then one day they were rushing to leave for school. Mel grabbed her keys and yelled for Serena, who came out of her room, head bowed, and rushed for the door. As Mel came up behind her to go out, she caught a glimpse of Serena's profile, half hidden by her hair. 'What's on your face?' she asked.

'Nothing.'

'Nothing?'

'Nothing. Can we go? I'm going to be late.' Serena turned her face away towards the door and reached for the doorknob.

'If it's nothing, let me see your face,' said Mel, teasing. She expected Serena to laugh and turn to her, but Serena raised an elbow to ward her off and went to open the door. Mel was shocked. 'Rena!' she said sharply. 'Look at me!' She'd never been a yelling mother, and she hadn't had cause to shout at Serena for years, so it surprised her as much as it did Serena, who dropped her guard for a second and looked up. She was wearing a full face of make-up: a lot of badly applied foundation that was far too dark for her, heavy black eyeliner and mascara and an awful frosted-pink lipstick. Mel couldn't help herself. She burst out laughing. She caught herself immediately, and tried to look stern and say something that sounded reasonable, but the damage was already done. Serena turned away from her and slammed into the bathroom, locking the door behind her.

Mel knew better than to pound on the bathroom door, or stand outside nagging about how they were going to be late. She waited quietly until Serena emerged, her face washed and her eyes a little red. They left the flat together, and as they walked along the road, she said quietly, 'I'm sorry I laughed. I was surprised, that's all.'

Serena didn't say anything. It was unlike her: she usually entered into any debate energetically. Mel didn't quite know what to do with her silence. She tried again. 'I appreciate that you want to wear make-up, but it's not ideal to wear it to school. And it's probably also best to buy stuff that's good quality and suits your colouring. Did you borrow that stuff from a friend?'

Serena still didn't say anything, but when Mel turned to look at her, she nodded almost imperceptibly.

'I'm happy to take you shopping at the weekend,' Mel said. 'I can't afford to buy you loads, but we can get a few bits. Good-quality stuff. Okay?'

Again, there was a tiny nod.

'But you can't wear it to school, okay? In the evenings or at weekends is fine.'

No nod this time, just a tiny clench of the jaw. Mel knew

it well. It meant Serena didn't agree, but wasn't going to have the argument now. Well, one thing at a time. The morning had been quite traumatic enough. But she couldn't resist saying one more thing.

'Serena, when girls your age wear make-up, it makes you look older. It makes you look . . . well, it makes it hard for people to know how old you really are, and they might . . . get the wrong idea. Just . . . be careful, okay?'

This time, Serena actually snorted derisively. Well, let her snort. On balance, Mel thought, she'd handled it rather well.

Except she hadn't. Serena refused to go make-up shopping with her. She wanted to go with her friends. And despite Mel's ban, she wore make-up to school every day, at first applying it subtly, then less so. Mel tried joking, nagging and eventually yelling, but Serena persisted, and in the end Mel gave up. It didn't seem a big enough issue to allow it to cause a permanent rift between them. Then Serena started wanting to buy her own clothes, and to go shopping without Mel. She wanted to go to Camden alone with friends, and Mel said no to that, but finally relented when Serena begged and said they would be going with a friend's older sister who was eighteen. Mel met the sister, who seemed sensible enough, handed over twenty quid and sat at home chewing her nails until Serena came back. She'd bought a black lacy skirt, very early Madonna, that looked like something Mel would have worn to a party in the eighties. Gradually Serena built up a wardrobe of stuff that she thought was quirky and interesting and Mel could see looked just like the clothes all the other girls in her circle wore. She begged to have her ears pierced, which Mel allowed and paid for, but then sneaked off with friends and had another two holes done at the top of her ears. Another screaming match ensued, there was more door slamming and the open channel of communication they had always seemed to have narrowed a little more.

By the time Serena turned fourteen, Mel found she was sharing her home with a sullen girl whose hair hung over her heavily made-up eyes, who slouched, kept earphones in at all times and wore a shocking pink, puffy body warmer over everything: jeans, her school uniform, her weekend outfit of too-short skirt, tights and Ugg boots. She spoke in monosyllables and exuded resentment from every pore. School, where she had always excelled, was suddenly 'boring', and her marks began to drop. And, in a heart-breaking blow to Mel's hopes for her, her piano practice tailed off and stopped, and she refused to go for any more lessons or gradings.

Then it got worse. Their system, since Serena was eleven, was that she would walk home from school alone and text Mel as soon as she was in the flat. Mel would then ring her on the landline as soon as she had a free moment at work and they would have a quick catch-up about their day. Mel could predict within a few minutes when Serena would text; the school was only a short walk from their home. But then the texts gradually started to come through later and later. If she rang Serena's mobile to check, Serena would hiss into the phone, 'Don't phone me! I'm almost home! I'm walking with Marina, okay?' And later, she would berate Mel for embarrassing her in front of her friends. After a while the texts started coming at the appointed time, but if Mel rang the landline Serena wouldn't answer. If she then rang Serena's mobile she would say she hadn't heard the phone, or that she'd just stepped out to take the rubbish to the bin. They were the most unconvincing stories Mel had ever heard. As far as she knew, it was the first time her daughter had lied to her. It broke her heart, but she knew if she persisted in nagging, or insisted that Serena ring her back from the landline to prove she was actually home, there would be another flaming row and Serena would lie more and tell her less.

As the months passed, things only got worse. Mel felt she was treading on eggshells all the time. Any question she asked, whether it was about school, or friends, or plans for the weekend, was taken the wrong way. Serena accused her of prying, of being controlling, and constantly of trying to spoil her fun. It was appalling, because Mel could see no way to get through to her. The sweet child she'd raised had disappeared, to be replaced with this sullen and selfish girl. Mel didn't like her very much, but she couldn't stop loving her, and constantly fearing for her safety and her future.

Mel, standing at her office window, sighed. It was dark outside. Serena was now fifteen, and they were living an uneasy truce, but only, Mel knew, because she was asking no questions at all now. She no longer expected a text from Serena after school, and she was sure her daughter usually came home only minutes before she got in from work herself. Serena stuck roughly to the curfew Mel gave her, but only because she knew Mel would cut off her allowance if she didn't. It was a far from ideal situation, but Mel consoled herself by thinking that she'd seen no evidence of drink or drugs, and Serena seemed happy to hang around with her friends from the girls' school and there were no boys on the horizon. Most aspects of her 'rebellion' seemed pretty innocent so far. If any of these more hazardous things should present themselves, well . . . to be honest, Mel didn't know what she would do.

She glanced at her watch. It was 5.15. Nearly time to go. She wandered into the tiny kitchenette, which was already clean and tidy, and absent-mindedly wiped the sink and the countertop one more time. Then she meandered back to the window. She could see down on to the platform at Finchley Central Tube station. There were crowds of commuters returning from work. As she watched, a train from London pulled in and a great knot of people spilled out and began filing towards the stairs. She watched them disinterestedly, but a flash of bright pink caught her eye, only because it was the same cerise as the puffa jacket Serena always wore. She looked again. Although the person wearing the jacket was far away, it really did look just like the jacket Serena wore. And the wearer was about the same height and build with dark hair.

Mel watched as the figure disappeared into the stairwell, and she waited to see if she would come out of the station exit and walk up the hill towards the building. She did, and as she stepped under a streetlight, it was instantly clear that it was Serena – Serena in ordinary clothes, not school uniform. She was walking with a tall, skinny person, almost certainly male, although Mel couldn't tell for sure because he or she had a hoody on with the hood up concealing their face. It wasn't someone Mel recognised. Serena was laughing, and she saw her point at Mel's building and say something. On the corner of the main road, she said goodbye to the tall person, who headed off up the high street. Serena jogged in the opposite direction, obviously hurrying to get home before Mel left the office.

Mel felt cold. There was no way Serena could have gone home after school, changed, caught the Tube into town and got back by 5.15. She must have bunked school. Mel had obviously been kidding herself. Whatever Serena was up to, it obviously wasn't totally innocent, and it wasn't harmless. She was going to have to do something, something decisive and firm, before Serena went off the rails completely. The trouble was, she didn't have a clue what.

9

JUNGLETOWN NOW

They had all learned a great deal in the few days they had been open, not least that there was an endless amount of tidying and cleaning involved in the day-to-day operation of the shop. At 7 a.m. on the day of the launch party, Jo was crawling around the shop on her hands and knees. She had a bottle of white spirit and some cosmetic cotton pads, and she was cleaning scuff marks off the walls where crowds of energetic little boys had kicked and scraped them. They were all exhausted to the point of slightly hysterical giggling. Lee stood at the counter compiling press packs, Zach was playing quietly with a puzzle and Imogene was asleep in her push-chair. Holly and Mel were filling balloons from a helium canister they had hired, occasionally breathing some in and launching into a chipmunk-style rendition of 'I will survive', and Mel's fifteen-year-old daughter Serena, who had reluctantly been dragged along, had been sent to stand outside the coffee shop and bring back caffeine and sugar supplies the minute the place opened.

When Serena returned, she was greeted with a cheer and they all gathered around the counter with their cups and muffins to go over the plans for the day. 'The photographer will be here at nine,' Jo said, checking her list. 'She'll get some shots of the shop before people arrive. The cupcake lady said she'd deliver between nine and nine thirty. What time is the face painter arriving?'

'I asked her to be here before ten to set up. I thought we could put her table over there,' Holly said, pointing to one of the back corners of the shop.

'Maybe on the other side,' Mel said. That's right in the way of the coconut ball-throwing game. She might not appreciate being hit on the head with a coconut, even if it is a soft foam-rubber one.'

'Good point,' said Jo. 'On the other side then. Mel, what are the RSVPs looking like?'

'Well, if everyone who's said they're coming comes, we'll have people queuing outside all day,' said Mel.

'That's great. We can probably count on half to two-thirds of them actually showing up. As long as there's a buzz in here the whole day, I'll be happy.'

'What's the final word on the press?' Holly asked.

'Both local papers are coming – that reminds me, they're also bringing photographers. But they said they want candid shots of the shop full of people, not set-up shots. We've got two listings magazines coming – both have said they'll do an editorial piece on us if we buy an ad, and at last count, about five mummy bloggers.'

'That's amazing!' Holly said admiringly.

'Well, that was my job.' Jo smiled. 'Getting bums on seats.'

'Fabulous,' Holly said. 'Now, if we're all done, I want to check stock one last time. We made quite a few late sales yesterday, and I want to make sure we have everything out that we need.'

'Balloons,' said Mel. 'Serena, can you give me a hand? We need another twenty or so.'

As her team headed off to complete their tasks, Jo reached for her bottle of spirit, but Lee put his hand on her wrist and drew her into his arms.

'There might not be time to say it later, and we'll probably be too knackered tonight, so I'm telling you now that I'm so proud of you my heart could burst.' He kissed her sweetly and then more passionately, and for a second they forgot the shop, the other people in the room and their two children in the back office. Serena broke the spell by snorting and yelling, 'Get a room!'

Jo giggled and stepped away, but as she turned she saw both Holly and Mel looking a little wistful.

From nine thirty, half an hour before they were even due to open, there was already a small crowd outside, peering in through the windows. Mel and Serena had done an impressive job with the balloons, and the shop looked like party central both outside and in. Daniel and Chris arrived to lend a hand and to bring additional T-shirt stock, for which Holly was very grateful. The last-minute tasks took them right up to ten o'clock, when Jo gathered everyone together. 'This is it, people,' she said. 'Thank you for all your work and patience. Today is make or break. Let's make it count!' Then she took a deep breath, walked over to the door and turned the key.

First through the door were Lee's parents, who had come to fetch Zach and Imogene and take them back to their house in Pinner for the rest of the day. They were full of admiration, and Lee's mum insisted on buying a few T-shirts for Zach, even though Jo said she shouldn't, and that Zach had all the clothes he needed. At points in the morning, the shop was uncomfortably full, and Lee, Daniel and Chris took turns to be doorman and restrict the flow of people into the room. At the busiest point, Serena said a mumbled goodbye and slunk off, pretending not to hear Mel's questions about where she was going and when she might be home. The photographers from the local papers had arrived, and were struggling to get shots in the crush, and Jo had to elbow a few paying customers aside so they could take the pictures they needed. Mel was on hand to smooth ruffled feathers with a free cupcake and an offer of face-painting for the little ones, and everyone seemed to go away happy.

Miranda came with her children and Holly's mum, who was a little overwhelmed by the noise and buzz, not to mention the constant risk of being knocked flying by a fast-moving small boy at waist-height. Holly eventually ushered her next door to the coffee shop and got her a cup of tea and a bun. Miranda oohed and ahed, and bought a few things for Oscar. Holly was rushed off her feet refilling the racks, answering questions on sizing and giving advice to customers. Chris and Daniel had stuck around and they proved invaluable, fetching and carrying, and it turned out Chris was a dab hand with an iron (he told Holly he had learned in the cadets at school), so eventually he just stayed in the back room, pressing things and putting them on hangers for Daniel to bring out.

There was a brief lull around lunchtime, but only long

enough for Mel to run a Hoover around the floor and for everyone to do a quick tidy and regroup. The afternoon rush was slightly less frantic than the morning, but the shop was still constantly full. At around three, Jo looked up and saw Louise, the woman who had run the business course, come through the door, holding the hand of a little boy of about three, with flaming red hair. She was no longer pregnant, and the tall man she was with, who was handsome and greying, had a tiny baby in a sling on his front. There was another couple with them, with toddler twins in a double buggy. Louise came over and greeted Jo with a hug and a kiss.

'You did it! This is absolutely fantastic!' she said with warmth and enthusiasm. 'I'm not even slightly surprised you got it off the ground, but it's even better than I could have imagined! And I'm so thrilled you connected with Daniel and Chris. They emailed to tell me you gave them their big break.' She introduced her husband, Adam, and her little boy, Peter. Adam shook Jo's hand, and gently tipped forward to show her the sleeping infant on his chest. 'This is Florence,' he said. His voice was deep and Scottish, and the pride he clearly felt was unmistakable.

'This is my sister, Rachel, and her husband, Richard,' said Louise, indicating their companions, 'and their twins, Jago and Xanthe.'

Jo left Louise and her entourage to have a look around, and went to spend a little time chatting up one of the influential local mummy bloggers who had just arrived. The blogger wanted a few pictures, so Jo asked Louise if she could borrow her little boy, who was very sweet-looking. They slipped one of the Monkeyman T-shirts on over what he was wearing, and he posed patiently for a few pics, playing with some of the equipment, holding a balloon and having his face painted.

Jo couldn't help noticing, out of the corner of her eye, that Louise's sister's twins, now out of their pushchair, were a pair of destructive and under-disciplined monsters. The little boy – Jago, was it? – was a thrower: he hurled balls, bricks and anything else he could get his hands on. He almost flung a cupcake with deadly accuracy at a rack of white T-shirts. Luckily Holly, who was also watching in horror, stopped him at the last second. His sister was a whiner, and if she didn't get her way, a screamer. The mother seemed mostly preoccupied with trying to placate her, mainly by pleading and offering all sorts of bribes. Louise's brother-in-law, a tall, blond man who looked extremely posh, seemed too preoccupied to help with his children at all. He was walking around the shop, scrutinising every item of clothing, then squatting down to look at the play equipment. Jo was rather surprised. She wouldn't have thought it was his kind of thing. He didn't pick anything up, so he clearly wasn't interested in shopping for his kids. Then she saw him make his way over to the counter and engage Lee, who was on till duty, in conversation. Jo turned her attention back to the blogger, who had finished taking pictures and had an enormous list of questions for her.

The rest of the day passed in a haze of narrowly averted crises, hurried conversations, friends kissing Jo and congratulating her, and endless, endless smiling. When they finally closed the doors after the last customers had straggled out at six o'clock, Jo sank down and sat on one of the big ladybird beanbags on the floor. She was vaguely conscious from the ache in her back and legs that it was the first time she had sat down all day. Holly was tidying up and straightening garments on their hangers – surely, Jo thought, for the thousandth time that day, while Mel was cashing up the till. Lee had already left to fetch the kids from his parents' place and would return with two bathed and fed children, ready for bed in their pyjamas, and one of his mum's homemade lasagnes. Jo was, both literally and figuratively, finished. Holly eventually stopped tidying, went into the back room and returned with a chilled bottle of Cava and three glasses. Jo managed a faint cheer from her beanbag, and Mel nodded enthusiastic assent. Jo knew she should lead the others in some kind of post-mortem of the day, but she just didn't have the energy. There had been hitches, there were things she knew she wanted to change, but overall, the day had been a huge, storming success. She was going to have a glass of bubbly, limp home with her family and sleep for twelve hours solid. Everything else could wait until tomorrow.

After the launch, the first few weeks were rather an anti-climax. The bloggers and the local press were all very generous in their assessment of Jungletown, but it brought a trickle rather than a flood of customers. Jo wasn't worried; she knew the real success of the business would lie in word-of-mouth and building a loyal customer base and it would take a little longer, and sure enough, as they began their second month of trading, there was a noticeable rise in the number of customers, and more and more of them mentioned that they had come because they had heard about the shop from a friend. They weren't bringing in millions of pounds, but they were covering costs and salaries and paying back the bank, and as far as Jo was concerned, that was all she hoped for at this early stage.

She and Mel had worked out a rota that suited them both, and most of the time they managed to balance working in the shop with their respective family commitments. For Jo though, the guilt was always there. She flew away from the shop every day as soon as her shift finished, taking paper-work to do when the kids were in bed. Even though Imi seemed perfectly happy at the childminder's and Zach loved nursery, she felt awful that she wasn't with them. On the days when the rota didn't allow her to pick them up at the normal time, and they had to stay later or go to a friend's, she was consumed with guilt and distracted at work. When she was with them, she found herself relaxing the rules, giving them more treats and letting them get away with naughtiness. As a result, Zach particularly pushed his luck and started answering back. Then she'd end up yelling at him, and she would be consumed with guilt all over again. One day, she was doing a lightning-fast handover to Mel, flinging things into her handbag as she prepared to rush out of the door. Mel followed her around, making notes, handing keys, phone and umbrella to her and generally looking like the picture of calm and competence. Jo stopped for a moment. 'How do you do it?'

'Do what?'

'Balance it all. Serena, work . . . and as a single parent? Didn't you go out of your mind when she was small?'

'Of course,' said Mel. 'All the time. I felt bad I wasn't working harder, and awful I wasn't with her more. I felt like I wasn't doing anything well.'

'That's exactly how I feel! So what did you do?'

'What does anyone do? I fudged it, compromised and eventually learned to live with the guilt. Can't change it, have to live with it.'

Holly filled in if it was necessary, but she mainly concerned herself with keeping the shop well stocked with fresh and exciting clothes. In the lead-up to Christmas they did a roaring trade. Holly had not only sourced loads of cute novelty Christmas jumpers, hats and baby clothes, she'd also bought a selection of soft toy dinosaurs and jungle animals, and set up a temporary gift section. Harassed mums who had to take their kids shopping were thrilled to come to Jungletown and be able to browse in relative peace while their kids worked off some festive-season madness on the play equipment.

By the day before Christmas Eve, they had had a better month than November, even though they had only traded for twenty-three days. It was a good thing, as they received notice from the council that there would be major roadworks on the pavement in front of the shop between Christmas and New Year. It would be a real struggle to get customers in and out.

'The last thing we need is someone falling or hurting themselves just outside the shop,' said Jo.

'And we could do without everyone tracking in mud and cement dust,' Mel pointed out.

'Let's close for a few days,' said Jo. 'We were going to struggle with staffing anyway, as you'll be away, Mel. We'll reopen on the second of January with a kick-ass January sale.'

The three of them went to the pub over the road for a Christmas drink after they closed. It was a frosty winter's evening, and through the pub window Jo could see her bright and sparkly shop. It gave her a warm glow inside, as did the mulled wine. What had been a dream in the summer was now a steadily growing reality. Contrary to her fears and worries, she seemed to be balancing the needs of her family with the business, and she had made two great new friends in Mel and Holly. The new year could only bring good things. She was sure of it.

'Cheers, girls!' she said happily, raising her glass.

'So, Holly, Mel's off to Devon, I'm going to have a craaaazy time in Hertfordshire . . . what does Christmas hold for you?'

'Oh, we're all off to Oxfordshire, to my brother's place. It should be a fairly toxic family Christmas, I imagine. I'll be the embarrassingly single, quirky sister, to be passed around at cocktail parties and forcibly introduced to awful, unsuitable men fresh from their first divorce.'

'So sorry,' said Mel. 'It does happen. If you resist for long enough, they give up after a while. My friends accept that I'm a dried-up old spinster now, and they leave me alone.'

'You not spending Christmas with family?' Holly asked her.

'No. I don't see my family,' said Mel, and her suddenly prickly tone made Holly realise this wasn't a line of discussion to pursue. But then Mel brightened and started talking about her plans. 'We have a long-standing tradition where we take a house in Devon with a crowd of friends. We take long walks on the beach, lie around and play board games, and we have a non-traditional traditional Christmas dinner: no turkey, because we all hate it, but a lovely roast lamb and plenty of wine.'

'And no passive-aggressive family crap?' Holly laughed. 'Sounds like heaven.'

'It is pretty cool,' said Mel, her smile a little tight. 'Serena's always loved it, but she seems less keen this year. She says she'd rather we stayed in London. I've convinced her to go, but every year, she's going to object more.' She didn't add that the only reason Serena had stopped yelling and sulking about the trip was because she had heard her dad was going to be there. Bruce came along about one year in every three. The old university friends Mel was going with were friends of his too, and it was a good way for him to see Serena over the festive season. Mel didn't think Serena was keen to see her dad because she was such a devoted daughter. Mel knew Bruce had a new job and was making more money, and she had a suspicion he had promised Serena some kind of special Christmas present. Well, whatever it took.

She had never told Serena she had seen her the day she skipped school, hoping it had been the first time, but she had reinstituted the home-from-school calls with new firmness, and she made sure she walked with Serena all the way to school each morning. She didn't make a big deal of it – just said she needed the exercise and that now she needed to be at work a little later, it was a good way to stretch her legs. Serena grumbled and sulked, but Mel knew she was at least getting her through the school gates every day.

Mel pulled her attention back to Holly and Jo. Jo was describing Christmas at her parents' place in Stevenage. 'I'm looking forward to some lovely free time with Lee and the kids between Christmas and New Year. But Christmas Day . . . oh boy. My parents know we see a lot of Lee's parents because they live closer, and to be honest, since my mum broke her hip, they're not up to babysitting the kids on their own. But they're jealous of how much Lee's folks see the kids. So if we're there for Christmas, they overcompensate horrendously. They buy them way too many presents, and tomorrow they'll want to drag us off to see Santa at every awful shopping centre within a twenty-mile radius. I haven't had the heart to tell them that Zach's decided he's terrified of Santa this year, so it's not going to go well.'

'Oh dear.' Holly giggled. 'Families, I ask you . . .'

But Jo was just getting started. 'A few days of being together twenty-four seven will also give my mum plenty of time to criticise everything I wear, say and do. Oh, and my mother equates food with love, so there'll be snacks and treats and meals at hourly intervals from the minute we arrive, and she'll be mortally offended if we don't eat absolutely everything.'

'Ah,' said Holly. 'Your mum is the opposite of mine. My mum thinks enjoying food is somehow unladylike. We're all supposed to compete to have the smallest portions and leave the most food on our plates, so we can look elegant.'

'Sound like we'll both be in food hell,' said Jo.

'Sod that!' said Mel. 'I love my food and I'm not afraid to say it. Anyone fancy sharing a plate of chips?'

'I fancy the chips,' said Holly. 'Don't fancy sharing.' She gestured to a waiter and ordered three portions of fries.

'Aren't you mum types supposed to be home for supper?' asked Holly, licking ketchup off her fingers. 'I told my mum I was out for dinner, so I'm off the hook. But aren't you expected to produce balanced meals for your families when you get in?'

'Lee will have fed the kids before he comes to pick me up,' said Jo, mopping up a glob of ketchup with her chip. 'We've been living on scratch meals ourselves for the last few weeks, both too tired to cook proper stuff. So this is the substitute for the stale cheese and chutney sandwich that would probably have been my dinner.'

'Serena's staying at her friend Marina's house tonight,' said Mel.

'Marina?' Jo smiled. 'Serena and Marina?'

'Yes, yes, I know,' said Mel, 'when they were little we called them the rhyming twins. Anyway, Serena won't eat anything I cook at the moment anyway. It's all "disgusting", apparently. She keeps trying to tell me she's lactose intolerant, which doesn't seem to stop her eating McDonald's cheeseburgers – just my macaroni cheese or cottage pie with cheese on top. Seems to me she's more home-cooking and vegetable intolerant.'

Jo laughed. 'And there was me thinking the fussy eating ended when they stopped being toddlers.'

'I think for teenagers it's a new way to assert their independence, or to prove how interesting and quirky they are.'

'Yawn,' said Holly drily.

'Yawn indeed.' agreed Mel. 'Another drink, you two?'

Jo glanced at her watch. 'I'd love to, but Lee's coming to pick me up right now.' She got up and kissed the other two warmly. 'Have a fab Christmas, you two, or as fab as it can be. And here's a little something to make things sweeter.' She handed them each an envelope. 'It's just a little bonus, not as much as I would have liked, but something to say thank you, from the bottom of my heart, for making the shop a success.'

And with another hug for each of them she dashed out into the chilly night air to meet Lee, and Christmas had begun.

10

HOLLY NOW

Christmas was just as hideous as Holly had expected. Just after Holly arrived at David and his wife Desiree's house on Christmas Eve, there was a cocktail party. Judith pleaded exhaustion from the journey and went up to her room, avoiding the party altogether. It was a bit rich, as it had only been an hour and a half's drive up the A40 and miraculously they'd seen very little traffic, but Judith got away with it nevertheless. Sadly, Holly had no such excuse. She decided to go all out, so she dressed in a festive, bright red Doradolla dress, tidied her hair, which in the busy rush of the festive season she hadn't had time to have cut, and put on make-up. A pair of killer, sky-high patent leather heels completed the look. If she had to suffer a tedious gathering of David's stuffy academic friends, she might as well look fabulous.

It turned out to be a gross miscalculation. There were no single men at the party, as it turned out, but there were a great many married ones, who were all there with their rather frumpy, M&S-wearing wives. It seemed that in academic circles, dressing-up was considered a little vulgar, and as a result, Holly stood out like a tall and rather exotic flower.

The husbands flocked around, and one by one tried ponderous flirtatious lines on her. One or two found a reason to graze a hand across her bottom, ostensibly by accident, or stand too close and leer down her cleavage. She would have been hot with embarrassment, if she hadn't been frozen by the icy glares of the wives. At exactly 10 p.m., she pleaded a headache and escaped upstairs. She was tempted to wedge a chair under the doorknob of her bedroom, in case any of the most persistent letches followed her upstairs, but she thought that might be a bit melodramatic.

When she woke up in the morning, she thought that perhaps she had overestimated the reaction she'd caused the night before. Maybe she was just flattering herself, she thought, pulling on some clothes to go downstairs. But Desiree's frosty reception told her that she was not. Desiree was a professor of mathematics, a steely-eyed woman with a cap of short grey hair and a very serious manner. Many of the women at the party would have been her contemporaries and her friends. Holly didn't know how to apologise, or even how to bring it into the conversation. 'Sorry I dressed like a dancer from the Moulin Rouge last night,' seemed rather a poor opening gambit. How about: 'I wouldn't touch any of your friends' grotty husbands with a bargepole, so they're quite safe'? No, that wouldn't work either. In the end, Holly made no mention of the night before. She wished Desiree a merry Christmas and asked if she could help herself to some coffee from the cafetière.

There wasn't much conversation that morning. David seemed not to have noticed the drama at the party the night before, but he didn't emerge from behind his laptop, even though it was Christmas morning. His children were teen-agers, a boy of fifteen and a girl of fourteen, both utterly without conversation and completely engrossed in their mobile phones. Judith sat as close as she could to the radiator and sipped a cup of hot water and lemon, without saying anything at all. David's family were staunch atheists, so no one would be attending a Sunday-morning church service, and opening the presents would have to wait until Miranda and her family arrived just before lunch.

Holly tried her best to keep busy, repeatedly offering to help Desiree with the lunch, but Desiree had a system and a schedule, and she was going about the necessary tasks with grim and scientific efficiency. There was no call for a vegetable peeler or assistant turkey baster. After an hour or so of awkward silence, Holly was desperate to escape, even for half an hour. David and Desiree had a fat spaniel called Nietzsche, so she offered to take him out for a run. At the sound of his name, Nietzsche opened one baleful eye from his spot at Judith's feet by the radiator and regarded Holly blankly. He didn't even bother to open the other eye. He looked as if he wouldn't run if you set Godzilla on him. He was her only hope of escape though, so Holly dashed upstairs to grab a coat and gloves, pulled on her boots and found Nietzsche's leash. Yanking on a woolly hat, she whistled with an energetic desperation, and, thank God, Nietzsche lumbered to his feet and waddled into the hallway. 'Back soon!' trilled Holly, and set out into the crisp December morning.

David and Desiree's house was on a busyish road, but there was a big field just a few blocks along, and that was

Holly's destination. She thought that on Christmas morning it would be deserted, but it was quite busy with dog walkers and a fair number of parents with kids who were trying out Christmas presents: remote-controlled planes, new bicycles and so on. It felt considerably more festive than the house she had just left. It was a mild day, and there was a brilliantly blue sky overhead. Nietzsche didn't seem to want to gambol about like the other dogs, but he was quite content to amble next to Holly, sniffing at the ground and any trees or poles they passed. 'Reading the news,' David called it. Holly was just happy to be out of the oppressive atmosphere and, if she was honest, away from her mum, whose refusal to eat was beginning to annoy her profoundly. It was time to move out. She'd had very little time to spend what she was earning, so she had some money put aside. Maybe in the new year, she'd go looking for a flat close to the shop. With a bit of luck, she could be moved in within a few weeks. It would be nice to be near Miranda and the kids too, she thought. She was very fond of Oscar, and now Martha was more used to her, she was less painfully shy. Yes, new year, new flat, and maybe, just maybe, it was time to think about looking around for a new man? Nothing serious, just a bit of light-hearted fun.

The idea struck her like a blinding flash, or, at least, that must have been what it was, because even though there wasn't a cloud in the sky, she saw an intense burst of light, and the next thing she knew, she was lying on her back on the grass, gazing up into the blue. It took her a good ten seconds to work out what had happened. The first clue was that Nietzsche was licking her face and his breath smelt horrible. The second was that her head hurt. A lot. And the third was that she could feel something wet trickling down one side of her face into her hair. She had clearly been struck in the head by an unidentified flying object.

The fourth clue came when she heard a man's voice close by. He was saying something, but either she was concussed, or it didn't make sense at all. 'Feathers,' he was saying, agitatedly. 'Feathers and crumpets and balderdash.'

Concussion. That must be it. She stared into the sky some more. It was a very pure blue. She could lie there, looking at it, forever, if it weren't for the fact that the ground was cold and very definitely wet, Nietzsche's halitosis was overpowering and she was now sure that the wet stuff running into her hair was blood. She raised a shaky hand to touch her head. Ouch. Yes. There at her temple, that was where the cut was.

'Don't touch it,' said the male voice, calmer now and more in control. 'You'll only make it bleed more.'

Holly turned her head slightly to see who was speaking. It appeared to be a boy of about seven. That was who was kneeling closest to her. He had a shock of pitch-black hair and very blue eyes and, it seemed, a deep, manly voice.

'What happened?' she said, deeply confused.

'We hit you in the head with our boomerang,' said the little boy, in a little-boy voice.

'Can you sit up?' said the manly voice, and Holly realised that it hadn't been the little boy who was talking to her in that deep voice, but someone else. She struggled into a sitting position to have a look at who it was. Well, that was a big mistake, as the act of sitting up made her head feel like it was splitting open and brought on a wave of nausea so intense she retched audibly.

'I'm sorry, you must feel terrible. Look, is there anyone I can call? Can I ring your husband? Do you have any kids here with you?'

'No husband,' said Holly. 'No kids. Just a ditzy mother and a houseful of siblings who hate me.' And she started to cry. She was vaguely aware that that might not be the information the speaker was looking for, but that was what came out. This was turning into the worst Christmas ever.

'Okay,' said the man, rather hesitantly. 'Well, I can see you need stitches, so I'm going to put you and your dog in my car and run you down to A&E.'

'You can see I need stitches?' said Holly sarcastically. 'What are you – a doctor?'

'Well, yes, I am actually. I'd stitch you up myself, right now, but I'm not in the mood for a malpractice claim and a massive legal bill.'

Holly raised her head painfully and looked at the speaker for the first time. He was a grown-up version of the small boy who was still kneeling beside her. The bigger edition also had a shock of black hair and blue eyes, but he looked about thirty-five years old.

'Well, thank you, Dr Sarcastic,' she said. 'I'll quite happily do without your field-hospital ministrations, if you don't mind. I'll just go home, and take it from there. It's not far from here at all.'

She tried to stand up, but her knees just didn't seem to want to support her, and she lurched alarmingly off the vertical. She peered back across the field; the short walk to the gate and then down the road to David's house suddenly seemed impossibly long. The man stood too, and gently took hold of her elbow.

'Look, I really can't let you go in this state. At least let me walk you home, and then take you to hospital. Please. I feel so awful. I'm supposed to heal people, not brain them with boomerangs.'

He had a fair point, and besides, Holly might have been able to get herself home, but not herself and Nietzsche, who had found a new lease of life from all the excitement and was bounding around her in circles, tangling his leash around her unsteady legs.

She handed the leash to the boy and let the man take her arm. Together they crossed the muddy field and made slow progress back to David's house. Miranda's car was in the driveway, and Holly's heart sank. She didn't fancy making an entrance in front of the whole family, covered in blood and mud and trailing a pair of complete strangers. She stood on the driveway for a second, then, leaving the man and his son behind, limped around to the kitchen door. She tapped on it softly and Desiree opened it impatiently, obviously annoyed at the intrusion on Christmas morning. When she saw Holly's blood-covered face, she looked alarmed, but at least she didn't scream.

'Look, it's nothing to worry about,' Holly said as cheerily as she could manage. 'I had a little accident in the park. Here's Nietzsche.' She handed over the leash, and Nietzsche trotted inside, padding mud all over Desiree's spotless kitchen floor. 'Some nice people I met in the park are going to whizz me to A&E. I'll be back as soon as . . . well, start lunch without me.'

Before Desiree had time to say anything, she turned and walked back to the man and his son, who were waiting on the driveway. 'Is your car nearby?' she asked. 'Because I don't think I can walk much further.'

'As it happens, it's right there,' said the man, pointing back down the road. He indicated a muddy estate car that was at least ten years old. Well, he clearly wasn't one of those Harley Street plastic surgeons, thought Holly.

'If it's okay with you,' said the man, as he helped her into the passenger seat, 'I'm going to drop Finlay off with his mum. We were only supposed to be gone for half an hour, and she'll be worried where he is.'

'Of course,' said Holly. She was finally sitting down somewhere dry and warm. He could go anywhere he liked as far as she was concerned. She rested her aching head gingerly on the headrest and closed her eyes. They drove for just a few minutes, and then stopped outside a tidy but modest house. The man and the boy hopped out of the car and went to the door. When the door opened the boy went inside, and Holly could see the man talking to a woman standing just inside the house. She couldn't get a good look at her, but she registered a woman of about her height with long, straight dark hair. He was only gone for a few minutes, and then he ran back and jumped into the car. 'Right. Let's go,' he said.

'Your wife must be very understanding,' Holly observed, 'you disappearing like this on Christmas Day.'

'Yes, well,' said the man, 'it's not every day I brain

someone with a boomerang. These are exceptional circumstances.'

'This is a first for me too,' said Holly. 'I've been hit with frisbees before. Ninja throwing stars, custard pies, even small children. But never a boomerang. I thought they were supposed to come back to the thrower.'

'I'm revising my opinion of this particular one,' said the man, glancing at the offensive object, which lay on the back seat. 'I don't think it is a boomerang. I think it's just a bloody big stick.'

'Where did you get it?'

'Where does anyone get one? Just like any other twonk who visits Australia, I had to have one. I went to Perth for a conference, and I brought it back as a gift for Finlay.'

'I'm Holly, by the way.'

'Fraser. Fraser John.'

'Fraser John? Are you—'

'Saying my name backwards? Heard that one.'

'I was going to say, are you any relative of Augustus John.'

'You've heard of Augustus John?'

'He's one of my favourite painters.'

'I'm impressed. Well, there is a family connection, but a very distant one involving grandparents being third cousins twice removed or something.'

They pulled up outside the hospital. 'I hope it's not too busy,' said Fraser. 'I also hope you don't get some nervy medical student stitching you up.'

'Thanks, I feel better already,' joked Holly, getting out of the car.

As it happened, they were lucky on both counts. Although

the A&E was thinly staffed, they were too early for the rush of alcohol-related incidents and she was quickly seen by a relatively senior doctor. Fraser shamelessly pulled medical rank and stood over the doctor as she cleaned Holly's head and put a few tiny stitches in the cut.

'It's mostly under your hair, so you should barely be aware of a scar,' said the doctor, pulling off her gloves. 'Now I know you've had a bad bang on the head and you feel pretty rotten. I don't think you're concussed, but it's best if someone keeps an eye on you for the next twenty-four hours.' She looked meaningfully at Fraser.

'Oh, it won't be him,' said Holly cheerfully. 'He has to get back to his wife.'

The doctor was far too professional to say anything, but Holly saw her press her lips together disapprovingly. She suddenly felt awful. Had she made Fraser look like a faithless bastard, in A&E with his battered floozy on Christmas morning? She looked over at him, and saw that he too had his lips pressed tightly together, but it was because he was trying not to laugh out loud. She noticed that he had a very appealing twinkle in his eye when he smiled. He pulled himself together.

'Shall we get you home? We wouldn't want your turkey to be all dried out.'

'Indeed we wouldn't. I like a nice moist turkey.' Holly said, getting up, and for some reason, that set them both off, and they left the A&E chortling together.

As they drove back to David's house, Fraser said, 'So what do you do? For a living, I mean.'

'I work in kids' clothing. I supply the clothes for a new

shop in North London. I design and make some, and source the others. If you're ever in that neck of the woods, do pop by. Finlay would love it. It's like a combination play area and clothes shop, especially for boys.'

'Sounds scary.'

'Well, I think it's pretty cool.' She pulled her wallet from her pocket and extracted a business card, which she put on his rather dusty dashboard. 'Well, if you're ever passing . . .' she said, 'or your wife is, you should check it out. Or she should. I know it's unlikely, but if you ever do visit London . . .' She needed to stop talking. She was beginning to ramble. It must be the blow to the head. It couldn't be that she was attracted to this man – he was someone else's husband, for heaven's sake. She had to get a grip. She closed her mouth firmly and vowed not to speak again for the rest of the journey. There was an odd and awkward pause and she was aware of Fraser glancing sideways at her.

'Where is your shop?' he asked.

Damn. Now she had to speak to answer his question. 'East Finchley. The address is on the card,' she said.

'That's not a million miles from me,' he said. 'I live in Acton.'

'But I thought . . .'

'Finlay lives with his mum. We're separated. I'm only here for Christmas Day.'

Well, that was a very interesting turn of events, thought Holly. But before she could ask any questions, they pulled up outside David's house.

Fraser insisted on taking her inside and speaking to the whole family. He gave them some advice on painkillers and on what symptoms to look out for should Holly become unwell. He apologised to Holly again, and to the family for disrupting their Christmas Day. They all seemed charmed by him, and Judith, who had been sitting quietly by the window, surprised them all by smiling and saying, 'Do stay for a drink, Dr John!'

He turned to look at her, and crossed the room to shake her hand. 'You must be Holly's mum,' he said, smiling gently. 'I see her in you.'

'I am.' Judith's smile was almost girlish.

Fraser took her hand. 'I'm very sorry I can't stay. I wish you well, all of you. Have a good Christmas.' And he was gone.

When Holly went through into the living room, Miranda made a fuss of her and insisted she sit down in a comfortable chair. She dashed off to get Holly a cup of sweet tea. Martha came over, shyly at first, and then, emboldened, peered at the stitched cut on Holly's head. Eventually she clambered on to the arm of the chair and proceeded to give Holly an almost forensically detailed examination. She kept saying, 'Is it sore? Is it very sore?' with a small child's ghoulish fascination.

With Miranda and family in the room, the mood lifted a little and Christmas lunch was a reasonably jolly affair, marred a little for Holly by the fact that she was sitting opposite her mother, whose pathetic demeanour was beginning to get right on her nerves. The food was delicious, but Judith pushed hers around her plate without actually eating any of it. Knowing her, she was probably offended that Desiree had cooked the entire meal without her help or advice. It was such an attention-seeking ploy that Holly wanted to shake her. Once David had polished off a bottle of good claret, he proceeded to regale the company with the story of Holly's femme-fatale appearance at the party the previous evening. At first Holly thought Desiree must have had a good whinge to him, but it turned out the most corpulent and unattractive of David's professor friends had rung up asking for Holly while she was at the hospital, and had made it clear to David what a hit she had been with the men at the party. Paul, Miranda's husband, joined in the teasing, and Holly tried to smile and take it in good part, but her head was aching and all she really wanted to do was crawl into bed. She couldn't drink any alcohol, because of the blow to her head and the painkillers, and as result, the afternoon seemed very long. As soon as the kids had opened their presents after lunch, she made her excuses and went up to her room. Miranda called after her that she would check on her every half an hour, but Holly didn't care. She slipped between the sheets with a sigh of relief and closed her eyes.

As she dozed off, it occurred to her that there would be worse things than crawling into bed with handsome Doctor Fraser John. Just for a cuddle, of course. She hoped very much that he might take her up on her invitation and pop by the shop, or even just ring her. Well, well, well. Maybe she was back in the game. It had turned into a rather interesting Christmas after all.

11

HOLLY NOW

'New year, new energy, new changes!' Holly announced, spreading her arms wide as she came through the door on the first trading day after the Christmas break.

'Aren't changes new by definition? Isn't that tautology?' said Jo, glancing up from the sheet of paper she was looking at.

'Tautology? Is that the study of taut, muscled male bodies?' said Holly, bounding over and kissing Jo on the cheek. 'Happy new year, m'dear.'

'And to you.'

'Speaking of changes . . . new glasses?'

'Not new – *first* glasses. I'm devastated. I've never needed them before. Suddenly, over Christmas, I realised I couldn't read the instructions on a packet of fish fingers, and when I read anything else I had to hold it really far away. Lee made me go and get my eyes tested. And here we are: Grandma Jo.'

'No, not so much grandma, more sexy librarian, I'd have said. What do you think, Mel?' Mel had just come in from the back room, carrying a stack of folded T-shirts.

'About what?'

'Jo's glasses.'

'Glasses? Oh. Are they new? Did you not have them before?' said Mel. She sounded distracted. She looked round for somewhere to put the T-shirts.

'Everything okay, Mel?' asked Jo. 'How was your Christmas?'

'Oh, it was okay,' said Mel, sounding none too convinced. 'Same old, same old. It was lovely, but Serena's dad got it into his head that it was appropriate to give her a laptop for Christmas.'

'A laptop? Wow. She must be thrilled.'

'She was. So thrilled that she hasn't come out from behind it for more than ten minutes since she got it. We had to prise it out of her hands to make her join us for Christmas dinner.'

'I suppose you have all the parental controls things set up on it.'

'Well, yes – our friend Hamish was there and he works in IT, so he set it all up.'

'Should be fine then, shouldn't it?'

'Should it? I mean, I'm a computer moron. I use email a bit, but I'm not on Facebook or Twitter or anything. I wouldn't have a clue what sites she's going to or what she's doing.'

'I don't know a lot,' said Jo, 'but I think if your mate set controls, there'll be a limit to what she can access. Did he give you passwords and stuff?'

'Yes. He asked me for ones I could remember, so I've got all that written down and tucked away in my underwear drawer. I know she'd never go looking in there.'

'What does she say she's doing?' asked Holly.

'Oh, you know, chatting to friends, playing games, watching videos on YouTube . . .'

'I'm sure it'll be fine,' said Holly soothingly. 'Probably useful for homework and stuff. Just give her a little talking-to. Tell her never to share personal information like her phone number or where she lives with anyone she doesn't know.'

'I can tell her,' said Mel dubiously, 'but to be honest, telling Serena things hasn't got me anywhere for a while.' She tried to smile. 'So how were your Christmases? Holly?'

'Well, on Christmas morning I got whacked on the head by a boomerang hurled by a handsome doctor and ended up in A&E.'

'Of course you did. Is that a euphemism for something rude that you young people do that I wouldn't understand?'

'No, I really did. I took my brother's dog for a walk and got brained by a boomerang. Look.' Holly lifted her hair and showed them the scar. She'd had the stitches out the day before, and the scar was a neat, but still livid, red line.

'Good grief,' said Jo. 'Are you all right?'

'Fine. It made Christmas more interesting and slightly less deadly than it might have been. I tell you something though. If I've learned anything this festive season, it's that I have to get out of my mother's house. She's drooping around like a wilting lily and it's driving me completely mad.'

'I don't know how you've stuck it for so long,' Jo observed. 'I know I couldn't go back and live with my parents now. I did it for a while after uni, and it was a nightmare. Once you've lived independently, it's hard to go back.'

'I think I was in such a state when I first arrived back from South Africa, I didn't really think about it. But it's definitely time. I thought I might look for somewhere in this area. Where would you recommend?'

'Well, you want somewhere where it'll be easy to get to and from work, with reasonable access into town, I should think,' Jo said.

'And I guess somewhere not too expensive,' Mel chipped in.

'Exactly,' Holly said. 'I'd like a place of my own, even if it is just a studio. I think I'm getting too old to share.'

'Hang on a sec,' said Jo, dashing into the back room and coming back with the local paper. 'We can have a look in here. Even if there isn't anything you like, you can get an idea of prices and locations, and maybe pick up the names of a few estate agents.'

'Shouldn't we be getting ready to open up?' asked Holly.

'Things are actually pretty much ready,' Jo said. 'I came in yesterday to get things organised. I've set up all the sale rails and repriced everything. All we have to do is unlock the door and hope the hordes descend. Now come on, let's find you a flat.'

They went through every page of the property supplement, and at the end of the exercise, Holly felt really down. Anything in East Finchley, Muswell Hill or its environs was right out of her price range. Places towards Finchley Central weren't cheap either, and if she thought of going further out, to Colindale or Edgware, transport links became more of a problem. Perhaps she would have to consider a flat share after all.

The day was pretty quiet, and they certainly weren't over-whelmed with customers. By mid-afternoon, Jo was beginning to get a bit antsy, so Holly sat down at the computer and designed a simple and bright sales flyer. She called Jo into the office to see the design. 'I'll go to the print shop and get a few hundred run off, and then I'll walk around and pop them through people's doors.'

'Thanks,' said Jo, patting her on the shoulder. 'That's a great idea.'

An hour and a half later, Holly began working her way up and down the residential roads that led off the high street, slipping a leaflet through each door. It was already dark, a crisp and clear January evening. She admired the big old houses as she walked along: the few where the curtains were not closed revealed warm, beautifully deco-rated interiors. As she reached the end of one road, she came upon an entrance to a pretty park. Now this would be a great place to live, she thought. In the next road along, she began working her way up one side of the road when a flash of yellow on the opposite side caught her eye. It was a hand-lettered sign Sellotaped on the downstairs window. 'Top-floor flat to let. One bedroom,' it said, and below, 'Enquire within.'

Holly didn't hesitate. She crossed the road and knocked on the door. The house was old. The outside hadn't been recently renovated like the houses either side of it, but it was clean and well kept. There was a tidy front garden with rose bushes, and the front door was a dark bottle green with an old-fashioned rippled glass panel. At first it seemed as if there was no one home, although she could see lights on inside. But after a longish wait, she saw someone walking slowly towards the door. It creaked open, and Holly saw an elderly man. He seemed very old, maybe eighty or more, and extremely thin. He didn't look frail though, and he had a strong, angular face and eyes that looked at her sharply.

'Er, hello,' she said. 'I saw your sign in the window. Is the flat still available?'

'Who are you looking for?' said the man. 'You and a bloke? You and three kids? A friend and ten other friends?'

'No, just me. Me and . . . well, me. I work around the corner.'

'Doing what?'

'I'm the designer and clothing buyer for Jungletown, the children's clothing shop.'

'And you get paid a proper salary?'

'I do.'

'I'd need to see evidence of that. Boyfriends?'

'None right now, and never more than one at a time.'

She rather liked his blunt, almost rude manner. He clearly wasn't going to let her through the door if he didn't like the answers to his questions.

'And where are you living now?'

'With my mum in Ealing. I lived in South Africa for ten years, and came back to the UK six months ago.'

He peered at her for a long moment. 'All right. You can have a look,' he said grudgingly, and opened the door wider. There was a small hallway area, and then two matching doors, side by side. They were both smooth, golden wood, not painted or varnished, but oiled, with old-fashioned, gleaming brass doorknobs. Holly stepped into the hallway.

The old man took a key from a hook on the wall and unlocked the right-hand door. As he pushed it open, he suddenly turned back to Holly. 'You're not in a band, are you? Or an orchestra? I'm not having a bloody violin screeching above my head at all hours.'

'No. You might sometimes hear a sewing machine, but that's about it.'

He nodded, and stumped off up the stairs. Holly followed him.

The staircase was the same oiled wood as the door, with a satin-smooth banister rail. Although it was dark, the street lighting revealed that there was a jewel-coloured stained-glass window on the landing. They got to the top of the stairs and the old man flicked a light-switch. The flat was simply beautiful. There were two big rooms, simply decorated, with high, pressed steel ceilings and polished wooden floors. The period details had been carefully restored. There was a small kitchen, newly refitted with blond wood cupboards and a granite countertop. The bathroom had floor-to-ceiling tiles in a dove grey and elegant fittings that looked brand new. It didn't look like a rental property at all; it looked like someone had spent time and money to make a beautiful home. Holly stood in the middle of the living room and looked around. She would love to live there, but she knew straight away it would be way out of her price range. The old man watched her, and waited for her to say something.

'It's lovely. Just lovely,' she said. 'What an amazing renovation job.'

'I did it all myself,' said the man, and for the first time, the gruff edge was gone from his voice and there was a hint of pride. 'My wife and I bought this house in 1963, and we lived here all our married lives. She died two years ago. Nearly fifty years we had together.'

'I'm sorry.'

'No, you're not sorry. Of course you're not. You never knew her.'

'I'm sorry for your loss.'

'Yes, well. The kids couldn't get on my back fast enough to sell the place and move to a "retirement community".' He spat the last two words as if they tasted bad. 'But I wasn't having any of that. Still, the house was too damned big, so I thought, what if I make it into two flats? I'll live downstairs, take in a tenant upstairs, make a bit extra to top up the pension, and really piss my kids off.' He cackled at the thought. 'I've been in the building trade all my life, so I just tackled each room like a project. And I think it looks all right.'

'It looks more than all right. It's stunning.' Holly looked around the living room again. It wasn't just that the flat was beautiful; it had a warm heart. He might be a gruff old bugger, but the love he had felt for his wife, and the pride in his craftsmanship, shone through in every detail.

'I can't believe you're not fighting off prospective tenants.'

'You're the first to have made it through the door,' the old man said. 'I've had a few I just didn't like the look of, and at least three that were bloody estate agents.'

'Estate agents?'

'I'm not having some poncey little twat called Farrell with mirror shades and two phones and a BMW earning commission on something I can manage myself.'

At this, Holly burst out laughing. 'The Farrells of the world don't stand a chance against you.'

He smiled. 'That's right. What's he going to earn commission for? I can get a lease form in WH Smith's. If something breaks, I'll fix it. If you don't pay your rent, I'll change the locks.'

And here, Holly thought, came the crunch. 'And the rent would be . . . ?'

'I haven't decided yet.'

'Okay. Do you have a rough idea?'

'Well, I think rent should be based on how much trouble a tenant is going to be. So definitely more for children, pets . . .'

'Musical instruments . . .' Holly chimed in.

'Scratching the floors, stupid questions . . .'

'Sewing machines?'

'Don't mind sewing machines. My wife liked to sew. It's a good noise.'

'So I ask you again . . . the rent would be . . . ?'

He looked at her long and hard. 'What can you afford?'

She looked back at him. She had to be realistic. It wasn't even as if her job was a-hundred-per-cent secure, working for a start-up business never was. She would love to live in this flat: she liked the old man, she adored the flat itself and the location was ideal. She named a figure. It wasn't the maximum she could pay, but it wasn't far off. She knew the flat was worth more, but she wasn't going to be bullied into paying more than she could afford. There was a long pause.

'I wondered if you'd take the piss one way or the other,'

he said, 'but you didn't. I know I could get more, but I like you, and that's a good enough offer, and that's enough for me.'

'So . . .' Holly said, not quite daring to believe it, 'I can have it?'

'We'll have to do all the usual checks, but yes. Can't see why not.'

She wanted to hug him, but she was sure that would be one of the items on his list of things that would make him change his mind about letting to her, so she contented herself with holding out her hand and shaking his energetically. 'I'm Holly, by the way. Holly Evans.'

'Bob.'

'Bob?'

'Yes.'

'Bob the Builder?'

'That's right. And I've never heard that one before. Not. Any more smart jokes like that, young lady, and I'll put your bloody rent up. Now, would you like to come downstairs for a cuppa?'

Holly went back to Bob's a week later with bank statements, employment references and, embarrassingly, a note from her mum saying she was a good tenant. Bob, true to his word, had got a standard lease form. On the last page, he had written in dark, spidery handwriting:

Additional clauses

No rubbish music
No long-haired boyfriends tramping up and down the stairs at all hours

Use teak oil on the doors and wood fittings, none of your supermarket furniture polish
Come for tea once a week

Holly handed over her paperwork, signed the lease, carefully initialled each of the handwritten 'clawses' and handed Bob a cheque for the deposit and first month's rent.

'Right, young lady,' he said, 'I'll check out your references and bank the cheque. But unless you hear from me to the contrary, I'll expect you to move in at the end of the week.'

It was good news, but of course, there was a catch. Holly had nothing to move. She had had no furniture of her own in Damon's lavishly appointed house in South Africa, and she hadn't bought anything since she'd been back in the UK, as she had been at her mum's. She could fit pretty much all her worldly goods into the back of her mum's car. She didn't own a plate or a knife and fork, let alone a bed or any furniture to sit on.

She hoped her mum might let her take the bed from the room she'd been sleeping in, and possibly the armchair. The rest, she'd have to buy. When she mentioned her move to Jo, Jo offered her their old sofa. It was perfectly sound, but the upholstery had taken the brunt of three years of Zach – not a problem for Holly. She bought some lovely plum-coloured fabric and spent one late night making a fitted slipcover for the sofa and new cushion covers. Then she borrowed her mum's car and spent a morning racing around IKEA, list in hand. She came out with a table and chairs and a couple of bookshelves that she would need to assemble, very basic crockery and cutlery and a few saucepans, and some bright throws and pillows. The rest would have to wait. But there it was: she had the basis of a home, the first she could call entirely her own. She would be moving that weekend and she just couldn't wait.

When she got back to her mum's place, she opened the door and called out, 'Mum, could you give me a hand? I've got a stack of stuff to unload from the car.'

'We're in here, dear,' called her mum.

We? Who could be visiting at this time of day? Holly went through to the kitchen, and found her mother sitting at the kitchen table opposite Miranda. The first thing she registered was that Miranda had neither of her children with her. The second was that her sister had clearly been crying.

'What's going on?' Holly asked. 'What's wrong, Randa? Are the kids okay?'

Miranda shook her head. 'The kids are fine. Sit down, Holly.'

Holly felt cold. Something was obviously very wrong. 'Okay, hang on,' she said, irrationally trying to postpone the moment. 'I just need to lock the car. It's got half of IKEA in it.' She walked back to the front door and held up the key remote. As she heard the locks in the car clunk shut, she somehow knew that when she walked back into the kitchen, something in her life was going to change forever.

Miranda had got up and put the kettle on and was bustling around getting cups and milk and sugar. Holly sat down next to her mother, whose small thin hands were resting on a folded piece of paper. They were all quiet for a minute, but Holly couldn't bear it. 'Look, just tell me. What is it? Is it Paul? Or David? Did something happen to David?'

'No, dear,' her mother said softly. 'It's me.'

Holly looked over at her mum and saw her, really saw her, for the first time in months. She had been so wrapped up in her own life, and so irritated by her mother's feeble behaviour, that she hadn't been paying attention. Judith's skin was pale and dull and looked loose and sagging, and she was very, very thin. She'd always been slim, but now that Holly looked at her, she realised she could see the outline of her jawbone under the skin. She was almost skeletal. How could Holly not have noticed?

Judith pushed the piece of paper she had been holding across the table to Holly, who unfolded it. The letterhead said, 'Dr E.K. Madison, Oncologist'. Holly swallowed hard. She skimmed the letter, but to be honest, it didn't make much sense to her. She registered the words 'stage four' and 'cancer', but that was about it. She looked up at Judith, her eyes wide.

'I've been having some tummy problems for a while now.'

'A while?'

'A couple of years. I kept thinking it would get better, but it just didn't. I didn't want to bother the doctor . . .'

Holly frowned. She could imagine how her prudish mother would hate walking into the doctor's and discussing her bowel problems. She would have been mortified. But what had that reticence led to?

Judith continued. 'Well, it has got a lot worse recently. I've been in some pain, and I couldn't seem to keep anything down. Miranda noticed that I'd got thin, and she nagged until I went to get checked out.'

Miranda. Miranda had noticed, not the daughter who

lived with Judith and saw her every day. Holly felt as if she'd been punched in the stomach.

'Well, the doctor examined me and referred me to this specialist.' Judith indicated the letter. 'That was only a few days ago. I thought it would take ages, but my doctor must have thought it was a bit of an emergency. And . . .' she hesitated. Miranda came back to the table carrying three mugs of tea. Judith looked at her, rather helplessly. 'You tell Holly, dear.'

'It's bowel cancer, but it's spread . . . to quite a lot of Mum's organs. They say they can operate, but there isn't a lot they can do.' Miranda burst into tears again and got up from the table to get a tissue.

'So . . .' Holly managed. She wasn't going to cry like Miranda. She could barely breathe or speak, but she was damned if she was going to cry.

'Well, dear, the doctor told me I could have surgery, but it would be very invasive and painful and wouldn't get rid of all of the cancer, and I could have chemotherapy, but the side effects would be dreadful. And with both courses of treatment, my chances are still rather poor.'

'So . . .' Holly said again.

'Well, I've decided just to have medication for the pain, and let nature do the rest,' said Judith calmly.

'So you're just going to GIVE UP?' The words exploded out of Holly before she could stop them. 'You're going to refuse all medical intervention and just sit there and FUCKING DIE?' She was faintly aware that she had just sworn in front of her mother for the first time ever, and that she was screaming at a dying woman, but neither of these things bothered her.

She saw only a red mist of fury. How could Judith be so pathetic?

'You've got grandchildren, for God's sake! Martha's only little and Oscar's just a baby! And what about my children? What about the children I haven't had yet that won't know you? You can't! You just can't!' And then the tears came. Holly put her head down on the table and sobbed like her heart was being torn from her. Judith said nothing. She just gently stroked Holly's hair, like she used to when Holly was little.

A short while later, David arrived. Miranda had rung him and he drove over once he understood the seriousness of the situation. He spent some time trying to talk Judith out of her position on refusing treatment, but for once in her life, she was adamant and refused to be moved. By eight that night, she was shaking with exhaustion and excused herself to go to bed. The three siblings sat around the kitchen table, cups of tea untouched in front of them.

'So what do we do now?' said Miranda helplessly.

'Well, the first thing I'm going to do is talk to that doctor,' said David. 'He hasn't been very clear in that letter about the prognosis. How are we supposed to plan? What are the real chances of success with treatment? Is surgery or chemo a better option? We need some facts.'

'I don't think there are facts,' said Miranda. 'Only odds, and he seems to think the odds are really poor.'

'Well, what about a second opinion? A different specialist?'

'You can try. But Mum seems pretty sure that she's had all the medical opinions she needs. I think she knew even before we went to see the doctor how serious this was.'

'Don't be ridiculous, Miranda,' barked David. 'How could she *know*? She's an old, sick, rather pathetic woman.'

'She's only sixty-two,' said Miranda reasonably. 'Hardly old.'

'Nevertheless,' said David impatiently, 'she's not some kind of soothsayer who can peer into her own body. For God's sake, the woman can't even send an email.'

For some reason, this made Holly snort with laughter, her only contribution to the conversation so far. Her siblings were playing their roles in this drama so well: Miranda was concerned and compassionate, David forceful and practical. But what was her role? She felt numb. Cold, afraid and numb. She had been so focused on her own life, she hadn't even noticed her mother was ill. She had just been irritated by her, like the selfish, self-involved teenager she was. Except that she wasn't a teenager. She was a soon to be thirty-one-year-old woman, who should bloody well have known better. And now, when her mother needed her most, she had her life in the back of a car in the road outside, and she was about to move away.

As if reading her thoughts, David turned to her and said, 'Well, the one good thing is that you're here to keep an eye on her.'

Holly didn't know what to say, but Miranda waded in with, 'Oh no, but Holly is about to move out. Weren't you starting to move today, Holls? That's what Mum said.'

'Well, you can't go,' said David briskly. 'Not the way things are.'

Holly wasn't entirely sure what she was going to do, but David's smug bossiness really got to her.

'I've just shelled out a couple of thousand pounds in rent and a deposit. I've signed a lease and I have a carful of furniture. I can't just not go.'

'All of those things are reversible,' said David. 'I'm sure you can take the stuff you've bought back to the shop. And any reasonable landlord would excuse you from the lease and return the money. If you've signed with an unreasonable one' – his lip curled as if he thought that was highly likely – 'we can use my lawyer to put pressure on them. They'll soon give in. Someone needs to be here, and it makes sense that it should be you.'

'Why, David? Why am I more responsible for her than you are? Why don't you move in here? Or Miranda?'

He looked at her like she was crazy. 'Because I have a home. A proper home, not a room in some squat somewhere. And a job, and a family. And Miranda has a home and a family too. You're the one who's spent the last decade roaming around footloose and fancy free. It's time to take some responsibility.'

Holly said nothing. She just got up from the table and walked out. As she opened the front door, she heard David say, '. . . running away. Like she always does.' She could hear Miranda's placatory murmur, although not what she said. She got into her mum's car, and without thinking drove around the North Circular to East Finchley. When she'd signed the lease, Bob had given her keys, so she opened the door and started to carry stuff up the stairs to the flat. The car had been absolutely rammed to the roof, but once she'd lugged all the boxes up the stairs, they made a sorry, small pile in the middle of the living room. The flat-pack furniture was all still in its boxes, and even when she laid all the kitchen stuff out on one counter, it looked pathetically inadequate. She wandered back into the living room and sat cross-legged on the floor, looking out of the window at the branches of a big tree that was illuminated by the street light. Curtains. Fuck. Curtains. She didn't have any curtains. She was thirty years old, about to become an orphan and she didn't even have curtains. She wished she could go and buy a lot of alcohol and get very drunk, but she didn't have a bottle opener or any ice, and anyway, she couldn't drink because she had to get her mum's car back.

When Bob tapped hesitantly on the door and came in, she was sitting with her head in her hands. She was too tired and sad even to cry. She could see Bob's olive green trouser leg and carpet slipper beside her, but she didn't have the strength to raise her head. She heard the clink of glass against glass, and Bob held a bottle of beer in her line of vision. 'I know you have to drive, but you can have one,' he said.

'Thanks.'

'Had some bad news?'

'Yes.'

'Need a bit of time to think things over?'

'Yeah . . . I—I don't know if I'll be able to take this place after all, Bob . . .'

'Well, that's a pain in the arse. I don't want to have to go down WHSmith's to get a new lease form and fill it in and all.' He paused, and then said diffidently, 'Look. Take a week or so. Sort yourself out. I haven't got around to banking your cheque yet, and I can hang on to it for a bit.'

'You're a nice man, Bob.'

'Now, don't you go spreading that around. I have a reputation to protect, you know.' He clinked his beer bottle against hers, and she heard him shuffle out and close the door behind him.

12

MEL NOW

Things between Mel and Serena seemed, temporarily, to have reached a peaceful place. Since they had returned from Christmas in Devon, Serena had been keeping better hours, hadn't skipped school once, as far as Mel could tell, and was generally more civil, even friendly. Mel hated to admit it, but it seemed Bruce's gift of the laptop had turned things around. A bit of freedom and access to her own computer had made Serena very happy. Not that Mel had had much choice in the matter, as the first time she knew about the computer was when Bruce gave it to Serena on Christmas morning.

And, to be fair, so far so good on the whole computer thing. They had set limits on the hours Serena could access the Internet: a two-hour window each weekday evening and longer at weekends. Her IT-whizz friend Hamish had assured her he had limited the websites Serena could access and he had given Mel the web address for the monitoring website so she could look at Serena's Internet history, but so far, she hadn't done this. Firstly, because while things were this good, it seemed unnecessary, and secondly because now that she had the laptop, Serena seemed happy to come home and spend time in her room, rather than being out roaming the streets. As her hours on the Internet were limited, she must be using her computer for other things – Mel could often hear music playing, so she reckoned that was a major part of it. She hadn't been at all sure about the whole thing when Bruce first gave Serena the laptop, but he seemed, on balance, to have been right. Having a laptop in her room meant Serena could type assignments for school instead of handwriting them, for one thing. And as her handwriting was as bad as Mel's, that could only be a positive.

One Thursday morning, Mel was at home. She wasn't due at work till midday, so she was using the morning to give the flat a quick once-over. She put through a few loads of laundry, mopped the kitchen floor, cleaned the bathroom and set about giving the flat a thorough hoover before she left for work. Serena was off to stay with her dad that weekend, a rare occurrence, and Mel would be working long hours at the shop while she was away, so she wanted to get all the housework out of the way.

She wasn't planning to clean Serena's room. She hadn't done that since Serena had turned thirteen and started yelling at her every time she came through the door. She nagged periodically and got Serena to pick up all her dirty clothes and put them in the laundry basket in the bathroom, or kept on at her until she brought dirty plates and cups out to be washed, but by and large, she left her to it. If it wasn't actively unhygienic, it seemed best to leave her to have her own space. But today, Serena was out, and her door was slightly ajar. Mel could see the fluff and dirt on the carpet on the other side of the doorway. She had the hoover out. She might as well run it over Serena's carpet. It wasn't as if she was going to do a major clean.

She pushed the door open and went in. The room wasn't terribly untidy: there was a pile of clothes on the end of the bed (which wasn't made), but at least there were no dirty dishes or food containers, and the floor was relatively clear. The waste-paper basket was full, but she could empty that – she had a big black bin liner with her to empty all the bins in the flat. She pulled the waste-paper basket out from under Serena's desk and tipped it into the bag. The bin was very full and a few bits spilled out on to the carpet. She bent to pick them up. There were a few soiled cotton buds, a tissue and a distinctive piece of red and white cardboard. Mel was streetwise enough to recognise a piece of card torn from a Rizla cigarette paper package. She also knew that a fragment of a Rizla packet meant that (a) you'd had a whole packet of cigarette papers at some point, and (b) when rolling a cigarette, or possibly a joint, you knew enough about what you were doing to use a piece of the package rolled into a cylinder as a makeshift filter. She sat heavily on Serena's desk chair.

So at best, Serena was smoking roll-up cigarettes. Quite possibly, she was smoking marijuana. Mel couldn't stop herself. She took the bin liner and tipped its contents on to the floor. It made an almighty mess, but she sat picking through each piece of rubbish to see what else she could find. There was nothing else terribly incriminating: lots of crumpled pages of half-done schoolwork and an enormous amount of junk-food packaging. There were also a few beer bottle tops, but in the greater scheme of things, she wasn't terribly worried about that. But Rizlas? Rizlas were not good.

Mel finished picking up all the rubbish and set about hoovering the carpet. In order to clean under the desk, she pulled the chair right out, and in doing so, jogged the computer mouse that Serena had attached to her laptop. The computer hummed and lit up. She must have left it on and let it go into sleep mode, rather than switching it off completely. Damn! Well, as long as she didn't touch anything, hopefully it would put itself back to sleep before Serena came home from school. Serena's desktop wallpaper was a picture of some awful grime group that she loved. They were all standing in front of a graffiti-covered wall and making gun shapes with their fingers and pointing at the camera. Yawn, thought Mel. How unoriginal. Unlike her room, Serena kept her computer desktop very tidy. There were a few progam icons neatly lined up along the left-hand edge, but that was all. Mel's own computer desktop was covered in random programs, copies of pictures and documents she'd opened or downloaded. Hamish was always on at her to file or delete things so she didn't lose them or clutter up her hard drive, but she couldn't be bothered. She knew where things were, more or less. It seemed Serena was a lot more disciplined.

Mel should have walked away, but a tiny voice said to her that if there was a Rizla packet at the bottom of Serena's bin, what else was her daughter hiding? She didn't know the first thing about looking for things on a computer, so she clicked on the 'Start' button and looked at the menu that came up. There was an option for 'Recent Items', and she chose that. There were fifteen or so items listed. There were about ten Word files that were clearly school coursework. Then there were three video files. Mel clicked to open one and saw it was a pirate copy of a film. She sat through the title sequence to see what it was, and it was *Hannibal*. She checked the other two video files: *American Psycho* and *28 Days Later*. All 18s, all films she would have prevented Serena from watching had she known. But how did Serena get them? Had someone lent her a DVD that she'd copied on to her computer? That seemed unlikely . . . Mel didn't even know if it was possible. But if not, where had she got them? From illegal file-sharing websites? But how was she accessing them when Hamish had set all the parental controls?

The last two files in the 'Recent Items' list were photos, and Mel had a feeling before she opened them that she would wish she hadn't. She was right. In the first picture, Serena was in a bathroom, not theirs, one at someone else's house. She was standing at right angles to the bathroom mirror, wearing just a bra and pants, and the angle of the picture told Mel she had taken it herself with her mobile phone. Like Mel, she was small and compact. Unlike Mel, she had quite big breasts, and they were spilling out of the bra, a sexy black lace one that Mel had certainly not bought for her. Why would Serena take a picture like that? Why was it on her computer? Did it mean she had posted it somewhere? Or sent it to someone? If so, whom?

But the second picture, which showed Serena lying on her back on her own bed, was even more worrying. Not so much because of what she was wearing – a T-shirt and very short shorts, but what horrified Mel was firstly the look of naked, adult sex on Serena's soft, teenage face, and secondly the camera angle. The picture had been taken from over by the window, looking down on the girl lying on the bed. That meant that Serena couldn't have taken it herself. Someone had been in this room, and had taken an intimate picture of Mel's teenage daughter. The kind of picture you took of a lover.

She felt sick. Sick, angry, powerless and very, very alone. She didn't know how to handle this. Serena was only fifteen, and she clearly had a secret life that was much more adult than Mel had imagined. It seemed to involve both sex and drugs. What was Mel to do? She knew from experience that confronting Serena would end badly. There would be screaming, and then there would be a wall of silence. And if she admitted she had seen the pictures or the contents of Serena's bin, she would be forced to explain that she had been in the room and had used the opportunity to look at Serena's private things. She knew that the betrayal of trust would slam doors closed and that Serena would never forgive her and never tell her anything again. She was walking on eggshells with her as it was. Was the Rizla packet Serena's, or had someone else left it there? Who had taken the picture of her on the bed? Who had seen the picture of her in her underwear? Who had helped her to get around the controls on her computer? It seemed there was one, or more than one, mysterious figure in Serena's life, convincing her to get involved in things she shouldn't. It would help to know who they were, and what exactly she was dealing with, before she started asking Serena questions.

Mel looked at her watch. She was already late for work. She closed the last picture on the computer and put the mouse back exactly where she had found it. She pushed the desk chair back in, grabbed the bin bag and the hoover and left Serena's room.

That evening, when she came back from work, Serena was in the living room, slumped on the sofa, watching an Australian soap opera. Mel looked at the back of her head. This girl, this child, had come from her body. She had thought she knew her better than anyone in the world, that they were partners for life. But it seemed Serena was a stranger. If Serena had secrets, she would have to have secrets too. If she was going to watch over her daughter and protect her, she would have to learn to be sneaky. She called on all her acting experience, took a deep breath and said, 'Hi,' in the most breezy, indifferent voice she could manage. In response, Serena muttered darkly, something Mel didn't quite catch. 'What was that?' she said, because that was what she would say if today was a normal day, a day the same as any other.

'Why did you go in my room?' Serena said. She didn't seem angry, just petulant.

'I was cleaning and your door was open so I thought I'd give it a quick hoover and empty the bin.' And before Serena could say anything else, Mel said, 'I got pizzas for dinner. Hope that's okay.'

She went into the kitchen and started putting things away. She was shaking, but she thought her performance had been convincing. Serena had a day off school the next day, Friday, as there was some sort of staff training. Bruce would be coming over to collect her in the morning to spend a long weekend with him. She would take the laptop with her, that was a certainty. But Mel had already decided to try to meet up with Hamish, who, she hoped, would shed some light on how Serena had bypassed the parental controls. It was a first step, a small one, but it was something, and she had to do something. She had to.

Bruce arrived the next morning. He was half an hour late, which was no big surprise; he was always late. It was just particularly infuriating that morning, because it meant Mel had to leave for work as soon as he arrived. She had been hoping to invite him in for a cup of coffee, so they could have a talk about Serena. But she'd been late for work the day before, and lenient though Jo was, she wouldn't take kindly to Mel opening the shop late. All she had time for was a quick, 'You're late. We need to chat at some point. I have to go.' She kissed him quickly on the cheek, grabbed her bag and ran out of the door. 'Bye, Serena, have fun!' she yelled, as she headed for the stairs. At any other time, she would have gone in and said a proper goodbye, maybe given a few instructions about homework over the weekend, and she would definitely have kissed Serena goodbye. But she just couldn't bring herself to go near her daughter. If she did, she would either weep, or slap her, or hold on to her with all her might and never let her go.

When Jo came in at noon so Mel could take her lunch break, she walked up to the sandwich shop. On the way, she rang Hamish, the IT expert. Hamish was a big, shy man, never married, who had been part of Mel's circle for as long as she could remember. He liked to sit in the corner at social events, sipping a beer and listening to the conversation. He was a man of few words, but when he did offer comment it was often dry, witty or surprisingly insightful. He and Mel had never really socialised one on one, tending to see each other as part of a large group. But tonight, that would hopefully change. Hamish answered his phone after a few rings, sounding a little out of breath and slightly surprised. 'Melster!' he said warmly. 'Don't often see your name coming up on my phone. What can I do for you?'

'Mr Hamish,' Mel said, 'I wondered what you were up to this evening.'

'Oh, you know, the usual: threesome with Beyoncé and Angelina, a little light skydiving and a lobster barbecue on the beach.'

'So you're free?'

'As a bird. What do you have in mind?'

'I thought I'd win you over with my awe-inspiring spaghetti bolognaise and a bottle of Tesco's finest Vino de Special Offero, and then pick your brain on what my wayward daughter's been up to on her laptop.'

'Throw in a Viennetta and I'm all yours,' said Hamish.

He arrived just before eight. He looked very large in Mel's small flat, a shambling, tall man who had worn the same Buddy Holly-style spectacles for as long as Mel had known him. He invariably wore rather baggy trousers and jumpers in shades of olive green and brown, and his shaggy hair looked as if he cut it himself.

Mel wasn't much of a cook, but she knew how to make a big bowl of pasta, and she could grate Parmesan with the best of them. She made a small salad, but didn't go to town on it, guessing rightly that Hamish wasn't much of a lettuce man. They chatted easily over the meal. Hamish had been working as the IT manager for a charity for the last seven years so he didn't have much to report about work that was new, but he had recently bought himself a cottage down in Devon, near the area where they all gathered for Christmas. He'd got it for a song because it was practically a ruin, and he'd been going down there most weekends to work on it.

'I'm lucky to have caught you in town then,' said Mel.

'It is a bit unusual for me to be here, but they're putting in new windows this week and the house is basically a few walls surrounding some large gaping holes. Not really where you want to spend a January night.'

'Not ideal. So what's the plan, ultimately? A holiday home? Let it out and earn an income?'

'Well, the plan, if I can make it work, is to move down there permanently.'

'Wow. And what about work?'

'Chuck it in.'

'And do what?'

Hamish blushed. He actually blushed. 'Well . . . write.'

'Write? I didn't know you wrote.'

'I don't tell people, because they mainly take the piss, but I write fantasy.'

'Fantasy?'

'You know, like science fiction, but with goblins and elves and stuff. I've been doing it for years.'

'And are you . . . ?'

'Published? Well, yes. I've had a series of books published by a specialist fantasy publisher.'

'Since when?'

'The first one was about ten years ago.'

'Ten years? And you've never told us?'

'You never asked. I tend not to talk about it. It's one of those things, like trainspotting, that if people know, they either think you're a hopeless anorak, or they ask lots of stupid questions.'

'Like I'm doing now?'

'Well, so far your questions haven't been too stupid.'

'So, here's a stupid question: do you make a living doing it?'

'Well, not really. I've been putting the money I've earned away since I started, and that was how I put the deposit on the place in Devon. But then last year my agent called me—'

'You have an agent! Oh my God, you're famous and you have a secret life, don't you?'

'And there's our first stupid question. No, I'm not famous. I'm mildly well known in one tiny circle of nerds. Anyway, my agent called, and told me they'd sold the series in America. So now I'll be pulling in the medium-sized bucks. Not an enormous amount, but enough to give up my job, which bores me to tears, and go and sit in my cottage in Devon and write.'

Mel sat back and took a sip of her wine. 'Well, I never, Hamish. You're a dark horse, you are. I had no idea.'

'Well, now you do, so can we drop it? No Gandalf jokes, okay? No Hobbit quips? And please, please don't ask me if I earn the same as that J.K. Rowling.'

'I wouldn't dream of it.'

'Now, talk to me about our Serena,' said Hamish, briskly changing the subject. 'What's going on there?'

'Well, remember the laptop Bruce gave her?'

'Of course. I set all the permissions on it and got it going for her.'

'Well, I have a feeling she's managed to bypass them.'

'Is it here?'

'No. She's gone to Bruce's for the weekend and taken it with her.'

'Well, the first step is to have a look at the monitoring site. That way we can look at her web habits and see where we go from there.'

Mel stood up and pointed to her ancient PC in the corner, but Hamish actually snorted, reached into his bag and pulled out a sleek compact laptop. Within seconds he had booted it up and connected to Mel's Wi-Fi.

He went to the site and Mel told him her log-in details. He sat quietly staring at the screen for a minute or so.

'According to this, the last time she logged on to the Internet was about four weeks ago.'

'But she's been on loads since then. Of course she has.'

'I'm sure she has. She's somehow found a way to switch off the parental controls entirely.'

'How?'

'Well, it's not that difficult. If she knew where to search, there'd be cheats and instructions on all sorts of sites. Or she could have got someone to do it for her.'

'She must have known she'd be found out.'

'She probably has a good idea about how computer phobic you are . . .'

'I'm not computer-phobic!'

'Okay, maybe not phobic, but you're not exactly Ms Techno-Literate though, are you?'

'Well, maybe not.'

'So she probably gambled on the fact that once you'd got me to set up the safeguards, you either wouldn't know how to check, or you wouldn't bother. At least for a while.'

'Or maybe,' Mel said, her voice cracking a little, 'she didn't care.'

'What do you mean?'

'I think she just doesn't care what I think any more. Somehow, and I'm not sure how, I've become the enemy. We used to be so close, and now all her energy seems to be devoted to lying to me and trying to do stuff against my wishes. This is all going to end badly, whatever I say. I mean, I'm playing the whole scenario out in my head. I'll ask her why she bypassed the safe-surfing controls, and she'll yell at me and say all I do is restrict her freedom and ruin her life. Then I'll yell back, and I'll have to play the stern-mum card and take the laptop away, and then she'll hate me even more, speak to me even less and feel she's even more justified in lying to me and sneaking around behind my back.'

'Oh dear,' said Hamish, and he looked very uncomfortable. This was clearly too much for him to handle. Whether he was uneasy with Mel's frankness, or with the insight into ugly mother–daughter stuff, or whether he thought Mel was just plain wrong, she had clearly dragged him way, way outside his comfort zone.

'I'm sorry, Hamish. I'm just venting. This is so hard though. There's so much advice to tell you how to raise a baby, but dealing with a teenager, well, these are uncharted waters. But I know they're my waters, and I'm sorry to have pulled you in, if you know what I mean.'

'It's okay,' said Hamish, rallying. He was nothing if not brave and polite. 'I'm sure you'll work it out. Listen, I must go. Last trains and all that. Thanks for dinner.' He gave her an awkward kiss on the cheek and was gone.

There were two alternatives, Mel thought. She could curl up in a ball on the floor and sob, then finish the bottle-and-a-half of wine left from dinner, then throw up and sob some more. Or she could wash the dishes. She went for option two. She had to be at work at eight the next morning and the tear-stained, red-wine-hangover look wouldn't go down at Jungletown.

Once she started, she couldn't stop. The cooker got a thorough clean, the floor was mopped and she was busy scrubbing the countertop viciously when the phone rang. She leapt to get it. It was just after midnight, and a call that late could only be bad news, but then she saw on the caller display that it was Hamish. She hesitated for a second and then answered it. Maybe he'd left something behind and would need her to send it to him. He started in without preamble.

'It seems to me that this is Coventry.'

'What?'

'You. Serena. This is a Coventry situation. Sort of.'

'Coventry? In the Midlands? What? Why?'

'You must know the story of Churchill in the war,' Hamish said.

Mel was baffled. She had no idea what he was talking about. 'Refresh my memory,' she said encouragingly.

'The Allies had captured a German Enigma machine.'

'Enigma machine? Sounds like some kind of science fiction—'

'It was a highly complex machine to send and receive messages in code,' said Hamish impatiently. 'Anyway, the Allies cracked the code—'

'I don't see what this has to do with Serena's laptop—'

'Let me finish! Anyway, because they were receiving and decoding the German messages, they knew that the Germans were planning to bomb Coventry. But if they told the people of Coventry and evacuated the town, then the Germans would know their coded communications were being read. So Churchill had to let them bomb Coventry, and loads of people died!' Hamish finished triumphantly. There was a long silence.

'So, who's going to die?' asked Mel tentatively. 'Am I Coventry? Or is Serena? This really doesn't help, Hamish.'

'No!' said Hamish. 'Serena's the Germans!'

'She's a Nazi?'

'You're not getting it. Maybe it isn't the best analogy I've ever come up with. But look at it this way: what if you could keep an eye on her online life without her knowing? Like you said, if she finds out you know she's doing stuff behind your back, then she'll find different ways to hide things from you. Let her bomb Coventry and think she's got away with it. And after that, you'll be watching her.'

'How?'

'Social media.'

'What?'

'Facebook, Twitter . . . you have heard of those, haven't

you? If she's getting involved with the wrong people, she'll be contacting them online. I don't think you'll find anything incriminating by looking at files on her laptop. And if she catches on that you're monitoring her computer access too closely, remember she can just as easily access social-media sites on her phone, if she has a Smartphone.'

'She does,' said Mel. 'I hadn't thought of that. Well, I don't know the first thing about Facebook and Twitter and stuff, but I'll can learn. And Hamish . . . thanks.'

'Don't mention it.' He sounded embarrassed. 'I've known Serena since she was a little speck. I want to do my bit to keep her safe.'

13

HOLLY NOW

She had done nothing; made no decisions, not told anyone
. . . she had been living in limbo for a week. Some of her
things were piled on the floor of the flat in East Finchley,
but most of them remained in the room at her mother's
house in Ealing. She was still sleeping in Ealing, but she
hadn't asked Bob to tear up her cheque, and he must have
banked it by now. So through her own inertia, she was committed to the flat, but she couldn't see how she could move
there.

With Judith's illness out in the open, it was amazing how
quickly the house became a place of sickness. Now Judith
had made her decision not to accept treatment, and people
had found out about her diagnosis, she seemed suddenly
to age. The consultant she had seen prescribed painkillers,
which seemed to give her some relief, but made her sleepy
and vague. There was a fairly constant stream of visitors –
Judith's parish priest, friends from the church – and Holly
had to manage them all. Judith wasn't always up to seeing
people.

Whenever Miranda came to the house, she spent her time

wandering around in a red-eyed daze, touching things and moving them, starting tasks she didn't finish, and then suddenly bursting into tears, upsetting Judith and the children if they were there too. She was very much more a hindrance than a help, Holly thought, as she emptied yet another half-drunk cup of tea down the sink. Holly herself kept things together by staying fiendishly busy. If she wasn't working, she was busy getting Judith's life in order, making sure she had all her paperwork up to date and that all the medical professionals knew what was needed and when.

Holly stayed in the house pretty much all the time. She could do most of her work from there, either over the phone or via the Internet. She still hadn't told Jo what was going on, although she stayed in daily communication with her. She kept their conversations on a very brisk, businesslike level. She didn't have the strength to tell Jo yet. In fact she wasn't ready to tell anyone, because when she did it would become real. In the house, with Judith, with the mounting piles of medical paraphernalia and the sympathetic murmurings from visitors, it was very real, but contained. But if she told her friends and colleagues, then the cancer would take over all aspects of her life and she just wasn't ready for that.

After a full week had gone by, her mobile phone rang, and she saw from the caller ID that it was Bob. Time to face to the world.

'Hello!' he yelled down the phone. She knew enough about him to know that he was a little hard of hearing and that using the telephone probably made him even more bad-tempered, so she decided to keep it brief. 'Hi, Bob,' she said loudly and clearly.

'Ah, so you can see it's me then? Where you been?' he barked.

'Remember the night I was there, when I had some bad news? It's my mum. She has cancer.' Holly was proud that she managed to keep her voice steady. It was the first time she had said it out loud.

'Bad?'

'Very bad.'

'Well, I suppose you want out of your lease then?' yelled Bob.

'No,' said Holly emphatically, surprising herself. She hadn't known exactly how she felt until the words came out of her mouth. 'No. I'm not paying rent here at my mum's, and I do want the flat. I want a place of my own to go.'

'Sure?'

'Sure. I may not be there much for the next little while, so I'm going to have to owe you on those weekly cups of tea, but I'll pay my rent and bills, and I won't make a noise.'

'Fine,' Bob barked. Then he paused, and said in a more normal tone, 'I lost my old girl to cancer. Cancer's a nasty bitch. Give your mum my best.' He didn't say goodbye, but Holly heard the old-fashioned phone receiver clunk down at his end.

She let out a deep sigh. Well, at last that decision was made. She'd have to start telling the other people in her life soon. Judith was managing better now her pain was controlled and she kept telling Holly that it was fine for her to go out. But sooner or later Judith's condition would deteriorate and Holly knew she wouldn't even be able to fulfil her work commitments then. Besides, she was well overdue some time in the shop. Checking stock levels remotely and phoning in orders was no substitute for being on the shop floor, seeing what people liked and what they didn't, and checking that things were displayed to their best advantage. She knew that when she went there she would have to explain about her mum. It was only fair to Jo and Mel to give them as much warning as possible. Speaking to Bob hadn't been as bad as she'd feared, so while she was on a roll, she might as well do it. That said, Bob's abrupt manner and gruff sympathy kind of worked for her. She hadn't cried yet, but she suspected that if Jo or Mel hugged her, or was nice, she might just dissolve into a sobbing mess. Well, there was nothing to be done. She had to go. She dropped Jo a quick email, saying she would be in at ten the next day.

She was up at seven to shower and blow-dry her hair. She felt she needed some armour, so she wore a favourite dress in a deep maroon and put on rather more make-up than she would usually wear for a weekday. She helped Judith to wash and dress, and made sure she had the telephone within reach, as well as a plate of fruit (which was all she seemed to want) and some water. Once she was sure her mum had everything she needed, she left to catch an eight thirty bus. She came through the door of the shop fifteen minutes earlier than she expected to, and Jo and Mel were both sitting at the counter. They heard the door, and when they saw it was her, both rushed over in great excitement. Did they know? How had they heard?

'Aren't you the dark horse!' exclaimed Mel.

'What?'

'That's one hell of a secret to keep!' said Jo.

Holly didn't know whether to burst into tears or run out of the door, but through her confusion, she saw their faces were full of excitement, not sympathy. They were talking about something else altogether, clearly. She played it cool. 'I don't know what you're talking about.'

'A certain very handsome doctor just stopped by, said he was "in the area" and wondered if you might be about.'

'What?'

'I assume he's the one who brained you with the boomerang,' Mel said drily. 'Black hair, blue eyes, irresistible boyish grin?'

'He . . . what? He came here?' Meeting Fraser John seemed like something that had happened to someone else, a very long time ago. She'd forgotten she had given him her card. In fact, she'd forgotten about him completely.

'Yes,' said Jo, smiling. 'He was a bit awkward and gawky, spent some time looking around the racks of clothes, chose something for an older boy . . .'

'Yes, he has a son,' Holly said faintly.

'Then, when he was paying, he ummed and ahhed and then asked if you were here.'

'We told him you'd be in for ten, and he said he might come back. I think he went next door for a coffee or something,' said Mel.

Holly knew she couldn't see him. Not that he didn't seem like a lovely guy, and very interesting, and not that it wasn't very flattering that he'd trekked all the way to East Finchley to see her, but today wasn't the day for it. She had steeled herself to tell Jo and Mel about her mum. She was holding it all together by a thread. Polite chat, or flirtation or whatever might be required if she saw him face to face . . . well, she just wasn't up to that.

'Did you say I would be here at ten?'

'Yes,' said Jo.

'Look, girls,' Holly said hurriedly, 'I . . . I just can't see him. I'll explain why later, but can you put him off? Tell him I rang in sick or something, or I'm very delayed, but please . . . I don't want to see him. okay?'

Jo and Mel looked stunned, but they could tell that she wasn't kidding. She was about to step behind the counter to go into the back office to hide, when they all heard the bell on the door tinkle. One look at Mel's rabbit-in-the-headlights expression told her who had come into the shop.

Holly summoned all her strength, turned and smiled.

His smile was warm and wide, so she knew he hadn't heard her saying she didn't want to see him. He was lovely-looking, although shorter than she remembered – only a little taller than she was. The words were out of her mouth before she could stop herself. 'You looked taller when you were leaning over me.'

Mel and Jo burst out laughing like a pair of embarrassing schoolgirl best friends.

Fraser took it very calmly. 'Yes, I prefer to render women insensible so they're flat on their backs when we first meet.'

'I didn't mean . . .'

'Don't worry.' He grinned. 'I'm not offended. Unless you

used to be really tactful and the blow to the head knocked that right out of you. Am I likely to get sued?'

'No, no,' she said weakly. 'I made a complete recovery. I am as you see me . . .' And here she ran out of words. What did he see? Even though she had dressed with care, she knew she had lost weight and that she was pale and probably haggard under the make-up.

'You look . . . possibly in need of a coffee. Could we go next door?' Fraser asked. Holly turned to Jo, hoping against hope that Jo would say that she needed Holly in the shop. But Jo smiled sweetly and said, 'Off you go, take your time.'

Holly had been at work for the sum total of four and a half minutes, and she found herself being ushered back out again and into the coffee shop next door. She murmured what she wanted and sat at a table by the window while Fraser collected their order. Maybe while his back was turned she could make a run for it. He was a nice guy, good-looking, and she had discovered as they had passed through the doorway together, nice-smelling too. But this was not the time. Not even close. She was only just keeping it together as it was. It was so bloody unfair that the very first time she had met someone she thought she could really like, and it was possible he might like her back, she was in no position to even consider it. For the next few months, her mum had to be her whole world. There was no space for romance. Not only that, but no man would want to stick around the full spectrum of craziness and grief that undoubtedly lay ahead. There was nothing for it. She had to be calm, very cold and very forbidding, and send him on his way thinking she wasn't interested at all. She'd be the ice maiden. Steely. Like

Cruella de Vil but with better hair. Fraser slipped into the seat opposite her and put the tray down.

'So how's your mum doing?' he asked gently. And Holly burst into tears.

She learned that the crackly paper napkins supplied by the coffee shop were useless for absorbing tears and snot, but extremely effective at spreading mascara across her face. She sobbed like a small child and Fraser held her free hand, and then she excused herself and went to the bathroom. She washed all the make-up off her face and splashed her red eyes repeatedly with cold water, but somehow the tears just kept leaking out. She couldn't hide in the bathroom forever, mainly because someone kept knocking on the door, so she grabbed a great wodge of toilet paper and, squaring her shoulders, returned to the table. She sat down opposite Fraser, who was making patterns in the cinnamon on the top of his cappuccino.

'How did you know?' she asked.

'I'm a doctor. I couldn't tell you exactly what's wrong with her, but I do know what a gravely ill person looks like. And you look . . . a lot more strained than you did the day we met, even though no one's tried to decapitate you with a traditional weapon today. So I put two and two together.'

'Bowel cancer. Stage four. She's refused all treatment.'

Fraser nodded. She appreciated the fact that he didn't utter platitudes or offer sugary sympathy. Instead, he asked about the support they had. 'Have you contacted your local hospice?' he said.

'Hospice? It's not that bad. I mean, I know she's sick, but you go into the hospice when you're going to die, don't you?'

'Not at all. They're there to give you whatever support you need with illness. Their first step will probably be to put you in touch with the Macmillan nurses. You're going to want them. They're all about practical help.'

'She's going to die. She *wants* to die. What help could we possibly need?'

'You could do with help with all sorts of things. Her financial affairs might need sorting out. What about palliative care? What about someone to come in and help you look after her? You can't be there twenty-four seven. What about getting a disabled badge for the car to make it easier if you need to take her for a doctor's appointment? And what about comfort and support and counselling for you?'

'Counselling?'

'Caring for a very ill person can wear you down. You're allowed to ask for help.'

'I'm not, you know. I'm the selfish cow who didn't even notice she was ill. I was so wrapped up in my own crap, and so busy being annoyed with her like a sulky teenager, I didn't even notice she was dying. I don't deserve help. I deserve a slap.' And she was off, sobbing again.

It was the furthest thing from an enchanting first date Holly had ever had. They alternated chat about cancer nursing with bouts of Holly weeping hysterically. It wasn't her sexiest look. She compared it to her carefree first meeting with Damon – all glamorous outfits, champagne and rampant sex. Fraser had met her twice – the first time she'd been unconscious and covered in mud and blood, and the second she'd been the heartbroken snot factory. But somehow, he seemed to take it in his stride. She liked his calm, practical demeanour. He was open and honest, kind, but didn't mince his words. He was full of practical advice, but also gentle and understanding when it all got too much for her. All in all, he was a sterling bloke, and she wanted to fancy him rotten, but the timing was awful. She wasn't going to bet on their long-term future, that was for sure. And anyway, who was to say he had had romantic intentions towards her at all? Maybe he'd just come to the shop to check she'd recovered from the boomerang accident, or maybe he genuinely was looking for an outfit for his little boy. Whatever his intentions, she was in no condition, or in any position, to take him up on any romantic overtures, or even an offer of friendship. And she wouldn't be, for a long time. Still, he was lovely, and he was the first person other than her family she'd been able to discuss the whole cancer and Mum thing with. As a doctor, and an outsider, he was perfect.

She looked at her watch regretfully. 'Look, I'm sorry. I have to get back to work. I'm also sorry I was such utterly miserable company.'

'Well, it seems as if we're destined to have high drama every time we meet. Last time you bled, this time you cried. What can I hope for next time?'

'Oh, a custard-pie throwing incident at the very least.' Holly managed a weak smile.

'Is that when you put me in custardy?' He grinned.

'That's terrible. That's the worst joke ever.'

'Really? I've got loads more if you want to hear them. They crack my patients up. Try this one: Knock, knock.'

Holly sighed. 'Who's there?'

'Europe.'

'Europe who?'

'No, you're a poo.'

Holly couldn't help herself and she guffawed at that. 'Your patients love your jokes? Please tell me you're not a proctologist.'

'No, I'm a paediatrician.'

'Well, that makes sense, at least.' Holly glanced at her watch again and grimaced. 'I know I have to go back to work,' she said, 'but would you walk around the block with me, just for ten minutes? I need to compose myself. No point in going back in there looking like a total wreck.'

'You don't look like a wreck, but I'm more than happy to walk,' Fraser said.

As they turned the corner into the road where Holly's flat was, she saw Bob coming the other way, his shopping bag over his arm. She raised a hand in greeting, but he was too busy staring at Fraser with ill-concealed distrust.

'Hey, Bob,' said Holly.

'That's not a bloody boyfriend, is it?' Bob growled.

'No, no, just a friend,' Holly assured him. Bob grunted and walked on by without speaking to Fraser at all.

'Sorry,' said Holly.

'Is that your bodyguard?'

'No, my landlord,' and Holly explained about the flat and how kind and understanding Bob had been. They stopped outside the house. 'I'd invite you in . . .'

'But Bob would never approve. I understand.' Fraser smiled.

'No, no, I was only going to say that I really do have to get back.' Holly smiled weakly. 'Look . . .' She stood awkwardly, not sure what to say. In the end, she held out her hand to him. 'Thanks. I'm sorry you got to see me in a great puddle, and I'm sorry we didn't get to talk about anything but my awful situation, but thank you. Telling you really helped.'

'It's a pleasure,' he said, squeezing her hand briefly. He took out his phone. 'What's your mobile number?'

She rattled it off. He typed it into his phone and then hit dial. Her phone rang in her bag and he cut off the call. 'Now I have your number and you have mine. Please use it, Holly, I mean it.' Then he looked at her . . . really looked, deep into her eyes, and she knew for sure that his intentions were more than friendly. She was pretty sure he wanted to kiss her, but she was glad, in her fragile state, that he didn't. Instead, he walked her back to the shop, gave her a friendly one-armed squeeze around the shoulders and was gone.

Holly came back into the shop just as two mums with two kids each left, carrying Jungletown bags. The shop floor was temporarily empty of customers. Jo was sitting behind the till and Mel was giving everything a quick tidy. They both looked up as she came in. She knew her face was blotchy and devoid of make-up.

'Holls, have you been . . . crying?' asked Jo. 'What did that guy do?'

'It wasn't him. He was great. Look, you two, can we sit down for a minute? I've got something to tell you.'

Having gone through the whole thing with Fraser, it was a lot easier telling the girls. When they were sympathetic, she managed not to cry. She answered all their questions without falling apart.

'Listen, Jo, I haven't been around a lot in the last week

or so, and I can't promise how much I'll be around in the next while. This isn't a predictable situation. I know we're running things on a shoestring as it is, so . . .'

'Let's not talk about work right now,' said Jo soothingly. 'You need to focus on your mum. We'll find a way to work around it.'

'Are you sure? I mean . . . what about placing orders? And making the clothes?'

'Do what you can from home, and we'll see how we go.'

'Thank you so much. You're amazing.'

'No, I'm not. I know what it's like. My grandpa died of cancer and my grandma spent years looking after him and the house and their business. I know how hard it can be.'

'My dad died of cancer too,' said Mel quietly. 'It puts a hell of a strain on the family.'

'Wow,' said Holly. 'I didn't realise . . .'

'Pretty much everyone's going to encounter it at some point in their lives,' said Jo. 'So let us help you, in any way we can, okay? Now, do you need to get back?'

'I'm okay for a bit. She was doing pretty well this morning, and Miranda's going to pop in later.' Holly stood up abruptly. 'Now, let's look at stock levels. What's selling? What's not? And what do we need to get in?'

The afternoon's work left Holly feeling energised and capable, and she carried that feeling all the way back to Ealing with her on the bus. She burst through the door, calling a cheerful hello, and the intense quiet and indeterminate medical smell hit her like a wall. She stood in the hallway for a second, trying to find the courage that she'd built up through the day. 'Mum?' she called out.

'In here, dear,' said Judith's voice faintly. She was in the kitchen. Holly was surprised. She'd have thought Judith would be settled upstairs in her bed by now.

She went through and found Judith sitting at the kitchen table.

'Where's Miranda?'

'She had to get the children home for bath- and bedtime. She made a lovely stew though. Do have some.' Judith indicated a saucepan on the hob.

'Have you had any? Can I serve some for you?'

'I had a little. I'm not very hungry, dear.'

There was a plate beside the sink, with a tiny portion on it, which as far as Holly could see had not been touched.

'Oh, Mum, you haven't eaten anything.'

'I just can't face it, Holly dear. I'm fine, really.'

Holly found she was ravenous. She served up a plateful of the stew, which was fragrant with thyme and full of vegetables and big chunks of tender beef. Miranda had left a French stick, and she broke a piece off to mop up the gravy. She sat down opposite Judith and began to wolf down her food.

'It's such a nice stew,' Judith observed. 'It's good to see someone enjoy it.'

Holly wondered if her mum was having a go at her un-ladylike eating, but when she looked up, Judith was smiling with genuine pleasure.

'How was it at work?'

'Good. I got a lot done, and Jo says she's happy for me to work mainly from home . . . for the moment.'

'That's very kind of her. Is that possible?'

'Mostly. It should be okay.'

'Well, if you do need to go in, of course you must. I'll be fine, really.'

Holly nodded, but didn't respond. Judith had got significantly weaker over the past few weeks, and there was no reason to think that the deterioration would slow down or stop. Very soon, she wouldn't be fine at all.

'So, how was your day, Mum?' said Holly, mopping up the last of the stew gravy and licking her fingers.

'Oh, lovely, dear. Miranda made such a fuss of me, and the children are angels, but . . . well . . .'

'Were they noisy? Did they wear you out?'

'No, no, not at all. Miranda does talk rather a lot though, doesn't she?'

Holly smiled. 'I think she does sometimes, especially when she's upset or worried.'

'Sometimes it's nice to have a bit of quiet,' said Judith. 'So when they left, I thought I'd just sit down here and do my nails, but . . .' She faltered. She held up one of her slim hands, and Holly could see that it was shaking. 'Silly really,' said Judith.

'Would you like me to do your nails, Mum?'

'Would you, dear? I got Miranda to bring my manicure set down, but I forgot to ask her to bring the nail polish. I can probably manage the trimming and filing, but I just don't think I can paint them.'

'Let me do the whole thing,' said Holly, jumping up. She put her plate in the sink and washed her hands. 'I love giving manicures.'

She got a big bowl from the cupboard and filled it with

warm water. She put it on the table and instructed Judith to soak her hands in it. She ran upstairs and collected soap, lotion, nail-polish remover and various other beauty supplies from her room. She went into Judith's room, where her bottles of polish were lined up on a little shelf on the dressing table. There were seven or eight, and they were all almost identical shades of pearly pink. Holly smiled. She had never seen her mum wear any other colour. She chose one at random, then nipped back to her own room and grabbed a few bottles of polish from there too.

Back downstairs, she gently washed and then dried Judith's soft hands and then cleaned off the old nail polish. As she massaged cuticle oil into her mum's hands, she was struck by how beautiful they still were. Judith had fine bones, and she had always taken good care of her skin. Her nails were naturally well shaped, if now a little long. Her ill health meant that the skin was dry and her cuticles were a little ragged, but Holly could fix that. She worked in silence, gently massaging and stroking.

Judith sighed. 'Oh that's lovely. You could have been a beautician, dear.'

Holly smiled. She leaned over her mum's hands and began tidying her cuticles. Then she carefully filed each nail into a neat oval.

'Right. Now to paint,' she said, and she lined up the bottles of nail polish. 'I bought one of your pink polishes down, but I thought you might fancy a change.' From her own collection she had brought a pillar-box red, a sparkly lilac and an elegant opaque taupe.

'Oh, I don't know, dear, probably the pink,' said Judith.

'Come on, Mum, try something different! It won't kill you.'

Was there a way to grab words out of the air and stuff them back into your mouth and unsay them? Holly would have given anything to be able to do it. 'God, Mum! I'm so sorry.'

'About what, dear?' Judith looked up, her clear blue eyes innocently enquiring. And then what Holly had said dawned on her, and astonishingly, she laughed. For Judith, it was quite a big laugh, more than her usual polite titter, though not quite a belly laugh.

'You know, you're quite right. It won't kill me. Now, let's see . . . I'm not quite ready for the red, I don't think. And the lilac is a bit . . . well, Martha might like it, but it's not really me. But what about this one? What would you call this? Beige? Fawn? Mink?'

'Mink, maybe,' said Holly quietly. 'Or maybe taupe?'

'Taupe indeed. Let's have that one.'

The silence which before had seemed companionable, now seemed a bit awkward. Holly cast about for something to talk about.

'Oh my goodness, Mum, guess what? Remember the doctor who bashed me on the head with the boomerang on Christmas Day?'

'How could I forget?'

'He came into the shop today.'

'Really? By accident?'

'No, he knew I worked there. I gave him my card.'

'So he came to see you?'

'Yes,' said Holly. 'Yes, I think he did.'

'And is he . . . ?'

'Single? Yes.'

'Well then,' said Judith. 'That's very nice, dear.'

'Nothing's going to happen,' Holly said defensively. 'It's really not the right time. I have enough to deal with right now, and it's too soon after Damon, and . . .' She stopped talking, and instead concentrated on painting perfect strokes of the polish on to Judith's nails.

'Well, you must do what you think is best, dear,' said Judith. 'Only . . .'

'Only what?' said Holly, expecting a lecture about how nice doctors don't come along every day and how she wasn't getting any younger.

But instead Judith just said, 'The heart does what it does. You can't always decide who you fall in love with, or when.'

And before Holly could ask her what she meant, Judith said brightly, 'My, that colour is very smart, isn't it? I shall look like that Kirstie Allsopp off the television.'

14

JO AND LEE NOW

Jo

He was so familiar, Jo thought. The man was browsing through the racks of clothing, picking up items and looking at the labels. She had seen him before, but she couldn't put her finger on where or when. He was a most unlikely visitor to the shop: he was dressed in an expensive suit and shoes, impeccably groomed and without a small child. She assumed he was a wealthy local, passing en route to the station. Maybe she had just seen him in the coffee shop or on the street. But no. She was sure, at some point, she had been introduced to him. She was alone in the shop, so she couldn't ask one of the others if they recognised him. Mel would be taking over at lunchtime for the afternoon shift, and Holly had rung to say her mum wasn't doing too well, so she would be working from home for the whole week. She was almost tempted to sneak a picture of him with her phone to send to Mel, Holly and Lee to ask who he was. It was really bugging her. But then he took a pair of T-shirts off the shelf. They were the same size, one in blue and one in red. He brought them to the counter. Something about the T-shirts clicked a switch in Jo's head. Why would you buy the same shirt in the same size in two different colours? Either you loved it so much you wanted your child to wear the same cartoon shirt day in and day out, or you had twins. Twins. He was the father of twins. He was Louise Holmes-Harper's brother-in-law, the one with the awfully behaved twins with the posh names. Jago and something. From the depths of her memory, she dragged up a name and prayed it was correct. 'Richard?' she said, as she took the T-shirts from him.

He looked astonished. 'Yes.'

'You're Louise's brother-in-law. It took me a while; I've been watching you since you came in, trying to work out where I knew you from.'

'Very impressive. You must have quite a memory for faces.'

'I do. But it also meant so much to me that Louise came to the launch and brought her family with her. She was such a support to me. To be honest, I couldn't have started this shop without her.'

'Louise is an amazing woman,' said Richard.

'So, if you don't mind my asking, what brings you to this part of the world? If I remember correctly, you live down south, near Louise.'

'That's right. Surrey,' he said. Jo busied herself with putting the clothes through the till and packing them in a bag. Richard handed over his credit card. He didn't answer her question though, just waited for her to finish. She felt a little uncomfortable. He wasn't rude or abrupt, just quiet, and he seemed to be watching her rather closely. Oh no, she thought. He wasn't one of those predatory posh men, was he? Maybe he'd come back to the shop alone so he could make a move on her. Because she was tall, blonde and striking, Jo had always had plenty of approaches from men. She was used to graciously declining, but a pass from Louise's brother-in-law would be embarrassing to say the least. She gave him her best cool, professional smile. 'Is there anything else?' she said briskly.

'There is, as a matter of fact,' he said. Uh-oh, here it comes, thought Jo, but she couldn't have been more wrong. 'I'm interested in what you've created here. This shop. Extremely interested. I think it has a future. I think there is capacity to expand the concept, way beyond what you have here. But you're going to need help. I'd like to meet with you to discuss it. Can we have lunch at my club? How about, say, Friday?'

Jo couldn't come up with the words to reply. She just stared at him, her mouth slightly open. He interpreted her surprise as hesitation, and handed her his business card. 'Ring my secretary and set it up. If Friday doesn't work for you, she can tell you which other slots I have free.' He smiled, picked up the bag with the T-shirts and left.

The shop was quiet after he'd gone, so she took his card into the back room and googled him. He worked for an investment bank and was obviously successful. She couldn't begin to understand what the investment bank did, but she was fairly sure that they didn't put money into one-woman businesses in East Finchley. It all seemed very strange. When Mel came in at midday, she didn't mention Richard's visit, just filled her in on a delivery they were expecting that afternoon and set off to fetch the kids. To be honest, she wasn't sure what Richard saw in the shop that made him want to invest in it. They had been quiet for all of January so far, and Jo was actually quite worried. They would just about break even that month – that is, she would be able to pay her suppliers and a wage to Holly and Mel – but only if she took nothing out herself. It wasn't like she was sitting on a secret gold mine.

That evening after the kids were in bed, she curled up next to Lee on the sofa. 'I had the oddest experience today,' she began, and told him about Richard coming to the shop and what he had said.

'So he said "help",' said Lee. 'That was the word he used?'

'Yes, why?'

'He didn't say he wants to invest in the business.'

'No.'

'Well, it all sounds a bit odd. Like you say, it's not like the shop is bringing in millions. You're doing okay, but not brilliantly.'

'I know.'

'What's your gut feeling?'

'He seemed genuine. It's an odd thing to say about a banker, but it didn't feel like he was feeding me a line.'

'So what's his motivation?'

'I don't know. Maybe I should speak to Louise about it, see what she says.'

'Well, if you think it wouldn't put her in an awkward position, maybe that's a good idea.'

The next day, Mel was on the morning shift, so Jo was at home and she rang Louise's mobile. Louise didn't answer, so she left a brief message asking her to call back, but without saying why. Louise rang back within the hour.

'So sorry I didn't pick up,' she began. 'Tiny baby, poo explosion. I'm sure you know what I mean. I had to shower her down and change all her clothes, then clean the bath-room. Life with small children is so glamorous.'

Jo laughed. 'Been there, done that.'

'So how are you? How's business?' Louise asked. Jo listened to see if there was a hint of extra meaning in the question, but it just seemed a friendly and genuine enquiry.

'Okay. Good December, quiet January,' said Jo.

'Well, nobody has it easy right now,' said Louise. 'Belts are tight, people aren't spending much. Keep your costs down, keep marketing like mad and hope for the best, that's all I can say.'

There was no doubt Louise had no idea about Richard. Either that or she was a very good actress, and from what little Jo knew about her, that just wasn't her. What she'd liked about Louise from the start was her direct manner and honesty.

'Louise, this isn't just a social call. I had a visitor at the shop yesterday, and I wanted to talk to you about it. It was your brother-in-law, Richard.'

'Richard?' If Jo had had any doubts left, they were dispelled by the surprise in Louise's voice. She clearly had no idea. Jo ran through what Richard had said to her, and Louise listened without asking any questions. When Jo had finished, she said, 'I'm going to give Richard a call, and I'll ring you back.'

She was true to her word, and rang back within ten min-utes. 'Richard genuinely does want to get involved in your business. It's not for the bank. It's in his personal capacity.'

'What do you think I should do?' asked Jo.

'I can't advise you on that. All I can say is this: Richard's a banker by trade, but he's not a bullshit artist. He is genuinely interested. The question is, is it what you're looking for? Only you know the answer to that.'

Until she heard what he was offering, Jo didn't know the answer, but it seemed Holly did. When she tentatively told Holly and Mel the next day, Holly just stared at her.

'What? Are you sure? Are you sure he wants to buy in?'

'I'm not sure about anything. And I won't be, unless I go to the meeting and see what he has to say.'

'Please, Jo, please be careful. Don't agree to anything, don't shake on anything and don't give him too much information. Not before you've put any proposal he has in front of a lawyer.'

Jo smiled. 'I'll be careful, I promise.'

'I'm sorry, it's just . . . I had a business. I let someone buy into it and I lost everything.'

'I don't know what this guy wants to give us. It might not be an offer of money at all. He just said "help". And I know it ended badly for you, but it doesn't mean every experience will be like that.'

'I know,' said Holly, calming down slightly. 'It just . . . well, the idea of it freaks me out.'

'I understand,' said Jo. 'But at the very least, I want to hear him out. For his family connection to Louise, if nothing else.'

'It does seem odd to me,' ventured Mel. 'I kind of remember him from the launch day, and the description you give makes him sound like a banker wanker, if you'll pardon the expression. What interest could he possibly have in a little suburban shop, miles from where he lives?'

'I don't know,' said Jo. 'When you put it like that, it does seem strange. But I won't know unless I talk to him, will I?'

She rang Richard's secretary, who set up a lunch date for the end of that week. Lee took a day off work so she could go and not worry about the time and picking up the kids. In the morning, Jo took herself off to the hairdressers and had a blow-dry and a manicure, to give herself a little polish and courage. She dug out a suit from her working days, a classic Chanel-style knee-length skirt and cropped jacket in a dusty pink. Thankfully, it still fitted her. Discreet make-up, pearl earrings, low-heeled but elegant shoes, and she was ready to go. Lee, who was sitting on the floor doing play-dough with Imogene, gave a low whistle when she walked into the living room.

'Bloody hell. You're working that sexy businesswoman look,' he said, and stood up to look at her more closely, then drew her into his arms. He kissed her softly and whispered, 'Don't be in a hurry to take that off when you get home. You look delicious.'

'Mamma!' gurgled Imogene and toddled up, her doughy hands reaching for Jo's skirt. Lee broke free and snatched her up in his arms, covering her little face in kisses. 'All right, little miss, let's let Mummy go to her meeting without play-dough accessories. See you later, love. Knock 'em dead. Oh, by the way . . . do you want to take my iPad?'

'And do what? Show him how good I am at playing Fruit Ninja? Let him watch an episode of *Bob the Builder*?'

'I don't know . . . I just thought it would make you look professional.'

'It would, if I had some whizzy presentation of the figures with pie charts and stuff, but I don't. I just have my little balance sheet, and a folder of press cuttings.'

'That sounds fantastic,' said Lee firmly and loyally. 'Now go. Take the car and park at the station so you don't have to walk in those shoes. If we go anywhere it'll be to the park, and we'll walk there. And have fun.'

He held Imogene off to one side so she couldn't touch Jo, and leaned in to kiss Jo softly at first and then very much more passionately. 'Now go, before I put a DVD on for the kids and rumple your suit.'

Jo giggled. 'Why, Mr Hockley, you've still got it. You've made my knees go all funny. I'm quite collywobbled.'

She blew a kiss to Imogene, who wasn't particularly interested in her departure, blew Lee a saucy kiss over her shoulder and headed out of the door.

Lee

Lee sat back down on the floor, put Imogene on his lap and reached for a lump of play-dough. 'All right, lovely, what do you want Daddy to make now?'

'Poo!' said Imogene delightedly.

'Well, that shouldn't stretch Daddy's artistic talents too much. I can manage that.'

They played contentedly for a while longer, then Lee read Imogene a couple of books. She went soft and quiet in his arms so he knew she was getting tired. He changed her and gave her some milk, and she curled up obediently in her little toddler bed for a nap. He tidied the house and made a plate of sandwiches for lunch. He checked his watch, and there was a good hour before he had to go and pick Zach up from nursery. He knew Imi would sleep until he transferred her into the pushchair to walk to Zach's school. He had an hour. A perfect, silent, uninterrupted hour at home, and he could do anything he liked.

He quite fancied sitting on the sofa and surfing the TV channels, or reading a magazine, but those pursuits seemed too mundane for such rare and precious time, so instead he dug in his desk drawers and found his old college pencil case. Inside were some ancient charcoal sticks. He took out a few sheets of textured drawing paper and found a board to press on, and then sneaked into Imogene's room and sat on the edge of the armchair where Jo used to breastfeed. He looked at his daughter's perfect face, her little lips pink and pouted in sleep, the sweep of lashes touching the swell of her cheek and her rather dramatic dark brows curved under the mad tangle of her hair. He began to draw, trying to capture the essence of her face with the charcoal lines. The first drawing was a disaster. It was stiff and wooden, and it made Imi look like a rather scary doll. He tried again, remembering the feel of the charcoal in his hand, and finding the natural arc as he drew. The result was slightly better, and he felt he had caught the shape of her mouth particularly well, but the hair wasn't right and her eyebrows looked wonky.

The third drawing was better still, but, Lee felt, too fussy and mannered. He did a series of five more, and with each he tried to capture the essence of Imogene's face with fewer and fewer lines. Some of them worked, some of them didn't. He suddenly glanced at the clock and realised that they had to leave in ten minutes. He put his drawing things away in his desk. He knew from experience that he would need to leave the drawings for a little while before he looked at them again to get a real sense of whether they were any good. He washed his hands and got the pushchair ready, then gently scooped a sleepy Imogene up and slipped her into the cosy cocoon of the pushchair. He pulled a woolly hat on to her head, yanked on his coat and a scarf and set off to walk to Zach's school. It didn't matter if the drawings were terrible, he realised as he walked in the crisp, cold sunshine. He had just spent the most fulfilling and creatively satisfying hour he had had for ages.

The weather was too cold for the park, so they came home for sandwiches and then Lee and Zach played an indoor ball game with a pair of Lee's rolled-up football socks, while Imi giggled and was the piggy in the middle. Later, he bundled them both up and they walked to the shop to get a few things for dinner. It was almost four o'clock, and while Lee wasn't worried, he was aware that lunch would be long over and he hadn't had a text or call from Jo. He hoped it was because it was all going so well, and not because she was depressed and wandering the streets of London alone.

He took a moment to check his work email. There was very little, not just because everyone knew he was out of the office, but because things at work were quiet. Not just quiet, worryingly silent. Custom typography was a luxury, and in these economic times, one that many companies were having to forego. A beautiful individual typeface or logo was a lovely thing, but when marketing and advertising budgets were being slashed, losing that was an easy way to trim costs. The company had seen a marked decline in their revenue over the previous year, and Lee knew his bosses were worried. They'd already had to let three junior designers go, and Lee was under no illusion that his job was secure. If he lost it, what would he do? The shop wasn't bringing in anything like enough money; he knew Jo hadn't paid herself anything at the end of January. He'd have to find work, and find it fast. There was usually graphic-design freelancing to be had, but it would mean a lot of travelling and working in strange offices, and there was no guarantee of work. Well, he'd cross that bridge when he came to it.

As he shut down his email, his phone rang. It was Jo, sounding breathless, obviously calling as she walked along. 'Hi, love, so, so sorry,' she began. 'I've just left the restaurant and there just wasn't a chance to nip out and ring you earlier.'

'No worries, everything's fine here. The kids are playing a game that involves a cardboard box and two wooden spoons. No injuries so far, but lots of laughing. How did it go?'

'It went . . . wow. Well, it wasn't at all what I expected, and I'm very surprised, but it's a long story. I'll tell you everything when I get home.'

'But it was good?'

'I don't know. It could be good, or it could be impossible. There are just so many things . . . so many problems . . . Lots of things we need to discuss. Look, I'm sorry I'm being cryptic, but just let me get home. I'm dying to see you and the kids, and once they're in bed, we can talk.'

It didn't take her too long to get back, and she came through the door, looking beautiful and smelling of the cold and the outside world, just as Lee set plates of dinner in front of the kids. She kissed him, then sat down between the children and helped them with their meal. Zach chattered away nineteen to the dozen about his day, and Imogene banged her spoon and squealed in delight. She managed to flick a baked bean on to Jo's lap. Jo laughed, grabbed a baby wipe and scrubbed the stain off her expensive skirt, then leaned in and kissed Imogene's chubby cheek. Lee watched her and thought he had never loved her more than he did right that minute, his clever, resourceful wife, mother of his precious children and builder of a successful business. He'd known from the first time he'd seen her at that student party all those years ago that she was something special, but he hadn't imagined she'd get more special as the years went by.

They got through the bathtime and bedtime routine, although it took an extra twenty minutes or so to calm the kids down. Although Jo did go out to work, a day at home with Daddy, and Mum coming home late, were out of the ordinary, and like all small children, Zach and Imogene saw it as an excuse to get madly excited. Eventually they were both in bed, and Lee went downstairs to finish washing up. Jo came down a few minutes later. She was still wearing her suit skirt and blouse, but she'd replaced her heels with fluffy animal slippers.

'Sorry, I know you were loving the sexy librarian look

earlier, but my feet were killing me,' she said, kissing Lee on the cheek.

'I don't know. I could be persuaded by the gorilla feet. It's kind of animalistic.'

'Wow, I know keeping the romance alive in a marriage takes imagination, but that is impressive.' She gave him a squeeze. 'Tea or wine?'

'Not that fussed either way. What would you like?'

'Well, I stayed on the fizzy water at lunch so I could keep my wits about me, so I would say definitely wine.'

'Wine it is then,' agreed Lee. Jo opened a bottle of red and carried it into the living room, grabbing glasses as she went. Lee finished up in the kitchen and followed her.

They settled on the sofa and sipped their wine in silence for a few minutes. Eventually, Lee said. 'Okay, go. I can't take the suspense any more.'

'Well, he seems a nice enough guy. I think he's nicer than he used to be, if that makes any sense. He seems to be on the point of a big epiphany.'

'Epiphany? What, like a religious vision?'

'No, not religious as such, but he seems to be reassessing his life and wanting to do something different.'

'Because . . . ?'

'Well, he says it's having kids. He's been in high finance all his life, working all hours, doing deals, making pots of money, as far as I can ascertain, but he wants to do something . . . his words were "a bit more meaningful".'

'Like caring for orphans in Romania? Eradicating rinderpest?'

'Bear in mind he was an investment banker. His idea of

"a little more meaningful" may be slightly more modest than that.'

'So his idea is . . . ?'

'He thinks Jungletown is an amazing business idea, but that it could grow exponentially and open stores nationwide, and beyond.'

'Nationwide?' said Lee incredulously.

'And beyond. He seems to think it would do especially well in Australia. Apparently conquering the American market is part of the five-year plan, but we wouldn't be tackling that quite yet.'

'And how does he plan to go about this?' asked Lee.

'Well, he's talking about significant financial investment from himself and a few friends. He proposes that he comes on board as Chief Financial Officer, I stay as founder and Creative Director, and we go from there.'

'And his banking job?'

'He wants to quit. He sees this as – quote – "downsizing".'

'I don't know what to say,' said Lee.

'It's okay, you can laugh. I did. All the way home.'

'So what do you . . . think?'

'Think? Well, it's amazing that he sees so much potential . . . I mean, I just wanted to open a little neighbourhood shop, something to make a bit of money and fit in with caring for the kids . . . but . . . a multimillion-pound operation? Stores everywhere? Franchising?' She sighed, long and deep.

'That still doesn't tell me what you think,' said Lee.

'There's no point in saying what I might or might not think, Lee. It's just not possible. I thought about it on the way home, and even if I wanted to do it, what about the kids? We stick them in care from seven till seven while I go off to my high-flying business empire? And what if I had to go away on trips? If we went nationwide, there'd have to be travel . . .'

'But in an ideal world . . .'

'What – an ideal world where my children don't exist?! That's scarcely an ideal world, is it?'

And to Lee's surprise, she burst into tears and began to sob. She rested her head on his shoulder and cried and cried. Lee had hardly ever seen Jo cry, and other than putting his arms around her and holding her tight, he didn't have a clue what to do.

15

RICHARD THEN

Confidence is a funny thing, Richard thought. Nobody was born with it. People who were smooth, open and affable and who exuded power and self-assurance hadn't always been like that. He believed that deep down inside, everyone was a small and rather frightened child, hanging back, afraid to get something wrong. Nobody was naturally charismatic. Some people learned early on in life to fake it, and they kept faking it until it became second nature, or at least until they believed their own press and really did think they were amazing.

At twenty-five, he was still deep in the 'faking it' phase. Yes he was a successful trader on the floor of a major multinational investment bank. He already owned his dream car (a vintage Porsche), and a delightful Docklands apartment. He was never without a beautiful woman on his arm or in his bed. He knew he was reasonable-looking, and by the standards of most people, extremely successful. Nevertheless, he couldn't shake the feeling that one day, as he sat at his desk, a heavy hand would fall on his shoulder, and a deep voice would say, 'Richard Anthony, no one was fooled. You're a fake. Out you go.'

His lack of confidence came, he thought, from his rather commonplace beginnings. He'd been born the eldest child in a very ordinary middle-class family living in one of the slightly less posh parts of Kew. His mum was a music teacher, and his dad was a solicitor. His father, Matthew Anthony, had been born Matteo Antonioni, the only son of Italian immigrants who ran a small restaurant in Bethnal Green. Matteo's parents had literally worked themselves into an early grave to give their son the finest education available. They both died when he was in his early years at university. He repaid their efforts by becoming a modestly successful lawyer, marrying a beautiful blonde English rose and anglicising his name. Mario and Rosa would not have recognised the polished man with his clipped vowels that their son became. Matthew was even more ambitious for his son, whom he named after the Lionheart – Richard was the most English and heroic name Matthew could think of, and he hoped it meant his son would leave his Italian peasant roots far behind.

Richard's mother, Elizabeth, was a fierce disciplinarian and expected a lot from her son. Music was everything to her, and she taught him to read music before he could read words, and play the piano before he could use a pencil. It was this intensive tuition and these high expectations that revealed Richard's golden ticket: a pure, clear treble voice and a perfect ear. Elizabeth took him to audition for the Westminster Abbey choir school, and by the time Richard was eight, he was boarding full-time and singing in the cathedral every day. He found it frightening and lonely at first. He would ring his parents every evening and beg to come home, but they were both immovable and just kept repeating how it was a once-in-a-lifetime experience and he would thank them when he got older.

He did get used to it eventually, and loved the camaraderie of the small group of boys. His talent led to a music scholarship to Harrow School when he was thirteen. He had been there just eighteen months when his voice broke, and the fluting treble was replaced with a very average tenor. He was still musical however, and continued with the piano up to Grade Eight, but he knew that, despite Elizabeth's efforts, music would never be his career. He felt that he had been faking it as a member of Harrow's exclusive community, riding on his musical talent, but he believed it wasn't enough. He began to work harder at his academic subjects. He mistook his classmates' easy confidence for cleverness, and he always felt he wasn't quite keeping up, even though his marks were excellent. He knew he was bright, but he didn't think he was exceptional, so he studied intensively to make up for what he saw as his lack of talent. It paid off, unsurprisingly, with outstanding results and a place at Oxford to read Politics, Philosophy and Economics. He worked just as hard there, with equally gratifying results. With a first-class honours degree under his belt, he went straight into a graduate programme at an American bank, and was swiftly headhunted to work at the one where he was currently employed.

The Abbey, Harrow, Oxford . . . Richard's CV read like that of someone who had been born into a lifetime of privilege, like so many of his co-workers. But he knew that everything he had was as a result of his parents' ambitions, a lucky talent and some very hard work. If things had gone a little differently for both his father and him, he might well have been Ricardo Antonioni, head waiter at his grandparents' restaurant in Bethnal Green. He was extremely careful about the way he spoke and the way he dressed. He wanted to fit in apparently effortlessly, but that took a lot of money and thought. His friend William, whose father seemed to own most of Berkshire, wore scruffy corduroy trousers and drove a twenty-year-old Range Rover that smelled of dogs, but Richard knew he couldn't get away with that. Not when the ancestral home was a three-bedroomed 1930s house just off the A315.

But one day, everything changed. He hadn't had cause to go into the PR department of the bank for some time, but he had been sent a press release to approve which concerned a deal he'd just done, and it was full of errors. Not small ones either: the name of the key client was misspelled, and the total value of the deal had an extra two zeroes, which took it from a big deal to the GDP of a small country. He scribbled all over the printout in angry red ink and went storming off to PR to find the R. Holmes who had made such a pig's ear of a simple job. When he found him – or more likely her – some ditzy poppet on work experience no doubt – he was going to tear a strip off them.

Except when he walked into the department, he was stopped short by quite the most beautiful girl he had ever seen. She was standing in the middle of the room with her back to him, and when he entered, she turned to look at him. She looked a little like Alice in Wonderland grown up, with a smooth sheet of fine blonde hair and a slender figure, and the finest creamy skin Richard had ever seen. As he walked towards her, he found himself staring at her mouth. Her upper lip was beautifully, classically shaped, but her lower lip was somehow a little too full. There was something so soft and inviting about it. He wanted to touch it with his finger and see if it was as soft as it looked, and then he wanted to kiss her and never stop.

He managed to pull himself together before he ended his career with a charge of sexual harassment in the workplace, and said brusquely, 'I'm looking for R. Holmes. The R. Holmes who wrote *this*.' He waved the offending piece of paper.

'That's me,' said the angel. 'Rachel. What can I do for you?'

There were so many answers to that question. Richard took a deep breath and went for, 'There are a few mistakes in it. Could we go through it?'

She beckoned him over to her desk and they sat down. He felt awful for all the angry red marks on the page, but he managed to put his criticisms to her gently and politely. She was mortified to have got so much wrong. 'I'm so sorry,' she kept saying. 'So, so sorry. This was my first go at a press release by myself. I should have been more careful. I'm so sorry.'

She promised to get a revised version to him by the end of the day. He couldn't think of a reason to stay in her office, and in fact there were any number of pressing matters awaiting his attention, so he reluctantly left and went back to his desk. She made him feel shy and gawky, but immensely protective at the same time. She was so lovely, but, he felt certain, completely out of his league. And even if that wasn't the case, how was he to make a move to get to know her better without looking like a sleazy perv? In the macho, male-dominated atmosphere of the bank, he was sure she spent a lot of her time fighting off advances from predatory traders. If he went and begged to take her out, spouting assurances about how he 'wasn't like those other guys', wouldn't that make him exactly like those other guys? And if, by some slim chance, she said yes, he'd have to put up with all sorts of teasing and ribald comments from his colleagues. Maybe it was best just to do nothing at all.

He'd talked himself into this position so firmly that when Rachel emailed him the revised press release, he responded with a curt 'That's fine, thank you for your prompt turn-around' and left it at that. However, he didn't forget her. Whenever he walked through the building and passed the PR office, he would glance in and look for her. When he went to the kitchen to make coffee, he would hope against hope that she would take a break at the same time. And in the mornings and evenings, he would pray silently that she would get into the same lift as him. It happened rather seldom: obviously they were on different timetables. After a few weeks, he thought of her a little less. He was caught up in a fiendishly complex deal, and it absorbed all his time and attention.

Until Justin Thackeray. Thackeray, a trader at Richard's level, was a burly, rugby-playing toff whose neck was wider than his head and whose ego was fatter than both. He was loud, brash and pushy. He believed that he who shouts the loudest does the best. He bulldozed over people in meetings and liked to yell at underlings. He treated everyone around him as inferiors: his fellow traders, who in his opinion, all knew nothing; anyone more junior in the company; all women, all foreigners, all politicians and anyone outside the world of finance – they were all scum to him and were spoken to accordingly. Richard had seldom disliked anyone as much as he disliked Justin Thackeray.

Late one Friday afternoon, after the UK markets had closed, the office was quietening down, and people on the trading floor were beginning to relax a little and chat to one another. Justin was still barking at full volume into his phone. Rachel walked into the room – she was obviously passing through on her way to somewhere – and Justin slammed down his phone and yelled, 'Oi! Blondie!' at the top of his voice. Rachel turned at the sound. Justin beckoned her over and she approached his desk hesitantly. Justin tipped his chair back. He kept beckoning until Rachel was standing in front of his desk like a schoolgirl called in to see the headmaster. Several people at the surrounding desks, including Richard, had stopped what they were doing to watch. Justin glanced around, enjoying the fact that he had an audience. 'Are you the brainless bint who wrote this?' he said, lazily waving a piece of paper under Rachel's nose.

'Er . . . yes,' she whispered.

'Listen, poppet, you might have a pert pair of tits and a cute behind, but you can't write for shit. I wouldn't wipe my arse with this.'

The room was silent. Rachel took a long shaky breath. Richard could see she was about to cry. 'What . . . exactly is wrong with it?' she whispered.

'You tell me, sweetheart, you tell me. You're the fucking

English graduate. You tell me what's wrong with it. Go on.'
Justin held the piece of paper out towards her and Rachel
reached out a trembling hand to take it, but he snatched
the page away, crumpled it up and threw it at her. It hit her
in the chest. There was a gasp from one or two people in
the room, and a couple of Justin's toadying friends laughed.

Richard didn't know how it happened. He had no memory
of getting up from his desk or walking over, but the next
thing he knew, he was leaning over Justin's desk, inches
from his sneering face. 'Listen, you nasty little bastard, if the
only way you can show you're a man is by bullying young
women in public . . .'

Justin stood up. Richard straightened up too and they
faced off across the desk. Justin had two inches and probably
three stone on him, but Richard had right on his side and
adrenalin flooding his every cell. Justin wasn't stupid. His
beady little eyes left Richard's face and darted around the
room. He could sense that the mood in the room had turned.
He laughed harshly. 'Whatever, Dicky-boy.' He tossed his head
at Rachel, sneering, 'I'll get someone else to write this.
Someone with a fucking clue,' and he sauntered out of the
room.

When Richard looked at Rachel, she was looking at him,
her blue eyes round and wide. 'Thank you,' she said.

'Don't mention it. He's a prick who needed to be put in
his place.'

'Could I . . . ?' Rachel hesitated. 'Could I buy you a drink
to say thank you?'

And Richard, still full of bravado and confidence, said,
'Only if I can buy you dinner afterwards.'

He took her to a little Italian restaurant that he knew nearby. He had enough family heritage to know that the food was excellent, and the little alcoves were private and candlelit. Within just a few hours, he had learned a lot about her and she about him. Normally on a first date, he would have given the briefest outline of his growing up, leaning heavily on the Harrow and Oxford parts, and omitting the Italian peasant grandparents and the scholarships that had got him his education. But he was honest with Rachel. He wanted her to know him, really know him, as he was, from the very beginning. Her own background was equally commonplace She told him she had grown up in Manchester, and for the first time he noticed a breath of the North in the way she spoke. She had come to London to do a degree in English, and then a diploma in public relations. They had all had work placements in their final year, and as it happened, Rachel's had been at the bank. 'They offered me a full-time job straight away,' she said. 'I'm not sure why. I'm not very clever, or business-minded. I was surprised, really.'

Richard knew the lecherous head of human resources, and he had no doubt that Rachel's slender ankles, blonde hair and innocent demeanour had had something to do with her being hired.

'So if you're not business-minded,' Richard said, 'is this not what you want to do with your life? What's the dream? Is it the arts? Writing? Acting? Music?'

'Oh no,' Rachel said, looking surprised. 'All I've ever wanted is to be a wife and mother.'

Richard nearly fell off his chair. He usually went out with

polished, sophisticated women who also worked in the City. They would never dream of admitting that they wanted commitment, let alone marriage, and no one ever mentioned children. Many of them were probably waging long-term, carefully planned campaigns to land themselves a rich husband, but you would never know it from speaking to them. But Rachel had just laid her cards on the table. She didn't know how to play the game at all. She knew what she wanted, and she saw no reason not to tell him. Richard knew he should be terrified. But he wasn't. He was enchanted.

There was something so fundamentally delicate and vulnerable about her, something in her that made him yearn to protect her. The first date became a second, then a weekly event, then twice a week, then every night. After three months, Richard knew he loved her. After six, he knew he wanted to marry her. He bought a ring, a simple but large solitaire-cut diamond on a platinum band, and put it in his bedside drawer. Not only did he love her, he knew she loved him. He knew she looked to him for care and protection. Yes, it was an old-fashioned relationship, almost Victorian, he liked to think, but it suited them both. Seeing himself through Rachel's eyes, Richard could glimpse a man he could be proud of, a man with class, power and brains. The man he had been pretending to be for years was real in her eyes, and it made him feel ten feet tall.

He knew that a proposal to Rachel had to be perfect. Not only because he knew he wanted to spend his life with her, but because Rachel so loved weddings and everything around them that she had been keeping scrapbooks of dresses, rings, and flowers since she was about ten years old. Her expectations would be very high. In the end, he went for the restaurant where they had had their first date. She noticed when they arrived that the room was very quiet (deserted in fact, since he had booked the whole place for the evening), but he told her it was just because they were early. There was a single white rose at her place setting, and champagne in an ice bucket. She smiled and lifted the rose to smell it. 'You spoil me,' she said. Richard raised a hand to summon the waiter, who came over and expertly uncorked the bottle. 'Ah, Giuseppe, we need glasses,' Richard said. This was the prearranged signal. Giuseppe nodded and retired, then returned with two glasses. As he put Rachel's glass in front of her and began to fill it, music began to fill the room, a plaintive tune on a single violin. Giuseppe filled Richard's glass, smiled and melted away, just as the violinist emerged from the kitchen.

'Rachel,' began Richard, and when he looked at her lovely face in the candlelight, his eyes filled with tears, 'will you do me the honour . . . ?' He was choking up. 'Will you do me the honour . . . ?' He took a ragged breath. 'Rachel, you're the light of my life . . .' and at that moment, the candlelight caught the enormous diamond at the bottom of Rachel's glass. She gasped and lifted the glass so she could see the ring.

The wedding, a year later, was perfect in every detail. Rachel gave up her job six months after they got engaged and spent all her time planning the big day. Once they were married, she moved into Richard's riverside apartment and redecorated it magnificently. Richard couldn't believe how she transformed his life. His clothes were impeccable, their home was beautiful, every meal was a delight and she kept their family finances in perfect order. While she had had no appetite for the business world, she was born to be a home-maker. They began to entertain, and he discovered that for all her ditzy manner in the workplace, she was a wonderful hostess. She was an accomplished cook and an even better baker. She created beautiful tables, brilliant guest lists and made the whole thing seem effortless. He lost his last vestiges of awkwardness and inferiority. With Rachel as his wife, he felt like a king.

After a year or so in the riverside place, Richard suggested that as they were planning to start a family, they might want somewhere a little bigger. Rachel had already researched schools and they settled on an area of Surrey that met her high standards. Richard left her to do the legwork, and she shortlisted three houses for them to see together. They viewed them all in a day, and chose the one she had already set her heart on. And so, on their second wedding anniver-sary, they took possession of a beautiful six-bedroomed sprawling house in Surrey with a big garden and a wonderful airy playroom.

Richard couldn't believe his luck. He had found his soul-mate, she loved him too, they had plenty of money, a beautiful home and a perfect marriage . . . except. Except. They had stopped using contraception as soon as they had got married. 'I'm ready whenever,' Rachel had said. 'It'll happen when it happens.'

But it didn't happen. After a year or so, Rachel went for some blood tests and an ultrasound and was told that every-thing seemed fine. After another year, she went for more comprehensive tests, and she begged until Richard went and had his sperm checked. The problem was definitely with Rachel. She had fertility treatment, which did nothing except make her feel extremely ill. Then they went through two rounds of IVF, both of which failed. By the end of the second round, the strain was beginning to tell. Rachel was terribly thin, and she looked permanently drawn. Then, to make matters worse, her sister, Louise, fell pregnant from an ill-judged one-night stand with a married colleague. When Rachel found out, she was devastated, and it nearly destroyed the relationship between the sisters.

Just before her thirty-fifth birthday, Rachel went to see her gynaecologist. He told her that she had gone into early menopause and that any future attempts at IVF would have to be with someone else's eggs.

Rachel, ever groomed, ever organised, always on the go, went to bed for a week. Richard gently suggested the possibility of adoption, but she wouldn't hear of it. She lay in their big bed, her hair dirty and lank on the pillow, with tears leaking non-stop into the white linen. Richard's heart ached for her. He couldn't give her a baby, the one thing she wanted, the only thing that would make her feel complete. After years of feeling like her knight in shining armour, he felt like a foolish failure.

But help came from a most unlikely source – Rachel's sister Louise. She worked very hard to win Rachel's trust again, and involved her in caring for her little boy, Peter. When Peter was a year old, Louise volunteered to be Rachel's egg donor. Rachel wrestled with the idea. The baby wouldn't be hers by blood, but it would be of the same bloodline.

Eventually, they decided to give it a try. The gamble paid off not once, but twice: Rachel fell pregnant with twins, a boy and a girl. Richard had feared it might be odd, but it wasn't. Even before the twins were born, he had all but forgotten that they weren't Rachel's children by blood, and so had she. Other than Louise, her husband, Adam, and Louise and Rachel's brother, Simon, no one else knew.

Overnight, Rachel had the family she had always dreamed of. She was exquisitely happy pregnant, and when Jago and Xanthe arrived, she lavished them with all the love in the world. The light didn't just come back on, it glowed from her like a lighthouse, and she was the happiest woman in Surrey.

At first, Richard was happy simply because she was happy, but as the twins grew, they stopped just being blobs who ate and slept. They became feisty, fascinating little individuals, and he fell in love for the second time in his life. Jago was boisterous, funny and cheeky, and Xanthe was quieter, but extremely determined . . . a miniature Rachel. He didn't know it was possible to love someone so small so much. Loving them made him reassess everything. He started thinking about the state of the planet, so he got rid of his enormous Porsche four-by-four and bought matching hybrid cars for himself and Rachel. He worked to build closer relationships with both his family and Rachel's. But most of all, he started to reconsider his work life. He didn't want to keep working thirteen-hour days, getting home when the twins were already asleep, and he didn't want to work in banking at a time when people saw it as the root of the financial crisis. He wanted Jago and Xanthe to be proud of their dad. He wanted to do something they would think was cool, and that they could relate to.

When Louise invited them to the opening of Jungletown, he went reluctantly. He liked family outings, but it was a long trek around the M25 to visit some funny start-up boutique. He didn't see the appeal, but Louise was very enthusiastic about it, so he was happy to go. The truth was, Louise had given him and Rachel the greatest gift possible. She'd given it graciously and had never asked for any acknowledgement or repayment. Privately, he thought it was possible that Louise was really an angel, and if she'd asked him to swim the Channel for her, he would have tried.

He was amazed when he saw the shop though. It was a brilliant idea, wonderfully designed and executed, and someone had taken trouble over every single detail. It screamed potential. He'd thoroughly enjoyed being there, and went away feeling the trip had been well worth it. He assumed that was the end of it, but over the days and weeks that followed, Jungletown kept popping back into his head. He kept thinking of ways in which the concept could be expanded. He started jotting down ideas, then making more comprehensive notes. It took him a long time to connect his interest in the shop to his wish for a career change. But when it came to him, it came as a blinding flash. What if he could be involved? What if he could grow the shop into a company, and meet his own work/life goals at the same time?

One evening, when the twins had finally been coaxed into bed, and the final boisterous noises had died down from upstairs, he and Rachel sat eating their dinner. He'd been thinking about Jungletown all day. He had meant to plan what he was going to say, but instead, he just blurted it out.

'Love, do you remember the shop opening Louise took us to?'

'Of course. It was wonderful,' Rachel said. 'Jungle something. I wish there was one close by . . . and I wish they did more girly clothes. I'd be in there every week.'

'I thought it was a brilliant idea too. I've been thinking about it a lot, and, well, what if I got involved?'

Rachel put down her fork and gave him her full attention. One of the things he loved best about her was that she always sensed when he was serious about something, and she listened properly. 'Involved?' she asked. 'In what way?'

He started to outline his initial thoughts, hesitantly at first, and then more enthusiastically. Rachel listened, added a few thoughts of her own and helped him to clarify a few points. Finally, she said firmly, 'Well, you need to go and take another look. Quite a few more looks, and you'd need to meet the woman who owns it and see what you think of how they operate day-to-day. You need to be sure.'

The next day, for the first time in his career, Richard pulled a sickie. He went into work and double-checked that he had no meetings that afternoon. At lunchtime, he told his PA he had a terrible headache and was going home to rest. Instead, he jumped on the Tube and headed north to East Finchley. He felt very conspicuous, walking up the high street in his City suit, so he took off his tie and loosened his top button. He walked hesitantly into Jungletown. It was around two o'clock, and the place was buzzing with mums shopping and children tearing around and playing. There was no sign of Jo, the woman who owned the place. Instead the shop was being ably staffed and managed by a short, compact woman with spiky hair, who looked like she might have been a street entertainer at some time. She was always on the move, advising a mum here, throwing a ball with a toddler there, ringing up a purchase with a smile and answering the phone at the same time. Whoever she was, she was worth her weight in gold. If the company grew as Richard imagined it might, she'd be a brilliant staff trainer.

He stayed just long enough to get a good feel of what was going on, but not so long as to be conspicuous or creepy. He chose two pairs of handmade jeans for the twins and paid for them. He certainly had some food for thought. The shop had looked great at launch, and was clearly still doing well, but there was so much scope for growth and improvement. On the train back home he wrote four pages of notes on his iPad.

He went back a couple more times. Each time the short woman was working, and once he saw a tall red-headed girl behind the counter as well. She reminded him a little of Louise. He spent a long time looking at his financial position. He believed he could make the business work and make money, but it would mean a significant investment. He planned to invest some of his own money and then bring in a few other private investors. He made a list of people he would consider approaching. In terms of his private finances, there was a big enough nest egg that he and Rachel wouldn't need to compromise on their lifestyle, at least for the moment. And as long as he made a success of the business, they could continue that way.

When he finally had all the plans in place, he made one last trip. He had got used to seeing the short woman in the shop, so he was surprised to see Jo behind the counter. He had meant to make a more formal approach to ask her to meet, but she caught him by surprise when she recognised him from the launch and remembered his name. He gave her his card and asked her to contact him. Walking back to the station, he found himself trembling a little. It was ridiculous. He did multimillion-pound deals for the bank all the time without breaking a sweat. But there was something about this little suburban shop and the opportunity it offered that made him excited. Would Jo be interested? Could they make it work? He hoped so. He hoped so very much.

16

MEL NOW

'So how was school today?' Mel said, putting cottage pie on Serena's plate and adding a spoonful of peas, carefully placing them so they didn't touch the cottage pie at all.

'Hmm.'

'Any homework?'

'No.'

'Plans for the weekend.'

'Yeah,' said Serena, pushing the food around her plate, but she didn't expand on that statement.

'I'm working Saturday morning, but I'm off from about two. Fancy an early-evening film and a pizza? I'd love to see the new X-Men thing.'

'Can't.'

This was hard work. She was trying to be pleasant and open, but so far hadn't managed to get more than a single syllable out of Serena. She'd been making a gentle effort for weeks now, making sure they had nice home-made meals and sat together to eat, suggesting outings that she thought Serena might enjoy, chatting about her own day to try to encourage Serena to talk about hers. But she was knocking her head against a brick wall. It wasn't as if Serena was rude, or even resentful. She was just . . . uninterested. It was as if she endured time with Mel because she had to, but her real life was going on somewhere else, and she was waiting for this interruption to end so she could get back to it.

She watched Serena carefully separating the potato from the mince, and eating mouthfuls of each in turn, then eating a few peas. She'd always liked all her food groups separate. As a small child, she had been a good eater, but fussy about presentation, and would refuse to eat her meal if one thing flowed into another. She had thrown the biggest tantrum of her childhood aged five because Mel had accidentally dropped some carrots into her rice. Mel's heart ached with love as she looked at Serena's bowed head. It wasn't just that she was worried about what Serena might be up to, she missed her. She missed her company, her laughter, her ferocious opinions. She tried a new conversational tack.

'I joined Facebook today.'

That got Serena's attention and her head snapped up. 'You what?'

'Jo set up a Facebook page for the shop, and I wanted to be able to see that, so I joined. It's very interesting. I found a bunch of people I was at uni with. It's weird. You can see people's pictures and everything . . . their holidays, their children . . . It's like popping into their houses to snoop through their photo albums.'

'Don't friend me,' said Serena, before she could stop herself.

'What?'

'Don't try to add me as a friend; I'll say no. It's so lame being friends with your mum.'

'I . . . okay. I wasn't going to, but okay.'

'And don't post any lame baby pictures of me, or add any of my friends.'

'Okay.'

'I'm going to my room now,' Serena said, standing up, and then adding belatedly, 'Thanks for dinner.'

Mel heard her door close, and then the hum of her computer coming to life. She wanted to smile, because she knew perfectly well what Serena was doing: checking all her Facebook settings to make sure none of her friends, her pictures or any of her statuses were visible to anyone who wasn't her friend. She'd entertained a faint hope that when she said she'd joined Facebook, Serena would want to be her friend, and that she could be open about it, but it seemed that wasn't going to be the case. Of course, she'd already had a look at as much of Serena's profile as was visible. She couldn't see any pictures except the profile one, a fairly innocuous one of her with two female friends, their arms around each other's necks, laughing. But she had been able to see her friends' list, and it was enormous: more than seven hundred people. Most of them seemed to be kids from schools in the area. Surely Serena couldn't know that many people. She must be adding friends that she didn't know, or barely knew, maybe people she'd met once.

Mel thought about it while she cleared the table, washed up and wiped down the kitchen surfaces. Then she logged on to Facebook, and sure enough, Serena's profile was even more tightly locked down. She couldn't even see the friends' list now. She searched for a couple of Serena's friends how-ever, and their profiles were completely visible. She spent an hour or so looking at the pictures they had up, the language they used, the conversations they had. Then she logged out and sat staring at the sign-up screen. What if Serena got a friend request from someone she *might* know, but couldn't put a face to? Someone whose profile looked like that of loads of the other kids she was friends with?

Could she create a fake profile . . . another teenager, someone Serena might want to be friends with? She didn't know enough about Facebook to know if it was possible, or if she would be found out. Was it criminal? She had no idea. She checked that Serena's door was firmly shut and there was music playing in her room, and then she rang Hamish.

'It's the lovely Miss Grey!' Hamish's voice was full of warmth.

'How are you?'

'In the midst of an edit of my new book. Trying to get the trolls from one side of the mountain to another in a snow-storm. You know how it is – tricky stuff.'

'Ah, those pesky trolls,' said Mel. 'Never go where you want them to.'

'Indeed, too true,' said Hamish. 'Now, to what do I owe the pleasure of this call? I'm sure you didn't ring me just to talk trolls.'

'Well, in a manner of speaking . . .' said Mel hesitantly. Now she had to say it out loud, her idea did sound slightly mad. 'I was wondering . . . what you knew about anonymity on the Internet. You know . . . like . . . fake identities.'

'Trolls?'

'Not really. More . . . well, social media profiles that aren't . . . actually . . . real people.'

'I'm not sure what you're getting at,' said Hamish. 'Are you worried that some of the people Serena is friends with might not be who they say? I wouldn't be surprised – it's dead easy to set up a fake Facebook or Twitter account – all you need is an email address, and you can get one of those in minutes. You don't even need to enter real information.'

'Really?' said Mel. 'That's very interesting.'

'I did speak to her about the whole social-media thing,' said Hamish. 'At Christmas. I told her not to accept anyone as a friend that she didn't actually know personally. Just because you have mutual friends doesn't mean the person is someone you want to have access to your life.'

'Mutual friends?'

'Yes. When you get a friend request from someone, it tells you if you have any friends in common. So she might be more tempted to say yes to someone because they know people she knows, even if she doesn't know them directly. It's one of the things that makes the whole world of social media so damned risky, especially for kids.'

'Wow. Well, thanks, Hamish. That's all very useful info. Look, we must get together for dinner again soon . . .' Mel was trying to work out how quickly she could get off the line to see if all the things Hamish had said were true. Could it really be that easy?

'Okay,' said Hamish, and she could hear the hesitation in his voice. It sounded almost like suspicion. 'Chat soon. Oh, and Mel?'

'Yes?'

'You wouldn't be thinking of doing something silly, would you?'

'I don't know what you mean.'

'I know you're worried about Serena. I know she's shutting you out. But . . . well . . . if she felt you had betrayed her trust . . . the damage it would do . . . It would be crazy to do anything that might make her feel that way, wouldn't it?'

'Of course,' said Mel. 'Of course. I would never do that.'

She forced herself to ask a few friendly questions about Hamish's cottage, and they made a vague date for a few weeks' time and then said their goodbyes.

It was an insane idea, Mel thought. Hamish was right. But somehow, the scheme wouldn't go away. Could she do this? Should she? And if she did do it, what would her alter ego be called? Lauren Smith. She didn't know why – the name just popped into her head. She chose a date of birth, making the fictional Lauren about six months older than Serena. She went into Hotmail to create an email address. (Hamish was right – it took seconds.) Within minutes, she had added the email address and been verified, and Lauren Smith, aged sixteen, had a Facebook profile. She added her to the network for a nearby school, one with a large student body. Now for a profile pic. She fetched her old albums from the bookshelf and leafed through until she found a photo of a long-forgotten university friend, a girl called Megan. They'd all gone to Brighton for a weekend and Megan had been standing on the beach, looking out to sea at sunset. She had long, straight blonde hair and she had been wearing a big floppy straw hat which partially obscured her face. The picture had the hazy, glowing retro look of those Instagram pictures. Mel chuckled: it was the perfect image. She popped it on the scanner and uploaded it. She'd need more pictures, but that would take time. She also knew if she added Serena as her first friend, Serena would smell a rat and refuse the friendship request, so she clicked on the profile of Serena's best friend, Marina, randomly picked thirty people off her list of friends, and sent them all a friend request. Some might say yes, some would ignore her, but she could begin to build a list of people of the right age from the right area.

She glanced at the clock. It was one in the morning. There was no glow of light shining out from under Serena's door so she must have gone to bed. Mel stood up and stretched. She had made a good start. She'd soon be able to have a good look at what was going on in Serena's life. She turned off her computer and all the lights, brushed her teeth and climbed into bed. As she was drifting off, she felt a moment of unease. What kind of mother spied on her child? She knew it was something many people would disagree with – Bruce, for one, would be horrified, and Hamish's reaction to the very idea had been negative. But she knew she was doing it out of love and concern. It was because she cared so much. She knew what it felt like to do without that concern, and even if Serena didn't seem to want it, she was sure it was for the best.

It took a few days, but she started to get a few friends. The boys she had requested were the first to accept. She decided Lauren was a big cat fan, so she added some images of cats with funny slogans and a few statuses about maths homework and the weather. She found a couple of mass party pictures with loads of people from the local area tagged in them and tagged herself. She even found a free image on Google of a blonde girl running on a beach. You couldn't really see her face, so it could easily be the same girl as the one in her profile pic. The whole profile was slightly patchy, but beginning to look believable. Mel presumed that most teenagers weren't all that interested in the details of each other's lives; they were too busy obsessing about themselves. Certainly, no one seemed suspicious. She kept adding friends, and when she reached fifty, she risked sending a friend request to Serena.

She sent it late one evening, when Serena was already asleep. She checked Facebook sporadically during the following day, but Serena hadn't responded. That evening, Mel said barely anything over dinner. After they'd eaten, unusually Serena settled on the sofa to watch some US show on television. Mel went into the kitchen to wash up. She was jumpy as a cat, and kept glancing into the living room to see if Serena was still there. She made tea, and went through just as the show finished. She handed Serena a mug and sat down beside her on the sofa. 'How was your day?' she said chummily. 'Tell me about school. How is it?'

'Fine,' said Serena, and immediately got up to go to her room. Bingo. The concerned-mum card worked every time.

As soon as she heard Serena's door close, she switched on her own machine and logged into Lauren's profile. She sat staring at it for a good ten minutes, willing something to happen. Would Serena see through it? Would she just ignore the request? Serena wasn't a stupid girl. Mel had all but given up when a little red notification popped up. She clicked on it, her hand trembling on the mouse. 'Serena Grey has accepted your friend request'.

She wanted to cheer. Any feelings of guilt she pushed firmly to the back of her mind. What she was doing was for Serena's own good. She wanted her to be safe, that was all. She went on to Serena's profile immediately. Right at the top of the page she saw it: 'Serena Grey is in a relationship with Jason "Triggah" Cook'. Serena's wall was full of posts from school friends, candid photos from parties and school, and a very high proportion of messages from this Jason 'Triggah' Cook.

So Serena had a boyfriend. She had suspected as much, but now she knew. She ignored the pain in her heart that something so enormous had happened in her daughter's life, and Serena had chosen not to share it. She clicked through to Triggah's profile. Thoroughly locked down. His profile picture was an image of the one from X-Men with the weird spectacles, so she didn't even know what he looked like. She sent him a friend request. She'd have to wait to learn a little more about this guy.

17

LEE NOW/THEN/NOW, JO NOW

Lee now

Lee's boss, Anna, had her head in her hands. In Lee's experience of the working world, walking into your boss's office and finding her with her head in her hands was never good. It meant either she'd done something wrong, or you had, or someone had, but if it was a headache for your boss, it was going to be a headache for you. 'Anna?' he said softly. She looked up, and the expression on her face did nothing to boost his confidence.

'Lee, come in,' she said. 'What can I do for you?'

Anna was a few years younger than Lee. She was a fiendishly smart, Cambridge-educated woman who had started her career in advertising as a copywriter and had soon found her real strength lay in management. She had been an enormous success since she had taken over running the font foundry – she was shrewd, witty and charming, and the clients loved her. She kept a tight rein on every project, watching the budget and the deadlines like a hawk. She was always positive, motivating the team and getting the best out of everyone. To see her down and, Lee had to admit, looking scared, was distinctly worrying.

'I just wanted to check what time the brownie people are coming in.'

'Oh,' said Anna, and to Lee's horror, looked as if she might cry. 'The thing is, Lee, they're not coming.'

'Oh, did they reschedule? That's great. I wanted to try a new colourway.'

'No, they're not coming full stop. They've pulled the plug. They've lost the distribution deal with Tesco and the whole thing's on hold.'

'What?' said Lee blankly. 'How . . . ? What? Hell, Anna, what does that mean for us?'

The brownie account had been the best thing to happen to the company in months. Mrs Huston's Delightful Home-Made Brownies was a boutique brand of melt-in-the-mouth desserts, which would be distributed in supermarkets and delis around the country. They had come to the font foundry to have a bespoke typeface designed for their logo. They had loved the result so much they had asked the company to do all their packaging design and all the advertising. It was a massive account, the biggest the foundry had had in over a year, and it was going to save them all. And now it was gone.

'They'll pay us for what we've done so far,' Anna said, 'but that's not even a quarter of what we thought we'd be billing on this. It's a huge loss.'

'How huge?' Lee asked.

'Huge. I don't think anyone understands how close to the wind we've been sailing. But without the brownie money . . .'

'Jobs will be at risk?'

'I don't want to say too much,' said Anna, remembering her position. 'It's unprofessional, and it's not fair to dump this on you. We'll make it work, somehow.' But her smile, normally wide and infectious, was weak and completely unconvincing.

Lee went back to his desk and sat down. He'd had his head down, working furiously all morning, but without the brownie deal, he had nothing to do. He assumed there'd be housekeeping to handle soon: the final transfer of any files and suchlike, but that was not a job for now. He glanced at his watch. Ten to twelve was early for lunch, but what the hell. He grabbed his jacket and set off into the watery February sunlight. He got a sandwich and a cup of coffee and found a bench in the square. There were very few people out and about: it was early for the lunchtime crowd. There was a homeless man sleeping on the next bench, and a couple of trendy types in square-rimmed glasses talking loudly and pointing at an iPad . . . obviously some sort of out-of-office brainstorm. Nothing like a spot of cold and damp to focus the creative impulses, Lee thought wryly.

What he'd witnessed in Anna's office was serious. Even if she wouldn't say it, he knew they'd have to lay someone off. As senior designer, he thought his job was probably safe for now, but one, or maybe both, of the remaining juniors would have to go, and possibly some support staff as well. Awful news in these difficult times. There just weren't the jobs out there at the moment.

A young couple came into the square, the man pushing a pushchair. He was wearing a suit and tie, and his wife was more casually dressed. Lee guessed she had brought the baby in to visit Daddy at work and they were having an early lunch. Jo had often brought Zach in when he was small, but once Imi was born, she found the Tube journey with two kids and a pushchair too stressful, so she stopped. The mum sat down on a bench and unwrapped sandwiches, and the dad lifted the child out of the pushchair and swung him into his arms, swooping him round and making him fly like a plane. Lee smiled, seeing the delight on the little boy's face and hearing him chortle. He was used to being away from Zach and Imogene during the day, but seeing this sweet little red-faced chap made him miss them.

The mum had got up now, and all three of them were playing a silly game that involved one of the parents hiding behind a tree and jumping out to scare the little boy and the other parent. Lee found himself observing the yellowish rays of sunlight and the way the little boy's bright red coat stood out against the iron-grey trunks of the bare trees. It would make an amazing photograph, or even better, a spectacular painting. He scrabbled in his coat pocket and came out with a stubby IKEA pencil and a receipt from the sandwich shop where he had bought his lunch. Resting the scrap of paper on his thigh, he sketched the scene in outline. Maybe he could turn it into a little painting later . . . something in bright, opaque acrylics perhaps. He was dying to snap a photo with his phone, but he knew the couple would think he was some kind of freak, taking pictures of their kid. He'd have to remember the colours and details of the scene.

He supposed he should get back. Word of the brownie account would have filtered through the office and the mood would be dark. He really should go. He'd been away a good while, and the bench he was sitting on was freezing. But he couldn't bring himself to move.

Lee then

At nineteen, after a year of living in uni halls, Lee moved into a room in a house in New Cross, near the station and within walking distance of all of his lectures. The house was at the very bottom end of the range of student digs: draughty, cold, in poor repair, with black mould on the walls and ceilings in the bathroom and an immovable layer of sticky grime over everything in the kitchen. Lee didn't know or particularly like his housemates, but his room . . . he loved his room. He'd been lucky enough to get the big front bedroom. He paid a bit more than his housemates, but it was totally worth it. The room was enormous, with an expanse of bare wooden floor and a high ceiling, and an enormous bay window overlooking the street, which allowed light to pour in. The wallpaper was dingy and peeling in places, the window was not double-glazed and was so ill-fitting it let in icy winds and even rain, but the space and the light were amazing.

Lee didn't have much stuff: he had a single bed, which he kept pushed right into a corner, and his few clothes were neatly folded away in the small wardrobe he had brought from his parents' house. The room was always swept and dusted, and he had a little handheld floor polisher that he used once a week. He liked it to be neat and clean, but not for show, just because then he had all the expanse of floor ready to be covered in paper at a moment's notice. And it usually was. He spent every spare minute drawing and painting.

Sleep was a luxury Lee couldn't afford. There was so much to do. He loved his lectures and practical classes and devoured everything that he learned, but he believed that the only way he would develop as an artist was to keep creating. His brain went at a thousand miles an hour, bursting with ideas, overflowing with what-ifs, and he had to get them down on paper, or gather people to create collaborative works, or write, write, write into the night. He wanted to do everything, be everything, make everything. Other students around him saw uni as a time to get drunk and get laid, to cruise along doing as little work as possible in order to maximise the time for partying, but to Lee, that made no sense at all. He had a powerful sense of urgency . . . he couldn't shake the feeling that if he hadn't created a major artwork by the time he was thirty, it would all be over and he would be a failure. The problem was, he didn't know what form this artwork would take. He loved to draw, especially in charcoal, but then he also loved to paint in oils or acrylics: bold, bright works. He found theatre immensely inspiring, and music filled his soul. He wrote too, compulsively and prolifically. He had read somewhere that to get really good at something, you needed to spend ten thousand hours practising it. So if painting, drawing, music, writing and theatre were his five passions – imagine if he gave twelve hours a day to practising one of these. Fifty thousand hours, divided by twelve, divided by three hundred and sixty-five days in a year (weekends off were for wimps . . .) he would be proficient in roughly eleven and a half years' time. That would be too late. He'd be thirty-two and hopelessly past it. He needed to focus more. But how could he focus when he didn't know which of his passions he could be best at?

His mum had laughed when she'd come down from Pinner to visit him in his digs, bringing a basket of food and a blanket, because she knew he didn't have one and would never go out to buy one. 'Good grief, Lee!' she'd said when she saw the room. 'You're living like some kind of mad monk!'

'I love it, Mum,' he said defensively. 'I've got it just the way I want it.'

'Well, I can't imagine the girls are flocking to share it with you,' said Betty tartly. 'As for the rest of this house . . .' It seemed there were no words in Betty's schoolteacher vocabulary to finish that sentence. 'A flame-thrower's too good for it,' she said eventually.

'I know it's not smart or clean or anything,' said Lee earnestly, 'but I do such amazing work here. I think I could stay here forever.'

'Maybe, love. But life does move on. You're so sure about what you want now, but you might find that changes. Life has a way of making decisions for us.'

Lee now

No point in getting up now, Lee thought. He felt certain that his bum had actually frozen to the bench and he'd do himself an injury if he stood up suddenly. The couple with their toddler were long gone and the square was beginning to fill with local workers, grabbing a few minutes of sunshine over lunchtime.

Life had made a load of decisions for him, he thought. Skinny, Afro-headed nineteen-year-old Renaissance Man would have despised thirty-seven-year-old font-designer Lee, with his suburban home and family and secure job. He'd have called him a total sell-out, and while Lee would defend to the hilt every choice he had made, his concern was not the choices he had made, but the ones he hadn't. He had willingly chosen his career path, his marriage to Jo and his children, and he wouldn't change any of that. But he hadn't chosen to give up on being an artist. That had just happened. Somewhere along the line, his dreams of creating something arresting, meaningful and beautiful had fallen by the wayside. And here he was, on the cusp of middle-age, sitting on a bench in Über-trendy Hoxton, worrying about brownie packaging. Well, if the deadline for doing something awesome by the time he was thirty had passed him by, what about setting a new deadline? What about forty? Maybe it was time to change the course of his life, forcibly and dramatically. And in the process, could he help Jo to realise her dreams too?

Gingerly Lee stood up from the bench. His legs were stiff and cold. He shook them out and walked briskly around the square three times. Then he went back to work, walked into Anna's office and said, 'Can we talk about voluntary redundancy?'

*

'You fucking what?' Jo exploded, when he told her that evening, after the kids had gone to bed. 'My God, Lee, have you lost your mind? You can't just chuck in your job on a whim. You know what the market's like – there are no other jobs out there. We've got a mortgage to pay . . . I can't believe . . .' She stopped, quite clearly at a loss for words.

'Okay, firstly, I didn't chuck in my job. I said to Anna that I might consider voluntary redundancy, but I would have to talk to you.'

Jo took a deep breath. 'So talk.'

Lee sat and looked at his hands for a minute. 'I think . . . sometimes the universe, or God, or whatever, gives us a sign that it's time to make a change. And I think we've had loads of signs over the last while and I don't want to ignore them.'

'Like what?'

'Like you starting the shop and loving it, but feeling torn between that and the kids. Me loving spending time with the kids. The offer from Richard Anthony. Trouble at work for me; we lost the brownie account.'

'The brownie account? Why?'

'Tesco pulled out, so the whole thing's on hold.'

'Anna must be gutted.'

'She is. I know she's going to have to let someone go, and I also know it probably wouldn't be me . . . it would be some of the juniors and I know how desperately they need their jobs.'

'Lee, *you* desperately need your job! We need it. I don't see how you think we're going to—'

'What if you take Richard up on his offer?'

'And what? Become a high-powered career woman who sticks her children in childcare sixty hours a week? Which we pay for *how*? I might ask.'

'What if we don't? What if I stay home with them? You could work as hard as you wanted to and not feel a moment's guilt, because I'd be the stay-at-home parent. Imi wouldn't even need to go to the childminder any more. Anna said that if I did decide to leave, she'd want to retain me as a freelancer, and I'm sure I'd be able to get a few other free-lance clients, so I wouldn't be bringing in nothing.'

'But I would still feel guilty, because it wouldn't be me looking after them.'

'Jo . . .'

'I know. I know it's ridiculous.'

'It is. The kids may like the idea of a stay-at-home parent but they do have two parents, and it could be me just as well as you. Now you're not breastfeeding, I can do every-thing for them that you do. I've loved the time I've had with them since you started working on the shop. They love being with me too.'

'I know they do,' Jo said, a little miserably.

'You don't have to sound so sad about it. Could this be Jo the control freak creeping in here?'

'You don't have to sit there being right all the time.' Jo managed a weak smile. 'So if we did it – *if*, mind you, I'm not convinced yet . . .'

'You'd be able to focus on growing the business to its full potential and it would give me space to do some of the things I want to do.'

'What do you want to do?'

'I . . . I want to be an artist, Jo,' Lee said quietly, as if he was confessing some kind of shameful deviance to his wife.

'You are an artist.'

'I'm not. I'm a crayon mercenary. A scribbler for hire. I want to do something that's real, that comes from the heart. The kind of stuff I was starting to do at university, except then I had no life experience and even less technique.'

'So what kind of thing?'

'I don't know yet. But I think if I'm at home, if my brain is free of day-to-day work stuff and I have some space and quiet, I'll begin to understand what it is.' He smiled wryly. 'Renaissance Man rises again, eh?'

Jo raised an eyebrow at this, but she didn't comment further. Maybe Lee would be able to manufacture more space and quiet in the average day looking after two toddlers and a home than she could.

'Let me think about it, okay?' she said finally. 'It's a big step, and I don't think it's a decision we can make right now.'

She got up and went into the kitchen to do the washing-up. As she scrubbed at a frying pan, she thought about what Lee had said. It was an astonishing, audacious and wonderful proposition. She couldn't imagine any of the other husbands of her acquaintance making an offer like that – to be a stay-at-home dad so their wife could pursue a career dream. Could they make it work? Who knew? If she could get past her own stubborn, egotistical need to be everything to everyone, if she could take a step back and let Lee do what she knew he was perfectly capable of doing, maybe they could. It was a huge decision though. They shouldn't make it right away.

But now, she thought as she rinsed out the sink and dried her hands, right now she would spend some time holding and loving her wonderful husband, because he was a gem beyond price, and he deserved to know it.

Jo now

'You'll be divorced within a year,' said Jo's mother abruptly. 'A house husband? Lee? Pottering about in a pinny doing your laundry? Running around after the children? No man would stand for that.'

'But it was his idea.'

'Of course it was. He's always indulged your every whim. He's just trying to make you happy.' Jo's mother snorted, as if trying to make someone happy was an aberration, or a weakness.

At that exact moment, Imogene fell over and bumped her head against the edge of the sofa, and Jo thanked her little girl silently. There was no way she would have been able to answer her mother without losing her temper.

It wasn't just geographical distance that prevented Jo from visiting her parents often, though it was convenient to pretend it was. It was conversations like these. Her father was a taciturn man, who very seldom offered an opinion on anything, but her mother always had something to say, and it was almost always critical. Jo dreaded visiting with the kids, because she knew her mother would criticise the way they were dressed, what they ate, their manners, the way Jo spoke to them, not to mention offering a thought or two on Jo's appearance. Jo's mother had always parented with a fine balance of bullying and guilt, and she always knew best.

It was for that exact reason that Jo had come here today. In a fit of masochism, she wanted to ask her mother's opinion on the proposed plan for Lee to give up his job and Jo to take up Richard's offer to expand her company. She knew that her mother would predict the worst possible outcome, and wouldn't hold back from articulating the worst of the things that Jo herself might fear. So far, Laura Morris had not disappointed. It wasn't enough for her to imply that Jo was a spoiled brat who was hell-bent on emasculating her husband. Clearly she wanted to break her children's hearts as well.

'What about Zachary and Imogene?' she asked plaintively. (Zach's name on his birth certificate was just Zach, not Zachary, but she refused to call him anything else.) 'Imagine how they'll feel when all the other children have their mum come and collect them from school and they're left with their dad? Everyone will think Lee is some kind of unemployed layabout.'

'Will they? And if they do, do we care?' Jo couldn't resist saying.

Her mother gave her one of her Looks. It was a brilliant maternal Look, which incorporated disappointment, pity and disapproval in a single glance. The Look used to devastate Jo, but she was kind of over it now.

'Really, Joanna,' Laura said. 'You don't seem to be taking this seriously at all.'

Jo's father chose that moment to wander into the kitchen.

'What isn't Joanna taking seriously?' he said. 'Is it laundry related? Or anything to do with potty-training? If it's either of those, I'm going back into the living room to watch the golf.'

Jo opened her mouth to answer, but she should have known better than to try. Her mother was much quicker off the mark than she could ever be. 'Joanna has come up with a hare-brained scheme where she goes off and becomes a high-powered career woman' – Laura said 'high-powered career woman' in much the same way she might say 'street-walker' – 'and she's making Lee give up his job and stay at home to babysit the children.'

'Firstly,' said Jo, hating herself for rising to the bait, 'it was Lee's idea to give up work, not mine. Secondly, I've had a significant offer of investment and help to grow my business and it's a great opportunity, and lastly, a father does not *babysit* his own children.'

'Do you want to take up this investment offer?' said Jo's father.

'Yes,' said Jo, rather surprising herself. 'Yes, I do. I'm proud of Jungletown, and I'm flattered that someone else sees so much potential in it. And I think if I didn't go for it, I would spend the rest of my life wondering what might have happened.'

'And Lee offered to give up working?'

'His company is in trouble. If he takes voluntary redundancy, he'll get a reasonable payout, because he's been there so long, and he'll still do some freelance work for them. He mainly sees it as an opportunity to pursue some projects of his own though.'

'Projects like what?' Jo's mother cut in.

'Artistic projects,' said Jo, expecting and getting a disdainful maternal sniff.

'Moneywise?' said her father, always a man of few words.

'The offer I've had on the business would pay me a regular salary. That's something I haven't been able to take so far. It'd be slightly more than Lee currently earns, plus we'll have Lee's payout and anything he brings in as a freelancer, and if Imi doesn't go to the childminder, that saves us quite a bit too. We'd actually be a little better off.'

'Hmm,' said Jo's father. 'Well, I don't see a problem.' Jo's mum blustered and made all sorts of noises, but she knew she had lost the argument.

Jo resisted the urge to cheer. It wasn't that she needed her father's approval, and it wasn't just from saying it all out loud, hearing her mother's objections and defending against them. The whole thing had made her realise that not only was the plan possible, it was something she really wanted to do. She wanted to take this new leap of faith in her life with Lee. It was huge, it was scary, it was potentially risky, but she wanted to do it, and she was so excited now she could barely wait to get home, grab Lee's hand and jump.

PART THREE

18

HOLLY NOW

Holly had not slept for four straight nights. Judith's pain medication made her restless and she groaned and cried out through the night, even though most of the time she was still asleep. Holly had moved rooms, into the bedroom next door to her mum's, and contrary to the family habit of a lifetime, they slept with both doors open so she could hear Judith if she needed her. Because there was no way to tell if Judith was calling her or merely shouting out in her dreams, Holly got up every time she heard her. For the last four nights, she had been up pretty much every hour. It wasn't even as if she had the days off to sleep and relax: she was still trying to get work done, and the house was still like a train station with medical personnel coming in and out, and a stream of people from Judith's church.

Holly was an atheist, but she had a grudging admiration for the effort the church people made. There seemed to be a rota, and someone came to visit every morning and evening. They never came empty-handed – everyone brought food. It wasn't as if Judith ate anything really, and Holly hadn't cooked for herself in weeks, but as twice a day, a meal for roughly four people was delivered, she couldn't keep up. There was so much food that the fridge and freezer were full and Holly had begun to palm dishes off on Miranda, on Mel and Jo, in fact on anyone who stood still for more than five minutes.

One morning, she found herself standing in the kitchen, staring blankly at an enormous apple crumble on the kitchen table. She had no idea where to put it. The fridge was crammed, the freezer was full and it was too warm in the house to leave it out. It smelled delicious, but she'd already had breakfast: one of the other church ladies had brought a basket of warm croissants. She could hear the soft sound of singing from Judith's room. There were four or five women up there, singing and praying around the bed. Holly's mobile rang. She answered without looking to see who it was.

'Hi, Holly,' said a male voice, deep and quite attractive. 'Are we still on for eleven?'

Eleven? Who was she supposed to meet? Was it work or a social engagement? How could she have made a date with Mr Nice Voice and not remembered it? And who was it? She pulled the phone away from her ear and glanced at the screen to see if caller ID could help. Daniel. Daniel? Did she know a Daniel? She must, if the name and number were stored on her phone.

'Um, eleven . . .' she said slowly, her brain befuddled with lack of sleep. She was too sluggish to make small talk to buy her a bit of time.

'If eleven isn't convenient, I can come earlier or later. I just got a car so I'll be driving over with all the samples.'

Daniel! Monkeyman T-shirt Daniel! Of course! Now she

remembered that they had made an arrangement weeks before for him and Chris to bring her a selection of new T-shirt designs to choose from. She felt awful. She knew the Jungletown contract meant so much to Outtake, and this meeting would be something Daniel and Chris would have worked hard to prepare for. She felt doubly bad because the shop did need new T-shirt stock. Postponing the meeting would let Jo down as much as it would the boys.

She snapped into action. 'Look, Daniel, I don't know if you know, but I've had something of a family crisis recently. My mum's ill . . .'

'Oh, I'm sorry,' said Daniel quickly. 'I didn't know. Would you like to reschedule? I completely understand.' He tried to sound professional, but Holly could hear the disappointment in his voice.

'No, no, no. I just wanted to say, if you don't mind, could you come to my house in Ealing instead of us meeting at the shop?'

'No problem. Give me your address and postcode. I have a satnav, so it'll be easy to get there. What about parking?'

'There are no restrictions in our road,' said Holly, grateful that he was being flexible and nice about the whole thing. If they were coming to see her at home, that meant she had a good hour to shower, drink two cups of coffee and wake up. And by eleven, the church singing should have stopped and her mum would likely be having a nap.

The best-laid plans, however, are so often thwarted. She was on her way up the stairs to shower, second cup of coffee in hand, when the doorbell went. It was two blokes who had parked their extremely large delivery van across the driveway. Another gift from David, Holly surmised. She wished her brother would let her know when stuff was arriving. He was obviously feeling guilty that he wasn't able to spend much time with his mum, so he kept throwing money at the problem. He'd sent a sheepskin mattress cover to prevent bedsores, a massage pad, and a walking frame to help Judith to get into and out of the shower. The latest offering was a simply enormous recliner chair with a motor, so that if the person sitting in it was too weak to stand up by themselves, the seat would tilt from horizontal to vertical and lift them into a standing position. It was a very thoughtful gift and must have cost a lot, and Holly was sure Judith would be grateful, if she ever came down into the living room to sit in it. But however wonderful the chair was, it was sodding gigantic and extraordinarily heavy, and it took two deliverymen fifteen minutes of huffing, puffing, manoeuvring and swearing to get it into the house. Holly knew Judith would worry about the paintwork in the hall, so she darted around nervously, trying to stop them scuffing every surface on their way in. Once it was finally in the living room, one of them insisted on explaining to Holly how it worked. He did this extremely slowly, pointing at the pictures in the brochure as if she was a slightly backward small child. Two or three times, he said, 'Just give the instruction book to your hubby, and he'll get it going.' Just standing next to the delivery chauvinist made her eyes water. The man was clearly a stranger to the morning shower and to antiperspir- ant. So while she would have loved to take the instruction booklet, roll it up and shove it where the sun don't shine, she wasn't getting any closer than she absolutely needed to.

He then produced a wodge of paperwork, pulled a pen from behind his ear and ponderously insisted on her initialling each page and signing to show she had received the chair in good order. Through all of this, Holly kept glancing nervously at the carriage clock on the mantelpiece. Daniel and Chris would be arriving in a very short time, and she was still unshowered, her teeth were unbrushed and her hair was scraped into a scruffy topknot. She was also wearing holey tracksuit bottoms and an ancient faded red T-shirt, and she was, she realised from the goggle-eyed stare of the deliveryman's gormless mate, braless.

Once she had shoved Stinky Hardy and his pervy friend Laurel out of the door, she headed for the stairs again. Surely the church ladies must be on their way soon. But it seemed they were well in the groove, because the singing reached a new, almost gospel fervour, and she could hear someone proclaiming loudly as they sang and prayed. She tiptoed to the top of the stairs. Could she make a dash to her bedroom to grab some clothes without being seen? And what if the boys arrived when she was in the shower? Would the church ladies know to let them in, and would they terrify the living daylights out of them? She'd better skimp on the shower and just brush her teeth and tidy herself up . . . and put on a bra. She was going to be meeting with two hormonal teenage boys. For the love of God, definitely put on a bra.

She stepped on to the top step, remembering too late that it creaked. Naturally, it did so in a rare moment of silence in the prayer-and-song marathon in her mum's room. She'd have to make a run for it. She was in mid-scuttle when someone popped out of her mum's bedroom. Holly's heart sank. It would have to be Angela, a large-boned Nigerian lady of formidable temperament. Angela would stare you down through her thick, Dame Edna spectacles and would tell you what you thought about anything. She was also very hands-on. 'Oh, Holly,' she boomed, and grabbed both of Holly's hands firmly in her own, 'you are suffering so much. You are crying for your mother day and night. I know. I know.'

'Oh, I—' said Holly weakly, trying to claim back her hands and failing.

'She is bad, your mother. What do the doctors say? It will not be long. I know this.'

'They don't know—'

'Of course they don't know. Doctors know nothing. Only God knows. And God is calling her. He told me.'

Holly didn't even attempt to answer this. She was quite sure that if anyone was being told what to do in Angela's relationship with the Lord, it was God doing the listening.

'I will pray for you in your suffering,' Angela announced and, keeping an iron grip on Holly's right wrist, placed a heavy hand on Holly's forehead, closed her eyes and began to intone, 'Oh Father, look upon this poor girl, so broken with grief that she is not even dressed at eleven in the morning, and be merciful . . .'

God was listening, it seemed, and He was merciful, because at that exact second, the doorbell rang. 'I'm so sorry,' breathed Holly, and slipped out from under Angela's weighty hand. 'I have to get that. Um . . . Amen.'

There was no time to go to her room and tidy up. She ran down the stairs, and took a moment to tidy her hair and rearrange her T-shirt so it was slightly less apparent that she was hanging free, as it were. Daniel and Chris would have to come in and then excuse her for a moment or two. She opened the door, and was a little surprised to see only Daniel there. He noticed her glancing past him, and said, 'Oh, it's just me. Chris is back at the workshop, printing T-shirts for a band. I hope that's okay.'

'It's fine,' said Holly, smiling tightly, very conscious of her unbrushed teeth. 'As you can see, I'm not really . . .'

'You said your mum's ill . . .'

'Yes. She's upstairs and some of her church friends are there. This morning things have all gone a bit mad . . .'

As if to confirm this, Angela boomed, 'Hallelujah!' from the bedroom upstairs. It was so loud that Daniel jumped a little and a dog across the road barked. Holly couldn't help but giggle, and that made Daniel laugh too. 'Look, come in,' she said. 'I'm so sorry it's like this. Go through into the kitchen. The tea things are all out on the countertop – help yourself, and give me ten minutes upstairs to sort myself out, okay?'

'Okay,' he smiled, and bent to pick up the box of T-shirts at his feet. She pointed him in the direction of the kitchen and then raced upstairs. Not even Angela could stop her now. She dashed into her bedroom and grabbed a pair of jeans, underwear and a top, then whisked into the bathroom and locked the door. She took two minutes in the shower, brushed her teeth, tidied her hair, put some clothes on and was back downstairs well within the ten-minute limit.

To her surprise, she found Daniel up to his elbows in the sink, washing up the dirty cups, plates and mugs that seemed to multiply alarmingly every day in the kitchen, even though Holly herself hardly ever had time for a hot drink and her mum never wanted one. 'You didn't have to . . .' she said.

'It's no bother.' He smiled at her over his shoulder. 'My grandpa was ill for about two years . . . emphysema. We spent a lot of time at his house. There was always something going on – carers, or someone helping him with oxygen, or deliveries – and the one thing I could do to help and stay out of the way was wash up. It always needed doing.'

'Emphysema? I'm so sorry. That must have been very hard for you to see.'

Daniel nodded. 'It's horrible, listening to someone gasp for breath, and eventually just run out of air. Awful.'

'Was he a smoker?'

'Two packs a day for forty years. I tell you what, I don't need warnings on the pack to tell me how bad it is.'

'So I'm guessing you don't smoke.'

'No way.' Daniel smiled. 'Never have, never will. Well, except for the occasional . . .' He touched his thumb and forefinger to his lips and narrowed his eyes, and then grinned at Holly.

'Ah,' said Holly, understanding.

From upstairs, Angela let rip with an echoing and extended 'Aaaamen,' and the other women echoed it. Holly giggled. 'Did you have the Amen Brigade coming to see your grandfather too?'

'No, he was a socialist and an atheist. He wouldn't even let the parish priest through the door.'

Angela launched into a heartfelt rendition of 'Kumbaya'.

'He wouldn't have been able to say no to Angela,' said Holly, pointing to the ceiling. 'Nobody does.'

Daniel rinsed the last cup and put it on the dish rack, dried his hands and came over to the table. 'I made you a cup of tea,' he said. 'I hope that's okay.'

He had wiped down the kitchen table too, and laid out the new T-shirt samples neatly in rows for her to see. Holly found herself looking at him closely. He was just nineteen, she thought, but he seemed older. He was quiet and considerate, not all over the place and self-obsessed like so many teenagers were. He was a lovely kid. His parents must be very proud.

She turned her attention to the T-shirts. She picked up each one and examined every seam and every detail of the design. The quality of the shirts themselves was better than the first batch Chris and Daniel had done. The designs were a mixed bag: some were too edgy for small children, but a few were great. Monkeyman seemed to have acquired a sidekick called Super Squirrel, and the Super Squirrel T-shirts, all printed in white on bright red, green and cyan backgrounds, were surefire winners. Holly rather fancied one for herself. 'You should so do these in adult sizes,' she said, holding a crimson shirt against her front. She looked up and caught Daniel staring at her chest. He looked up and caught her eye and blushed a deep red. Bless him, Holly thought. Under the composed exterior, he was just another horny young guy.

She made sure to keep her distance and act in a quietly professional manner for the rest of their meeting. She didn't want to make him feel uncomfortable. She selected some designs and sat down and wrote an order for the sizes and colours she wanted there and then. Holly knew that Daniel and Chris were still running their little business on a shoe-string and that there was no way he could carry the cost of the order without payment upfront. She rang Jo and told her the value of the order, and Jo said she would transfer fifty per cent of the payment straight into Outtake's account. When she told Daniel, he looked extremely relieved. He packed up the samples, and Holly walked him to the door. 'Oh wait!' she said suddenly. 'I bet you and Chris could take care of something for me.' She dashed back into the kitchen and returned with the apple crumble. 'There isn't room for this anywhere in the house. Please eat it, and get the dish back to me sometime, okay?'

'Thanks so much, Holly,' he said, taking the apple crumble. 'As always, it's a pleasure to do business with you.' She smiled at his formal tone. But then he dipped his head and looked at her with big serious eyes. 'I know how hard it is, what you're going through,' he said hesitantly. 'With my grandpa it was very difficult, and really long. So if you need anything, anything at all, even if it's just to get out for a little while, go for a drink, talk . . . I'm there, okay?' He managed to embarrass himself again with this little speech, so he blushed once more, gave her a sweet smile and sauntered off down the path. His visit had made Holly feel so much better she couldn't quite believe it – and not only because they had got the T-shirt order out of the way.

The next few days were gruelling. Judith's pain relief seemed to have stopped working, and very suddenly she seemed to have become weaker. Holly rang their GP, who made a rare home visit. She spent a long time with Judith and then came to find Holly, who was sitting at her computer at the kitchen table trying to work. 'The medication she's on isn't working as we'd hoped,' said the doctor. 'And I don't want to up the dose because there will be side effects. I think it's best if you go and see the palliative-care experts at the hospice.'

'The hospice?' said Holly, and she couldn't hide the wobble in her voice.

'They're the experts at this. They can make her as comfortable as possible and work out a pain regime that works better and has fewer side effects.'

Holly nodded, shaken. She hadn't imagined they would need the hospice so soon.

'It's not a bad place,' said the doctor soothingly. 'Odd though it sounds, it's quite cheerful. You both might like it there.'

Holly thought that was unlikely, but she sat there while the doctor rang the hospice and made an appointment for them for the following day. She took down the details and agreed she'd get her mum there for ten. She remembered her talk with Fraser about the hospice. How was he? she wondered. There was no point in dwelling on it. He hadn't rung her, and she certainly didn't have time to ring him at the moment.

The hospice was at the hospital itself, and Holly drove them there in the morning. Just getting Judith into and out of the car and into the hospital made her realise how weak her mum had become in just a short time. Judith leaned heavily on her arm, and walking from the car to the reception area seemed to wear her out completely. She was pale and shaking as they came through the door. 'Can I just sit down for a moment, dear?' she said softly. Holly glanced at her watch nervously. Their appointment was in two minutes and she wasn't sure where in the hospital they needed to be. How was she going to get Judith there? She went to the reception desk, and waited to speak to the harassed-looking woman who was simultaneously talking on the phone, trying to enter details into a computer and arguing with a persistent man who wanted change for the parking and wouldn't take no for an answer. Holly touched the man on the arm.

'Do you need change for a fiver? Here.' The doctor had warned her about the parking charges, so she had gone to the bank and got a ton of pound coins in preparation. The man grabbed the coins, thrust his crumpled five-pound note into her hand and thumped off without saying thank you. Holly stepped up to the counter. The woman was now typing at breakneck speed, with the phone wedged between her ear and her shoulder. It was clear from her side of the conversation that she was placing some kind of supplies order. She didn't look up or acknowledge Holly's presence. Holly stood there for about a minute, then glanced nervously over at Judith, who was sitting tipped slightly to one side, as if she didn't even have the energy to straighten up. 'Excuse me . . .' Holly said hesitantly.

The woman looked up at her as if she had done something unmentionable on her desk. 'Can you not see I'm busy?' she said sharply.

'I can, but—'

'Stand behind the line and wait,' the woman barked. Holly took a step back in surprise. Clearly courtesy was too much to ask. They were now several minutes past the appointment time, and Holly was afraid they wouldn't be seen. She would feel awful if she had dragged Judith all the way here and they had to go back home again without sorting out the pain regime. She took a step forward again. 'Look, I'm sorry to disturb you,' she said firmly, 'but my mother over there has cancer, and we're here to attend the palliative-care clinic at the hospice. Could you please just tell me where to go? Or would you like me to fill out one of these staff-assessment surveys?' There was a stack of cards with tick boxes on the counter, and she picked up the top one and showed it to the woman. The woman took the phone away from her ear and glared at Holly. She opened her mouth to speak, but Holly cut in. 'And before you accuse me of being rude and abusive, I have been neither. I've just asked you to do your job, pleasantly and politely, and to help a sick person.'

The woman looked long and hard at Holly, obviously weighing up the chances that she would make an enormous fuss if she resisted further.

'The hospice is outside, behind this building. You need to go to the end of that corridor, turn left, take the lift down to the basement, then go out of the exit doors, left at the end of the path and the hospice building will be in front of you.' Holly looked down the corridor. It looked long. Impossibly long if she had to get Judith to walk down it, and then there were lifts and paths and more to contend with. The woman saw her expression, looked over at Judith and said abruptly, 'You'd better put her in a wheelchair. They're over there.' And then to dispel any notion that she was showing an iota of compassion, she added, 'Health and safety.'

A wheelchair. It made sense, but it made Holly's heart ache. Judith had always been so poised, so straight-backed, and putting her in a wheelchair would make her seem like a sick old woman. It was a realistic solution though. Holly went over to the row of chairs and fetched one, which she pushed over to where Judith was sitting and engaged the brakes.

'Mum, it's quite far to the hospice, so I thought it might be easier . . .' She began to explain, but Judith seemed relieved.

'Thank you, dear. I was hoping you'd get one.'

She levered herself out of the chair she was sitting in and sat unsteadily in the wheelchair. Holly helped her to get her feet up on the footrests. Her ankles were so thin it was a wonder they could hold her up at all, and her feet, always slim and elegant, were heavily veined and very cold. Holly swallowed hard, brushed her hand over her eyes and straightened up. 'We'd better get going, we're late already,' she said brightly, and began to push Judith down the long corridor.

They were alone in the lift, and Holly took a moment, standing behind Judith, to take a few deep breaths so she'd be composed and not weepy when they arrived. Judith turned her head slightly and glanced up at her, and Holly managed a small smile. 'You're doing a fine job, Holly,' Judith said quietly. 'I don't know what I'd do without you.'

Holly gave her mother's bird-like shoulder a little squeeze as the lift doors opened.

The hospice, once they found it, was surprisingly bright and airy, with pot plants and prints of Impressionist paintings on the walls. It didn't feel overly medical. The receptionist here was the antithesis of the woman downstairs: she smiled at them both warmly. 'You must be Judith,' she said. 'Welcome.'

'I'm so sorry we're late . . .' Holly began.

'Not to worry. We know parking and getting here can sometimes be a bit of a nightmare. Judith, shall I take you through? The nurse is ready to see you, and is this your . . . daughter?'

'Yes, this is Holly,' said Judith.

'Holly, maybe you'd like to help yourself to a cup of tea or coffee?' The woman smiled again, and pointed to where Holly would need to go. She came out from behind her desk to take charge of the wheelchair. Holly hesitated for a moment. Maybe she should go with Judith? But Judith reached back and patted her hand.

'You wait here, Holly dear. I'll be fine. And I'll ask the nurse to write everything down for you.'

The woman took Judith off into a nearby consulting room. Holly wandered in the direction the woman had indicated. She found herself in an open lounge area, lit by a big skylight. There was a table set up in the corner with tea and coffee supplies and plates of biscuits, and a comfortable-looking seating area with a selection of magazines, books, and toys. In the middle of the room there was a circle of tables where a group of eight people were having a watercolour painting class. Someone had set up a simple still life in the middle of the circle. There was a round stool draped in a cloth, with a loose arrangement of fruit and flowers on it, and the people were all having a go at reproducing the arrangement with varying degrees of success. From the wigs, hats and bald heads in the circle, Holly guessed these were cancer patients. She didn't want to interrupt, so she edged her way over to the table and made herself a cup of coffee as unobtrusively as possible.

As she stirred her coffee, one of the students pushed her chair back and said, 'That's me. I don't think Vermeer's going to be bothered by my incursion into the still-life market any time soon.'

The woman got up and came over to the drinks table. She smiled at Holly. 'Could you pass me a custard cream?' she said. Holly held out the plate of biscuits and the woman took one, hesitated for a second and took another two. She was young, probably only a few years older than Holly herself. She was wearing a brightly coloured knitted hat, and Holly could see from her lack of eyebrows that she had no hair at all. She had a pretty, lively face and a wicked smile.

'Thanks. I'm Erin,' she said, holding out her hand.

'Holly, hi,' said Holly, shaking hands. 'I'm here with my mum . . .'

'She here for treatment?'

'Yes, they're trying to sort out her pain meds.'

'Ah, well, she's come to the right place. They're awesome here. With the last round of chemo I couldn't stop throwing up, so I came in and stayed for a few days and they sorted me right out.' Erin stirred some sugar into her coffee.

'I hope they can help her,' said Holly, and something about Erin's normal tone and matter-of-fact attitude made her feel wobbly again. Her hand was shaking so she put down her cup. Erin noticed and looked at her. 'You must be finding this all very hard. I often think it's just as difficult for the family and the carers.'

It was Holly's turn to stare. 'How can you say that? I'm not going through any of the things my mum is, or you are. None of the pain, none of the fear . . .'

'Well, it's not easy going through it, I'll give you that,' said Erin, 'but the other side can't be easy either. Seeing it all. Not being able to help. I think it's often the little things that freak people out. My mum was wonderful and very supportive when I had the mastectomy, but me losing my hair? She hated that. More than I do, to be honest.'

'I had to put my mum in a wheelchair to get her here,' said Holly. 'That freaked me out.'

'First time?'

'Yes. The worst part was, she wanted to use the wheelchair. She's always been so elegant, so genteel, but she sat in the wheelchair like an old, sick person.'

Holly was very aware that she was pouring out her problems to a woman with cancer . . . a woman her own age who would quite likely never be an old person. But Erin didn't seem to have a problem with that.

'You're going to have lots of moments like that,' she said, munching on her second custard cream. 'And you'll probably cry a lot and panic a lot. But there are also times to laugh. Life goes on, you know, if you'll pardon the cliché. I always thought that out of suffering comes great art, but

I tell you what, I can't be suffering nearly enough. Look at my painting! It looks like a dog crapped next to that apple!'

Holly followed Erin to her chair. Her painting was dreadful. So bad that Holly laughed, which delighted Erin.

'Wow, harsh!' she said delightedly. 'Everyone's a critic.'

'What made you take a watercolour class?'

'Oh, this isn't a class, just a weekly get-together. We come and do an activity of some kind, eat too many biscuits and bitch about our bowels and our sore feet . . . it's great! You should have been here the week we had the rookie volunteer who got us to do needlework. We had to make tapestry bookmarks.'

A few people in the group looked up and laughed at the recollection, and one of the other women said, 'Needlework? What the hell was she thinking?!'

'Why is that funny?' said Holly, confused.

'One of the side effects of some of the chemo drugs is a thing called peripheral neuropathy. Basically you lose sensation in your hands and feet,' Erin explained. 'So we were all stitching away, and we all kept stabbing ourselves in the fingers without knowing we were doing it.'

'Some of us have clotting problems too,' a bloke across the circle chipped in.

'It was a bloodbath!' chuckled Erin. 'We all thought it was hilarious, but she was mortified. She kept running around trying to patch us all up with gauze and plasters, and apologising like mad.'

And so it was that Holly found herself giggling with a group of dying people, when the nurse came out to speak to her. She turned around, mortified that she was being so frivolous in this place of heartache, but the nurse seemed to think it was all perfectly normal.

'Holly?' she said enquiringly.

'Yes, that's me,' said Holly, looking around for somewhere to put her coffee cup.

'Dump it on my painting,' Erin suggested. 'It can only improve it.'

'We've agreed with your mum that she should stay in here for a few days,' explained the nurse. 'Come through and see her. We're just settling her into her room.'

Holly followed the nurse through to a private room, where she found Judith being helped into bed.

'We're going to adjust her medication levels and try a few different options,' explained the nurse. 'We'll be trying to get her as comfortable as possible, and set up a regime you can continue with at home.'

Holly nodded. Judith already looked a little less strained. 'You okay, Mum?'

'Much better, thank you,' Judith said. 'But I don't have any of my things with me. Could you pop back home and bring me my bathroom things and a clean nightie or two, and my dressing gown and slippers?'

'Of course.'

'And, Holly, when you come back, do you think you might do my nails for me again?' She managed a smile, and whispered, 'I think I might be ready for the sparkly purple now.'

'Why, Judith Evans, you devil!' Holly smiled, and kissed her mum's soft cheek.

It took her an hour to drive home, pack everything into a bag and get back to the hospice. When she got there,

Judith was fast asleep, and for the first time in weeks, her face was relaxed, as if she was not in pain. Holly quietly unpacked Judith's things, putting her book and spectacles within easy reach and all of her toiletries neatly in the little private bathroom. She sat quietly by the bed for another half an hour or so, but Judith didn't wake up. She was getting the rest she so badly needed, so Holly scribbled a quick note to say she had been there and where everything was, and then she headed off.

It was strange to come home to the empty house. Holly couldn't help thinking that it wouldn't be all that long till Judith wouldn't ever be here again. Even though the morning at the hospice had made her feel a little better and stronger, the quiet in the house was oppressive. She resolved to pack a bag of clothes and go and stay in the flat in East Finchley for the few days till Judith came home again. She'd use the time when she wasn't visiting her mum to work in the shop and start making her flat a home.

She fired off a quick text to Miranda to update her on the situation, and she was busy packing her own things into a bag when the doorbell went. No doubt it was another church casserole. She considered not answering at all, but her conscience got the better of her, and she dashed down the stairs. She opened the door to a small, elegantly dressed man of about seventy. 'Good afternoon,' he said. 'Is Mrs Judith Evans receiving callers?'

'I'm afraid not,' said Holly. 'She's spending a few days in the hospital.' She didn't want to say 'hospice'. It seemed too scary and final. 'I can tell her you came by though. Who shall I say . . . ?'

'I do beg your pardon,' the man said formally. 'Christopher Benton. I'm an acquaintance of Judith's from the church.' He offered her his hand to shake. Holly couldn't help noticing his hands were soft and well cared for, and that he was very smartly turned out – crisp shirt, neat tie that looked like an old school one, a razor-sharp crease in his trousers and shoes polished to a high shine.

'I'm Holly, Judith's younger daughter,' she said. 'Would you like to come in for a cup of tea?'

'If it wouldn't be too much trouble,' said Mr Benton. 'I would like to hear how Judith is getting on.'

Holly took him through to the kitchen, which was mercifully clean and tidy. She didn't think he was a mug sort of man, so she made a pot of tea and got out two of Judith's china cups and saucers. Christopher Benton stood quietly by, and when she gestured to the kitchen table, drew out a chair, did that trouser-twitching thing old men do to preserve the creases, and sat down, straight-backed.

They exchanged a little halting small talk about the weather, but Holly could see that Mr Benton (she couldn't think of him as Christopher) was uncomfortable, and suspected that he was mustering up the courage to say something. She tried to give him an opening. 'So, have you known my mum long, Mr Benton?'

'Yes,' he said. 'Yes, for some years.' He paused, and carefully set his teacup back on the saucer. 'The thing is, Holly – may I call you Holly?'

'Of course.'

'Well, the thing is, until . . . some months ago, I would have said Judith and I were rather more than acquaintances. Or friends.'

Well, well, well. Holly was dying to ask a million questions, but instinctively she sensed the best way to proceed was to nod and let Mr Benton tell the story at his own pace.

'Judith and I met eight years ago, when I joined the church. I started to come to the services after my wife died. I liked the music, and the company, and I found it made a bit of a change in my routine. Everyone was very kind and welcoming, but when I first got to know Judith – it was during a Lent course of lectures about a year after I first joined – well, I felt I had met a kindred spirit. Someone with similar values. Of a similar . . . class.'

Holly could see why he would think that. Judith's genteel manner and quiet grace would certainly have appealed to an old-fashioned gent like Mr Benton. He continued. 'After we had known each other for a year or so, I ventured to invite her to a concert at the Wigmore Hall. And she accepted. We had a lovely time, and a week later, I invited her to another event, and that was most pleasant too. And so on.' He took a careful sip of his tea. 'We began to go out in the evening about once a fortnight, and to meet for a coffee or lunch once in a while. I liked to think we were . . . courting.' He managed a weak smile. Holly had never heard someone use the word 'courting' in an actual real-life conversation before. 'That sounds lovely,' she said encouragingly.

'Well, I thought so,' he said. 'But then, about eight months ago, everything changed. Judith suddenly began turning down my invitations. She kept making excuses. For example, she'd say that she had other things to do, or that she didn't want to see a particular film . . . I let it go for a while, and then one day, when she'd finally agreed to meet for a cup

of tea, I asked her if she had been avoiding me, and she said
. . . well, she said her daughter was coming back from South
Africa – I assume that's you . . .'

'Yes,' said Holly briefly, not wishing to interrupt his flow.

'And that she didn't think it was appropriate for her to
be . . . "dating", she called it, with her daughter in the house.
She told me not to ring her up any more, and that we would
just see each other at church.'

'Oh,' said Holly, really just to say something, and then
she closed her mouth, which had been hanging open in
shock.

'Well, yes. I was rather surprised, and I couldn't see that
an adult child would object to their widowed parent having
a companion—'

'I wouldn't have objected at all. Of course not. I would
have been thrilled for her,' said Holly.

'Well, that's what I thought. And I must confess, I was
rather upset and hurt. But then, when I heard about her
illness . . . well, first, I wanted to see her and say how sorry
I was. And secondly, when I thought about it, I realised that
might have been why she broke it off. Not because of you
at all, but because she knew she was ill.'

Holly nodded.

'I hadn't seen her at church for some weeks, but then
her name cropped up in the prayer list for the sick. I went
to ask the vicar, but he said he couldn't give me any details
. . . but then, when we were having coffee after the service
on Sunday, I overheard Angela Joba saying she'd been here,
praying for your mum, and I suspected that her illness must
be serious.' He looked to Holly for confirmation. She nodded.

'I thought that might be the case,' he said. 'And I thought long and hard about it, and I thought that even if she thinks she doesn't want me here, I want to be here. I want to offer my support. Even if she won't see me. Perhaps I could do some errands for you both. Shopping, or driving maybe.' He brightened suddenly. 'Perhaps I could do a little in the garden. I imagine you wouldn't have had time for that.'

'Oh, Mr Benton,' said Holly, 'that's very kind of you, but I wouldn't dream of—'

He cut her off. 'I would like to do something,' he insisted. 'Judith brought a ray of light into my life, and I've missed it very much. If she needs help, it would mean a great deal to me to be able to give it.'

Holly paused. 'Well, you're absolutely right. I haven't had time to do anything in the garden, and Mum does like to keep it neat.'

He nodded, satisfied. 'I'll come by with my gardening tools at the weekend, shall I? With spring on the way, there'll be plenty to do.'

He stood up then, happy to go, and thanked Holly very much for the tea. She saw him off down the path and watched him get into his car, a gleaming little dark green Rover, which he obviously kept in impeccable condition. He drew on his driving gloves and pulled slowly and carefully into the road. Holly waved him off, but as soon as he rounded the corner, she dashed back into the house and grabbed her mobile. Miranda answered on the second ring.

'Oh my God!' Holly began, without bothering even to say hello. 'Did you know Mum had a *boyfriend*?'

'A what?'

'A gentleman friend! A beau! A bit on the side!'

'No, she didn't!'

'She did! I just met him! He came over here!' Holly knew she sounded like an excited nine-year-old, but this was the first hint of fun, light-hearted news she'd had in ages. 'His name is Christopher Benton and he's a . . . what's the word? A very dapper gentleman. She knows him from church, and they've been going to films and concerts and dinner for years. He says he was "courting" her.'

Miranda gasped. 'Oh my word! Mum's often mentioned she was going out, but she always said, "I'm going with my friend from church," and I never asked who the friend was. I just assumed it was one of the ladies from the Mothers' Union.'

'Oooh, she's a dark horse.' Holly giggled.

'So what's he like?'

'Very trim, very, very smartly dressed, a little older than Mum, I'd say. Apparently about eight months ago, she broke it off. She told him it was because I was coming back from South Africa to live with her. But he thinks – and I agree – it's because she knew she was ill.'

'That makes sense,' said Miranda. 'She's very private.'

'Well, he wants to do stuff for her, even if she won't see him. He's offered to sort out the garden.'

Miranda sighed. 'That's so romantic . . . him toiling outside, gazing up at her window . . .'

'It's quite sad though, isn't it? I hope she will see him. He's obviously smitten with her.'

'Well, it's her choice; she might not want him to see her when she's so thin and ill-looking. She's very proud.'

'I know, but . . .' said Holly, and at that moment her phone bleeped. 'Randa, I've got another call coming in. Can I ring you back?'

'Not to worry. I've got things on the cooker. We can chat later,' Miranda said, and rang off.

Holly took her phone from her ear and was surprised to see that the incoming call was from Fraser. So surprised that she fumbled answering it and cut him off. Damn. She tried to ring him back, but it went straight to voicemail, no doubt because he was leaving a message for her. She waited impatiently for her message tone to bleep, so she knew he'd rung off. She didn't bother listening to his message, just rang him straight back.

'Sorry, being a phone klutz,' she said.

'You sound cheerful,' he said, and she felt a little fizz of excitement at his deep voice and the smile she could hear in it.

'Ah, I was just having a good gossip with my sister about our mother's secret boyfriend.'

'Sounds intriguing.'

'So, Dr John, what can I do for you?' Holly let her voice sound slightly flirtatious. Why the hell not?

'I was just ringing to check up on you. See how it was all going.'

'Well, it's going like terminal cancer, really,' said Holly bluntly. 'We're taking it one day at a time. She was struggling with pain, so she's staying at the hospice for a few days while they sort out her medication.'

'Sounds like a good idea,' said Fraser. There was a pause.

Seize the day, thought Holly. It wasn't as if she often had a free evening.

'So are you busy this evening?' she said casually. 'Fancy a bite of dinner?'

'You didn't listen to my message, did you?' said Fraser.

'No, I just rang you straight back.'

'I rang to ask you out for dinner. So great minds, obviously . . .'

Holly smiled to herself. 'Well, then we're in agreement. Dinner it is. Where would you like to go?'

'Also mentioned in my message. I thought if you'd spent time in South Africa, you might appreciate the little bistro near me, where they do traditional South African dishes, Malay curries and so on, and some lovely seafood. I don't know if you like seafood . . .'

'I love seafood, but you had me at Malay curry,' said Holly.

'I can pick you up,' said Fraser. 'Is seven okay? Are you up in East Finchley? Shop or flat?'

'I'm at my mum's place in Ealing, so not too far from you at all,' said Holly checking her watch. It was six already. 'Give me a bit of time to sort things out in the house though. Can we make it eight?'

Fraser agreed, she gave him the address and they rang off. Holly would have to move fast. There was nothing in the house for her to sort out, but any amount on herself that needed doing. Her personal grooming of late had left rather a lot to be desired. She needed to wash and blow-dry her hair, pluck her eyebrows, shave her legs . . . and as for her bikini line . . . Not that Fraser would be seeing her bikini line, but it didn't hurt to be neat and tidy.

She was lightning quick in the bathroom, and her hair, for once, was relatively well behaved. But finding something to wear was another matter. She hadn't been paying much attention to food, so she'd lost weight, and a few of her standby outfits designed to dazzle hung loose on her, especially around the boobs. Not a good look. She didn't have time to whip out the sewing machine and take anything in either. In the end, she went for jeans (her skinniest jeans, she was pleased to note), and a soft turquoise cashmere jumper. Her feet hadn't changed size, so she could go to town on the shoes. She didn't want to wear massive heels, as Fraser wasn't all that tall, so she went for her favourite soft brown leather boots, a gift from Damon when he went on a business trip to Florence. She had thrown out pretty much everything he'd given her, but the boots had been too beautiful to part with. She kept her make-up subtle and simple, and with ten minutes to spare, she went into her mother's bedroom to check out the ensemble in the full-length mirror on Judith's wardrobe door. It was odd being in Judith's room without her there. Holly resolved not to look at the bed, with the dent from Judith's head still in the pillow, or at the bedside table, which was laden with pill bottles and medical paraphernalia. It looked and smelled like the bedroom of a sick person. In a funny way, it was worse, because for as long as Holly could remember, her mum had always been very private about her room. The children weren't allowed in if she wasn't there, and she had always kept it neat and clean. Now it was the centre of the house and any number of people trooped in and out every day. That must be hard for her, Holly thought, and resolved to be firmer about keeping people out and keeping it tidy, as her mum would like it. She looked herself up and down one more time. She looked slim, well groomed and casual . . . a definite improvement on the last two times Fraser had seen her. The outfit was rather plain, though. It would definitely be enhanced with a piece of jewellery – not something quirky or gaudy, just a simple gold chain. Judith had just such a thing, and she had let Holly borrow it in the past. Holly was sure she wouldn't mind if she took it for the evening. She'd mention it to her mum when she visited her in the hospice the next day.

Holly went over to the dressing table (noting with sadness that it was dusty) and opened her mum's jewellery box. Holly's own jewellery was a crazy tangle of strings of beads, earrings and oddments stuffed in an old tobacco tin; Judith's jewellery collection was the opposite. On the top tray she had all her earrings neatly paired and lined up in straight rows, with her bracelets on a roll of velvet. Necklaces lay in the tray beneath. Holly lifted off the top tray and quickly found the fine gold chain she'd been thinking of. She put it on and glanced in the mirror. It was the right choice and finished the outfit perfectly.

She lifted the earring tray back into place and went to shut the box, but the lid would not come down flush so she could close the clasp. She opened it again and jiggled the top tray, to make it sit evenly, but she could feel that it and the tray below were rocking, as if there was something big and awkwardly shaped in the box below. She lifted both trays out, expecting to find bulkier costume jewellery or something similar in the bottom section, but she was surprised to see that it was full of letters. She could see the top one was addressed to Mrs Judith Evans. It had been opened but was still in its envelope. The handwriting was rather beautiful and old-fashioned, written with a fountain pen, with an even, forward slope, as if the person who wrote it was used to writing a lot by hand. The postmark was recent. Holly lifted the letter and saw another one below addressed in the same handwriting. She riffled through the pile and there were a lot of letters, perhaps thirty or forty, all clearly from the same person. Holly had seen plenty of examples of her father's handwriting so she knew the letters were not from him, and besides, the most recent postmark was just a month or so ago. Who was her mother's correspondent? Judith had never mentioned a friend that she wrote to regularly, but then she had also never mentioned that she'd been dating someone for some years. Maybe they were love letters from Christopher Benton? It seemed Judith was a woman with hidden depths. Holly couldn't bring herself to read any of the letters. It would be a dreadful invasion of Judith's privacy. She carefully aligned the letters again, making sure the most recent one was on the top, just as she had found them. Then she gently replaced the trays in the jewellery box and closed it, successfully this time. Just as she took a step back, she heard the doorbell ring. Fraser. Speculating about her mother's secret life would have to wait.

The bistro was lovely, a homely, warm place with mismatched chairs and scrubbed wooden tables, and old South African advertisements printed on tin framed on the walls. It was run by a couple from Cape Town, who had brought a little taste of the open sociability of their countrymen to London's suburbs. Fraser had clearly done his homework, or been there before, because as soon as they arrived, he ordered a bottle of an outstanding South African Pinotage that Holly remembered drinking with Damon. African jazz played softly, and the host lit the old paraffin lamp that stood on their table.

'This place is amazing,' smiled Holly. 'It makes me homesick.'

'Homesick?' Fraser asked.

Well, it was my home, for ten years. I haven't been back here long enough for this to feel like home.'

'Wait till you taste their bo-bertie.'

'You mean bobotie?' said Holly. 'Curried lamb mince and egg topping? They do that? Wow. I love that.'

'Save some space for the milk tart,' cautioned Fraser.

'Oh, I think I'm in heaven.' She grinned. 'I didn't have lunch either, so I'm starving. I hope you're not one of those blokes who thinks girls should pick at a lettuce leaf, because I'm likely to stuff my face like one of those competitive eaters.'

'You say the sexiest things.'

'Wait till I undo the top button of my jeans to make more room. You won't be able to resist me.'

If the time they'd met in the coffee shop had not been a first date, Holly began to think that this definitely was. Fraser was acting differently around her. He no longer seemed to be the concerned doctor (or boomerang hurler). He seemed to be taking the role of an attentive man, clearly showing interest in her as a woman, and she was enjoying every minute of it. It was the best date she had been on in years. Come to think of it, it was the only date she'd been on in at least five years. She had moved in with Damon pretty much the day she met him, so they'd never really dated, and there hadn't been anyone for a while before Damon, and definitely no one since. She knew she should feel awkward and shy, but Fraser was such fun to spend time with. He was quick-witted and funny, well informed on topical issues but not a bore, interested in her and her life, and happy to chat openly about himself too.

On their second glass of wine, she plucked up the courage to ask about his marriage.

'We were university sweethearts,' he said. 'We dated from halfway through the second year. She's also a doctor. We worked well as a team, and marriage seemed the obvious next step.'

Holly couldn't help thinking that was a terribly unromantic thing to say about your wife. He carried on. 'Both our careers went well, and we worked very hard. She was a GP; I worked at the hospital. Then Finlay was born, and . . . well, don't ever let anyone tell you that having kids will save a relationship. It won't. And it's hard. She really struggled, giving up work to look after him when he was tiny, and then when she went back, we fought all the time, about work and childcare and housework . . . everything became about scoring points: who'd worked the most hours that week, who'd changed the most nappies, who'd had the most broken night . . . it was like this awful, awful competition where we both had to prove how hard our lives were. Then I got offered a better position at the hospital in Hammersmith, and I decided to take it. I think that was the last straw. I woke up one day and I just thought, I have so little time with Finlay, and I want to enjoy it. I don't want to fight any more. So I moved out. That was about six months ago.'

'And she was okay with that?'

'She was furious at first. I think she thought I was supposed to stay there so she could be angry with me all the time. But we started having counselling together and things are getting better now. Having Christmas together was a big step, and it seemed to go okay.'

'And you see Finlay . . . ?'

'I normally go up one afternoon in the week, and every Saturday I take him to football. He comes to stay with me every second weekend as well. I think we have a better time together, and we spend real quality time too. I'm happier, he seems happier and I hope Lindsay's happier as well.'

'It all sounds very civilised,' said Holly, sipping her wine. They seemed to have done in the bottle of wine and without her noticing, Fraser had ordered another and filled up her glass and his.

'I hope so,' he said, smiling.

'So does this mean you're . . .' She didn't know quite what she was trying to say, and she had a sudden moment of terror that she'd got completely the wrong end of the stick and he was just being friendly. Damn, this dating/not dating thing was a minefield. She blushed furiously and stared down at her plate.

' . . . Ready to move on?' he said quietly. She would have loved to see his facial expression, but that would mean lifting her eyes from her plate and as her face was the colour of the wine she was drinking, that wasn't going to happen. She allowed herself a small nod instead.

'Did you actually listen to the voicemail I left you?' he asked.

'No.' She'd been too busy primping and exfoliating.

'I wish you had. It's a work of art. I sat in my office for an hour, and wrote down what I was going to say, and then read it in my best Radio Three classical-music-DJ voice.'

'Because . . .'

'This is the first time I've asked someone out. It's the first time I've been out with a woman who wasn't my wife, and I'm terrified. I'm so terrified I've accidentally drunk four glasses of wine and I'm going to have to put you in a cab home because I can't drive.'

'If it's any consolation, I'm terrified too. The last time I dated . . . well, it was a long time ago.'

'You can't tell me a woman like you has been single for a long time. You're not a nun, are you?'

'Far from it . . . just been recovering from a bad, bad break-up. That's why I came back from South Africa.'

'How bad?'

'He broke my heart, bankrupted my company, nearly landed me in jail and fled the country?'

'Wow. Sounds like a great guy.'

'Yes, well. All in the past now.' She smiled and said, 'Is there any more wine?'

Fraser picked up the bottle and peered at it quizzically. 'Nope, all gone. I could order another . . .'

'A third?'

'Hmm . . . maybe not.'

'Well, you'd better call me a cab then.'

'You're a cab.'

Holly smiled. 'Those jolly paediatrician jokes still working for you?'

'Well, the kids keep coming back.'

'I'm not sure it's for the jokes though.'

'So' – Fraser leaned back in his chair slightly – 'I *could* call you a cab from here, or you could come back to mine, which it so happens is just around the corner, and we could have another glass of wine, or a cup of coffee, or I keep an awful brand of neon-pink squash that Finlay likes. I could rustle you up a glass of that. And then I could call you a cab from there.'

'Wow, now that's an offer a girl would be crazy to refuse.'

Fraser paid the bill, and they left the restaurant. As they walked back to his flat, it seemed the easiest thing in the world to hold hands. He lived on the first floor of a rather nice house. Holly had imagined it would be a sad bachelor pad with make-do divorced-dad furniture and a sleeper couch, but instead it was a warm and cosy two-bedroomed apartment. He might have no interest in cars, but he had spent money and time to make a beautiful home. The living room had two enormous brick-red sofas, and a selection of kids' toys in a massive wicker basket under the coffee table. As soon as they arrived, Holly excused herself and went to the bathroom. She was nervous . . . Being in Fraser's apartment suddenly made this seem very real. She liked him a lot and was definitely attracted to him, but was she ready to sleep with him? Did he think she would? Damn! She was out of practice with this whole dating thing. She washed her hands, tidied her hair and contemplated putting on more lipstick, but then decided not to. She rinsed her mouth out with water, squared her shoulders and went back into the living room.

Fraser had put on some music and was sitting on one of the sofas. He smiled lazily at her as she came into the room. She went over and perched on the opposite sofa.

'So, Miss Evans,' he said in his best doctor voice, 'what seems to be the trouble?'

'Well, Doctor,' she said, 'I'm really not sure how to play this. I've got a case of the first-date nerves and I'm suffering from trembling knees. What do you prescribe?'

'Firstly, I would recommend you come and sit over here, on this sofa. The view is so much better.'

Holly got up and crossed the room to sit beside him. He was looking at the opposite wall, and she looked at it too. It was a big expanse of wall, and it was empty except for a small framed picture about the size of an A4 sheet of paper.

'The view's unusual,' she commented. 'What's the picture? One of Finlay's?'

'Not exactly,' said Fraser. 'Go and take a look.'

She got up again and crossed back to look at the picture. It was a small, simple pencil sketch of a sinuous naked woman. The style was familiar, but it wasn't until she glanced at the signature in the corner, that she realised. 'Oh my God, it's a Chagall. A real Chagall.'

'Indeed it is. I bought it when I moved here. Sold my very expensive car, bought the banger I drive now, and blew the money on that.'

'It's beautiful.'

'I love it. I can sit here all evening and look at it.' Fraser had got up too, and was standing beside and slightly behind her. She felt his hand touch the hair at her temple, lightly, so very lightly.

'The cut has healed beautifully,' he said. 'You're barely going to have a scar at all. Soon no one will know I tried to brain you with a boomerang.'

He kept stroking her hair and then lightly touched the side of her face. She leaned lightly against his hand and he seemed to take that as encouragement, as she hoped he would. He slipped his hand down on to her shoulder and turned her gently into his arms. It was a very, very tentative first kiss, feather-light on her lips, dry and warm. But he smelled so good, so very, very masculine, that Holly found herself sliding her arms around his waist and pulling him closer to her. The kiss deepened, and they fell in a tangle on to the nearby sofa. He slid his hands all over her body, as if he didn't know where to touch her first, and kissed her mouth, her ears, her neck, anything he could reach. It was clumsy, they kept elbowing each other and clashing teeth, gasping, 'Sorry,' and 'Oh God, you taste delicious,' and 'You too, but your elbow's on my hair.' It was so ridiculous, that, nice though it was, Holly felt herself starting to giggle. Fraser must have felt her smile against his lips because it made him smile too. The little bubble of laugher between them broke the tension, and they disentangled themselves and sat up, panting.

'Wow, am I out of practice,' Fraser said ruefully.

'Me too.'

'I was so hoping to impress you with my smooth moves.'

'I was enjoying your moves,' she said, taking his hand.

'There are spotty fifteen-year-olds with more impressive

moves,' he said. 'Look, I desperately, desperately want to carry on, and drag you into my bedroom and take off all your clothes, but . . .'

'But . . . ?'

'This is going to sound so stupid, but firstly, Lindsay will be dropping Finlay off here at eight tomorrow morning, and it would be slightly awkward if I was still in bed with you . . .'

'I see that.'

'And secondly, I haven't got any . . .'

'Oh.'

'I don't suppose you . . . ?' he said hopefully.

'No, I'm not carrying a pack of condoms like a modern woman should,' she said. 'I didn't think . . . well, that we'd get here so quickly.'

'Me neither,' said Fraser. 'But you're just so . . .' He leaned over and kissed her again. The temperature between them very quickly began to rise again.

'Oh God . . .' he groaned, breaking away. 'Right now, I'd willingly trade in the Chagall for a pack of three.'

'I should go,' said Holly reluctantly. 'We don't have to . . . do everything tonight. There'll be other nights. There will be other nights, won't there?'

'Please. Please can there be another night really, really soon?' he said. 'I'd say tomorrow, but I have Finlay for the weekend. Sunday night?'

'I don't know. I hope so. As soon as I know what's happening with my mum . . .'

'Listen to us . . . children, sick mothers . . . We have all the sexy banter, don't we?' He grinned at her.

She leaned over and kissed him softly. 'Welcome to adult-hood, Dr John. Okay. One of us has to be strong. I'm going. If you could ring for a taxi for me, I'm going to get a glass of the radioactive squash you promised me.' She got up and walked towards the kitchen, very aware that Fraser was watching her shapely behind in her jeans and very glad that he was.

19

MEL NOW

She was addicted. She logged on to Facebook at least ten times a day, to check if there'd been any action on Serena's wall, and to see what 'Triggah' was up to. He obviously thought he was quite the gangster, but according to his date of birth he was just sixteen, and he was still in school. It wasn't the same school as Serena, and it wasn't a very good school, but he was, at least nominally, still in formal education. It was something.

Serena posted on his wall all the time. Often it was just a 'luv ya babes', or a heart, or she'd put a YouTube link to some hideous song. Mel couldn't understand what they saw in the terrible music, but it seemed to be the thing that united Serena with this boy. He'd sometimes 'like' her posts, but didn't respond very often. He seemed to have stopped posting on Serena's wall as much as he used to. In fact, when Mel looked back, he hadn't posted anything there for several weeks.

She checked Facebook using her phone, but if she wanted to look at pictures in more detail, she preferred using a computer. Of course, it was risky to do it at home, because while Serena usually disappeared into her bedroom and stayed there, she might emerge at any moment, so Mel could never relax. If Serena was out, she stayed online continually, in case there were updates or pictures posted, and she kept a constant eye on any events Serena said yes to attending. So far, she hadn't lied outright to Mel about parties she was going to, but she knew that she had stretched the truth a bit about who was going to be there or, if she was sleeping at a friend's house, how late she stayed. Mel felt much more in control now: as if she was a secret guardian angel watching over Serena. She knew that if Serena knew, she wouldn't see it in the same way at all, and she kept promising herself that she would stop once she was confident that Serena wasn't doing anything stupid, or as soon as she felt Serena was old enough to look after herself.

But then everyone started talking about the party. It started with a boy at Triggah's school posting an event he called 'Free House'. Mel thought maybe he meant free house music, and that he was hosting some kind of gig, but she soon worked out that his parents would be out of town and that he'd be throwing a party with no adult supervision. People kept joining the event and there were soon over a hundred, including Serena and Triggah. Some wit posted, 'Are we drinking your dad's booze cabinet, or do we bring our own? and that led to a flurry of comments, suggesting that if people clubbed together, someone's brother could be persuaded to go to Costco and get enough beer to get everyone slammed. Then a post appeared that chilled Mel to the bone: 'J says he'll come with draw and pills.' She didn't know what 'draw' was, but in conjunction with 'pills', it didn't sound good. If she was to hazard a guess, it was probably a term for marijuana. She was no blushing innocent, and she'd smoked plenty of it when she was younger, but she'd heard that what was out there now was much more potent than the stuff they'd had as teenagers. Besides, Serena was so young, and if she was off her face, at an unsupervised party full of strangers and the hideous Triggah, who knew what might happen?

Mel didn't know what to do. So far, Serena hadn't mentioned going to a party that weekend, but she had developed a pattern of announcing her social plans only just before they were about to happen. Mel might once have thought it was the spontaneity of teenagers, but now she was a little wiser, she knew it was because that way Mel would have little time to check up on Serena's story or ask too many questions. She had to stop Serena going to that party. Could she invent some kind of family emergency? Commit them both to a social occasion somewhere? She knew if she did, Serena would just beg off and make an excuse. Maybe she could get Bruce to invite Serena to do something. Serena would go along with whatever her dad asked, but when Mel rang Bruce's mobile, he didn't answer, and then sent her a text to say he was in Spain for a fortnight. Nice of him to let her know.

She was thinking of inventing a deathly illness and begging Serena to stay home and look after her, but it would seem very out of character, and besides, she knew she wasn't a good enough actor to pull it off. The difficulty with being Serena's online friend was that she couldn't take that friendship into the real world, or even do anything to draw attention to herself. She thought of posting as Lauren and suggesting that the party might be raided by the police or something, but then everyone would want to know who she was and how she knew. She felt powerless. Maybe not knowing was better than knowing and not being able to stop things happening.

Late on the Friday afternoon, she was sitting at the computer in the office at work, staring at the screen, waiting for Jo to arrive so they could cash up and close the shop. The last customers had left about five minutes before and she knew no one else was likely to come in. There was a post on the Facebook page for the party that had her flummoxed. 'Sum1 getting NOS,' it said. 'Bring balloons.' What the hell was NOS and why was it related to balloons? Some kind of party game? She wished she had some way of decoding this cryptic youth-speak. She looked out through the open door of the office and saw Jo's car pull up outside. Jo got out and set about unloading the kids from their car seats and getting her things together to come in. Mel didn't want to have to explain why she was on Facebook on the work computer, let alone logged on with a fictitious profile. She was about to close down the Facebook profile and go out to meet Jo, when she saw a little red notification flag come up. She clicked on it. 'Jason "Triggah" Cook sent you a message.' She opened the link. It took her to a private message, and Triggah had written a single word: 'Peng,' Peng? What the hell was peng? Jo was coming through the door, and Mel quickly closed the browser window.

She went out on to the shop floor to meet Jo. Without thinking, she said, 'What's peng?'

'Pen?'

'No, peng. P-E-N-G. it's something I . . . heard Serena say.'

'In what context?'

'I can't remember.'

Jo looked surprised. 'I don't know, it's not one I've heard before, but youth slang moves so fast. We wrinklies can't be expected to keep up.' She thought for a second. 'Tell you what . . . I remember Lee saying that when they're working on youth campaigns and want to use the right slang terms, they use Urban Dictionary.'

'The what?'

'It's an online slang dictionary that anyone can contribute to, like Wikipedia. Try looking it up there.'

'Thanks, I will,' said Mel, as if it wasn't a big deal. She went over to the till and she and Jo went through the day's figures while Zach and Imogene played in the play area. Since Jo had decided to say yes to the big investor, she wanted much more detail on the day's sales and the traffic through the shop, Mel was usually very good at keeping notes on people's browsing habits and what their kids got up to while they were looking at the clothes, but for the last few days she'd been so distracted she'd been a bit sloppy. She could see Jo wasn't very pleased with the level of feedback she was getting.

'Look, I'm sorry. I've had terrible period pains all day. I haven't been at my best,' she said. She felt awful lying to Jo, but she wasn't going to admit to spending the afternoon Internet-stalking her own daughter.

'That's okay,' said Jo. 'Go home and rest. We'll get some better data tomorrow.'

Mel excused herself and headed for the door. She couldn't wait to get home. She'd tried looking at websites on her phone a few times, and she just couldn't get on with it. She wanted to be able to sit at her PC and and look up this Urban Dictionary. When she got home, Serena was slumped in front of the television, watching a DVD of something violent that involved cars roaring around and crashing a lot. Often, when Mel came home and Serena was in the living room, she would make an excuse and go to her room, but today, she glanced up, but stayed on the sofa watching the film. Damn. Mel went through into the kitchen and started preparing dinner. She was itching to switch on her PC. She put her head around the door and said, 'Any home-work to do?'

'Done it,' muttered Serena.

'Great!' Mel said brightly.

Eventually, the swelling music suggested that the film was finished and Mel assumed that Serena would then head for her bedroom, but she switched over to a music channel and sat in the same position, watching music videos.

Mel dished up dinner and carried plates through into the living room. 'Let's eat in front of the telly for a change,' she said cheerfully, handing Serena her plate. 'Is there anything we could both watch?

'*EastEnders*?'

'Too depressing,' said Mel.

'There's that American comedy thing on E4,' Serena said.

'Perfect.'

With years of practice, Mel knew how to infuriate Serena when they watched television. She'd just sit there and ask really stupid mum questions until Serena had had enough and stormed off to her room. She started as soon as the show came on. 'Now, who's that? Is he the same one we saw in the other show? The one about the school?' Then she tried, 'Is he married to the blonde one or the skinny dark one? I can never tell these pretty American girls apart.' And finally, 'Why is that funny? I can't bear those American laugh tracks.'

But to her surprise, Serena answered all her questions and sat quite quietly on the sofa. She picked at her dinner, but for once didn't complain about Mel's cooking. It was more as if she just wasn't hungry. She seemed very subdued. She wasn't often vibrant or chatty any more with Mel, but this seemed different . . . as if she was sad rather than sulky.

Mel finished her dinner and held out a hand for Serena's plate.

'Are you done?'

'Yes, thanks. Sorry. It's nice, I'm just not very hungry. Mel nearly fell off her chair. Serena had been polite! Something must be wrong. Why today? Normally she barely saw her in the evenings, and now, today, when Mel was desperate to get to her computer, Serena was moping on the sofa. She'd try being extra chummy. That would surely get Serena to flee to her bedroom. She took the plates through to the kitchen, and dug around in the freezer. She came up with an ice-cream lolly and carried it through to the living room.

'Maybe this will cheer you up,' she said, and handed Serena the chocolate ice cream. Then she sat beside her daughter on the sofa and grabbed the throw off the back of the sofa to spread over both of them.

'Thanks, Mum,' said Serena in a small voice. She pulled the throw up to her chin, and sat nibbling at her ice cream in tiny bites. Mel knew she should ask what was wrong, but in all likelihood, Serena would either say, 'Nothing,' or would yell at her for being nosy. Mel kept sitting beside her on the sofa, itching to get moving, but eventually the restlessness got the better of her. She jumped up and headed for the kitchen, where she washed up noisily. Then she thumped back into the living room. 'Are you going to be long in here?' she asked briskly. 'Only I want to hoover.'

'Hoover?' said Serena blankly. 'It's the middle of the night!'

'It's only eight o'clock, and I just have so much to do over the next few days. I need to get these things done.'

'Okay . . .' said Serena rather dubiously. She clicked the television off and, wrapping the throw around her shoulders like a superhero cloak, shuffled off to her room. Mel felt a pang. Maybe Serena had wanted to talk. Maybe she'd been about to open up, and she, Mel, had missed an opportunity. But she'd gone too far down the path she was on. She had to see what was going on with Triggah and the party – see the whole thing through.

Damn. Now she would actually have to hoover. She dragged the machine out from the kitchen cupboard with a clatter, and ran it over the living room carpet in the most cursory of ways before she pushed it back into the kitchen, not bothering to put it away properly, and switched on her PC. Oddly enough, there was no music coming from Serena's room.

She ran a Google search and easily found the Urban Dictionary website Jo had mentioned. She began by looking up some of the words she had seen in the discussions on the party page. She had been right that 'draw' was a term for marijuana. And NOS, it seemed was Nitrous Oxide – laughing gas – which the kids inhaled for a brief euphoric high. It wasn't illegal, but another Internet search suggested that it probably wasn't entirely safe either.

Finally, she typed 'peng' into the search box. Multiple definitions came up, but the first one was: 'Fit, sexy, good-looking, hot, fuckable'. Well, that cleared that up. Serena's boyfriend was trawling around on Facebook telling other women he thought they were hot. Classy. Maybe his behaviour was the reason for Serena's subdued mood that evening. The question was, what should she – as Lauren – do about it? It was probably best to just ignore it. She shouldn't respond. But as she sat at her computer, she got more and more angry. Whatever she might think of Triggah, Serena had picked him and had invested her heart in him, and it seemed he was a slug. But just how much of a slug was he? She couldn't resist prodding him slightly to see just how slimy he would turn out to be. She hit 'Reply' and spent some time trying to come up with a response that would not give her away as a fake. Eventually she opted for, 'Havnt u got a gfriend?' That should be pretty safe. She hit 'Send'. He must have been online, because he replied pretty much immediately. 'Nah,' he said. 'Not relly. You goin Alexs free house Sat?'

Well, that settled it. He was a vile little opportunist. She wanted to march straight into Serena's room and say to her,

'Your boyfriend is a disgusting little worm, did you know that?' But of course she couldn't. Firstly, Serena had no idea she knew of Triggah's existence or his place in her life. And secondly, even if she could get around that, what would she say? 'I know he's a pig because he's been hitting on my fictitious online persona, the one I use to spy on you'?

In the morning, Serena seemed a little happier. Mel guessed that during the course of the previous night, she'd heard from Triggah. Either that, or she was just getting excited for the party that night. She hadn't actually asked to go out yet, so Mel tried offering some alternatives. 'Hey,' she said when Serena sloped into the kitchen at around eleven, 'that vampire film opened last night. How about we splash out on some VIP tickets and I'll take us to Pizza-Express for dinner after?'

'Hmm,' said Serena. 'Coffee?'

Mel switched on the kettle. 'Or if you don't feel like a film, we could go bowling. Or invite someone for dinner. Shall we see if Hamish wants to come?'

Serena didn't answer, just made herself a mug of instant with three sugars and sank into a chair at the kitchen table. Mel busied herself with kitchen tasks – packing away clean dishes, wiping surfaces, humming to herself. Pretending that this was a normal weekend and a normal conversation. But it seemed Serena wasn't going to answer unless she pushed. Eventually she said, 'So what do you think? Film? Dinner? Bowling? Dinner party?'

'I can't,' said Serena. 'Sorry, I meant to tell you. Izzie's having a sleepover. Loads of us are going.'

Izzie and Serena had been friends since junior school.

Not close friends, but always in roughly the same circle. It was one of those friendships that seemed more about competition and bitchiness than affection. Izzie was a brittle, insecure girl who looked as if she had something to prove. Her parents were very rich, but time-poor. They were always at work or out of the country, and they tended to throw money at Izzie and her younger sister to assuage their guilt. She wasn't necessarily popular for herself, but the kids were not averse to spending time in her huge house with its pool table, home cinema and frequent lack of parental supervision.

'Really?' said Mel carefully. 'You didn't mention it before.'

'We only decided yesterday.'

'And will her parents be there? I know they're away a lot.'

'They are away, but there's an au pair there to look after her little sister.' Serena knew how to play the game. 'You can meet her when you drop me off, if you like.'

I bet I can, thought Mel. I also bet Izzie's slipped her a few quid to keep her mouth shut about the girls going out for the night. She had met the au pairs at Izzie's house before. They tended to be moody, disinterested Eastern European girls who saw the job as a stopgap. But without causing a major row and arousing Serena's suspicions, there was no way she could put her foot down and say no. Serena had slept over at Izzie's many times before.

Mel was working at the shop from twelve until four, and she worried and fretted through her shift, but couldn't come up with a feasible way to prevent Serena going. When she got back to the flat, Serena had packed a small rucksack, ostensibly with pyjamas, toiletries and clothes for the next day, but Mel was sure the bag actually contained an outfit for the party. Together, they walked over to Izzie's house. It was only a few blocks away, but in a more affluent part of the neighbourhood.

Mel rang the bell, and an expensive, sonorous clang sounded inside the house. She heard someone coming down the stairs and the door was opened by a Slavic-looking girl who would probably go on to a successful career as a ramp model following her undistinguished stint as an au pair. 'Yes,' she said with sulky insolence.

'Hi, Romana,' said Serena quickly. 'I'm here for the sleepover.'

Romana shrugged and walked away. Izzie came bounding down the big staircase. 'Serenie!' she squealed. 'You're here! We're going to have the best . . . sleepover ever!'

If Mel had been harbouring any hopes that the girls were actually planning a slumber party, they were dashed then and there. Izzie was a terrible actress.

Serena turned to her, her face guarded. 'See, Mum? We're fine. I'll text you before I walk home tomorrow, okay?' She was obviously desperate for Mel to go before Izzie let loose with any more unconvincing lies.

'Okay, love,' said Mel, fighting the urge to grab Serena's hand and drag her out of there. 'Have fun, girls.'

At ten o'clock that night, she couldn't take it any more. She had been pacing up and down the living room for an hour. What was going on? Where was Serena now? Was the party in full swing? She went into her room and changed into black jeans and a black polo neck and pulled on her black running shoes. All she needed was a black woolly hat and she'd be a cat burglar, she thought ruefully, looking at her reflection. She went to her PC and checked the location of the party . . . it was about half a mile away, closer to Izzie's house than their flat, but still within easy walking distance.

She took a detour to avoid crossing any possible routes Serena, Izzie and their friends might take, and ended up approaching the house from the other end of the road. If she hadn't been sure which house it was, as soon as she was within a few hundred yards, there was no doubt. Music blared and pulsed and every window seemed to be open. She could see flashing lights in the living room and the front garden was full of teenagers smoking and talking and laughing in that heightened, super-loud way they affected when they were in a big group. Kids were flowing into the house at quite a rapid rate. She knew there was no way she could go in without immediately being spotted as an adult. She crossed the road, and saw that there was an alleyway almost directly opposite the house with a big overhanging tree. If she stepped into the passage and hung back in the shadow of the tree, she could watch the house undisturbed.

There was no sign of Serena or Izzie, although there were an awful lot of young girls wearing very small dresses and very high heels. To Mel, they all looked far too young to be out at a party like this. People kept arriving and going in: in the first half an hour that Mel watched, she counted forty-odd people. Admittedly, it was hard to tell who was arriving for the first time, because people kept going in and out, standing in the garden to smoke, or just randomly wandering into the street and before going back into the party. They seemed incapable of standing still, as if they were scared that if they did, something more fun might be happening somewhere else.

Mel was getting cold, and she was beginning to doubt the wisdom of her actions. She had no idea what was going on inside the house and no way of finding out: Serena might be shooting up heroin in there for all she knew. And what if she saw her spying? The damage that would do to their relationship was incalculable. Also, what if Serena rang the flat looking for her and she wasn't there? Or went home for some reason? She decided that it made the most sense to head back to the flat, maybe send Serena a text saying something innocuous like, 'Hope you're having a nice time,' and hope for the best. She was about to turn and go up the alleyway before doubling back along the parallel street to go home when she heard a commotion behind her. A boy burst out of the door of the house, closely followed by two girls. In an instant, she recognised the boy as Triggah (and a ratty little individual he was too, with an overlarge baseball cap and his trousers worn at gangster level, showing his boxers). The two girls were Serena and Izzie. Izzie immediately backed into the shadow of a house and stood sobbing, her arms clasped around her body. But Serena was screaming and raging. That was the noise Mel had heard . . . her own daughter screaming.

'I can't believe you!' she screamed at Triggah. 'You disgusting bastard! With my own friend! At a party with all my friends! I hate you!'

'Yeah, well . . .' said Triggah, who actually looked quite pleased with himself. Clearly he thought this made him seem like quite the stud. 'Whatever,' he finished proudly.

Whatever it was Serena saw in this boy it clearly wasn't his conversational skills. Serena was sobbing, a real body-shaking, heartbreaking cry. She kept screaming at Triggah, but Mel couldn't hear what she was saying. Then Triggah said something to her and laughed, cruelly.

Serena stared at him, horrified, and pushing past him, she ran down the path and away down the road. Mel could see her weaving and stumbling. She was obviously very drunk. Mel thought for a split second, then sprinted back down the alleyway, up the parallel road and around the corner. She had guessed right: Serena had turned towards home, and was half a block away, still running and lurching, half on the pavement and half in the road. Mel stepped into her daughter's weaving path.

'Serena!' she called. 'What's going on?' She hoped, in Serena's drunken state, she'd assume their meeting was coincidental.

'Mum!' she gasped. Mel held her tight and Serena's body shook and convulsed in her arms.

'Oh,' Serena said suddenly, apprehension in her voice. Fortunately Mel was thinking fast. She spun her daughter around and bent her at the waist, just as Serena started to vomit. She held Serena's hair as she retched and cried. Once the vomiting had stopped, she looped an arm around Serena's waist and together they walked home. Serena didn't ask what Mel was doing there. She was too drunk, too distressed and too exhausted.

In the early hours of the morning, Mel found herself sitting on the bathroom floor with her daughter's head in her lap. Serena would doze for a while, then wake up crying, drag herself up to retch in the toilet for a while, then collapse back into Mel's lap. She kept muttering and talking about Triggah. At one point, she fell into a restless sleep, her eyelids fluttering, then woke up and looked up into Mel's eyes. 'I can't believe he did it, Mum,' she sobbed. 'I can't believe it.' Then she fell asleep again, but woke up a few minutes later, continuing the conversation as if there had been no break. 'He said he loved me. Yesterday he said he loved me. And now he says I'm a frigid bitch.'

Mel was cold and aching, but sitting on the floor, stroking her little girl's head, holding her close and looking at the long sweep of wet lashes on her cheek, she felt choked with love. She had done the right thing. If she hadn't been online, she would never have known about the party. The end had utterly justified the means. She had been there to catch Serena when she fell.

20

MEL THEN

The patent leather shoes were squashing her toes so badly she wanted to cry. They were too small, but her mum had said she would have to manage. They had to wear smart shoes for the funeral, and these were the only decent pair Mel had. They had been bought for Christmas the year she turned seven, and that was more than a year ago now, and she had grown. She sat on the cold wooden pew and tried to pull her skirt down under her, but her mum put a hand on her leg to stop her fidgeting. She looked up at her mum, who was wearing a small black hat with a bit of netting to cover her eyes. She was very thin. She had spent months looking after Mel's dad when he was ill and then working nights in the betting shop. Her lips, coated in very bright red lipstick, were thin and pressed together. She wasn't crying. And Mel didn't think she would cry. Dad's illness had been so long, so painful and drawn out, that they'd all cried themselves out. Mel wasn't going to cry either. She was relieved it was over . . . that her dad's terrible, rattling breathing that had echoed through the house day and night, had finally stopped. She felt bad that she was glad it was finished, and she was sure that it made her a terrible daughter.

The whole neighbourhood had turned out for the funeral. Her dad had been a popular man before he got ill, and everyone was sorry that he was gone now. Mel had lived her whole short life in this grim little town in Shropshire. She knew every single person in the church. Everyone was there, from the lady who ran the corner shop, to the head teacher from Mel's school and her mum's workmates from the betting shop.

Mel turned in her chair and peered over the back of the pew to see who else was there. There was her friend Matilda from school, with her mum and dad, and a group of big, awkward-looking men. She didn't know their names, but she knew they were long-distance truck drivers like her dad had been. Her mum suddenly pinched her hard in the leg. 'Face the front!' she hissed furiously. Mel's eyes filled with tears. She didn't want to face the front and have to look at the horrible polished box that had her dad in it. And the pinch had really hurt. But she knew her mum had done it because she was also upset and scared and this day was horrible. She was only eight, but she understood, so she faced the front and sat quietly.

In the days that followed, people kept dropping by with things to eat and offers of help, but within a week or so, the visits had dried up and it was just Mel and her mum alone in the house. Mel could see her mum was struggling. It wasn't just the loneliness. It was the lack of money, the bills that kept coming in, the problems with the house that she had no way of fixing. She seemed to be angry all the time. Mel tried to be as good as she could. Even though she was boisterous and outgoing by nature, she was always quiet at home, did her homework and helped out around the house. But she couldn't help it that she grew out of her coat, or that there was a school trip to Ironbridge and she needed money for the coach, and she hadn't meant to break the plate when she was washing up. But it seemed whatever she did her mum found annoying or difficult, and she was always sighing and saying, 'Oh, *Melanie*,' or shouting at her, or telling her to be quiet. She wished she knew what to do to help her mum, but it seemed to her that the only thing she could do that would really help would be to disappear and stop being a bother who kept costing so much money.

Her mum had to work longer and longer hours at the betting shop just to make ends meet, so most days Mel would walk home from school and let herself in with the key she wore on a string around her neck. Her mum would have left a sandwich in the fridge for her (it was always cold and dry by four o'clock), and she would sit down and do her home-work at the kitchen table. Sometimes, when she was finished, she would watch some telly, cuddled in a blanket on the sofa, but she had to be careful to watch the time and turn it off before her mum got home. Otherwise she'd get, 'Oh, *Melanie*, do you think I'm made of money? Do you know what electricity costs these days?'

She knew better than to put the fire on, even when it was very cold. She got used to putting on extra jumpers and socks and shuffling around in her slippers like a pensioner, trying to keep warm. One Friday afternoon though, she was squarely caught out. She was huddled on the sofa watching

Morph and giggling, when she heard a key in the door. She looked up at the clock. It was only four thirty and her mum wasn't usually home before six. Mel jumped guiltily to her feet and ran to switch the television off, but as she did it, she realised her mum would have heard it as she came through the door. Mel stood frozen in the middle of the living room, certain she was about to be yelled at. But instead, she heard something she hadn't heard for months . . . her mother laughing.

She stayed where she was, and listened. Her mum said something softly in the hallway and laughed again, and then Mel heard another, deep voice. A man. Who could it be? Her mum's boss, Terry, from the betting shop? She couldn't think who else it would be . . . They never had male visitors. Her mum walked into the living room then, still talking and laughing over her shoulder. Her cheeks were pink from the cold outside, and she was smiling. Mel remembered then that her mum used to be pretty, very pretty, before worry and grief had made her thin and pinched.

The man with the voice followed her mum into the room. Mel had never seen him before, but she recognised his type: he was a big man, balding and red-faced with a neck as thick as his big head. He was twisting a woolly hat in his large fists. Without knowing how she knew, Mel was sure that the man was another long-distance driver, like her dad had been. He looked a bit like her dad had looked before he got sick, and he looked like his friends who had come for the funeral too.

'And who's this?' he said, noticing Mel, who was still standing in the middle of the room. Her mum hadn't seemed to have noticed her yet.

'Oh, this is our Mel,' said her mum dismissively. 'Some tea, Phil? How about a little something to eat?'

'Thanks,' said Phil. 'Don't want to put you out.' And he winked at Mel, who smiled shyly.

Her mum bustled into the kitchen and started banging frying pans and plates around. 'Egg and chips all right? Maybe a fried slice?'

'Got any beans?' said Phil.

'Course!' said Mel's mum. Mel looked at him open-mouthed. She would never have dreamed of asking for something extra for tea, and she'd have got a clip around the ear if she had. Phil smiled at her again, and opened his mouth as if to speak, but he clearly couldn't think of anything to say to an eight-year-old girl, so he shut it and wandered into the kitchen to chat to Mel's mum while she cooked.

Who was this man? And why was he in their house? Mel was dying to ask, but she knew she would never get an answer. She'd learned very early on that the best way to find things out was to sit quiet as a mouse and listen when grown-ups were talking. They soon forgot you were there, and as long as you didn't ask any silly questions, they would just keep talking. So over tea (the best tea she'd had in months), Mel learned that Phil had known her dad from the long-distance truck routes. He had been living in Newcastle, but something had happened with his wife (she wished she could ask what a 'hussy' was, but she knew it wasn't the time). Phil had moved back into the area with his son ('He's a couple of years older than you,' he said, turning to Mel. 'Look out for him at school.'). He'd come to live with his sister, so she could help him look after the boy when he was away on the road. He'd thought he would look up his old friend, and was sad to learn Mel's dad had died. However, when he found out his widow was working in the betting shop, he'd stopped by to pay his respects.

She didn't know what to think about Phil. He seemed a nice enough man and he tried very hard to be nice to her and was very nice to her mum. It was both good and sad to see her mum smile again, and laugh. Of course it was good she was laughing, but she was laughing for someone who wasn't Mel, and wasn't Mel's dad. It seemed very strange to have another man at their kitchen table.

On Monday, Mel went to school as usual. She had completely forgotten about Phil's son, and in fact, hadn't thought again about Phil. But at lunchtime when they were queuing to get their food, her friend Gillian nudged her and pointed. 'See the new one in the fourth year?'

Mel craned her neck and peered. There were a lot of big fourth-year boys close to the front of the lunch queue. As soon as she saw the boy, who was laughing and punching another boy on the shoulder, she realised he must be Phil's son. He was very big for his age and chunky like his dad, tending a bit to fat. He had very red hair, which was cut very short, and the same thick neck and round face as his dad. But where Phil was a sort of gentle giant, this boy just looked mean.

Mel's first impression of Phil's son was right. It was hard for anyone to start in a new school, where everyone had known each other for years, and probably much harder to come in halfway through the fourth year, so Patrick (that was his name) had obviously decided he wasn't going to win anyone over by being friendly or clever or good at sport. He decided to be the biggest bully, and win respect through fear and intimidation. He was easily the biggest boy in the school (rumour had it he had been kept back at his old school and he was actually nearly thirteen), and he used physical force on a daily basis. He punched anyone who argued with him, extorted money and food out of smaller children and soon gathered a sniggering cohort of other boys who had muscles and violence to offer rather than brains. The school had always been quite rough, but now, if you were small, or clever, or not good at keeping your mouth shut, it was just plain scary.

Mel was all three. She was tiny for her age and always had been. She was also fiendishly smart and had been an avid reader since she was four, so she was streets ahead of many of her classmates and always top of her class. It meant she was viewed as a bit of a freak, and to make up for it, she'd become the class clown. She was well liked in her year. It was always such a relief for her to come to school, after being so good and quiet at home, and she loved being a show-off to her classmates. But under Patrick's reign of terror, she was a natural victim.

Their first encounter happened when he and his friends were loitering in a corridor after lunch one day. Mel had to walk past them to get back to her classroom, and she kept her head down and tried to be inconspicuous. Patrick lazily stuck out a foot to trip her up, but she saw it and hopped over it like a little rabbit. She was about to break into a run and escape into an area where an adult might be, but Patrick lunged out and grabbed her arm roughly. 'Oi, little smart arse,' he said into her face, and she recoiled from his cheese-and-onion-crisp breath. He stared at her closely with his beady little eyes. She had no idea whether or not he knew who she was, or that their parents knew each other. It seemed not, because he came out with his standard request. 'Got any money?'

'Not that I'm giving you,' she said defiantly. She didn't know why she said that. It wasn't as if she ever had any money.

'Gimme.'

'No.'

'Gimme one good reason why I shouldn't pick you up and shake you till it falls out.'

'Because you'd have to get your knuckles off the ground and engage your slug brain, and by then I'll be gone,' spat Mel. Patrick's moronic mates laughed at this, and he turned furiously to challenge them. In that moment of inattention, Mel shook off his grip, ducked under his sweaty, beefy arm and ran. The angels were on her side, because as she rounded the corner, she ran into Mr Scribbins, the fourth-year teacher, a stooped, gloomy man. He caught her by the shoulders, 'No running, girl!' he barked, and Mel was sure she was in for a punishment, but in the next moment, Patrick came thundering around the corner after her. He stopped short. Scribbins was well known to be an extremely quick-tempered man, dealing out swift discipline with the edge of a wooden ruler, and even Patrick would not have wanted to endure that. He stood stock still and did his best to look innocent. But Scribbins had been a teacher for a long time, and he assessed the situation in an instant. He pushed Mel around behind him and gave her a little shove. 'Get to your room before you're marked late,' he said gruffly, but not unkindly. 'And Watkins . . . you and I will need to have a word in our room.' He grabbed Patrick by the collar, and headed off at speed. Mel caught a glimpse of Patrick's face as he went. He was furious, and she knew she hadn't seen the last of him.

In that first year, Patrick showed he would have done well in a regime specialising in torture. He wasn't academically clever, but he was immensely sneaky. Once he had set his sights on tormenting Mel, he found ample opportunity to corner her where nobody else could see and to hurt her physically in ways that left no marks. When he didn't hurt her physically, he liked to intimidate her and make her constantly jumpy. School became a source of terror and tension. Her marks began to drop, and she got very anxious. She couldn't sleep at night, and because she was too scared to sit and eat her school dinners, she started to lose weight. She knew there was no point in telling her mum about it. She wouldn't believe her and would say she was looking for attention. And she wasn't a sneak, so she wasn't going to go to a teacher or the principal. She stuck it out through the winter term and into spring, gritting her teeth and enduring each frightening day. She became adept at hiding from Patrick, and she kept reminding herself that unless he was even more boneheaded than she suspected, after July he would be off to the secondary school in the autumn. It was the only thing that kept her going, and she ticked off each day until the end of term in her diary.

The day the summer holidays began, Mel could have jumped for joy. She wouldn't have to see him every day now. After the holidays, he would be in the comprehensive, which was all the way over on the other side of town, and he would no doubt find a new victim. Or maybe there would be some much bigger boys who would give him a taste of his own medicine. Mel planned to spend her summer holidays in the garden at home. She had an enormous stack of books to read, which she'd got from the library, and she was determined to teach herself to juggle. It was going to be a wonderful summer.

But a week into the summer holidays, she was lying on her stomach in the garden, reading *The Hobbit*, when she heard the front door close and voices in the house. For the second time, she heard a deep male voice and her mother's lighter tones. She knew at once that it was Phil again. She felt sick. Had he brought Patrick with him? She jumped up, smoothed her shirt and shorts and slid her copy of *The Hobbit* under the rug she had been lying on. She knew from experience that Patrick liked to damage books, and it was a library copy she would have no way of replacing.

Her mum came out into the garden smiling and laughing, followed by Phil, who had Patrick trailing in his wake. Mel shifted from foot to foot, and when her mum asked her to get something for everyone to drink, was grateful to run into the house. She paused only to snatch up the book and the rug. She put the kettle on, and while it was boiling, ran up to her room to put on some jeans and shoes and hide her book under her pillow. As she turned to leave her room, she jumped with fright. Patrick was standing in her open doorway, staring at her.

'Did you watch me change? Pervert,' she hissed at him. She didn't really know what a pervert was, but she knew it was rude. She'd heard girls at school saying it. Patrick lunged at her, but she skipped out of his way and ran down the stairs. She was pretty sure he couldn't hurt her in her own house, not with his dad right there.

Her mum cooked a nice tea and they all sat around the kitchen table to eat it. Patrick scoffed everything on his plate and asked for more, and Mel's mum said something about how lovely it was to feed a boy with a good appetite. Patrick sneered at Mel across the table. She could barely eat a bite. She kept trying to wind her legs around her chair legs, drawing them in as close as she could, because he had already kicked her viciously in the ankle, twice. The first time she winced and jumped, and he said, 'Oh, sorry!' in a smarmy voice, as if it had been an accident. The second time she didn't react, even though his shoe scraped hard against her ankle bone and she was pretty sure he had made it bleed.

After they had finished dinner, Mel's mum suggested that Mel and Patrick watch some television. She and Phil stayed in the kitchen. Mel sat on an armchair, and kept a sharp eye on Patrick. The kitchen door was open, so she knew he couldn't hit her or hurt her, but she wasn't taking any chances. Surely he and his dad would have to go home soon? But after her mum had done the washing up, the grown-ups came into the front room. 'We thought we might go down to the pub for a quick one,' said Phil. 'Will you two be all right on your own? Patrick will look after you, Mel.'

'No!' gasped Mel without pausing to think. 'I . . . I've got a horrible stomach ache. Please, Mum.' She looked at her mum, trying to show with her eyes how desperate she was. Her mum looked hard and unmoved, and Mel thought she might have to burst into tears. But Phil came to her rescue.

'If the little one's not well . . .'

'She's fine,' said Mel's mum shortly.

'I'm not,' said Mel quickly. 'It's very sore.'

'Another time,' said Phil. 'Maybe we could get my sister to watch them both. Come on, Patrick. Home time.'

He put a gentle hand on Mel's mum's back and guided her to the door so they could say goodbye. Patrick got up to follow, stopping briefly to give Mel an agonising Chinese burn on her wrist. Mel huddled in her chair. Her stomach did hurt now. She'd be in no end of trouble with her mum. And she'd seen how she had looked up at Phil, and his expression when he'd looked down at her. Phil would be back, and Patrick with him. She trudged upstairs to her bedroom, hoping she could pretend to be asleep before her mum came back. When she got to her room, she found the copy of *The Hobbit* on her bed. He had ripped it in half.

That was the end of Mel's perfect summer. She never knew when Phil and Patrick would be coming around, so she lived each day in a state of apprehension. When they were there, she tried desperately to stay in the same room as her mum and Phil, but as they were trying to get to know each other, the last thing they wanted was a nine-year-old girl watching their every move. Her mum kept shoving her out of the room, telling her to go and watch television or play in her room. She didn't dare go to her room when

Patrick was round, because he saw it as a place to hurt her where the adults couldn't see or hear, and he took particular delight in breaking her things.

Thankfully, the adults never again suggested going out and leaving Patrick and Mel alone together, but about once a week they'd all walk around to the house Phil and Patrick shared with Phil's sister. She would keep an eye on the kids while Phil and Mel's mum went to the pub. Those were the best times for Mel, because Phil's sister, Gloria, seemed to be the only person who wasn't taken in by Patrick's smarmy insincerity and saw him for the bully he was. The first time they were both in her care, she waited until the door had closed behind the adults and then stood both kids in front of her. 'Right,' she said, folding her arms over her large, forbidding bosom, 'I'm going to do the ironing. Melanie, if you like, you can sit in the kitchen with me and watch the little telly or read a book. Patrick, you get yourself out in the garden. I know what you're like with littler ones, and let me tell you, it's not happening in my house. All right?'

Patrick opened his mouth and started to whine about how unfair that was, but Gloria lashed out and gave him a sharp clip on the ear, which had him howling. He trudged upstairs muttering blackly under his breath. Mel knew she'd pay for that when he next got her on her own, but for now, she was safe. She loved those quiet times, sitting in Gloria's kitchen, reading or drawing while Gloria got on with her household tasks. She wished with all her heart that her own mum could see what Gloria did quite plainly, but it was not to be. Her mum was sugary sweet to Patrick all the time, trying to keep on Phil's good side. Patrick was very good at being smoothly polite and sucking up to adults. Phil seemed to have no idea at all about who his son really was. He treated him with a kind of vague distance, and seemed to think any kind of hands-on parenting should be woman's work and therefore not his concern.

Mel wasn't going to let Patrick crush her spirit though, and she kept studying hard. She remained top of the class in most subjects. There was a small choir at school and she joined, loving the camaraderie of singing together. After the circus came to their town, she was inspired and taught herself to do the splits and Arab springs and to walk on her hands. She was popular at school, and enjoyed performing for her friends and in school shows. In contrast, Patrick was barely scraping by academically, and his dad and teachers all seemed sure he would simply leave school at sixteen and get a job. The contrast with Mel's academic success and popularity seemed to enrage him even more.

Over the next couple of years, her mum and Phil got closer, and one evening they came back from the pub breathless and laughing. Her mum held out her hand to show Mel her brand new sparkling engagement ring. What could Mel say? She smiled thinly and gave her mum a hug. They set a date for the wedding within just a few weeks: as it was the second time for both of them, it was just going to be a registry office do with a few sausage rolls and sandwiches in the pub after. Mel went along with all the preparations, and submitted to the scratchy taffeta dress her mum chose for her. She even sat quietly in the hairdressers the day before while they wound rags into her hair to make ringlets.

That evening, she and her mum sat opposite one another

at the kitchen table. Her mum was carefully painting her nails, her own hair up in rollers. The house was very quiet – the very last night when it would be just Mel and her mum, because the next day, Phil and Patrick would be moving in. Most of their stuff was already upstairs in boxes and bags. Mel watched her mum closely for what seemed like hours. She was a little plumper and softer in the face than she had been when Mel's dad had died. She looked pretty and happy, in anticipation of her big day. Mel so wanted to be happy for her, but then she started thinking about how, from tomorrow, her own life would change, never to be the same again. She didn't mean to do it, but suddenly the tears came, and once she began to cry, she couldn't stop. Her mum looked up in surprise. 'What now?' she said, a little impatiently. Mel got up and came around the table and buried her face in her mum's lap, in the way that she used to when she was a tiny girl. Her mum patted her hair lightly and exasperatedly, with the flat of her hand, trying not to ruin her nails. 'Don't be silly now,' she said. 'Is it your dad? Are you thinking about your dad, then?'

Mel hadn't been, but now she did. She imagined how her dad would feel if he knew how his daughter was being bullied and frightened by a boy who was coming to live right in her own house, and that made her cry even harder. Eventually she managed to gasp, 'Mum, please don't do it. Don't marry Phil. I'm scared of Patrick. He hurts me. Please don't.'

Her mum grabbed her then, with no thought for her nails, and hauled her to her feet so she could look her in the eyes. She was clearly furious. 'Listen, you selfish little cow, I'm getting married tomorrow. I need Phil. We need Phil. We need a man to care for us, and he's a good man. You've been a spoiled brat and an only child for too long anyway. It's about time you learned how to live with a brother. It'll do you good, and you're just going to have to manage. All right?' and she shoved Mel away, a little hard, so Mel stumbled and almost fell. Without another word, Mel turned and went to her bedroom. When she took off her jumper to go to bed, there were smears of red nail varnish under the arms, like blood.

She learned then and there that there was no point in speaking out, because her mother wouldn't help her. She got through the wedding with grim determination, and only sustained a few bruises from Patrick's pinching as they stood side-by-side during the speeches. She kept her head down at home, spending as much time as she could in the living room in plain view of the adults, or visiting friends' houses. She focused hard on her schoolwork. She knew that good marks could be her ticket away from home. She got a paper round, and with Gloria's help opened a Post Office account, where she put away every penny she earned. And she spent every spare minute she had working on her performing skills.

At fifteen, she finally and belatedly hit puberty. Although she was still petite, slim and wiry, she developed breasts and hips. She had always dreaded it, although she had known it would happen eventually. One day, she was out in the garden practising her acrobatics. She was standing on her hands when she saw Patrick come out of the kitchen door and stand staring at her. She was suddenly aware that her shirt was untucked and her midriff was showing. She jumped to her feet and tucked it in. His face was red and tense. 'Don't look at me like that,' she said harshly. 'It's disgusting.'

'Why?' he said, and grinned. 'It's not like you're my sister.'

She didn't want to run yet. She wanted to get her qualifications. She also knew that if she left home before she was sixteen, her mother would send the police after her. But she was pretty sure that if she was over sixteen, they would probably just let her go. So she stayed. It was like living with a time bomb. Patrick suddenly seemed capable of much worse than Chinese burns and trip-ups.

It was a Friday night, and her mum and Phil were out with friends. Mel had gone to bed early with a book. Patrick was out with mates, hanging around in the park and drinking. She was reading but she quickly switched off her light when she heard the front door bang open. She prayed that it was her mum and Phil. But then she heard his heavy and unsteady tread on the stairs. She huddled down under the blankets and pretended to be asleep. He threw her door open and she could hear him breathing heavily as he looked at her shape under the blankets. She didn't stand a chance against his strength and weight, so when he ripped the blankets off her, she lay there like she was dead. Through the whole, awful experience, she didn't even open her eyes.

She got up very early the next morning, packed the bare essentials into a bag and was outside the Post Office before it opened. As soon as she could get inside, she withdrew all her money. Then she went around to Gloria's house and pounded on the kitchen door. When Gloria opened it and saw her face, she drew Mel inside and shut and locked the kitchen door.

'What did he do?'

'He . . .' She couldn't say the words. She just shook her head, and closed her eyes. Tears leaked on to her cheeks. 'I've got some money. I need to get away.'

'Yes,' said Gloria. She didn't argue. She also, to Mel's surprise, didn't suggest they tell Phil or her mum, or call the police. 'I have a friend in London you can stay with. She's in an area called Streatham. I'll ring her in an hour. In the meantime, go upstairs and have a bath.' Gloria gave her a gentle push towards the stairs. That evening, Gloria put her on a coach bound for London. She handed her an envelope, stuffed with notes, and a piece of paper with her friend's address and telephone number on it. 'She'll put you up and get you into a school to finish your studies. We'll keep in touch through her. Don't come back,' said Gloria, and squeezed Mel's hand fiercely. Mel climbed on the coach and the doors hissed closed. She waved to Gloria through the window. She would never see her again: Gloria succumbed to lung cancer less than a year later.

As the coach pulled on to the motorway and Mel stared out at the setting sun, she wondered where her mum was, and what she was thinking. What would Gloria say to her? Would she come after Mel, or leave her be? Instinct told her her mum wouldn't come looking for her, and she was proved right.

She got to London, where she lodged with Gloria's friend Doreen, who was kind but distant. She soon saw Mel was more than capable of looking after herself, and left her to get on with it, which is exactly what Mel did. She got excellent O and A levels and won a place to study theatre at Goldsmith's.

She didn't miss her mum. Where the love should be in her heart was only an echoing emptiness, drained by years of disappointment. She had tried to speak out and had been shouted down, and even when Mel had been in danger, her mum had chosen to ignore it. Mel didn't know a lot, but she did know that if she ever had children of her own, she would listen.

21

LEE NOW

At the moment, Lee thought, his relationship with Jo seemed to consist of fleeting brushes. She would sweep past him in the morning, kissing his cheek as she rushed out of the house to get to work, and she would briefly rub his arm or shoulder as she fell into bed beside him late at night. If he saw her in between, she was always in motion, rushing from her desk to the door, flying out of the car into the shop, dashing into the bathroom to grab a few minutes with the kids as they played in the bath.

Richard had rented them office space in Angel, and together they had hired a small but high-powered team: a PR person, someone to scout locations and a fashion buyer. Holly was still in overall charge of the look of the range and the original designs, but Gary, the new buyer, was there to get stuff in bulk as they opened more stores. Jo had had to hire more store staff for the shop in East Finchley to help Mel, because she quite simply had no time to be there herself. Things were moving fast, but in a good way. Even though he missed her, Lee had to admit when he did see

Jo, her face was aglow with excitement. She was loving every second of this new adventure.

And Lee? How was he finding his new adventure? Stay-at-home dad extraordinaire? Primary caregiver? House husband? The first day was an unqualified disaster. He'd managed to get Zach ready for nursery, but hadn't got Imogene dressed or given her any breakfast. As a result, he ended up stuck in traffic on the way back from nursery with a hungry, screaming baby in pyjamas. Once they were home and he'd got her fed and dressed, he was exhausted. He had sat with her on his lap, watching some kids' TV, and then let her play on the floor while he tackled the breakfast dishes and put some washing on. Then she got tired and fractious and wanted to have a nap, and Lee put her down without checking the time. When he did look at the clock, it was only fifteen minutes until he had to go and fetch Zach. He hadn't made any lunch, or got a minute's creative work done. Off he went, back to the nursery, with Imi screaming in the back once again because he'd had to wake her up to put her in the car.

It was raining, so they couldn't go to the park or even play in the garden, so the afternoon was spent devising games indoors. All of a sudden, it was six o'clock. The living room looked as if a toy bomb had exploded, there was nothing for dinner, the remains of the sandwiches they had had for lunch were drying out on the plates that were still on the table and the load of laundry he had put on that morning was still lying, wet, in the machine. He was angry with himself. He felt like he had failed, and particularly failed Imogene, who seemed to have had a thoroughly miserable day.

He resolved to do better the next day, and he did. He had both kids dressed and fed well before it was time to take Zach to nursery. He'd worked out that Jo was right, and that walking with the pushchair was easier and less stressful than driving and having to find parking, so he did that. He timed Imi's nap so she had plenty of time to wake up naturally before they had to leave to pick up Zach, and he even managed to organise beans on toast for lunch and a pasta dinner before Jo got back from work. The same load of washing was still languishing in the washing machine, but what the hell. One day at a time. Each day got a little better and he got a little more done, and managed to keep both kids reasonably happy. By the end of the week, he was on his knees though. He felt much more exhausted than he ever had putting in a full week's work in an office. If he thought about why, it was because he would set out to do the simplest task, but never manage to complete it. Going out in the car, shopping, washing dishes, cooking . . . anything he tried to do meant he had to see what both children were doing, either engage them and get them ready to do it with him, or occupy them safely while he tried to do the task alone. Nothing ever got done without interruption either.

By the second week, he felt a little more confident, so while Zach was at nursery, he took Imi to a couple of the baby-and-toddler groups she had previously attended with Jo. The first one they went to was in a church hall. He still hadn't quite cracked timekeeping with a small child, so they were about fifteen minutes late. They walked in hand-in-hand, and the group of women sitting on chairs near the coffee table all turned to look at them. One woman smiled brightly and said, 'Oh hello, Imogene! Lily's over there, waiting to play with you!' She indicated her own daughter, a little girl of about Imi's age, who was banging two sauce-pans together in the kitchen corner. Imogene leaned against Lee's leg and hung on to his hand shyly. The women all turned back to their conversation. No one spoke to Lee.

He led Imi over to the kitchen corner and knelt on the floor. He passed her a spoon and a plastic bowl, and she began to play, keeping up a stream of babbling commentary as she went along. She and the little girl, Lily, didn't seem at all interested in playing together. Lee knew that Imi was still too small to play with someone, but she often liked playing alongside another child, as long as they didn't snatch things from her. He got off the cold lino floor and pulled up a chair. He was quite happy to sit near her and watch her play. Every now and then she brought him a plate with a piece of plastic food on it, and he obligingly pretended to eat it. She moved on and played with some bricks, then rode around on a little push-along car. Her coordination was good, probably from trying constantly to keep up with Zach, and Lee watched in pride as she propelled herself efficiently with her fat little legs.

After forty-five minutes or so, there was a snack break, and all the children sat on a big waterproof sheet on the floor and ate raisins and breadsticks. Imi scoffed all her raisins and helped herself from the bowl of the little boy next to her, then got up and hurtled off to the play-dough table for a while. Ten minutes before the end of the session, there was a singalong, and Lee sat with her on his lap while she clapped her hands to all her favourite nursery rhymes. She had had fun, but he could see she was exhausted, so he took her to the baby-changing area and changed her nappy before loading her into her car seat. She was asleep before they reached the end of the block. It wasn't until he got home that Lee realised that not one of the mothers in the group had even greeted him, let alone engaged him in a conversation.

He mentioned it to Jo later that evening. She was surprised. 'Really? I've always found that lot will never shut up. I mean, granted, they only talk about kids and babies, or pregnancy or birth if you're lucky, but they're normally very friendly.'

'Perhaps I was just so caught up in playing with Imogene that they didn't want to interrupt.'

'Maybe,' said Jo, but she didn't sound sure. 'Maybe . . . they're just not used to seeing a dad there,' she said thoughtfully. 'I've certainly never seen one there before. You are rather a rare bird, you know.'

'What, a stay-at-home dad is a rare bird? That's ridiculous.'

'In middle-class yummy-mummy playgroups like that one, you are. The dads just aren't around.'

'I suppose it might take them a few goes to get used to me. Maybe I'll have a T-shirt printed that says, "Freelancer, not unemployed layabout".'

'So the one I'm having made for you that says "Kept man" won't do?' Jo smiled and slipped her arms around his waist.

'Do you reckon "Gigolo" would be too much for the Baby Chickens Toddler Group?'

'Oooh, if you had a gigolo T-shirt, would it be white, and

very tight?' asked Jo, running her hands over his arms and shoulders.

'Well, if that's what my sugar mommy bought me, that's what I would have to wear,' said Lee, smiling down at her.

'Aren't sugar mommies supposed to be older?'

'Details, details,' he said, and kissed her.

He and Imi went to another toddler group on the Thursday, and there a few mums did at least try to talk to him, but he couldn't shake the feeling that they were just being polite. They asked after Jo, and asked how he was managing with Imogene, and then smiled indulgently when he played with her, as if he was doing something rare and unusual. When he got out a baby wipe and cleaned her face and hands after snack time, one of the women said, 'Look at that! So clever!' As if he was a small child himself. He couldn't believe that they all still lived in a society with such divided gender roles. Did their husbands not play with their kids? Was a man caring competently for his child such a rare thing that it merited comment?

That Friday afternoon, he took both kids to the park. He didn't want to admit it, but he was a little bored, and while they played he caught himself surreptitiously checking Twitter on his phone. He'd always thought parents who stood around in the park staring at their phones were terrible people, but he was beginning to understand that watching Zach climb the wrong way up the slide and then launch his way back down head-first over and over, or pushing Imi end-lessly on the swing was not the most stimulating thing he had ever done. He was relieved when he saw Holly's sister

Miranda come into the playground with her kids. At least here was someone he could talk to.

He hadn't seen her for ages, and he was surprised at how thin and pale she looked. She'd always been quite round, even a bit dumpy, but she had lost quite a lot of weight – maybe two or three stone – and not in a good way, Lee thought. It didn't look like healthy exercise and diet-inspired weight loss, more like the weight had fallen off because she wasn't eating, or sleeping. Her clothes were hanging loose, and she had dark shadows under her eyes. He knew it must be worry and strain about her mum. Her kids seemed unaffected, and he saw that little Oscar had just started walking. He was barrelling around the play area with that slightly forward stance and lurching walk brand-new toddlers use. He was a dear little chap, built like a prop forward, and he was cackling away to himself with pride at his new achievement. It was enough to make anyone smile, and Lee looked up and caught Miranda's eye and grinned. She managed a weak little smile, but looked as if tears weren't too far away. Lee went straight over. 'You look like you could use a coffee.'

'Do I look that bad?' she said, shocked. Lee could have kicked himself.

'No, not at all,' he said quickly. 'Sorry, that definitely came out wrong. You look a bit tired, that's all, and I know you've been having a tough time.' She managed a weak smile.

'I'm sure I look rough as anything. And I'm knackered. Yes, I would love a coffee, but we've just got here, so I can't really drag the kids off . . .'

'You stay here,' said Lee. 'If you wouldn't mind keeping half an eye on Zach, I'll go and get us a couple of takeaways.'

She smiled gratefully and nodded. Imi was playing in the little sandpit, so he scooped her up and popped her in the pushchair, then made a dash to the coffee shop and returned with two lattes and a couple of chocolate brownies.

The kids all seemed content to get on with their own thing and he and Miranda sat side by side on the bench, sipping their coffee. She held her cup with both hands as if she was cold. Lee didn't say anything, just sat quietly beside her. After a few minutes he took the bag with the brownies out of his jacket pocket and slid them across the bench to her. She peeked inside and managed her first real smile of the day.

'My favourite. How did you know?'

'You ordered one when we had coffee ages ago, that time I was looking after the kids when Jo went on her business course,' Lee said. 'I remembered you liked them.'

She stared at him like he was an alien who had emerged from his spaceship and come to sit on her bench. 'You remember that? It was months ago. Maybe a year?'

'Was it?' Lee said, a little embarrassed.

'You're the only man I've ever met who would notice stuff like that,' said Miranda. 'I've been married to Paul for twelve years. I don't think he could tell you what my favourite dessert was if you held a gun to his head.'

Lee glanced at her, a little surprised at how bitter she sounded. In his limited experience Miranda had always been gushy, a bit superficial perhaps, but always sweetness and light.

He sat quietly for another minute or so. Eventually, he said, 'I'm sorry. What you're going through, you and Holly, and your family . . . it must be so hard. How are you coping?'

'Holly is being amazing,' Miranda says. 'She has it much harder than me. She's there all the time with Mum, and it's so difficult.' She stopped short, as if she might have said more but had thought better of it.

'It can't be easy for any of you,' said Lee gently.

'I just wish I could do more,' said Miranda. 'I wish I could do anything. But every time I see Mum, I get so upset. She looks worse every time, even if it's only a day or so since I last saw her.' She took a sip of her coffee, and then the words started to spill out of her. 'My time with her is so limited . . . I always have the kids to worry about, and getting someone to look after them while I drive to Ealing and spend time with Mum and drive back . . . I worry all the way there and all the way back and the whole time I'm there . . . what if they need me? What if I can't get back in time? And then I feel bad, because I'm worrying about traffic on the North Circular, not giving Mum my full attention, and then there's all the things I used to do . . . the groups I was in and the PTA at the school, and just running my own household . . . Paul's dry-cleaning and shopping and cooking . . . and sometimes I let things slip and I feel bad about that too . . .'

What the hell was Paul doing through all this? Lee found himself thinking. Was he moaning at his wife that she hadn't collected his dry-cleaning while she tried to care for her dying mother and his children too? A tear brimmed over and slipped down her cheek. She turned away, mortified. 'I'm so sorry. I didn't mean to go on at you. You barely know me. Now there's another thing I can add to my list of things I'm doing wrong . . . ranting at strange men in the park.'

Lee put his coffee down and grasped her hand and held it on the bench between them. 'Okay, firstly, I'm not a strange man. Because of Jo and Holly, I do know what you're going through and I asked you how you were doing. And secondly, you're doing amazingly well. You're doing everything you could possibly do, and more. Give yourself a break.'

She looked down at her hand in his, and managed a little smile. 'Thanks. That's the nicest thing anyone has said to me in I don't know how long.' She gave his hand a little squeeze, then took her hand away and busied herself with getting a tissue out of her handbag. Lee looked up and saw that over by the swings there was a little cluster of women who had obviously been watching them. One leaned over and whispered to her friend. Fine, he thought. Let them gossip. If they were going to read evil intentions into him comforting a woman with a dying mother, then they needed to go and get themselves lives.

22

HOLLY NOW

Things at home continued to be difficult, but manageable. Judith's pain was better controlled, but she was very weak, and needed Holly on hand in case she needed to go to the toilet. Sometimes she even needed help to sit up in bed or roll over. Holly had never imagined she would care for another person's intimate needs until she was a mother. If you'd asked her six months before how she would feel about helping her mum pull her pants up, or wash in the shower, she'd have been horrified. But it had to be done, and in a funny way, it seemed like the most loving thing she had ever done.

Judith slept for long periods now, and often there wasn't anything to do but sit there in case she woke up and wanted anything. Because she was on morphine, her dreams were very vivid and she was often a little confused. She'd wake with a start and say something seemingly random.

'We can paint them terracotta!' she once said brightly.

'Paint what, Mum?' asked Holly.

'What?' said Judith. 'What are you talking about, Holly?' And when Holly tried to explain that she was answering

Judith, and asked more questions to see if she could find out what should be painted terracotta, Judith lay back on her pillows, and said angrily, 'Well, I don't know. I don't know what needs painting, and what is terracotta anyway?'

When she was awake and compos mentis, however, she wanted Holly to talk to her. She loved to hear about Holly's time in South Africa, about the markets where she worked, and the homes and gardens. She was fascinated to hear that many people had swimming pools in their gardens.

'My goodness,' she said once, 'It sounds as if the sun really does shine all the time there.'

'Pretty much,' said Holly. 'You could probably wear a sundress and sandals for eight months of the year.'

'Oh my, Holly,' sighed Judith. 'I do so wish I had come out to visit you when you were there.'

'I wish you had too, Mum,' said Holly. At the time, she hadn't been surprised that Judith never made the trip, and she hadn't missed her particularly. But when she thought about it now, she'd have loved to introduce her mum to some of her friends, take her shopping, widen her perspective. Judith seemed to have lived such a small life, and now it was too late to change that. It was no substitute, but Holly put together a slideshow of photos from her time in Johannesburg (edited to exclude any shots of Damon). She put it on her iPad and sat on the edge of Judith's bed, her arm behind her mum's thin shoulders, going through the pictures with her. Judith sighed at the landscapes, wanted to know all about Holly's friends, and exclaimed with joy at the pictures of Holly's Doradolla designs. It seemed to give her so much pleasure and pride. Why had Holly never done this before? For the life of her, she couldn't imagine.

It had been three weeks since she had last seen him, and Holly had not managed to have another date with Fraser. They had hoped to get together on the Sunday night after their first date, but Holly's mum had come home from the hospice that day. Since then, fate seemed to be conspiring against them. Whenever Holly could snatch some time away from the house, Fraser was working, or had Finlay with him. It was very frustrating not seeing him, but the anticipation made Holly want him more, and she was enjoying getting to know him better through their phone and text conversations. There was no doubt that the heat between them was still very real; they spoke on the phone every day, and sent a lot of text messages in between. These started out flirtatious and ended up downright filthy. They even shared a few late-night phone-calls which left them both gasping and desperate to be together.

Miranda helped with Judith as much as she could, but she could only manage a few hours on a weekday morning when her kids were at nursery and at the childminder's. Holly toyed with the idea of asking her to come one evening to sit with their mum when the kids were asleep, but she would have to explain why, and she somehow didn't think Miranda would be thrilled to mum-sit while she went out to shag a still-officially-married man.

David was no help at all. He hadn't even visited for the last few weeks. It wasn't as if he didn't care – he rang at least three times a week, and kept trying to buy things and pay for things, and he was always very willing to ring people in the care system and yell at them – but when he did come, he just didn't know what to do. He seemed to find the sight of Judith intensely distressing, and he just couldn't sit quietly beside her. He wanted to do things, to bustle around and make things happen. Privately, Holly found it easier when he wasn't there. His agitation was infectious and she found herself more focused on him than on Judith's needs.

Christopher Benton, true to his word, came by twice a week and worked in the garden. Holly had given him a key to the side gate, and he would quietly let himself in, mow the lawn, trim the edges, weed and tidy, and then let himself out. When Holly was in her mum's bedroom and looked out of the window, she would see him working industriously and neatly. However, every now and then he would glance up at Judith's window, his face full of yearning and concern. It seemed to Holly as if Judith was a princess locked in a tower, and he was a humble gardener without a hope of rescuing her. Or maybe Holly was over-romanticising the whole thing. Maybe he was just short-sighted. If Holly was there and not busy with Judith, she would go out and offer him a cup of tea. He would sometimes accept, but he would never come into the house. 'Don't want to track mud into your kitchen,' he'd say, and even though Holly protested that she didn't mind, he was adamant. She had told Judith a few times that Christopher was coming, but it didn't seem to have sunk in.

One day, however, Judith was slightly more alert and bright than she had been, and she asked to sit by the window. With a great deal of effort, they had got the enormous recliner up to her room, and it was a comfortable place for her to sit when she was up to it. She was enjoying the rays of spring sunshine on her face when Christopher started up the lawn-mower outside. Judith opened her eyes and asked, 'What was that?'

'It's Mr Benton, Mum. I told you he was coming to do the garden. He's just mowing the lawn.'

'Mr Benton?'

'Christopher Benton? From your church?'

'I know who he is,' said Judith, a little impatiently. 'Why hasn't he come in to say hello to me?'

Now there was a question Holly didn't know how to answer. Should she mention what Mr Benton had said to her about him and Judith courting? And what about the fact that she had sent him packing? Was it better to play dumb and act as if he was just another friend from church? Holly decided to go for a fairly neutral approach.

'I think he thought you might not be well enough to see him. He just wanted to do something to help.'

'Ask him to come in. Please,' said Judith.

Holly couldn't have been more surprised, but she was thrilled. She ran down the stairs and out of the kitchen door. 'Mr Benton!' she said. 'My mum is a little better today, and she would love to see you.'

'Oh no,' he said, flustered. 'I couldn't possibly. I don't want to intrude . . . the mud . . . I wouldn't want to incon-venience . . .'

'Mr Benton,' said Holly, patiently but firmly, 'she's a bit better today' – she leaned on the word 'today', so he would understand this improvement was very temporary – 'and she's asked for you, specifically. Please.'

He fussed for a little while longer and then said he would

go to the car to fetch his 'house shoes' and meet Holly at the back door.

With all the fiddling and faddling and adjusting he did, carefully removing his wellies by the back door, stepping in in his socks, sitting on a kitchen chair (trouser twitch before he sat down), putting on his shoes, tying his laces in perfect bows, asking to use the bathroom so he could wash his hands and comb his hair – Holly was beginning to worry that Judith might have passed on before he was ready. Somehow, eventually, she got him up the stairs and tapped lightly on Judith's door. They both popped their heads around the door, and it made Holly's heart ache to see that Judith had also made a little effort while they had been gone. She had combed her hair as best she could, although it had thinned and got rather long, so it didn't look as neat as it had always done before she got sick. She had also managed to put on a little lipstick and powder. She still looked deathly pale and her thinness was alarming, but she had a little colour and she managed a smile for Mr Benton.

He was very good, Holly thought. He smiled warmly at Judith and looked for all the world as if he had come to a routine afternoon tea party. He didn't allow himself to look shocked or sad at her appearance. He came over and took her hand, lightly holding her fingertips in a courtly, old-fashioned way, and inclined his head.

'So sorry I can't get up,' Judith said.

'Not at all,' said Mr Benton. 'It's very good to see you, Judith.'

'How have you been, Christopher?' she said. 'Do pull up a chair.'

He looked around and drew the stool from Judith's dressing table close to her chair. 'Not too bad,' he said. 'Just been out in the garden. Your lupins are coming on a treat.'

'Really?' said Judith. 'I'd have thought the snails would have got them.'

'Ah, they might have, but I make up this spray myself . . . one part Fairy Liquid, three parts water, and a secret ingredient. Keeps the snails right away!'

Judith managed a little laugh, the first one Holly had heard from her in months. 'Ah, now, Christopher. You'll have to tell me what the secret ingredient is. You can't keep me in suspense!'

Holly took a step or two back, towards the door. Neither of them seemed aware that she was there at all.

'Er . . .' she said softly, 'I'll go and make some tea, shall I?' But they had moved on to the best ways to encourage tomato plants to flower, and didn't hear her. She went downstairs slowly, and took her time making a pot of tea. When she crept back upstairs with it, she found Mr Benton quietly reading one of the classical-music reviews in *The Times* aloud to Judith. She put the tea tray down on the side table and slipped out again.

He came every day after that, and his company made an enormous difference. Judith made the effort to be up and dressed to see him if she possibly could, and he paid her compliments and made her smile. If she was too tired to get out of bed, he would draw a chair up close and read to her until she fell asleep. Holly found it very touching to watch them together, and she wished with all her heart that Judith had not sent him away all those months ago. They had lost so much time, and she was happy to see her mum experiencing some affection, and – dare she call it that? – love, in these last months of her life. She remembered the stack of letters she had seen in her mum's jewellery box. Were they love letters from Mr Benton? They must have been.

Holly wondered if there was any way Mr Benton might sit with her mum for an evening, so she could finally get out to see Fraser, but she didn't know how to ask him. He saved her the bother however. On the Thursday afternoon, he came down to find her in the kitchen. 'Oh, Holly,' he said, deferentially, 'I am so sorry to disturb you, but I was wondering whether you would mind my bringing a portable television here to put in Judith's room?'

Holly could have kicked herself. Why had she never thought of giving her mum a TV in the bedroom? 'There's no need to bring a portable one, Mr Benton. We could just move the set from the living room up to the bedroom. No one watches it downstairs.'

'Are you sure?' He looked very pleased. 'Only I noticed they're showing *Brief Encounter* on the television on Sunday evening, and it's a film we – Judith and I – very much enjoyed watching together once before. I thought perhaps she might like to see it again. It wouldn't inconvenience you for me to be here on a Sunday evening, would it?'

'Oh no . . .'

'I thought perhaps you might like to take the opportunity to go out . . . see some friends perhaps? I could cook Judith a light supper . . .'

'That would be brilliant!' Holly leapt on his offer with

alacrity before he changed his mind. It was a win–win situation. The elderly lovebirds would get an evening to themselves, and she could see Fraser. 'I'll get the television moved upstairs this afternoon!'

She ran to her room and sent Fraser a quick text message: 'I'm a free agent on Sunday evening. I can't stay out all night, but I'm sure we could get some things on our to-do list done in a few hours . . .'

He rang her immediately. 'Oh my God, you mean I actually get to see you?' he said excitedly.

'All of me, baby, all of me,' she giggled. He groaned at that.

'I can't wait. Listen, I've got Finlay for the weekend, but Lindsay's due to collect him from mine at five on Sunday. Can you get to me by six? Can you be naked by five past? Can I kiss you all over?'

'Yes, yes and yes. Can't wait.'

'Me neither,' he said. 'You have no idea.'

She was nervous about leaving Judith, but her mum was very encouraging. 'Go, have a nice time,' she said, when Holly tentatively said she was going to see Fraser. 'You've been stuck in this house day after day, looking after me. Christopher and I will watch the film and I'll be asleep by nine, I'm sure.'

Holly felt better after she said that, and she told herself that Mr Benton had her mobile number and she would be a twenty-minute drive away if she was needed. She was jittery and excited on the Sunday afternoon, and spent ages trying to choose what to wear. It didn't seem to matter terribly much, as Fraser had made it clear that whatever she was wearing was going to end up on the floor as soon as she came through the door. In the end, she went for a simple white cotton dress, a pretty lacy bra and matching knickers. She showered, plucked and primped, and was ready by five, then paced up and down, her stomach full of butterflies.

She checked her watch. Five thirty. If she drove slowly, she'd be at Fraser's bang on time. But she didn't need to worry about driving slowly, as it turned out. The traffic was appalling, and instead of getting there early, she began to worry she was going to be late. She was stuck for ages at a set of temporary traffic lights, and she grabbed her phone to let him know she was delayed, only to see that she had no signal at all. Well, she'd get there eventually. Luckily the traffic eased as soon as she got through the temporary lights, and she was outside Fraser's by five past six. She parked and hurried to the door, trying not to look too flustered in case he was watching from the window. She pressed the bell, and he buzzed her straight in.

She ran up the stairs to his flat, and saw he had left the front door ajar. Maybe he was already in the bedroom. She stepped through the door, closed it behind her and leaned against it. 'Right, Dr John,' she called out. 'I'm wearing a flimsy white dress, I'm carrying a pack of twelve ultra-sheer condoms and I'm kicking off my knickers . . . right now.' She reached up under her skirt and started to shimmy her pants down over her hips. She heard the kitchen door open, and looked up, expecting to see Fraser emerging carrying a bottle of champagne, or maybe wearing an apron and nothing else. Instead she saw . . . Lindsay.

She had to assume this was Lindsay: she was the same

height and build as the woman she had seen in the doorway at Christmas, all those months ago. And what other woman would be in Fraser's flat? Holly, ever dignified, pulled her knickers back up and let her skirt fall.

'I imagine I'm not the Dr John you were expecting,' said the woman coolly. This was definitely Lindsay then. She looked Holly up and down slowly, and then said, 'Fraser rang to say that he had a flat tyre and he and Finlay had been delayed. I assume he didn't get hold of you . . . ?'

Holly, who hadn't said anything since her unforgettable condoms-and-knickers pronouncement, fumbled in her bag for her phone. Sure enough, there were five missed calls and two text messages from Fraser, all of which had come through since she left the signal black hole. 'No,' she said simply. There didn't seem to be much else to say.

'And you are . . . ?' Lindsay said. She had a rather superior attitude that made Holly feel as if she'd been sent to the headmistress's office.

'Holly. Holly Evans,' she said, with more confidence than she felt. Part of her was mortified at the situation, and very aware that this woman was Fraser's wife and the mother of his child, and had been part of his life for a very long time. But another part of her was furious at Lindsay's high-handed manner. Fraser was her boyfriend (was he?) and she had every right to be here.

'And tell me, Holly Evans,' said Lindsay icily, 'do you make a habit of fucking other women's husbands?'

'What?' said Holly. She was properly angry now. 'You can't talk to me like that. Fraser isn't your husband any more . . .'

'I think you'll find he is.'

'You're legally separated . . .'

'We've had a brief trial separation and we're in the process of getting back together again, I think you'll find.'

'That's not what Fraser—'

'Told you? Well, I'm sorry, my dear, but you've been fed a line. We separated because he has a tendency to play away . . . silly little dalliances, nothing serious, but I found it hurtful. We're working through it, and he's been seeing a therapist . . . they're calling it sex addiction. Very American, isn't it?'

'That's not how he . . .'

'He told you we were having marital difficulties and were seeing a counsellor, didn't he? That's one of his favourite pick-up lines. Come on,' she said, looking at Holly with pity. 'You're a big, grown-up girl. A married man feeds you the "my wife doesn't understand me" sob story, and you believe him?'

Holly stared at Lindsay. What an idiot she had been. After Damon, she vowed she'd never get taken in by a man with a clever story again. But Fraser had been so convincing . . . all the bumbling, sweet talk about not having had a date in ages, about not having had sex . . .

As if she could read Holly's mind, Lindsay said coolly, 'He's probably also told you we haven't slept together in ages. But just so you know, I was here last night and we had sex. As we have throughout the separation. He's never been able to resist me.'

And to be fair, she was beautiful. She was wearing a slim-fitting black linen dress and her hair was a sheet of ebony. She made Holly, in her cotton frock and sandals, feel gauche and scruffy. 'They're on their way back now,' Lindsay said. 'It's probably best if you're not here, don't you think? I don't really want to introduce my husband's latest bit on the side to my seven-year-old son.'

Holly, who had not moved from her position by the front door, fumbled behind her and opened the door. The thought of bumping into Fraser and Finlay on the stairs or in the street was too awful to contemplate. She ran out of the building, fumbling in her handbag for her keys, and flung herself into the car. She roared off as fast as she dared, and as she swung around the corner into the main road, she saw Fraser in his clunky old car, coming the other way. He didn't see her – why would he be looking? And anyway, he had no idea what car she would be driving. The sight of his handsome profile, even though it was just for an instant, made her feel such a fool. How had she fallen for his lies? What an idiot she was. An idiot and a liability to herself.

She was home by six forty-five. Christopher and her mum were still watching the film. She tried to creep up to her bedroom as quietly as she could, but Christopher popped his head out of her mum's room. 'Hello, Holly,' he said, surprised. 'We weren't expecting you back for hours!'

'My plans fell through.' She managed a weak smile.

'What a pity,' he said gallantly. 'You look very pretty. Well, the gentleman's loss, I say. Why don't you come in and join us? The film is still on, I've just made some tea and I took the liberty of bringing Judith some of my home-made Bakewell tart. She doesn't have much of an appetite, as you know, so you'd do me a great service by having a slice.'

Holly paused for a second. Now that she thought about it, the very last thing she wanted was to be alone with her thoughts. She had the rest of her life to think about what a romantic disaster she was. 'Thank you,' she said as graciously as she could manage. 'That would be lovely.'

And so it transpired that at around the time she had expected to be licking the sweat off Fraser's naked body for the second or third time, she was watching Trevor Howard touch Celia Johnson on the shoulder while she nibbled on the last crumbs of Mr Benton's lighter-than-air pastry. Life, she concluded, is always full of surprises.

23

JO NOW

It was the Easter bonnet that did it. Jo was racing around the house, trying to coordinate a halfway decent outfit. She only had about twenty minutes before she had to race to the Tube station so she could meet Richard at nine at King's Cross to catch a train to Leeds to meet a potential supplier. She would have been up earlier and been better organised, but Imi had woken seven or eight times in the night, feverish and niggly. Jo wasn't sure if she was ill or just teething, but whatever was bothering her little girl, only Mummy would do. In the end, Jo had slept fitfully for a few hours, sitting up in bed with Imi on her chest. She was fuzzy-headed and clumsy this morning. Everything she wanted to wear seemed to be crumpled in the laundry basket. She would have had a go at Lee for not keeping up with the laundry, but she knew he'd had as hard a time during the day with Imogene as she'd had through the night. At 8.05, she was standing in the utility room in her bra and tights and dressing gown, ironing a dress that she hoped very much would (a) still fit her, and (b) be warm enough for Leeds. She glanced up through the door into the kitchen, where Lee was giving the kids their breakfast, and saw that Zach was weeping silently into his porridge. Lee hadn't noticed; he was too busy trying to coax a little food into Imi. Jo unplugged the iron and went through to sit next to Zach. 'What's wrong, sweetie?' she said, putting her arm around his shoulders.

'Go 'way,' he mumbled.

'Zach! Don't be rude to your mum,' Lee chipped in from the other side of the table.

'Come on, Zachy, why are you crying? Let Mum help,' Jo said, giving him a squeeze. She stole a glance at the clock. She was still in her underwear, not wearing any make-up and she knew she looked grey and rumpled from the interrupted night. If Zach was also getting ill, his timing couldn't be worse. 'Zachy? What's wrong, love?'

'You forgot to make my Easter bunnet,' he shouted.

'Your what?'

'My bunnet. It's the Easter parade at school today and we all have to have a bunnet and you promised we'd make one together and then you didn't make it and now I haven't got a bunnet and everyone will laugh at me.'

'Oh . . .' said Lee, realising. 'Easter *bonnet*.'

And with a start, Jo remembered. About a week before, she'd been sitting at her desk trying desperately to catch up on emails, and Zach had come to stand beside her and told her all about the parade at school and how he needed the best 'bunnet' because Joshua's mother always made the best ones and Joshua was a smelly poo. She'd stopped what she was doing, and laughed. 'We'll make it together, Zach, this weekend. Promise. And it'll be the bestest bunnet in town.'

'Should we ask Dad to help?' Zach asked.

'No, let's do it just the two of us,' she had said, giving him a cuddle. 'It'll be a special mum-and-Zach project.'

But in the mad rush of the weekend, with grocery shopping and catching up on housework, taking the kids to three different birthday parties and creating a PowerPoint presentation for the Leeds meeting, the 'bunnet' had slipped her mind totally.

'Oh, Zachy . . .' she said, looking helplessly at Lee. 'I'm so sorry, but Mum has to leave to catch a train in ten minutes . . .' Zach started to cry really hard now, and her heart ached. Lee shrugged, then he raised his eyebrows and Jo knew he had had an idea. He rushed upstairs, and within a few minutes was back with Zach's plastic fireman's helmet, a roll of small white price tag stickers, Imi's little toy bunny and some small Easter eggs that Jo had stashed in their bedroom ready for Easter morning. He opened the drawer they used for craft materials and got some Sellotape and a sheet of green paper.

'How about we turn this helmet into a hill, with the Easter bunny on top, and some eggs at the bottom? We can make bunny paw prints with these stickers, and grass with the green paper? What do you say, big guy?'

Jo mouthed, 'Thank you,' to Lee. He had saved her bacon again.

'No,' said Zach stubbornly. 'Mummy do it.'

'Honey, I can't . . .'

'Mummy,' said Zach, and he looked her squarely in the eyes. 'You promised.'

Jo stared at him for a moment, sighed and took out her mobile. Richard's phone went straight to voicemail. He must already be on the Tube. Thank God. 'Richard? It's Jo. I'm so sorry, but I've been unavoidably delayed. Catch the nine a.m. train and I'll be on the next one. I'm sorry, but it's a domestic emergency and I have to sort it out.'

'I'll finish ironing your dress,' said Lee.

'Right, Zach,' said Jo, picking up the green paper and a pair of scissors. 'Shall we put some lovely green grass all the way around the bottom of our hill?'

The finished 'bunnet' was a bit wonky, and held together by Sellotape, string and luck, and it was unlikely to last five minutes beyond the parade, but Zach went off to nursery happy. Lee dropped Jo at the Tube station, saving her ten minutes, and the train came mercifully quickly. She made it to King's Cross by 8.55, and caught up with Richard as he headed for the platform.

'I just heard your message,' he said. 'I thought I'd have to manage the presentation on my own.'

The presentation. A work of art that she'd spent hours on over the weekend, currently sitting on her home PC. She had meant to save it on to a memory stick or email it to herself, but in the midst of the Easter-bunnet crisis, had completely forgotten.

'Excuse me,' she said to Richard, 'I just have to ring Lee about something. I'll see you in a moment.'

He boarded the train and went looking for their seats, and she stood by the door desperately hoping she'd catch Lee at home before he and Imi went to their playgroup. He answered the home phone on the third ring and she sighed with relief.

'Love, I desperately need your help. I forgot to save my

presentation to my laptop and I'm about to climb on a train to Leeds. Can you email it to me now?'

'Of course,' said Lee, and she talked him through where to find the file on her computer.

She got on the train and found Richard sitting in first class. He had got them each a coffee.

'Can I have a look at the presentation en route?' he asked.

'Of course!' Jo said brightly. 'I just need to make a few tiny final adjustments.'

To her relief, Richard settled down to read the *Financial Times* on his iPad. She booted up her laptop. Try as she might, she couldn't connect to the Wi-Fi, so she spent a hair-raising few minutes trying to remember how to use her mobile phone as a modem. It seemed to work in principle, but kept dropping the connection. It took her twenty minutes to get into her email and download the presentation. Then Power-Point kept crashing. She could feel sweat blooming under her arms. She'd have to pop into the chemist at Leeds station and buy some deodorant.

Finally, she was able to load the presentation and spin her laptop around to show Richard. 'There,' she said, as calmly as she could manage. It was 9.30 a.m. Between the Easter-bonnet crisis, the sick baby who she'd actually forgotten to kiss goodbye, the neglected husband, the nearly absent presentation and her less than perfect outfit now sporting fetching sweat stains, it had been a disaster of a morning. A real swan day, where if she appeared to be gliding along serenely, it was only because she was paddling like a lunatic beneath the surface.

They were going to Leeds to meet a woman called Kimberley Lytton, a clothing wholesaler who imported a vast array of children's fashion from the Far East. Jo and Richard had agreed that the first and most obvious step in growing the business was to start stocking clothes for little girls as well as boys. Jo was adamant that the brief would be the same: hard-wearing and reasonably priced play clothes. Their buyer, Gary, had a long-term working relationship with Kimberley, and Jo and Richard had come up to meet her, see her operation and talk about a potential link-up and prices and quantities. Jo had desperately wanted Holly to come on the trip, but her mother was just too ill for her to be out of town. She had taken copious notes from Holly on what to look for in terms of quality, and she had a list of questions to ask about sustainability and working conditions in the garment factories, which were core values of the business and very important to her and to Holly.

Every now and then in your life, you will meet someone who, for no real reason, just rubs you up the wrong way, and the feeling might well be mutual. Maybe you're having a bad day, maybe they are. Maybe it's some kind of profound hormonal thing, or perhaps it's related to a historic but long-forgotten clash between your ancestors and theirs. Whatever causes it, it can be really very bad, and there is nothing you can do to change the way you or the other person feels. This was what Jo kept telling herself, as she sat across the boardroom table from Kimberley Lytton.

It had started badly, when Kimberley met them at the station. She had brought her car so she could drive them back to her premises, and she put Richard in the front beside her and Jo in the back. She chatted exclusively to Richard all the way to the business park where she had her warehouse and offices, and Jo had to sit in the middle of the back seat and lean forward uncomfortably to try to hear what was being said. Rationally, she knew that only one of them could sit in the front, but it annoyed her that Kimberley had automatically assumed it should be the man. If she had done her homework, she should know that Jo was the company founder and still the majority shareholder.

When they got to the business park, Kimberley ushered them upstairs to her boardroom. She had pulled out all the stops, and there was a delicious selection of pastries and sandwiches laid out, as well as coffee, tea and juices. Along the long wall of the boardroom, she had set up a clothing rack, with hundreds of sample garments.

'You're certainly well prepared,' said Richard.

'Thank you!' Kimberley giggled.

Jo caught herself mentally sneering. Firstly, in her opinion, women in their forties shouldn't giggle, and secondly, in her correspondence with Kimberley, she had specifically said that she wanted to present their current and future vision for Jungletown before viewing samples. Now she felt that whatever she said in her presentation, Kimberley had made up her mind about what they needed.

She stopped herself before the sneer registered as a facial expression and she tried very hard to smile and be pleasant. Don't make judgements too soon, she told herself. Kimberley was probably a perfectly pleasant woman, and she was obviously very successful. She was trying to make a good impression, that was all. She was just keen. Jo was very hungry, but she was damned if she was going to eat a croissant and then do her presentation with a flake of pastry adhering to her lapel, or worse, her face. She poured herself a sparkling water and sipped it, while the IT technician linked her laptop to the projector and handed her a remote mouse to change the slides. As she waited, she glanced over the selection of clothes. There was only one word for them. Pink. Unrelentingly pink. Every last T-shirt, skirt and dress was in a shade from strawberry milkshake to brightest cerise. She was sure she had spoken to Gary about the colour brief. Yes, Jungletown would now have a separate section with clothes for girls, but she had wanted the colours to reflect the colours they used in the shop: bright primary colours, vibrant jungle shades of green, orange and purple. She knew they would have to stock some items in pink, but she had been hoping to offer as wide a selection for girls as she did for boys. Well, maybe she would be able to get that across in the presentation. She hoped Kimberley would be paying attention and taking notes.

Jo loved to present. She knew she was good at it: three years of drama school had made her at ease in front of an audience, and she had a witty, lively style that won people over. She was well prepared for this: no one knew the business better than she did, and she had filled the presentation with enticing images of the interior of the shop, as well as Lee's artist's impressions of future, bigger stores. For the first time that day, she relaxed, and enjoyed herself. She could see Richard nodding and smiling, so she knew she had come across well, and when she finished, Kimberley's team gave her a quick round of applause.

'Questions?' she said brightly.

One of Kimberley's assistants put his hand up. 'The artist's impressions are great, but what will the girls' section look like?'

'The girls' section?' said Jo, a little confused. 'It'll look like the rest of the shop, continuing the jungle and tropical-island theme. Our current store is small, but in future stores, there'll be girls' clothes along one wall, boys' along the other.'

'Would you not consider having a castle theme? Or maybe a fairy grotto?' said Kimberley sweetly. 'That's very big, you know. Every little girl wants to be a princess.'

'Not in our shop, they don't.' Jo smiled. 'Every little girl that has come through our doors has loved the play area, and has wanted to be a pirate, or a ladybird, or a toucan.'

Kimberley sat back in her chair and gave a little half-smile to her assistant, which to Jo, who was already feeling sensitive, looked condescending. 'We've looked at the market,' Jo said, rather louder than she had intended to, 'and there is no one doing exactly what we are doing.'

'With all due respect,' said Kimberley, and her tone suggested that she didn't think much respect was due at all, 'we've been leaders in the little girls' fashion market for twenty years. We know what works.'

'More than one thing can work,' said Jo, a little tight-lipped. 'Little girls can wear colours other than pink. They can imagine being more than just princesses or fairies. And I do not want to look at the girls' section in my shops and see a sea of bubblegum pink.'

Richard interrupted smoothly. 'Kimberley, thank you for

your market insights. I think we've made our position clear. While I'm sure your pink selection is excellent, we will be looking for a wider range of colours.'

Kimberley nodded and made a note on her pad. It seemed that if the direction came from Richard, she was happy to take it. Jo was annoyed. She didn't want Richard to have to jump in and save her. She was perfectly capable of holding a meeting with a supplier, and she had done so many times before. She swallowed her irritation, smiled sweetly and said, 'Could we take a look at some of your samples?'

That part of the meeting went rather better: Kimberley seemed happy to talk fine detail with her, and they discussed fabrics, styles and lead times. Richard was no expert in the minutiae of garment buying and he sat back and let Jo go over each item and ask questions. At the end of the meeting, they had a long list of styles they liked and an agreement that Kimberley's team would come back to them with a wider range of colour options.

Jo relaxed slightly. It had gone better than she had feared. Everyone was standing around the boardroom and chatting and she picked up a checked gingham dress with a big bow sash and a broderie anglaise underskirt. 'This I love,' she said to Kimberley, trying to be genuinely friendly. 'I'd love to order one for my daughter.'

'You have a daughter?' said Kimberley, and raised an eyebrow.

'Yes, she's eighteen months old, and I have a son, who's coming up for four.'

'Wow!' said Kimberley. 'And who's looking after them today?'

Jo bit the inside of her lip hard enough to make it bleed. 'My husband is – he's a stay-at-home dad.' And even though she knew it was rude and unprofessional, she walked away.

On the train on the way home, she and Richard held a post mortem of the meeting. 'I could see you didn't like her,' said Richard mildly.

'Oh, could you?' said Jo sarcastically. 'Did it show?'

'It really did,' he said. 'And while I agree that her company probably isn't the right wholesale supplier for us, what if they were? You can't let personal feelings come into it.'

'That's where I disagree with you. Firstly, we would have to work closely with any supplier and trust them, and if that's the case, we have to know they have the same values and culture that we do. Secondly, I know my own business, I know what look we're trying to present, and I don't appreciate someone condescending to me and suggesting they know better. If she's a supplier, she should supply.'

'She does have significant expertise in the sector . . .'

'In one aspect of the sector. And I might have been more prepared to listen to her if she'd treated me like the founder of the company, rather than as your glamorous assistant. She asked me who was looking after my children!'

'And why shouldn't she ask you . . . ?'

'You told her you had two-year-old twins. She didn't ask *you* who was looking after your children today, did she?' Richard shook his head. 'Thought not. No one ever asks fathers. They just assume the wife is at home doing the job that she's meant to do. But if a woman has small children, the assumption is that she's letting her kids down by being out at work.'

She knew she was ranting, and she had to stop. The whole day had been a chain of disasters, beginning that morning with the Easter bonnet and the chaos at home. It had made her on edge and defensive all day, and maybe she hadn't been as objective and professional in the meeting with Kimberley as she should have been. She stared out of the window at the countryside, washed with rain. Was this how her life was going to be? Lurching from crisis to crisis? Crushed with guilt that she was letting her kids down, and then crushed with a different kind of guilt that she wasn't giving her all to build the business she loved and believed in? Never mind her husband, her extended family, her friends . . . the people for whom she currently had no time at all. There was another whole world of guilt there.

'Richard,' she said, 'how do you do it? How do you make it work?'

He looked up from his iPad, surprised. 'What do you mean?'

'Well, to get to King's Cross by nine, you must have left home at . . . what?'

'Seven.'

'Were the twins awake?'

'No. Neither was Rachel.'

'So you left without seeing any of them, and you'll be back home when?'

'I'm staying in town for drinks with an old work friend, so I shan't see the twins before they go to bed. Rachel might still be up, but I doubt it.'

'And how do you feel about that?'

'Well, sad that I won't see them of course, but they're

with Rachel. So I know they're happy and well. And we'll have fun this weekend. We're taking them for their first pony ride.'

'So you don't feel guilty at all?' Jo said incredulously.

'What's this all about?' Richard looked hard at her. 'What's brought this on?'

And before she knew it, the whole story of her hideous morning spilled out. 'So I'm sitting here crushed with guilt, because I'm a terrible mother, an incompetent business-woman and probably a rubbish wife and friend too. But is it just me? Or is it all women? Can men just go off and work without a moment's worry? Is it just working women beating themselves up, because they're running to catch up with themselves and failing at everything?'

Richard leaned back and put the tips of his fingers together as if he was a psychoanalyst and Jo was the patient. If there was a couch on the train, she was sure he would have told her to lie down.

'Now, I've been a husband for a lot of years,' he said. 'And as a man, when you come to me with a problem, my instinct is to offer practical solutions. But I know from years of living with Rachel that that isn't always what women want. Do you want me to commiserate and say that your life is dif-ficult and I'm so sorry? Or do you want my opinion on how to fix it?'

Jo laughed for the first time that day. It was exactly the argument she had with Lee all the time. When she had had a bad day, Lee would ask lots of penetrating questions about what had happened, and would often make suggestions about how she could have done things differently. In reality, what she usually wanted was a cuddle and a glass of wine and a bit of, 'Poor love,' while he stroked her hair. But this was different. She couldn't go on feeling like this, and Richard was a successful businessperson and a parent – and, more crucially, not her husband. Maybe he had some insights.

'Let's hear your opinion.'

'I didn't learn a lot in the world of banking that was useful,' began Richard, 'but one thing I did learn is that guilt is a useless emotion. It doesn't help anyone and it hinders you.'

'But how do I stop feeling guilty, when I can't—'

'Be everything to everybody twenty-four hours a day? You can't. So stop trying. Organise your life so that panic situations like this morning don't arise; give your kids the best of your attention when you're there, and trust that between you and Lee and the other people responsible for their care, they're getting lots of love and attention.'

'That's easy for you to say, but—'

'Here's what I think about your morning,' said Richard. 'Hire a cleaner so your washing and ironing is done, and housework isn't something standing in the way of family time.'

That was tiresomely practical, Jo had to admit. Someone who came to do the heavy cleaning once a week and dealt with a stack of ironing would lessen their stress significantly.

'Secondly, put everything in your diary. If Zach's Easter bonnet had been diarised, it would have happened.'

'But that's so clinical, making diary entries to remember to care for my children . . .'

'Did you remember without it?'

'No, but—'

'You're busy. Make a note. Why is that something to feel guilty about?'

Again, Jo had to nod.

'And do me a favour – ring up my technology guy, Angus. Get him to set up your laptop and phone and so on so you have what you need, when you need it. Arrange it so all your devices synchronise automatically and you always have all your files. You can't plan for everything. You can't plan for a sick child, an accident, or someone else's incompetence. But you can do a lot to make your life easier just by putting a few things in place.'

If Lee had made those suggestions, she would have yelled at him. She would have said he was accusing her of being a bad mother, or of being hopelessly disorganised. But Richard managed to sound dispassionate and practical about all of it.

'So if we're not going to go with Kimberley Lytton's company, what's the next step?' she asked.

'Well, I think we learned a lot from that meeting about what we do and don't want from a supplier, in terms of culture, financials and attitude. Let's put all those things down in a list and we can share it with Gary and Holly when we get back to London.'

'Good idea,' said Jo, opening her laptop and firing it up. 'Let me put a few things in my diary, and we'll get working on it.'

She opened a to-do list in her email program and wrote:

- Hire cleaner
- Online grocery shopping
- Book tickets for children's show at the arts centre
- Babysitter for Saturday night
- Take Lee out for dinner

'Right!' she said brightly. 'Item one: less than ten per cent pink stuff. What else is on our list?'

24

MEL NOW

Since the party debacle, Serena had been on especially good behaviour, but she had resisted all Mel's efforts to have a heart-to-heart chat, insisting she was fine, that going to an unsupervised party and getting drunk had been one-off mistakes she would never repeat, and refusing to expand on any of the things she had said when she was lying on the bathroom floor. 'I was drunk and crazy. I don't remember what I said, and I'm sure none of it was true.'

The morning after the party, when Serena was still asleep, Mel had gone around to Izzie's house. She rang the doorbell loud and long, and after three rings Romana, the sulky au pair, opened the door. She had obviously just woken up and she looked like a grumpy Persian kitten, all smudged eyeliner, ruffled hair and attitude. When she saw it was Mel at the door, her eyes widened.

'I think the girls are still asleep . . .' she began, playing for time.

'Serena is asleep, you're right. But she's asleep in her own bed, at home, after I found her drunk and crying in the street in the middle of the night. We're not even going to discuss what Izzie did to cause that. Please go and pack up Serena's things and bring them to me.' There was no real satisfaction in yelling at this girl, however petulant and lazy she was. But Mel had to yell at someone. She knew Serena would never forgive her if she yelled at Izzie, or if she got her hands on Triggah, which she would dearly love to do, so she continued, 'And you might as well start packing your own things; because I'll be letting Izzie's parents know that you let two fifteen-year-old girls go to a party where there was no adult supervision.'

When she got back home, Mel sat down at her computer and logged into Facebook. The first thing she saw was that Serena had changed her relationship status to 'single'. She breathed a sigh of relief. There were a few messages on Serena's wall from friends saying 'How RU?' and sending hugs and kisses, but she had not responded to any of them.

On the Friday afternoon nearly two weeks later, Mel's phone rang just as she was leaving the shop. She saw that it was Hamish and checked her watch: surely he must be in the middle of his work day?

'Hello, stranger,' she said. 'On a coffee break?'

'Well, a lifetime coffee break, as it happens,' said Hamish happily. 'I've given up my job at last.'

'Wow. Congratulations.'

'It's all a bit up in the air, to be fair. My flat in London has been sold, and I'm waiting for them to finish rewiring my cottage in Devon, so I'm living on a sleeper couch at my brother's place at the moment.'

'So unemployed and of no fixed abode?'

'Pretty much. I wondered if there might be a plate of that

fine bolognaise on offer at Mel's soup kitchen any time soon?'

'Well, I always do my best to help the homeless and indigent. Free tonight?'

'As it happens, yes.'

'I might be able to rustle up a chop or something for you, if you're lucky. Come around about six.' She hung up, smiling.

Serena seemed pleased that Hamish was coming for dinner, and even helped Mel with the cooking. When he arrived, she gave him a hug and sat talking to him in the living room while Mel finished preparing the food and set the table. Mel tried not to mind that Serena seemed to be much more chatty and forthcoming with Hamish than she ever was with her. Still, it was good to hear her giggle again. As she put the plates on the table, Serena came into the kitchen.

'Look at this, Mum!' she said, holding up a book. 'This is Hamish's latest. He brought me a copy, and he signed it and everything!'

Mel took the book from her. It was really odd, seeing Hamish's name printed on a book cover. She flipped to the title page, where he had scrawled, 'For Serena, Warrior Princess, and her awesome mum, Queen Mel, Love, Hamish.'

'It's for both of us!' said Mel, pointing to her name.

'Yeah, well, my name's first, and I'm reading it first.' Serena grinned. 'Is it ready?' she said, looking at the table. 'Hamish!' she bellowed. 'Come and eat!'

Hamish came in, and as they all settled down, Mel smiled at him. 'Thanks for the book.'

'Yes, well . . . I thought you might like to see what paid for the house you'll be coming to stay in.'

'Hamish says we can come down and stay whenever we want,' said Serena.

Mel looked at Hamish.

'The cottage has three bedrooms. I'm going to be rattling around in it, driving myself mad. Come and visit often. You'll save me from turning into a beardy weirdo who sits around in his pyjamas all day eating cereal out of the packet.'

'Well, we can't have that.'

Over dinner, Serena seemed happy to tell Hamish which subjects she liked (English and history), which of her teachers were idiots (Mr Norman for biology) and which of her friends were currently in favour – Marina, as always, two girls called Melissa and Heather, whom Mel had never heard of, who were apparently 'cool'. Izzie was right off the Christmas list, although Serena didn't say why. After dinner, she gave Hamish a kiss on the cheek, grabbed the book and gave it a flourish.

'I'll review it on Amazon if it's any good,' she said cheekily, and headed for her bedroom.

'She seems on good form,' said Hamish, leaning back in his chair and taking a sip of his wine.

'She seems like a changeling child,' said Mel. It was difficult not to resent Hamish, but she knew it wasn't his fault. 'You got more out of her in an hour than I have in month.'

'Well, you're the mum. I'm not.'

'What's that supposed to mean?'

'Don't you remember hating your mum asking about things? Thinking she was prying when she asked how school was?'

'Not really,' said Mel tightly. 'I didn't have that kind of mum.'

'Well, my mum asked all the time. Now I realise it was because she was interested. But at fourteen, I thought my life outside the house was hugely important and private. God knows, I had nothing to hide – I went to an all-boys' school in Amersham – but I was always telling my mum to leave me alone.'

'Well, maybe now you can understand why I . . .' Mel stopped herself.

'Why you . . . ?'

'Worry about her,' finished Mel. 'More wine?'

'I'm serious about you coming down to Devon, Mel . . . and I will still be in London a lot. If it helps having me around, talking to Serena . . . I'd be so happy to. I'm very fond of Serena. You know that, don't you? And you. I'm very fond of you . . .' Hamish stopped, and when Mel looked at him, she was surprised to see he was blushing.

He didn't stay for long after that – his brother lived in South London and he made noises about not wanting to miss the last Tube, but Mel suspected he'd let on more than he had meant to and was embarrassed. She hugged him goodbye, and after he left, stood in the hallway thinking about him – his large, reassuring presence, his gentleness, his way with Serena. If he did have feelings for her, might she reciprocate them? They'd been friends for years, and she had never thought of him like that before. But why not? Could she and Hamish . . . ? She had been single for so long, maintaining her independence, keeping her household going, looking after Serena, she had somehow never allowed herself to think she might have a romantic relationship of her own. But Hamish was a lovely guy, kind, reliable, financially solvent, and very attractive in a slightly shambling, bear-like way. Best of all, Serena already knew and liked him. So maybe . . . one day in the future . . . She shook her head. She would have to feel that things with Serena were more under control before she could ever consider it.

The next morning, she was busy with laundry when, to her surprise, Serena came out of her room, dressed, at about ten. 'Fancy some breakfast?' Mel said. 'I've got stuff for bacon sarnies . . .'

'I have to go to school,' said Serena.

'But it's Saturday.'

'Yeah, there's a thing,' said Serena unconvincingly.

'A thing?'

'It's a class project.' Serena was looking more and more uncomfortable. Mel knew she could push it, but Serena was looking so defensive already.

'Okay, will you be long?'

'A couple of hours.'

Serena pulled the hood on her jumper up over her head, stuffed her hands in her pockets and headed out of the door. True to her word, she was home two hours later, and took herself off to her room.

Three hours later, Serena's door was firmly shut and she didn't seem likely to come out of there before dinnertime, so Mel logged into Facebook as Lauren. There was a new post on Serena's wall. It was from Marina. 'How was this morning?' she posted. Serena answered almost immediately. 'Great. Hopey is amazing.'

Hopey? Who or what was Hopey? Mel looked it up on the Urban Dictionary. There were two potential translations: 'hopey' was a slang synonym for 'optimistic', or was used as a nickname for Barack Obama. She was fairly sure that neither of these applied in this case, so she had to assume Hopey was a person. But who? Surely not a new boyfriend, just two weeks after she had split up from Triggah? Hopey? What kind of name was that? It sounded like some kind of gangster nickname, or one of the grime or hip-hop artists Serena liked. But she couldn't have gone off to a gig at ten o'clock on a Saturday morning, could she? What if she'd hooked up with some bad-boy graffiti tagger? Or a drug dealer? And how was this person 'amazing'? What the hell did he do?

When she got to work on Monday morning, it was still bugging her. It was a bright sunny day, and the shop was very quiet. They had learned that bad weather was good for business, as mums could come in out of the rain and let their little monsters blow off some steam in the play area. The mums were usually so grateful that they'd buy something. But on days like this, with not a cloud in the bright blue sky, everyone with kids under school age would be at the park. Mel sat at the counter, doodling on a piece of paper and wondering about Serena and Hopey.

Holly was in on one of her rare days in the shop. She was doing a stocktake and starting to think about where they would put the girls' range when it was finally settled. She had the teenage boys who made the T-shirts coming in later too. Mel felt guilty; she knew she should be helping – counting things and so on – but so far Holly had refused all offers of assistance and seemed happiest to work alone.

'Are you sure I can't . . . ?' she said for the third or fourth time.

'I'm fine,' said Holly. 'Unless you're offering to do a coffee run. I didn't get much sleep last night.'

'Coffee it is,' said Mel, hopping off her stool. 'Latte?'

'Espresso. And a sticky bun.'

'Wow, that is bad,' said Mel. 'Your mum not doing so well?'

'She slept fine last night; it's just me. Insomnia, you know . . . boy trouble.'

'Oh no, not the handsome doctor?'

'Handsome shitbag, more like. Seems he's not separated from his wife at all. He just likes a little extra-curricular action.'

'And you found this out . . . ?'

'I went around to his and the wife was there. She told me.'

'Ouch.'

'Yes. And now he keeps ringing, and I keep rejecting his calls. I don't know how stupid he thinks I am. I want to kick myself for falling for his story. I'm just so angry. And therefore . . .'

'. . . You can't sleep. I'd be the same,' said Mel. It was rather odd to be sharing such intimate chat with Holly. She had always thought of Holly as much younger, although there was less than ten years in age between them. Holly had the bohemian, itinerant lifestyle Mel had lived a lifetime ago, before Serena. Holly was single, with no hint of kids on her horizon. Even though she was now caught up in all the responsibility around her mum's illness, she seemed to be in a very different place in her life. Mel hadn't thought they had much in common.

She popped to the coffee shop and came back with coffees for both of them and a range of sweet carb-laden snacks. When she walked back in, Holly was on the phone, obviously answering a customer query. She finished the call as Mel unpacked the goodies on to the countertop.

'You're a hero,' said Holly, biting into an apricot Danish. 'What do I owe you?'

'My treat.' They ate and drank in silence. Mel also hadn't slept very well, and the caffeine and sugar were a welcome boost.

'So who's Hopey?' said Holly out of the blue, and Mel spluttered cappuccino foam all over the counter.

'What?'

'Hopey. You've doodled it over and over on this bit of paper. Is he your bloke?'

'What? No. It's a name Serena posted on Facebook. It's bugging me that I don't know who it is. It's not a musician, is it? A band or a rapper or something? Someone I just haven't heard of?'

'Not that I know of, but if it's like a youth counter-culture thing, we're both too ancient to know for sure. When Chris and Daniel get here, we can ask them.'

Mel nodded. That seemed like a good solution.

They ate in silence for a while, and then Holly said gently, 'Is everything okay with Serena?' And Mel found herself talking. She had always been a very private person – she had friends, but not confidantes, and she tended not to burden people with her problems. Maybe it was because she wasn't all that close to Holly, or maybe because Holly was younger and might have some insight, she started to tell a – much edited – version of the things she had found out about Serena's secret life. She told her about the Rizla packet in the bin and the photos on the computer, and about finding her stumbling blind drunk out of the party and what Triggah had said to her. She didn't mention her Facebook stalking. Holly listened without comment. When Mel had finished, Holly said, 'I know this is going to sound weird, and probably not what you want to hear, but I think you might be over-reacting.'

'What?'

'I know that seeing your kid grow up, and having her keep things from you, is difficult, but let's look at the evidence objectively, okay?'

Mel wanted to protest, but she thought better of it, nodded and said, 'Okay, objectively, how am I overreacting?'

'Well, for a start, do you smoke?'

'No.'

'Well, if Serena did, you would smell it on her, guaranteed. You'd smell it on her hair, her clothes and her breath. So my guess is that the Rizla packet belonged to the boyfriend.'

'But the pictures . . .'

'She was in her underwear, right?'

'Yes.'

'And when the boy – what kind of name is Triggah, anyway? – when Triggah was yelling at her, he said she was a frigid bitch?'

'Yes, that's what she said.'

'I think she's still a virgin. I think he probably pressurised her into the pictures, but she refused to do anything more. So he went looking for it somewhere else. And he got it from her friend the bike . . . Izzie, was it?'

'I hadn't thought of that. But she's been bunking school . . .'

'I bunked school. I smoked, I got drunk and threw up, and I went out with all sorts of awful guys. And I think I turned out okay. Mel, I've only met Serena once or twice, but my instinct is that she's a good kid. She's sulky and secretive because that's what teenagers are supposed to be. But I think she's probably fine. Really.' And Holly squeezed Mel's arm.

'Thanks,' said Mel, and managed a smile. But she was far from convinced. She knew the world was full of perils. She knew how danger could be close to home – even inside your home – and without someone looking out for you, you were powerless. She wasn't ready to let her guard down. Not yet. And certainly not before she found out who the mysterious Hopey was.

Daniel and Chris came into the shop about half an hour later. They were lovely boys, the sort she had hoped Serena might meet and have as a first boyfriend. They were polite and neatly dressed, and the fact that they'd started their own business when they were still at school suggested a great work ethic. Mel caught herself thinking all this and smiled. She'd always thought of herself as such a hippie, but parenthood, it seemed, had turned her into a social conservative. Street-performer Mel would have scorned neatly dressed boys with posh accents, like Daniel and Chris, but it was all she wanted for Serena. After Triggah, she didn't want her daughter to go through any more heartache and disappointment. Maybe she could find a way to introduce them. The boys seemed to get on well with Holly – they all sat together in the back office, sorting through T-shirts and chatting. Daniel, the taller, good-looking one, seemed to be trying especially hard to impress Holly. He obviously had a crush, and small wonder – Holly was a gorgeous woman. He kept paying her compliments and trying to make her laugh. It was good to see Holly smile and giggle. She was taking so much strain with her mum being so ill, and the thing with the faithless married doctor didn't help at all. Some flirtation from a young handsome man, even if he was technically still a child, was good for her.

Mel served some customers and played a raucous game of piggy-in-the-middle with two small boys while their mum stocked up on summer clothes for them. The mum, who looked harassed and stressed beyond belief, was clearly very grateful to be able to look at clothes in peace while someone else dealt with her two boisterous little terrors. She ended up spending a small fortune, kitting both boys out and buying a few extras as gifts for friends.

'Thanks!' Mel grinned as she put the transaction through. She could almost hear the woman's credit card weeping.

'No, thank you!' said the woman, glancing nervously behind her as her boys swung from a jungle rope. 'This is the best shopping experience I've had in five years. If you stocked adult clothing, I might well move in!'

It was an interesting idea: if you were keeping the kids busy, why not let the mums shop for themselves as well as their kids? Maybe they could start with a maternity range. Mel made a mental note to mention it to Jo.

'Well, tell all your mates!' said Mel, handing the woman her bulging shopping bags. 'We'll be stocking girls' clothes as well soon.'

'Already tweeted about it.' The woman grinned. 'See you soon!'

Once the woman and her small savages had gone, Mel did a quick tidy. As she was finishing up, Holly and the Outtake boys came out of the office. Holly set about hanging some of the new T-shirts and the boys set off home. As the office was deserted, Mel took the opportunity to log on to Facebook for a moment to see what Serena had been up to. Marina had posted 'Hey babez, see you after school? Come to mine for coffee.'

And Serena had replied, 'Can't, seeing Hopey at 4.'

Mel checked her watch. It was lunchtime. Jo was coming in at three to do the last few hours in the shop. Mel could be outside Serena's school by three thirty, when classes ended, and she could see where she went after that. Whom she met. She had a bad feeling about this Hopey. She couldn't put her finger on why . . . somehow she didn't think it was just a friend. Serena was uncommunicative, yes, but she did mention her friends by name, and this was not a name Mel had ever heard from her.

As it happened, there was a builders' cafe across the road from Serena's school. They did a roaring trade at lunchtime, supplying sausages and chips to hungry teenagers. Mel got there at three twenty and found a table by the window. The cafe was quiet, and she grabbed a copy of the *Sun* from the rack of newspapers and ordered a tea. Although she had a good view of the road outside and the school opposite, she was partially concealed from view by a dusty plastic palm tree. If, by some fluke, Serena saw her or came into the cafe, she decided to say she had left work early and wasn't feeling well, so had come to meet Serena to walk home with her. It was most likely that Serena wouldn't see her, however. In Mel's experience, Serena, and teenagers in general, didn't notice things or people around them unless it was something that affected them directly.

At three thirty, kids starting trailing out of the school opposite. There were just a few at first, then a flood – groups of boys laughing and shoving each other, girls calling out to one another in piercing voices. Why were they all so loud? Mel watched from behind her pot plant. She knew from years of collecting Serena from school that she would be one of the last out. She always was. Sure enough, most of the kids had wandered off down the road towards the station or their houses, or got on the school bus, when Serena came out, her arm linked through Marina's. They had their heads close together and were chatting. They stopped outside the school and leaned against a low stone wall. Marina seemed to be waiting with Serena. Whoever Hopey was, perhaps he was meeting Serena at the school. She didn't seem to be going anywhere in a hurry. The two girls looked at something on Marina's phone, and then Serena got hers out along with a set of headphones and they took one earpiece each. Mel checked her watch. It was five to four. The cafe owner was pointedly sweeping the floor and moving tables and chairs. Clearly he wanted to close up. She had to hope that Serena's rendezvous would be prompt. She glanced up and down the road, expecting to see someone approaching on foot. There was no one who looked obviously like someone a teenage girl might meet – just a young mum with two toddlers and a couple of old ladies with tartan shopping bags on wheels.

Then, at one minute to four, a car came crawling along the road and pulled up outside the school. Serena looked up and smiled. She retrieved the other earphone from Marina, hugged her goodbye and ran around to the passenger door of the car. Somehow, Mel hadn't expected a car, and she stood up quickly to get a better look. It was a very ordinary car – a little silver hatchback, a Peugeot or a Vauxhall Corsa or something. She couldn't see the driver's face because of the sun's late-afternoon glare on the windscreen. Without thinking, she ran to the door of the cafe, oblivious to the man shouting behind her that she hadn't paid for her tea. She could see Serena clearly now. She was turned towards the driver of the car, smiling and chatting as she did up her seat belt. The car pulled out and headed down the road, past Mel, and turned left at the bottom. As it passed, she got a clear look at the person driving. He looked about fifty, wearing a suit and glasses. She had never seen him before. What kind of fifty-year-old man picks up a teenage girl from school without her mother knowing? Mel started to tremble with fear and anger. She had been in such a hurry to see the driver, she hadn't thought to take down the registration number of the car. With shaking fingers, she took out her phone and dialled Serena's number, but it went straight to voicemail.

She didn't think. She was panicking, crazy with fear and

desperation, so she just started to talk. 'Rena, I'm outside your school and I just saw you get in a car with a man. Is that Hopey? Who is he? What are you doing? What is he making you do? Oh God, Rena, ring me. Please just ring me. I don't know where you've gone and I couldn't get the registration number or I'd have rung the police. Rena . . . just . . . ring me, okay? I'll come and get you wherever you are.' She hung up, and started to cry. Mel couldn't remember the last time she'd cried. She turned back into the cafe and retrieved her bag. The cafe owner, seeing how upset she was, waved her money away when she went to pay for her tea.

Marina. Marina would know. She knew who Hopey was, and maybe she could tell Mel where they had gone. Mel stood on the pavement, looking wildly up and down the road, but Marina had gone. She took off at a run, heading for her house, which was on a main road close to the school. She arrived out of breath and rang the doorbell, but somehow, from the way it echoed, she sensed no one was home. She scrolled through the numbers on her phone and, to her relief, found one for Marina. She dialled it, but got a recorded message saying, 'The number you have dialled has not been recognised.' Marina must have changed her number.

This was a nightmare. She stood on the pavement, trembling and staring up and down the road, as if a solution might magically present itself. After a minute or two, she calmed down and sat on the low wall. She started to go through her phone methodically, looking for numbers of any of Serena's friends. She rang each one, trying to sound as calm as she could, saying that she had seen Serena get into a car with a strange man outside the school, and did any of them know who it might be, or where they might have gone? They all answered in monosyllables, and clearly none of them had any idea what might have happened. Tiresomely, they sounded mortified to be taking a call from Serena's mum, and it seemed to Mel that this constrained them from speaking openly. It was as if their embarrassment at speaking to her was more important to them than Serena's safety. In desperation, Mel even rang Izzie, who had the decency to sound properly shamefaced, but who also knew nothing. Hating herself for doing it, Mel asked Izzie if she knew how to get hold of Triggah.

'He's here with me now,' said Izzie in a small voice. 'And he also doesn't know where she is.'

There was nothing for Mel to do but go home. She didn't take her coat off, just sat in a chair, her bag balanced on her knees, and waited as the shadows lengthened.

It felt like hours, but was in fact just gone five thirty when she heard Serena's key in the door. She was too numb to feel relieved. She just stayed sitting where she was, bag on lap, waiting. Serena didn't come into the living room, but went straight to her bedroom. Mel could hear her banging around. After a minute, she carefully put her handbag on the floor and went to stand in Serena's doorway. Serena had a sports bag on the bed and was throwing clothes and school books into it willy-nilly.

'What are you . . . ?'

'I'm going to stay at Marina's,' said Serena flatly. Then she stopped what she was doing for a second, and looked at Mel. 'You're a freak, do you know that? What did you do?

Read my emails? Hack into my Facebook? Why couldn't you just ask me?'

'Because you never talk!' Mel didn't even bother to deny the allegations.

'I would talk. I would tell you things if you ever got off my back. If you ever let me have even the tiniest bit of fucking privacy!' Serena was screaming now, and it didn't seem the right moment to tell her off for swearing.

'I . . .'

'I don't know what you think I am. I don't know what you think I'm doing, but let me tell you, it's what's in your head that's wrong. I'm not an idiot. I can look after myself. And just because you're a weirdo who never ever has a boyfriend and thinks every man is a rapist or a paedo, doesn't mean I think that way. I'm going. And before you start ringing all my friends again, or calling the police, I'm staying with Marina's mum and dad. I'm not having sex with some old man, okay?'

She grabbed her bag, not even bothering to zip it up, tucked her laptop under her arm and pushed past Mel. Mel heard the door slam, and then everything was quiet.

25

HOLLY NOW

Judith, whose arms and legs were so thin you could see every ridge of bone under the skin, looked pregnant. Her skin was an alarming shade of yellow, and her belly was grossly swollen. Lynne, the Macmillan nurse, was scheduled to come on the Friday, but on the Wednesday Holly rang her in desperation and she came round within the hour. Holly sat downstairs in the kitchen and waited while Lynne spent some time with Judith. She felt sure that when Lynne came downstairs that the news wouldn't be good. There was no doubt about it: in the last few months Judith had got very sick very quickly.

Lynne, who was plump and pleasant, came down the stairs stripping off her latex gloves. 'Got the kettle on there, Holly?' she said. She bustled around making tea, and then sat at the table with Holly.

'Now I know that you must be worried about the way your mum looks today,' she said calmly.

'She looks awful, Lynne. Just awful.'

'It's because the cancer has reached her liver. That's why she's so yellow. The swelling is mainly fluid in her abdomen, and we can do something about that. I've rung the hospital, and they're sending over an ambulance. We're going to keep her in and we'll drain off some of the fluid. It's a minor procedure, she'll be awake throughout and it'll make her much more comfortable. More than likely, she can come home tomorrow.'

'So she . . .'

'She hasn't got long, but she's not quite on her way out yet.' Holly appreciated Lynne's blunt honesty. She was matter-of-fact, but always kind, and she always gave them all the information they needed. 'Now why don't you pop upstairs and pack a bag for your mum? She seemed worried about her jewellery. She wanted to take it all with her. See if you can talk her out of that – it won't be safe in the hospital.'

Her jewellery? How odd, Holly thought as she walked up the stairs. Judith hadn't worn any jewellery other than her wedding ring since she'd been ill. Why the sudden obsession? When she went into the bedroom, Judith was sitting up in bed, her jewellery box on her lap. She hadn't opened it, but she had her claw-like hands clasped over it as if she would never let it go. As soon as Holly saw the box, she knew why Judith didn't want to leave it behind. The letters.

'Mum,' she said gently, 'you don't need to take that with you. It'll be perfectly safe here.'

'What if I don't come back?' said Judith.

'Lynne says it's just a small procedure, and you'll feel much better and be home tomorrow.'

'What if I'm not home tomorrow? What if I die in the hospital? I need this.' Judith clutched the box tighter.

'Mum . . .' said Holly, sitting on the edge of the bed and

putting her hand over Judith's. 'I know you have letters in there, and I'll keep them safe. I promise.'

'How do you know? Did you read them? That's terrible! You should never read other people's letters, Holly! That's disgraceful!' Judith was so distressed that Holly wished she had never said anything.

'I didn't read them. I promise. I borrowed your gold chain weeks ago – I told you, remember? And the box wouldn't close. I saw there were letters, but I didn't even take them out. I would never read your private letters; of course I wouldn't.'

'I need them, Holly. They're all I've got.' There were tears in Judith's eyes. 'All I've got of him. Please.'

'Mum, they're much safer here than in the hospital. And you'll be back tomorrow.'

Judith shook her head. The tears were still trickling down her cheeks.

'Why not take one or two? Maybe not all of them. And not your jewellery box,' Holly suggested. Judith calmed down and nodded. 'That's a good idea,' she said, and with trembling hands opened the catch on the box. She lifted the trays out and handed them to Holly, then began to leaf through the stack of letters. She chose two from the very bottom of the pile. Holly fetched Judith's handbag, and Judith carefully slid the two letters into an inside pocket of the bag and zipped it up.

'We need to get the rest of your things organised,' said Holly, and she helped Judith to replace everything in the box and put it back on the dressing table. In a few minutes, she had packed a small overnight bag for Judith. Lynne popped her head around the door and said the ambulance was ten minutes away, and that the ambulance crew would come up to the bedroom to fetch Judith. Holly sat down beside the bed. Now Judith was not so agitated, she looked terribly tired.

'You all right, Mum?'

'Yes, thank you, dear.'

'Your letters are safe in your bag. I'll make sure it's right beside your bed when you're in the hospital, okay?'

'Thank you, dear.'

There was a long silence, and then Holly said, 'Mum? Who are the letters from? Mr Benton?'

Judith lifted her head from the pillow and looked sharply at Holly. 'Oh no, dear. Good heavens no. I got the oldest letter in the pile more than forty years ago. I only met Christopher a few years back.'

'Were they from Dad?'

'Oh no. They're not from your father. I never knew Charles to write so much as a postcard.'

Holly was desperate to know now. 'So who . . . ?'

Judith smiled. 'I know it's hard to imagine your dull old mother had a life before you came along. But I did. They're from the love of my life, dear. The one man I truly loved.'

Holly opened her mouth to ask more questions, but the doorbell rang and Lynne called up the stairs that the ambulance had arrived.

In the bustle of getting her into the ambulance and then getting her settled in the hospital, Holly had no further opportunity to question Judith. Once she was in her bed in the ward, she fell asleep immediately. The procedure wasn't due to be done for a few hours, so Holly was sent home. It wasn't until she was in the car and driving that she remembered something. The letter she had seen on the top of the pile had had a recent postmark . . . just a few months old. If that was the case, Judith's One True Love was still very much alive, and very much in evidence. So who was he? Where was he? And while she was thinking about identity, who the hell was Judith? Because she certainly wasn't the quiet, dutiful Christian widow Holly had always imagined her to be.

Holly got back to the house in Ealing and wandered through the quiet rooms. Although she was desperately tired, she felt completely wired, unable to settle. The last time Judith had been in hospital was the night she had gone out with Fraser. More fool her. Look at how that had turned out. She needed to do something: she couldn't just sit around in the house. The letters were calling her from her mum's room. It felt like they were yelling, 'Come and read us!' down the stairs. She had promised Judith she wouldn't, and so she had to take herself out of the way of temptation. If Judith didn't want to tell her about her mystery man, then that was her right.

Holly decided to go to the shop, spend some time checking over the stock, and then stay the night in her flat in East Finchley. She packed a change of clothes and her toiletries into a small bag and headed for the door. While she was looking for her keys, her mobile began to ring. She could see it was Fraser calling. She hadn't heard from him for a week or so, so she had assumed he had given up, but it seemed he was more persistent than that. She clicked

'Cancel' and cut off the call. Somehow, the phone ringing reminded her of Mr Benton. He would be coming around in the morning to work in the garden, and she didn't want him to find the house deserted and think the worst. She had his home number, so she rang him and left a message on his answerphone to explain where Judith was, and that she had gone to spend the night in her own flat.

As she stepped out of the front door of the house, she felt her mood lighten. An afternoon and a night. Infinite possibilities.

But when she got to the shop, it was mayhem. There seemed to be hundreds of small children running around and screaming and bashing things. Both Mel and Jo seemed to be able to function in this atmosphere without a problem – Holly assumed that having children of your own somehow made you at least partially immune to the noise of other people's brats – but she found it a struggle. There was no way she could assess the state of the stock in the monkey-house atmosphere on the shop floor, so she hid in the stockroom and shut the door. There really wasn't anything for her to do, so she spent a bit of time with paper and pen sketching out some ideas for dungarees and padded trousers for the winter range. But to be honest, she was bored. She wanted company, excitement . . . something that felt like life and liveliness, as an antidote to illness, death and sadness. When someone knocked on the stockroom door and she saw Daniel and Chris outside, they looked like the answer to a prayer.

'Delivery, miss!' said Chris cheekily, coming in with a box of T-shirts.

'Boys!' she said happily. 'You're a lovely sight. Please tell me you don't need to rush off.'

The boys looked surprised, and glanced at each other. 'No,' said Daniel. 'Is there something you need us to do?'

'Yes! I need you to come to the pub with me and sit in the garden and drink beer and shots until the sun goes down and possibly beyond.'

'Yes!' they chorused, full of enthusiasm. Holly wasn't sure if their excitement was at the prospect of her company, or at the possibility of her funding this drinking expedition. Either way, she'd take it.

The weather was glorious and the pub garden was inviting. Holly suggested getting a jug of Pimm's. Neither of the boys had tried it before, assuming it to be a parents' fuddy-duddy drink, but they loved it and within half an hour they were well into the second jug. Holly knew that Pimm's was insidious – it tasted like a soft drink, but the alcoholic effects could sneak up on you, especially sitting in the sun. But she had parked her car safely and only had half a block to walk to get home. The boys were another matter.

'Where are you parked?' she asked Daniel.

'In a side road. No parking restrictions.'

'How will you . . . ?'

'Get home? Bus, night bus . . .' He gave her a cheeky grin. 'Relax! Stop being a grown-up. Let's just have some fun.'

The boys argued about music and films, and they all had a good bitch about a reality TV show they'd been watching. Holly couldn't believe how good it was to kick back and talk nonsense. She stretched her arms along the back of the wooden bench she was sitting on and turned her face up to the sun. Real life was out there, and the awfulness of Judith's situation was always present, but for this afternoon, she could put it to one side.

She must have been quite drunk, because she scarcely registered when Chris kissed her on the cheek and left. He was taking his girlfriend to a film that evening. They'd started early, so it was only around eight o'clock when she and Daniel stumbled out of the pub. They were both ravenous, and she found herself in a neon-lit takeaway devouring doughy slices of pizza. Then they went to the off-licence and bought a couple of four-packs of lager and took them back to Holly's flat. They lay on big cushions on the floor and Daniel got some music going on his phone. Holly made sure it was very quiet, so as not to alert Bob to their presence. Daniel lay on his stomach, his hands folded under his chin, eyes closed, listening to the music. He was so beautiful, Holly thought, looking at his long lashes resting on his cheeks. He was, she thought drunkenly, the epitome of youth and life and health. The polar opposite to everything else in her life.

He opened his eyes and looked at her sleepily. 'So what's your story, Holly?' he said, rolling over and sitting up. 'Where's the handsome Mr Holly who should be looking after you? I can't believe you're single. You're so . . .' He didn't seem to have an adjective.

'Peng?' she said cheekily. 'Am I "peng"?'

'Peng?' he laughed. 'Where did you learn that?'

'Mel has a teenage daughter.'

'Well, yes, you are, as we young people say, bare peng. You're even piff.'

'Why, thank you, sir,' she smiled.

'You didn't answer my question. Where's your boyfriend?'

'Don't have one. Had a bad, bad, lying, cheating, stealing one in South Africa, met one here I thought was nice, turned out he was also a snake.'

'Snake how?'

Holly found herself recounting the story of Fraser and Lindsay. She left out the fact that she had been removing her knickers when she first saw Lindsay though. She thought the image might somewhat cloud Daniel's judgement.

'Wow,' said Daniel. 'Awkward.'

'It was.'

'Is there any chance . . . ? No. Forget I said anything.'

'Any chance of what?'

'Any chance the wife might be lying? I mean, it's her word against his, and just because your South African boyfriend was a bastard, doesn't mean all men are.'

'Maybe . . .' Holly said dubiously.

'Look, whatever's going on between them, it sounds a bit messy, and you might not want to be involved. But the guy seems really keen on you and it sounds like you liked him too. He deserves a chance to put his case. I think you should hear what he has to say.'

'That's very mature thinking.'

'That's me. Mature.' He grinned. 'Text him tomorrow. Not now. You're drunk.'

'Okay.' She smiled.

He laughed suddenly. 'What an idiot I am,' he said. 'Here I am advising you to ring some guy you like, when I want you to fancy me.' He stretched, and his T-shirt rode up, exposing a line of brown skin. Holly caught herself licking her lips. She couldn't be thinking . . . could she? Dear God, no. He was a child. Well, not a child. Nineteen. Technically an adult. And he'd made his intentions towards her perfectly clear. But then he was right about Fraser too – she should ring him, hear him out at least. And she had to fetch her mother from the hospital tomorrow, and then the whole horrible cycle of illness and impending death would begin again. She shook her head. She was tired of thinking, tired of arguing with herself. Why shouldn't she have just one, simple, meaningless night? Why not indeed? She sat up, took a deep drink from her beer, and then leaned over and kissed Daniel's wide, soft mouth.

He was just deliriously, splendidly lovely. He was life – vibrant, healthy, youthful life and she could have eaten him with a spoon. He was all smooth skin and slender limbs and powerful muscles. He was not a virgin, that was clear, and what he lacked in technique, he made up for in enthusiasm and stamina, and he was very willing to be taught. The box of twelve condoms Holly had bought weeks before was severely depleted by the time the sun came up.

Holly dozed for a few hours and woke up at ten. Leaving Daniel sprawled across the mattress in the bedroom, she tiptoed to the bathroom to shower. Remarkably, she didn't feel too hungover, and although she'd barely slept, she was very wide awake. She didn't regret her actions, but she was absolutely clear in her mind what the night had meant. She only hoped Daniel would feel the same. There was no possibility of a romantic relationship between them, and she felt awkward that they had overstepped the boundaries of their professional relationship too. She'd have to be firm but kind and explain it all to him when he woke up. If he ever woke up. He was a teenager, after all; he would probably sleep till the afternoon if she let him. Well, too bad. She'd have to boot him out sooner rather than later. She didn't feel like explaining to Bob the landlord who Daniel was or why he was in the flat.

She turned on the shower, which was very powerful (thank you, Bob), and began to shampoo her hair. The shower was as noisy as it was vigorous, and she was unfamiliar with the sound of her own doorbell. So when she came out of the bathroom wrapped in a (not very big towel), she was surprised to find the bed empty. She went through into the living room, which was empty too. Then she saw Daniel, a sheet loosely wrapped around his lower half, at the bottom of the stairs, opening the front door to admit Fraser. Fraser stood in the doorway. He looked up the stairs at Holly, then looked at Daniel. Then he looked again at Daniel, and Holly could see him estimating Daniel's age.

'I'm sorry,' he said. 'I seem to have got the wrong house.' And he turned and walked away. There was no way for Holly to run after him, not without being arrested for indecent exposure. Daniel, who had no idea what had just happened, shrugged and closed the door.

He bounded up the stairs to Holly and, giving her a cheeky grin, let the sheet drop. Then he saw her face.

'Oh my God,' he said. 'That was him, wasn't it? The doctor guy?'

Holly nodded.

'How did he know where to find you?'

'I don't know . . .' Holly said, and then she remembered pointing the flat out to Fraser all those weeks ago. Not that it mattered. As far as she and Fraser went, there were only so many excruciatingly embarrassing situations one relationship could stand, and they seemed to have covered them all.

Which left . . . Daniel. Pretty, young Daniel, standing naked in her flat. Daniel, who really shouldn't be there, should never have been there, but who was, very much, still there.

'Daniel . . .' she said, and even to her own ears her voice sounded mumsy and condescending.

He bent and picked up the sheet. 'I know. I'm going.'

Holly felt awful. 'I didn't mean . . .'

He smiled at her. 'Holls, I know what this was. I know it was a one-off, and that nothing more can happen between us. I'm sorry if it's ruined things with you and your doctor. But it was fucking fantastic, and thank you.' He leaned across and kissed her softly, went through to the bedroom and dressed, and was gone within minutes.

Holly went to the window and watched him saunter up the street. Against her will, she smiled.

26

JUDITH THEN

When the phone rang and Judith answered, she barely recognised Mrs Whittaker's voice.

'Judith dear, I've a terrible cold,' she croaked, then broke off to sneeze explosively three times. 'I'm so sorry. I do beg your pardon.'

'Bless you,' said Judith automatically.

'I shouldn't be in the surgery today, passing my germs on to all the patients. Could you pass by my house to collect the keys and open up?'

'Of course,' said Judith, although she was terrified at the thought. She was just eighteen, and she'd only been working at the surgery for six weeks or so.

'Don't worry,' said Mrs Whittaker thickly. 'You know what to do. Open up, open the curtains and make sure everything is tidy in the waiting room. Then check the doctors' consulting rooms and see they have all their instruments laid out. You've done it with me dozens of times.'

But never alone. Judith didn't want to make a fuss, as Mrs Whittaker really did sound so ill, but what if she made a dreadful mistake? Let one of the doctors down? She felt fairly confident she could manage the appointment book, answering the telephone and ushering the patients in to see the doctors, but she had always watched Mrs Whittaker do the doctors' instruments. She had never done it herself.

Mrs Whittaker dictated a list of each doctors' preferences. Dr Pine liked his stethoscope laid along the bottom of the instrument table, and the other instruments – the otoscope, tongue depressors and so on – in a neat row. Dr Mistry preferred to have his instruments in a fan shape. Judith scribbled everything down and then hurried to get dressed. She wanted to be there as early as possible so she didn't have to rush.

The surgery was quiet when she let herself in. She had never been in there on her own before, and she was used to the bustle of patients, the ringing telephone and the hiss of the sterilising machine. She spent a few minutes sorting out the waiting room – tidying the magazines, watering the African violet and running a duster over the windowsill. Then she tentatively opened the door to Dr Pine's consulting room. She straightened a few files on his desk, and fetched a clean white cloth from the drawer to cover his instrument table. Checking her list, she began to lay out the instruments one by one. Mrs Whittaker had said Dr Pine liked to have one thermometer dry and ready to use on his table, so she went over to the sink and picked up the jar of alcohol, which held ten or so of the thin glass thermometers Dr Pine favoured.

Three things happened in very quick succession. She heard a voice call, 'Mrs Whittaker, where's my—' Then there was an almighty crash, followed by another.

It took her a few moments to realise the voice belonged to Dr Mistry, who had burst into Dr Pine's office. The first crash had been the door slamming back against the wall, and the second had been the jar of thermometers falling from Judith's hands and into the sink. It took another few moments to see that a shard of glass from the jar or one of the broken thermometers had gashed the palm of her hand and blood was dripping into the mess in the sink.

'I'm so sorry . . .' Dr Mistry and Judith said simultaneously.

'I've made a dreadful mess . . .' said Judith.

'Only because I gave you a fright,' said Dr Mistry, coming closer to see. 'Oh, you've cut your hand. I'm so sorry, Judith.'

'But the thermometers are broken . . .' Judith was very distressed. She'd caused such chaos. What would Mrs Whittaker say?

Dr Mistry glanced into the sink. 'Only one or two are broken. And we can give old Pine my sterilising jar. He'll never know the difference. The most important thing is to sort out your hand.' He took Judith's hand in his and looked at the wound. 'I don't think it needs stitches, but come to my consulting room and I'll clean it and bandage it for you.'

Dr Pine had been Judith's GP since she was a tiny girl. He was abrupt and taciturn and his hands were always cold. She had been very nervous when her mother had organised this job for her in Dr Pine's surgery. She had little to fear however, because as a junior receptionist, she was all but invisible to Dr Pine, and she had never had cause to speak to the junior partner, Dr Mistry, before. Until now, as he carefully cleaned the cut on her hand and dressed it. His hands were gentle and warm and his tone was soothing. Once he had finished bandaging her hand, he looked into her eyes. It seemed to Judith as if he looked at her, really at her, as if he could see right into her mind. Then he seemed to catch himself, and he looked away, embarrassed.

She couldn't stop thinking about him after that. If she had to go into his room, she would dash to the bathroom to comb her hair and check her reflection first. But when she was in there, she was too shy to make eye contact. It was ridiculous, of course. She'd been going out with Charles Evans for a year already; he was a perfectly nice chap, someone she'd known at school. She knew Charles expected that they would get engaged within the next year or so. Her parents expected the same. Until that moment in Dr Mistry's consulting room, she had been looking forward with all her heart to the day Charles would propose.

She didn't know what it was about Dr Mistry. Was it his beautiful eyes, a brown so deep she couldn't distinguish the pupil in the darkness of the iris? Was it his slim, smooth hands, or his perfect skin? Or was it his gentleness or his scrupulously polite manner with the staff and the patients? She didn't think it was just because he was nice – she recognised that her reaction to him was physical and visceral. He leaned over her desk once to point out a name on something she was typing, and she caught a trace of the scent of his skin. She felt her heart thump and her blood start to pump, and she felt outrageously and inappropriately turned on. She might have been young and naive, but she knew that it wasn't a schoolgirl crush. It was proper, grown-up desire. Lust even. And astonishingly, she couldn't shake the thought that her feelings might be reciprocated. Every now and then, she would catch Dr Mistry looking at her – not glancing at her, or smiling in the affable, friendly way he did with everyone else, but staring, as if he was thinking things he shouldn't. At first, she would blush and look away, but she gradually became bolder, and she held his gaze, staring him down, daring him to look away first.

She had slept with Charles. It was the seventies, after all – nobody waited till they were married any more. It had been . . . all right, she supposed. She imagined it would get better when they were married and did it more. They both lived at home with their parents, so when they did get to do it, it was usually a rushed affair on the sofa or on one of their narrow single beds, when the parents were out. Also, when they got to do it more regularly, Charles might not be so overexcited every time and it might last longer. There never seemed to be enough time for her to get properly aroused, and if she was, certainly not enough time for her to get real pleasure out of the whole thing. She imagined that with Dr Mistry it would be a very different experience.

It was going to happen, somehow she knew it. And it would take the smallest thing. As it turned out, it was quite a large thing: a consignment of parcels from Dr Mistry's family in India, which was delivered to the surgery. When he came in and saw the stack of boxes beside Mrs Whittaker's desk, he smiled ruefully. 'I'm so embarrassed,' he said. 'My aunts worry that I'll freeze to death, or that I'm sleeping on the floor, so they send me things. Heaps of things. My flat's just around the corner. It'll take me a few trips, but I'll take them all home with me this evening.'

'Or I could help you,' said Judith. 'Between us, it would only take one trip.'

'Thank you, Judith,' he said. 'I would be so grateful.' And they exchanged a look so intense it felt to Judith as if it might set the papers on her desk alight. Judith wasn't quite sure how Mrs Whittaker had missed the bolt of energy that passed between them, but she carried on typing, unconcerned.

It was the longest work day of Judith's life. The hands on her watch crept around so slowly, she was convinced it had actually stopped. But eventually, years later, it seemed, it was five thirty and the surgery closed. Judith took a moment to visit the bathroom and comb her hair. She was being ridiculous. She was just going to be carrying some parcels around to his flat. He might offer her a cup of tea. That was all.

Except it wasn't all. An hour later, she was lying naked on his bed, making sounds she didn't know she had inside her. She had been absolutely correct. This was nothing like what she did with Charles.

At first it was all about sex. They would race around to his flat after work and tear each other's clothes off. But after a few weeks, they began to talk. His first name was Pravin, and he was clever, funny and very insightful. She loved to listen to him talk, and he seemed genuinely interested in her and in her thoughts. He was ten years older, and when she expressed an opinion about something he would question her closely, not to put her down, but to understand what she was saying. It made her more thoughtful, made her read more, made her try harder. They couldn't ever spend more than an hour or two together (she had told her parents and Charles she was working slightly longer hours), but those were the minutes in the day when she felt properly alive.

She didn't break it off with Charles, although she made excuses to avoid sleeping with him, and she didn't tell her parents or any of her friends about Pravin. They hadn't even really spoken to one another about what was going on between them, or what it meant, but she knew very well that it wasn't a conventional love affair, and it wasn't going to end in marriage and happily ever after.

She didn't expect it to end quite so soon however. She was at work one Monday morning when Mrs Whittaker came over and put a greeting card, still in its envelope, on her desk. 'Sign this for Dr Mistry, won't you, dear?' she said briskly.

'Is it his birthday?' Judith said, trying to sound unconcerned. If it was his birthday, she knew just what to do to celebrate.

'No, he's leaving,' said Mrs Whittaker. 'Didn't you know? He's going back to India at the end of the month to get married.'

Judith wasn't quite sure how she didn't faint or throw up on her desk, but she didn't. She just kept typing. 'I'll sign it later,' she said. She waited until the last patient from the morning round had left, and then grabbed a stack of files and went into his consulting room.

She shut the door behind her. 'When were you going to tell me?'

He looked up at her. 'Tell you what?'

'That you were engaged to someone else.'

'I've been engaged to her since I was seven years old. It's an arranged marriage, Judith. Not something I ever had a choice about.'

'But what about . . . ?'

'Us? What about us? What about the boyfriend you haven't broken up with? The parents you haven't told?'

'But . . .' She started to cry. He got up, put his arms around her and wiped away her tears.

'Don't. Please don't. Come to my flat tonight. We'll talk then.'

She rang her mum and made up a story about spending the night at a friend's house. Her mum was a little surprised – it was a week-night after all – but Judith stuck to her story. After work, she and Pravin went around to his flat. She sat on an upright kitchen chair and he sat opposite her. She didn't take her coat off.

'I love you,' he said simply. It was the first time he had said it.

'I love you too.'

'I didn't mean to fall in love with you.'

'No.' There was a long silence. 'So what do we do?' she asked.

'I don't know.'

They talked all night. They argued, wept and shouted, tore off each other's clothes and made love, dozed, laughed, cried and argued again. He explained that the wedding plans were far advanced and his family had invested heavily in it. Refusing to go ahead with it would cause his family to disown him and would bring untold agony to his parents. But for Judith, he would do it. If she was brave enough.

She thought about it – about asking him to give up his family and his future. About what her parents would say. About the scandal if she dumped Charles and ran away with an Indian doctor. And as the sun rose, she knew in her heart that she wasn't brave enough. No matter how much she loved Pravin, it was a course of action for a much bolder woman, a woman who didn't care what people thought. A woman who knew she alone would be enough for a man who had given up everything for her.

Finally, as the sun came up, she got out of his bed and stood naked by the window, looking out over the high street. She turned to look at him. 'I want one letter a year,' she said. 'For as long as you think of me, as long as you love me, wherever you are, I want a letter from you every year. And I'll write one to you.'

27

JO AND LEE NOW

Jo

It didn't seem a lot to ask, thought Jo. She didn't want to be a bitch or a nag, but every evening when she came through the door from work, hungry, tired, desperate just to spend some time with the kids, she'd say to Lee, 'Have you done anything about dinner?'

And he'd say, 'Oh, no, sorry. It just didn't occur to me.'

She tried taking something out of the freezer before she left in the morning. She tried mentioning dinner when she rang him at lunchtime. She even tried cooking double portions and leaving half in the fridge so he'd just have to heat something up. But every evening, she came home and there was nothing prepared, so she had to go straight into the kitchen and start making dinner, because if she didn't, the kids would get ratty and hungry, she'd end up giving them something quick like fish fingers, and she and Lee would end up eating at midnight.

It should have been a minor thing – something they could discuss light-heartedly, laugh about and forget. But it had got beyond a joke. Jo would start to get tense about it on her way home, and by the time she walked through the door and they had the now-familiar exchange, she'd be seething. She'd find herself wondering why he couldn't just take the hint, as she bashed saucepans and chopped vegetables as if she was trying to murder them. It was so unlike him. Lee had always been the perfect partner: competent, helpful, more than willing to do his fair share in caring for the kids and looking after the house. Sure, he'd never been a great cook, but he'd always given it a go, even if it was a chilli con carne, made with a bottled sauce and served with couscous because he couldn't cook rice. But his refusal to make dinner these days seemed almost deliberate, defiantly obstinate. She couldn't work it out, and she was too angry about it to discuss it without causing a fight. And frankly she was stretched so thin, and working so hard, she just didn't have time for a battle with Lee.

Richard didn't mess around once he got going, and in just a few months, they had launched a girls' range in the East Finchley store and signed leases on two further North London sites: one in Highgate and one in Mill Hill. It was brilliant, but it was madly hard work, and Jo felt like she had to be at the top of her game all the time. It was very important to her that the core values of Jungletown stayed the same, and it meant she had to be in every meeting. Richard called her a control freak, but he meant it as a compliment. She felt like she fought dragons every day; she'd had to learn so much so fast – stock control, investment, law and negotiation – and that was just the beginning. What they were doing now was so far beyond running a small neighbourhood store. And astonishingly, she was good at it. Really good. She tried to explain it all to Lee in the evenings after the kids had gone to bed. He listened, but as time went on, he asked fewer and fewer questions, and she felt he was just nodding along, not really paying attention.

She didn't want to talk about work so much, but it was all she thought about – work and the kids. She still felt terribly torn, and she missed Zach and Imogene desperately during the day. She wanted to spend every spare moment with them when she wasn't working, and she knew that meant she had become more indulgent. She would let them eat whatever they liked for breakfast in front of the TV, to minimise the trauma when she left them. She brought home toys and books from work so often that Zach had started meeting her at the door when she got home, holding out his hands for the gift he had come to expect. Both kids' behaviour deteriorated with her. When she was the main carer, she had been a firm but calm disciplinarian, and Zach and Imogene had generally listened when she told them what to do. Now she was a part-time parent, they both played up like mad. They could sense she was full of absent-parent guilt and would not lay down the law as before, and they made the most of it.

It all culminated one Saturday afternoon, with Zach and Imi throwing a stereo tantrum in the supermarket. She placated them as best she could and raced around, throwing things in her trolley at high speed. When she was in the queue to pay, she saw an elderly couple in the next checkout queue. They were looking at her pityingly. For an instant she saw what they did – her children, bickering and smeared with chocolate, and her trolley piled high with convenience foods.

She drove home too fast. 'Mummy, why are you crying?' Zach asked.

'Mummy needs to fix some things,' she said, wiping her eyes.

When she got home, she marched into the back garden, where Lee was tinkering with his bicycle.

'This isn't working,' she said. 'None of this is working. What are we going to do?'

He put down his spanner. 'What do you mean?'

'You never make dinner. You always wait for me to get home to do it and it drives me nuts.'

It wasn't what she had meant to lead with, but the words just came out.

Lee's face darkened. 'Fine, while we're throwing around "you never" and "you always" statements, you never, ever ask me how my day was, how I'm feeling or what work I've managed to do. You always march in here and interrogate me about the kids so you can tell me what I'm doing wrong, and then you talk about work. All. The. Time.'

Jo took a step back. She had never heard Lee talk with such bitterness and anger. She couldn't have been more shocked if he had slapped her.

'Oh,' she said. There was a long silence.

'I didn't mean it to come out like that,' Lee said. 'But I had to say something. It's been eating away at me, and you just marched out here and . . .' He looked over her shoulder. Zach and Imi were playing at the sand table, but he could see Zach was listening. Jo turned around and looked at the kids too. She turned back to Lee.

'Truce till the kids are in bed?'

'Yes.'

Later that night, they sat down to talk. The dinner thing, it seemed, was not Lee being thoughtless, but his own – admittedly passive-aggressive – way of suggesting that Jo wasn't doing enough around the house.

'When I went out to work full-time, I still did laundry, and helped with dinner and stuff,' he said.

'Fair point,' said Jo. 'I don't want to bicker endlessly about who does what chores. In future, can we just discuss it like adults?'

'I'd like to discuss lots of things like adults,' said Lee. 'I don't want to feel like I'm last on your list of priorities any more. I want time for the two of us. Just us. No kids. No phones, no email, no work talk.'

'Fair enough,' said Jo, although she had no idea how to carve that kind of time out of days that were already crammed full.

'Here's my idea,' said Lee. 'Let's make Friday nights date night. My parents can come and babysit the kids, and we'll go out. Every Friday night – for dinner, or even just a couple of drinks. We can talk and catch up. Maybe even flirt a little.' He managed a small smile, and Jo smiled too.

'That sounds great,' she said. 'If your folks don't mind.'

'They don't. I already asked them.'

She tried not to feel put out that he'd set the plan in motion without asking her first. It was a plan born of love, trying to make things better between them. And God knows, they had to do something.

The first date night started awkwardly. It had been so long since they'd been alone together and awake, they didn't quite know what to do. Jo got home from work to find her in-laws already there. She went upstairs and changed out of her suit and into a summery dress, and she and Lee kissed the kids goodbye. They decided to walk to their local pub, which had a nice garden.

'How was work?' asked Lee.

'Fine,' said Jo, but she didn't want to go on and on about work and upset him, so she didn't say anything more. 'How was home?'

'Fine. Imi's learned to sing "Baa, Baa, Black Sheep" so we had a few hundred renditions of that. Oh, and I hope you have some more of those make-up-removing cotton pads somewhere, because I went upstairs and found Zach had filled the sink with water and he was feeding them to his bath fish.'

Jo laughed. 'I can use loo paper to take off my make-up tonight. I can get more tomorrow.'

They walked in silence until they got to the pub, but it was an easy, companionable silence. They got a bottle of their favourite Sauvignon Blanc and found a table that caught the last rays of the evening sun.

'So what have you been doing with your creative time?' she asked. 'We haven't talked about it for a while.'

'That's because I haven't.'

'At all? Nothing?'

'I did a few drawings at first, even started a painting, but I didn't know what I was doing them for. I mean, were they exercises? Was I planning an exhibition? Or a book?'

'And did you decide what you were doing?'

'Well, I thought maybe a children's book, but I didn't have a definite idea.'

'So . . .'

'Well, there's so little time. I mean, between getting Zach out of the house and clearing up after breakfast, it's mayhem, And then I have to get Imi down for her nap, which is more and more of a struggle, by the way, and once she's down, that's my only time to put my feet up. If I turn on the TV, that's deadly – all of a sudden it's time to go and get Zach, or if I go on the Net . . . the other day I wasted an hour and a half watching Jimi Hendrix videos on YouTube. I don't even like Jimi Hendrix. And of course once Zach's home from nursery, you can forget it. It would be like trying to work in the middle of a cyclone. And that goes on day after day, and then suddenly, it's Friday and I haven't picked up a pencil all week.' He shook his head and took a sip of his wine. 'Sorry. I'm whining.'

'Yes,' said Jo.

'What?'

'Yes. Yes, you are. Who are you, and what have you done with Lee? You were always the most driven guy I've ever known. You never stopped. You always had an idea, and nothing would stop you working on it.'

'I know, but—'

'No buts. This is tough love. Get over yourself. Decide what you want to do, and do it. Once you start, you know the momentum will carry you.'

'I was only going to say it's a long time since I did a project where I generated an idea for myself, by myself. It's difficult to get back into that space, that's all. It would help me a lot to talk through things and brainstorm them with you.'

'Of course,' said Jo, squeezing his hand. 'Any time. You know that.'

They finished the bottle of wine, and laughed all the way home. Once Lee's parents had left, they made love on the sofa, and when they finally made it to bed, made love again and woke up still wound around one another.

She meant to make time to talk about Lee's book project in the week, but time got away from them. Suddenly it was Friday again, but they had both come down with such bad colds that they cancelled Lee's folks coming over and lay on the sofa together, watching a Bruce Willis film and sharing a box of tissues.

Lee

Nine days. Ten if you counted today. Ten days since he and Jo had talked about brainstorming his book project, and she hadn't so much as mentioned it. It wasn't like him to play games, but he was damned if he was going to be the one to bring it up. She had said she wanted to help, and he would wait until she said something. Yes, they'd both been ill this Friday night, but they'd had the whole weekend, and they were allowed to have proper adult conversations at times other than their Friday-night date.

'Daddy, can you walk slower?' Zach's voice cut through the fog of his anger, and he glanced back. Zach was trailing behind him, running and hopping to keep up. Lee had been pushing the pushchair with speedy fury.

'Sorry, boy,' he said, waiting for Zach to catch up. 'Want to ride on the buggy step?'

'Nah, only babies do that,' said Zach dismissively.

'Babies and . . . chariot drivers,' said Lee, lifting him on to the step on the back of the pushchair. 'Hold on tight!' He ran all the way to the nursery, keeping up a commentary about a chariot race, and arrived with Zach and Imogene both breathless and giggling.

'Good race, my lord!' he said to Zach, high-fiving him as he hopped off and tore through the gates into the nursery.

'Looks like you had a fun walk here,' said Miranda, who was checking the contents of Martha's bag before walking her in. Martha still liked to be taken right to the classroom and handed over to the teaching assistant, even though the children had been at nursery for almost an entire school year. She liked routine, and she liked things done the same way. Lee, who knew this, waited with his pushchair and Miranda's, as Miranda took Martha in and went through the ritual, kissing Martha goodbye and assuring her that she would be back to collect her at the right time.

Martha was wearing an old-fashioned smock dress in a deep berry purple, and Miranda was wearing a white blouse. Lee watched through the window of the nursery as Miranda bent over her daughter. The curve of her arms, the colours of their clothes and the dark curls of their hair mingling together made a beautiful arrangement of negative shapes and colours.

He walked home quickly and, unusually, Imogene fell

asleep in the pushchair as they went. He lifted the pushchair into the house so he could leave her sleeping where she was. He dashed to his desk and found some watercolour paper and pastels, and began to sketch Miranda and Martha from memory. It was one of those rare moments where economy of line and the right colour choice came together, and in half an hour he had drawn something very lovely. The two people in the picture were instantly recognisable, but it was the simple tenderness of the moment that made it work.

Lee sat back and looked at what he had done. For the first time since he had given up his job to be at home, he felt creatively satisfied. He carefully sprayed the drawing with fixative and waited for it to dry, then scanned it and saved it on his computer.

He put the original in a plastic sleeve, and when he left to collect Zach from nursery, he took the drawing with him. When he saw Miranda waiting by the gate, he felt unaccountably shy. He had assumed it would be easy to give her the drawing, but it suddenly seemed like a strange, and rather stalker-ish, thing to do. Then she turned and saw him and gave him such an easy, happy smile of welcome that his doubts were dispelled. He was just being silly. He drew the plastic sleeve out of his bag, and walking over to her, he held it out. 'Here,' he said diffidently. 'I drew it this morning and it turned out okay. I thought you might like it.'

He didn't mean to make her cry. He knew she was very sensitive, with her mum being ill, but he hadn't thought that a simple sketch would make the tears trickle down her cheeks. He patted her back awkwardly.

'I'm so sorry, she said, swiping the tears away. 'It's just so beautiful. Thank you.'

'No, thank you.' Lee smiled. 'You two looked lovely this morning – it gave me inspiration. It's the first thing I've drawn in ages.'

She looked worried. 'You shouldn't give it to me then. Don't you want to keep it?'

'I scanned it and saved it electronically,' said Lee. What he didn't say was that he didn't particularly want to explain to Jo why he was drawing pictures of Miranda and her daughter. Mainly because he didn't know why himself.

'Look . . .' Miranda hesitated, 'please come back to ours for lunch. It won't be much – just some pasta and salad. It's the only way I can think to say thank you.'

'Are you sure?'

'Absolutely. Martha would love to play with Zach, and the babies can crash around in the playroom.' She looked up at the sky. 'Besides, it's going to rain, so no one will be going to the park this afternoon. Come on.'

'Thanks,' said Lee. 'That would be nice.'

It was, oddly enough, his very first play date since he had been a stay-at-home dad. The mums who would ordinarily have had Jo over with the kids had never invited him. He discovered that it livened up his afternoon considerably, and that two adults looking after four children somehow seemed to have a much easier time than one adult looking after two. They all sat around the big table in Miranda's immaculate kitchen and ate big bowls of pasta. Both Zach and Imi ate much better than they would have done at home, because the environment was new and exciting. Then they moved into the playroom and Martha had great fun showing all her toys to Zach. The rain fell steadily outside, and while Miranda cleared up the kitchen and loaded the dishwasher, Lee sat at a table in the playroom keeping an eye on the kids. There were big sheets of paper on the table, and a bucket of thick wax crayons, and he absent-mindedly started sketching the brightly flowering shrub he could see through the rain-speckled playroom window.

Miranda came in and sat quietly beside him, watching what he was doing. She didn't say anything until he put the crayons down.

'I've never seen anyone draw like that,' she said. 'Not in real life. That's beautiful.'

'Thank you.'

'Do you miss working?'

'Well, I didn't get to scribble with wax crayons when I did work,' he smiled. 'But yes, I miss the discipline of creating every day. I'm supposed to be working on a creative project, a book . . . but I'm not getting anywhere with it.'

'A book? What kind of book?'

'Well . . . I thought maybe a children's book. I've done some sketches of kids . . . a little guy I saw in a park, Imi when she was sleeping, the one I did of you two today . . . and I thought I might be able to do something along those lines.'

'So what would the story be?'

'Not sure . . . I'm a bit stuck there.'

'I can't believe that. You have such an incredible imagination. I'm always amazed when I hear you playing with your kids. The things you think of! What were you doing when you arrived at nursery this morning?'

Lee laughed. 'Oh, we were having a chariot race. We narrowly avoided being eaten by lions and getting slain by a gladiator called Maximus.'

'You see? That's amazing! Couldn't you translate that into drawings? The amazing imaginary adventures of a dad and a little kid?'

'Amazing imaginary adventures . . .' Lee stared out into the rain-soaked garden. Ideas flooded his head: a man with his jumper half on, covering his head, the flapping sleeves becoming the tentacles of a giant octopus. A hoover that was also a dragon . . . household objects made magical and fantastical. 'Miranda . . . you're a genius!'

'Nonsense. It's all you, all your amazing mind and talent. Now I'm going to put on a DVD for the kids in the living room. Why don't you sit here and draw for a while?'

'I couldn't . . .'

'Why not? The kids'll be perfectly happy watching *Finding Nemo*, and we'll call you if we need you. Just draw, okay? Draw something amazing and imaginary.'

Miranda ushered all four kids out of the room, smiling at Lee as she went. He picked up a bright red crayon and began to draw.

PART FOUR

28

MEL NOW

If it had been anyone other than Marina and her parents, Mel would have gone around there, guns blazing, to get Serena out and bring her home. But Marina and Serena had been friends since they were tiny, and Mel considered Marina's mum Jane a friend. The night Serena stormed out of the flat, Jane stayed on the phone with Mel for well over an hour, reassuring her that Serena would be okay.

'She's just terribly upset,' Jane said, 'and you know how you two can wind each other up. When she's ready to talk, you'll be the first to know, I promise. Just give her a few days to cool off.'

It was one of the hardest things Mel had ever done. The flat was horribly quiet without Serena, and she wandered around aimlessly, unable to settle. She sat at her computer and started an email to Serena over and over, but everything she wrote sounded either accusatory, or as if she was sucking up to get Serena to forgive her and come home. She knew she had overstepped the mark, and that she would struggle to get Serena to trust her again. How could she fix it? And how would she find answers to the questions that continued to plague her? Who was the older man she had seen with Serena? Was that Hopey, or was Hopey someone or something else?

For three days, she waited. She jumped every time her phone rang, and when she was at work, she watched the door of the shop continually, praying that Serena would walk in. She barely slept at night, and when she did she was plagued by terrible nightmares, in which Patrick, back from the past, pursued Serena down dark alleyways. Jane kept in close contact, and reported that Serena seemed happier and more relaxed, but was still not ready to talk to Mel.

By the fourth day, she began to think it was quite likely that she might go mad if something didn't change. And when Marina came through the door of the shop, she was so wound up that she almost didn't recognise her.

'Hi,' said Marina warily. Mel glanced at Jo, who was working at the counter. She hadn't told Jo or Holly about the fact that Serena had moved out.

'Shall we go outside?' Mel said. 'Jo, I won't be a moment, okay?'

Jo nodded, barely looking up from her laptop screen.

Mel and Marina went out on to the pavement. Mel resisted the urge to grab her by the shoulders and interrogate her. With great effort, she waited, silently.

'Serena doesn't know I'm here,' Marina began. 'But I wanted you to know she's doing something – something she hasn't told you about.'

Drugs. Mel felt like she'd been punched. She knew it. She had always known it would happen. Was it heroin? She still hadn't said anything. She just nodded.

Marina continued. 'Mum and I talked about it, and we decided it's best if you just come and see.'

Mel imagined Serena lying on a filthy mattress in a crack house. Could she bear to see that? Would they be able to get her out?

'It's this afternoon,' Marina said, which Mel found a bit confusing. What was this afternoon? 'Anyway,' Marina continued, 'Mum's parked around the corner. Can you come now? It'll only be an hour or so.'

An hour? For some kind of intervention? What would they do? Where would they take Serena? Mel's mind was racing.

'Can you get off work?' Marina was asking.

'Of course, of course,' Mel said.

She went back into the shop and explained to Jo that she had a crisis with Serena.

Jo didn't hesitate. 'Go. I'm here; we've got the girls . . .' They'd taken on two college leavers, who were wonderful at playing with the kids and keeping the shop tidy. 'They can hold the fort, and I'm here to cash up and lock up if you don't make it back.'

'Thanks,' said Mel. 'Really, thank you so much.'

'Nonsense. You've always been a hundred per cent reliable. We employ people with families, and families have emergencies sometimes. Now go, and don't worry about us at all.'

Mel grabbed her bag and dashed out of the shop. Marina was waiting, and together they walked down the road. Jane was sitting in the car around the corner and they got in.

'We're going to be a few minutes late, but I don't think

it'll matter,' said Jane. 'It was a bit last-minute, but Marina and I decided you had to see this.'

'See what?'

'You'll have to wait and see,' Jane said. 'I promise you it'll be worth it.'

Mel was now thoroughly confused. Jane pulled off and drove through the busy streets from East Finchley through Hendon and into Colindale. They passed the RAF Museum and the police station and pulled up outside a lumber yard. Was this where Serena was? Had she found another dodgy boyfriend, who worked here? Was it the mysterious Hopey?

They got out of the car and Jane and Marina led Mel past the lumber yard and through some gates. She found herself outside a large prefabricated building. She seemed to remember it was, or had once been, a scout hall. Jane eased the door open, and putting her finger to her lips, she led Mel inside.

There were rows of chairs facing a low stage. Half the seats were taken, by a mixture of teenagers and adults. On stage, Mel saw the middle-aged man she had seen driving Serena away in the car. He was conducting a choir of about eight girls and boys who were singing an energetic gospel number without accompaniment. Mel scanned the faces of the kids in the choir, and the ones she could see in the audience. There was no sign of Serena. The little choir sang enthusiastically and well, and they swayed and did a little basic choreography with their song. As they finished, the crowd burst into loud applause.

The man turned to the audience and said, 'Ladies and gentlemen, the Swinging Hallelujahs!' There was another round of applause with some cheering and stamping. 'Right!' the man said. 'Give us a few moments to change over, and then we'll be having a duet from Melissa and Heather, followed by a very special solo number.'

Everything seemed rather haphazard and casual, but no one seemed to mind. Two teenage boys pushed an electric piano on to the stage. The man sat down at the piano and nodded, and two girls, both quite plump and shy-looking, climbed onstage and stood beside the microphones, watching him closely. The man nodded and began to play. The girls started to sing 'I Know Him So Well' from *Chess*, tentatively at first – but the man's sensitive support on the piano and his encouraging expression seemed to give them confidence. They reached the climax of the song, and while the harmony wasn't quite perfect, it was heartfelt and sweet. They got a storming round of applause and edged off the stage, blushing and thrilled.

The man stood up and said, 'And now, ladies and gentlemen, I give you . . . Serena Grey.'

Serena stepped up on to the stage. She must have been waiting in a back room, because until that moment, Mel had not known for sure that she was there. She looked small and nervous. Serena sat down on the piano stool. She didn't say anything – she just began to play and sing. She started with the Beatles' 'Yesterday', simply played and beautifully sung. She had been a talented musician as a little girl, but this . . . this was different. She was no longer playing the piano like a good exam student – she was playing with feeling and flair. She was playing like herself. And her voice was beautiful – deeper and smokier than you would expect from such a young girl, but with pure, very true high notes.

When she stopped, the room was silent for a few seconds and then exploded into a roar of noise. Serena smiled, and looked out into the crowd for the first time. She locked eyes with Mel and her face darkened. She half stood up from the piano stool, but then she looked from Mel to Jane, and something she saw in Jane's face made her sit back down. She rested her fingers on the piano keys and looked at them for a few seconds. Then she looked up and stared pleadingly at the man who had introduced her. He nodded, and that seemed to be the cue she needed.

'I wrote this song for my mum,' Serena said. 'I didn't think she would be here to hear it, but . . . she is.'

There was no way for Mel to know what Serena meant by that. All she could do was listen to the song. It was called 'The Lion's Roar' and it was about the fierceness of protective love. Mel wished she could remember all of it, because it was beautiful. But she was too busy crying with pride and shame and sorrow. She hoped that she would hear the song again and again. When Serena finished and the thunderous applause died down, the man said, 'That's it for the first half of our programme. We'll take a short break, and then we'll be back with some instrumental numbers.'

Mel made her way over to the stage. Serena was surrounded by a crowd of well-wishers, who were all hugging her and telling her how amazing she was. Mel waited until the last of them had moved away. She waited for Serena to come to her, and she waited for Serena to speak first.

'I wanted it to be a surprise.'

'It was a surprise,' Mel said. She couldn't keep the hurt out of her voice.

'Mr Hope came to our school about six months ago and did a workshop, and then said we could come to his classes if we wanted to develop our own style of music.'

'Why didn't you . . . ?'

'Because I knew you'd be all pushy about it, and want to know all about it, and want to tell me what to sing, and make me practise. Or you'd say it was a waste of time, and if I was going to do music again I should do the exams. I wanted to do it my own way.'

'So how did you . . . ?'

'Dad signed the permission forms and paid.'

Mel breathed in sharply. She should be more upset about that, but to be honest, she wasn't surprised. Bruce was very laid back and wouldn't have thought to ask any questions. Nor would he have thought to mention it to Mel. She knew it wasn't malice . . . he just didn't always live in the real world.

Serena continued. 'I wasn't trying to do a bad thing. I just wanted to do something . . . my own way. To show you I could.'

'Well, you showed me,' said Mel. 'You were brilliant. And I loved the song.'

Serena hunched over and chewed on her thumbnail. 'Not everything I do is bad, Mum. Just some of it is private, okay?'

'I know, but—'

'I know what you're going to say. The world is dangerous. I know. I know it is. And I know you think I haven't, but I have listened to all the stuff you've told me over and over.

I made a mistake with Triggah. And I might make more mistakes. But sometimes . . . you just have to trust me. Please.'

'I'll try,' said Mel. 'Will you please come home?'

'Okay,' said Serena. 'But, Mum . . . I know this sounds like I'm being rude, but I'm not. I think you have some issues, and I think, maybe . . . you need to talk to someone about them.'

Mel nodded, and she could see Serena was incredibly surprised to see that she agreed.

'When I was young – your age and younger – some bad stuff happened to me. And I think, maybe I've just never dealt with it. You're right. It's time.'

Serena touched her hand briefly, and Mel could have wept with happiness. 'Will you come and meet Mr Hope now?' Serena said. 'He really is amazing.'

She led Mel over to the man, who was chatting animatedly to three young guys. He smiled when he saw them approaching. The teenagers shook his hand and moved on, and the man came over to Mel and Serena. 'This must be your mum!' he said, offering his hand. 'Ian Hope. It's great to finally meet you. Serena's told me all about you. You work in that fantastic shop in East Finchley, I believe? Great idea. I wish my son was still young enough for us to shop there!'

He had warm, bright blue eyes and a smile that lit up his face.

'You're doing wonderful work here,' she said.

'I teach music in a private school nearby, but I believe music is something all kids should have access to,' he said. 'So I run a series of workshops in schools where there's no music in the curriculum, and then the kids that show interest, I invite to join these classes. We do this concert once a term for all the kids in the borough who are involved.'

Mel looked around. There was a loose group of teenagers singing an R&B song together, and a skinny boy was pounding a drum kit while a knot of kids looked on.

'There certainly are a lot of them,' she said.

'They don't want to do formal classes and exams, but they do need some guidance,' he said. 'I teach them to read music, and to make their own kind of sound, but with proper musical foundations.' He paused. 'She's astonishing, your daughter. She has perfect pitch, did you know that? She could go on to be classically trained, with that degree of musicality and that voice, but she seems happiest doing her own thing.'

'Letting them do their own thing,' said Mel. 'That's a tricky one, isn't it?'

'It is,' said Ian Hope. 'You need nerves of steel, and a lot of grace.'

Mel smiled. She couldn't help but like him. 'Well, I'm working on the nerves, but I have a long way to go on the grace. And thank you for today. You have no idea what it meant to me. Us.'

He smiled at her, a little perplexed by her comment. 'If you'll excuse me,' he said, 'I've got a double-bass player with stage fright who's going to need some moral support before the second half. See you next term, Serena!'

Grace, Mel thought. Grace and forgiveness and flexibility. She took Serena's hand and they walked to the door.

29

HOLLY NOW

The beginning of the end came much more quickly than Holly had anticipated. Judith came home from the hospital after the procedure to drain the fluid. She was more comfortable, but she was very tired. She slept almost all the time, and over the course of a few days, stopped eating. Holly was frantic, and begged her to have something – anything – but Judith waved all food away. She didn't even want to drink, but if Holly nagged for ages would suck on a few small ice chips to moisten her lips. She was cold all the time, and Holly piled blankets on her bed, almost concealing her tiny frame.

Lynne, the Macmillan nurse, came to see Judith, and when she came out of the bedroom, took Holly into the living room. 'She hasn't got long, Holly. Just a few days, I would say. The pain medication means she's comfortable, but she's going to sleep more and more, and slip into unconsciousness, and then she'll pass on. If there are people who want to see her before she goes, and people who want to be with her at the end, now is the time to call them.'

Holly nodded. She, Miranda and David had discussed what

they would do when the time came, and they had agreed that the three of them would be in the house. David and Miranda's spouses were ready to take over caring for children and homes so they could be with their mum without worrying, and David had taken leave of absence at work.

As far as Judith's friends in the congregation went, Holly passed the buck by ringing the vicar. He said he would let everyone know, and ask them not to visit any more. She knew Judith would want the last rites performed, and he came to do that while she was still conscious. Holly stayed with Judith for the service and found it very moving. Judith looked very peaceful once it was completed, and although she didn't speak, she squeezed the vicar's hand. Holly walked him out. He was visibly upset.

'Thank you, Father,' she said, awkwardly. It felt odd calling him that – he looked younger than she was, and she wasn't entirely sure he needed to shave yet. 'I've made a note of everything she wants for the funeral – the hymns and readings and so on – so I'll be in touch about that when . . . after . . .' Holly couldn't finish the sentence.

The vicar nodded. 'Your mum has been a part of our church for far longer than I have,' he said. 'I'm not entirely sure what we will all do without her.'

That took care of the larger church community, and mercifully, the vicar seemed able to keep Angela Joba and the rest of the singing-and-praying contingent away. Mr Benton still came every day, and he moved through the house like a small, silent elf, washing up, making tea and answering the phone. For the most part, he stayed away from Judith's room, only going in to sit with her if he was asked. Holly felt appallingly guilty every time she looked at him – he was clearly there out of selfless devotion to Judith, who quite obviously had never loved him in return. That said, she didn't seem to have loved Holly's father either. It didn't seem fair to have Mr Benton in the house doing things for Judith and for all of them when he had no idea about her secrets. Still, Holly didn't know how to send him away without hurting his feelings, so she let things carry on as they were.

With most things in place, Holly's final and most agonising concern was the writer of the letters. Would Judith want him to know she was ill? Would she want to see him before she died? Judith's best time of day was early. It was when she was most likely to be awake and lucid, so Holly sat by her bed one sunny morning and waited for her to stir. When Judith's eyes fluttered open, she helped her to sit up slightly and persuaded her to take a couple of small ice chips. It was a difficult conversation to have. How to begin? She had not said to Judith in so many words, 'You are dying.' She assumed Judith knew, but what if she didn't?

'Mum,' she began hesitantly, 'I'm trying to get things sorted for you – tying up loose ends.'

'Thank you, dear,' Judith whispered.

'. . . And I was wondering about . . . the man. The man who wrote you the letters . . . ?'

Judith's face gave no hint of what she was thinking, and she didn't say anything. Holly wasn't sure if she understood. She pressed on.

'Do you want me to contact him? Do you want me to ask him to visit you?'

'He can't come, dear . . . He's in India. Gone, never to return.'

Holly nodded. She was sure the letter she had seen hadn't had an Indian postmark, but Judith would know where he was, wouldn't she?

'Do you want me to let him know . . . that you're ill?'

Judith stared at the light coming in the window. 'You can read them . . . after I've gone. You'll understand then, my dear. Tell him then. Tell him after. Tell him . . . I don't need the letters any more.'

That afternoon, she slipped into unconsciousness. In the evening, Miranda and David arrived, and moved back into their childhood bedrooms. They set a schedule for the night – four-hour stints for each of them to sit with her, but in the end, no one wanted to leave her. They took turns to doze in the armchair, but they all stayed in Judith's bedroom, one of them holding her hand at all times. She made it through the night, and in the morning Lynne came and helped Holly and Miranda to remake the bed and make her comfortable.

Through the afternoon, rain battered against the window and a harsh wind blustered outside. Judith's breathing became rapid and shallow, then she would stop entirely for long seconds at a time. They would all lean forward wondering if that had been her last breath, but then she would gasp and begin to breathe again. It was unnerving, but Lynne had explained to them what they might expect, so they knew it was not unusual. Miranda was stoic, and sat without moving beside the bed, holding Judith's hand, but David couldn't bear it. He kept going in and out of the room, and his eyes were wet with tears. At one point Holly went downstairs to get a drink and found David standing outside the open back door, puffing on a cigarette. She had never seen him smoke before. She had no idea where he had even come by a cigarette.

He saw her and smiled weakly. 'I bought some on my way down. I haven't had one since uni, but I thought I might need them.'

'Knock yourself out,' said Holly. 'Whatever you need.'

'This sucks,' said David.

'Well, it sucks worse for her than it does for us. The least we can do is stick with her. I don't think it'll be much longer.'

'You're right,' said David, stubbing out his cigarette. 'Let's go.'

They went back upstairs. Holly was right. An hour or so later, Judith let out a long rattling breath. An expression passed over her face – the only word Holly could find to describe it was amazement, as if she had seen something wonderful – and the room went quiet. David, ever the man with the right words for an occasion, stepped to the bedside, crossed himself and said, 'Rest eternal grant to her, O Lord, and let light perpetual shine upon her. Amen.' It was just what Judith would have wanted.

Miranda began to sob as if her heart was broken, and David put a restraining hand on her arm. 'Lynne said the hearing can be the last to go. Let her go in peace.' Miranda gasped and was quiet.

'Goodbye, Mum,' said Holly softly. A Zulu farewell came to her and she said the words as best she could. '*Hamba kahle* – go well.' It was sunset.

They knew what to do – the hospice had given them instructions, so they rang the doctors' surgery, and one of the GPs was just coming off duty and came out to confirm the death. Then they rang the funeral home. Holly had not imagined how very difficult it would be to have strange men in the house, lifting Judith on to a stretcher and carrying her out. She had coped and been strong for all of it, but she just couldn't bear to watch Judith leaving her house for the last time, so she hid in the kitchen and smoked two of David's cigarettes. They made her feel incredibly ill, but they passed the time until the hearse pulled away.

And then there was nothing to do. It was just eight o'clock. David and Miranda could both have gone home to their families, but the three of them needed to be together. David walked up to the off-licence and came back with six bottles of wine. Miranda looked in the cupboards and freezer for something to eat, but none of them could face a reheated church casserole, so Holly rang the local Indian and ordered curry. They ate like starving animals. When they had finished, the tablecloth was stained with turmeric and oil and there were remnants of poppadoms and grains of rice everywhere. Judith would never have countenanced a takeaway and wine feast at the kitchen table. She didn't believe in convenience food, and she would have been horrified to see them eating straight out of the containers rather than using plates. In a funny way, that made it exactly the right thing to do on this of all nights.

They all drank too much wine, they reminisced, they cried, they laughed. They went into the living room and played some of Judith's old long-playing records. Then first

David and then Miranda fell asleep on the sofas. Holly sat sipping her wine and listening to her mum's Cliff Richard albums. She didn't know what she felt . . . it wasn't grief, not yet. She was relieved it had ended, but she also felt that it wasn't quite over. The funeral was yet to come, and there was still unfinished business she needed to complete for Judith. She got up from her chair and crept upstairs, careful not to wake her siblings. She opened Judith's jewellery box and retrieved all the letters, and also got the two Judith had put in her handbag to take to hospital. They were in chronological order, and, as Judith had said, the postmark on the oldest ones showed they had been sent from Mumbai (or Bombay, as it was then). But from 1995, the stamps changed to British ones and the letters had a Manchester postmark. The mystery man had obviously come to live in the UK. Judith must have been confused when she said he was still in India. He was only a couple of hundred miles away.

Holly's dad had died in 1992, so Judith was a widow by then. Why had he and Judith not met up? She picked up the most recent letter and turned the envelope over. There was an address sticker on the back: Dr P. Mistry, it said, with a Manchester address. Then she went back to the very first letter, dated some forty years before. The envelope was thin and the edges were frayed, as if the letter had been taken out and put back many, many times.

My precious Judith,

I arrived in Bombay last week, and it is as if I have come to a different planet. Everything seems strange,

but nothing is so strange as the great void in my
heart where you should be . . .

The date of the first letter was about six months before her mother and father were married. In the second letter, it was clear that Dr Mistry was also married, and working in Bombay. Holly read them all. None of the letters was long, and they told her the life story of this man, the man Judith had loved. A man who had married out of duty and had come to care for and respect his wife, but wrote words of love to another woman once a year. He had had a successful career and had fathered children, and was now a grand-father. When his oldest son decided to come and live in the UK, the whole family had followed and they all now lived in Manchester. From things he said in his letters, it was clear that Judith wrote to him too – he asked about things she had told him, and mentioned David, Miranda and Holly by name. It was also clear that in the intervening years they had never met up. Perhaps that was the reason, in her con-fused state, Judith had believed he was still in India. As long as he was married, her moral code and his would have pre-vented them from meeting. He might as well have been thousands of miles away.

When she had finished reading the last letter, Holly put them all carefully back in order. She got a shoebox from her room, put the letters into it and put them under her bed. She got a sheet of paper, an envelope and a stamp. 'Dear Dr Mistry,' she wrote, 'It is with sadness that I inform you of the death of my mother, Judith Evans. She asked me to let you know of her passing.'

Before she could fill the page with a million questions, she wrote, 'Yours sincerely, Holly Evans,' and made herself fold it and put it in the envelope. She crept downstairs and out of the back door, and walked to the postbox on the corner. The sky had cleared, and she stood watching the stars for a while. But she was desperately weary, so she walked back home, crawled into her bed and slept properly for the first time in weeks.

The sound of the side gate opening woke her early the next morning. Still very tired, she got up and pulled on a dressing gown. When she got out into the garden, Mr Benton was busy taking tools out of the garden shed. She walked out towards him. 'Mr Benton . . .' she began.

'I know,' he said. 'I felt her go, yesterday evening. And the vicar rang to let me know.' He nodded his head. He kept his eyes on the handle of the rake he was holding, and carefully brushed a loose petal off his lapel. 'Still, these leaves aren't going to sweep themselves up, are they? And she likes a tidy lawn.' He clearly didn't want to talk any more, and he began to rake up the leaves with precision.

The funeral was a week later, and Holly was astonished and touched at how full the church was. Mr Benton did a reading from John, that he knew Judith had particularly liked. The choir sang her favourite hymns, and it was all as correct and old-school as Judith would have wished. David did the eulogy, which was in essence a well-written and accurate biography, but not terribly emotional.

Then Holly stood and walked to the front. Her knees were shaking under her skirt, and she could only stop the trembling in her hands by gripping the edge of the lectern.

'My mum had beautiful hands,' she began. 'Very soft, with long, slim fingers and beautiful nails. When she became ill, one of the things I was able to do for her was give her a manicure. A few days before she died, I did her nails, and she asked me to paint them pillar-box red. If you knew my mum, that might surprise you – you probably thought of her as a pale pink woman. I know I always did. But for me, the great privilege of these last few months has been learning that she was anything but. She was a woman of many, many colours. She raised three children I hope she had cause to be proud of, she was a cornerstone of this church, and she inspired great love. I am sad that I only caught a glimpse of who she was so close to the end of her life. But I'm so glad that I saw what I did.'

When she got back to her seat, Miranda squeezed her hand tightly. She looked across at David, but his jaw was clenched, and he was gripping the knees of his trousers. She knew not to touch him or talk to him – he was only just holding it together.

When Holly stood up with David and Miranda to follow the coffin out to go to the crematorium, she spotted a tall, distinguished looking Indian man of about seventy, sitting at the back. He was alone, and he looked out of place – somehow she knew he was not just another member of the congregation.

Everyone was milling around outside the church and chatting. Holly accepted condolences from a few people, but then worked her way through the crowds to the Indian man.

'Dr Mistry,' she said.

'Holly. You look so like your mother,' he said. Holly was

astonished. She had never seen any similarity in their looks. 'She told me all about you in her letters,' he continued. 'She was so proud of your courage and your creativity.'

She didn't mean to cry. She'd held it together through the service, but she couldn't stop the tears that spilled down her cheeks at his words.

He touched her arm gently. 'I'm so sorry, Holly dear.'

She looked up at him. 'Holly dear – that's what my mum always called me.'

'I know. She called all three of you "dear". It was deliberate. She wrote once that she thought it was the loveliest endearment, because it means both beloved and precious.'

'This is hard,' Holly said. 'Not just her dying. This . . .' And she gestured at him.

'I can't expect you to understand,' said Dr Mistry, 'and I don't ask for your forgiveness. I loved Judith for more than forty years and I'm sad she's gone.'

'But she was married. To my father.'

'She was. And she loved him, and was always faithful to him. I love my wife too. We have a good marriage – it's an excellent partnership and we have wonderful children and grandchildren.'

'But you and my mother . . .'

'It was one letter a year. That's all. One letter where we could remember the very happy and brief time we had together, and where we could imagine a different life. A life we never had, and which would probably have been disappointing in reality.'

'I have the letters in Mum's . . . in my car,' Holly said. 'I had this mad idea I could put them in the coffin before she was cremated. I don't know why I thought that would be possible. I didn't just want to throw them away. Would you like . . . ?'

'Thank you,' said Dr Mistry. 'It would mean a lot to me to have them. I'll keep them with the ones that I have. The ones she sent me.' He walked with Holly to the car, and she handed him the shoebox tied closed with string.

'Thank you,' he said. 'And Holly, you spoke so beautifully in the church. I think she would have loved what you said. It was very brave of you.'

'I had to say it. She was more, so much more, than people knew. And if I hadn't said it today – here – it would never have been said. Because she's gone.'

He didn't answer, just nodded once and then walked away. She was glad he didn't say goodbye. She was sick and tired of saying goodbye to people.

Miranda came over to her. 'Who was that?'

'No one. Old friend of mum's,' said Holly. 'Let's go. Let's get to the crematorium and get this over with. The wake is booked for three and we need to get to the hotel.'

30

LEE NOW

'New York?'

'I know!' said Jo. 'Isn't it fantastic?'

'I . . . I don't know what to say. Is this Richard again?'

'No, it's me. I joined this online networking thing for women in business, and found this woman I was at school with – Verity Ellis. I'm sure I told you about it.'

Lee nodded. She might well have done. But as she talked about work stuff pretty much all the time, he tended to filter some of it out.

'Anyway, she moved to the States about ten years ago and she owns a bunch of clothing companies. She's terrifyingly successful.'

'So . . .'

'So she's been speaking to some of her investors, and they're looking for a children's clothing outlet to develop. She's showed them pictures of the East Finchley shop and the plans for the other stores we have in the pipeline, and they're keen to talk.'

'Develop it where?'

'America, I guess. New York to start with, then the West

Coast. We'd need to talk details. I know very little about it so far. That's why I need to go to New York. To meet with them.'

'Wow,' said Lee, and sat back in his chair, folding his arms.

Jo had just got home from a late meeting. The children were already in bed, and they were sitting at the kitchen table, eating the lasagne Lee had been keeping warm in the oven. She took a sip of her glass of water.

'What kind of "wow" is that?'

'The "wow" kind. Why?'

'Well, it didn't sound like the "Hey, Jo, I'm so proud of you, that's brilliant" kind of wow. Which was the kind I was hoping for.'

'It was that kind of wow. Of course it was. It's just a lot to take in.'

He bent over his plate and concentrated on extracting a strip of pasta with his fork. He couldn't look at her. He knew she was looking at him with that hard-eyed, thin-lipped expression that meant she was about to pick a fight.

'What's to take in? Nothing is decided at all. We get to go on a jolly to New York, I have a few meetings and we see what we think.'

'We? You and Richard?'

'No. I thought it would be fun if we went as a family. I've never been to New York. I want to see it with you and the kids.'

'But we wouldn't see it together. I'll be stuck in some overpriced, air-conditioned hotel room with two kids while you wheel and deal. The Americans are workaholics. You'd be in dinner meetings and breakfast meetings . . . Anyway, it would mean taking Zach out of school – and we can't afford it.' He knew he sounded petulant, and he didn't care.

'We can afford it.'

'Really?' Lee hadn't meant the comment to come out quite so sarcastically, but he couldn't take it back. 'I'm not earning right now, and I think it would be bloody irresponsible to blow money on a trip to the States just because you think you have the ready cash right now.'

He still couldn't meet Jo's eye, because he knew what she was thinking – that he wasn't earning because he hadn't done anything to get any freelance work. As it happened, he had been trying, but he'd had regretful 'Thanks, but no thanks'-type replies from everyone he'd approached, including his old company. He knew he needed to get a proper website up and start registering with agencies, but his work on the children's book was progressing, slowly but well, and he just hadn't had the time.

'Okay, well,' said Jo, and to his surprise, she sounded hurt rather than angry. 'What do you suggest? Shall I tell Verity we're not coming because my husband doesn't want to?'

'No. You should go on your own,' he said, feeling rotten for being so unsupportive.

'I can't!' He could hear the tears in her voice. 'I've never been away from the kids for more than a night. I've barely ever spent a night away from you. How can I go to the other side of the world . . . ?'

'It's not the other side of the world. It's a six or seven-hour flight. And the kids will be fine – they're not tiny babies any more.'

'But a week . . .'

'It'll fly by,' Lee said, trying to be kinder. 'If you think this is what you want, you should go for it.'

'I . . .' said Jo, and stopped.

'You what?'

'Well, I kind of wanted to know what we wanted. Not just me. I mean . . . if this American thing took off . . .'

'What are you saying?'

'I'm not saying anything.'

'Are they talking about you moving there?'

'Not me . . . us. And no, they're not. They haven't mentioned it. But it would be a possibility, I suppose.'

'Fuck me!' said Lee. 'Now you're moving us all over to the States? Our kids growing up American? And what about me? You might get a Green Card, but I'm damned sure I wouldn't . . . So what do I do? Sit at home and paint my nails?'

'Lee . . .'

'It would have been good if you'd run some of this past me first.'

'This *is* me running it past you! I finished the telephone conference with Verity an hour ago. I'm trying to discuss some of the things I thought about on the Tube on the way home! Jesus, Lee, you can't withdraw all your support and refuse to come with me or discuss it with me, and then yell at me because I haven't included you in my plans! You can't have it both ways!'

'Whereas it seems you get it any way you want it,' Lee said. He pushed his plate away. 'I'm not hungry. I'm going to work.'

'At what?' said Jo sarcastically.

Lee didn't answer. He went into his little study and slammed the door. He didn't draw or write, just sat fuming, playing endless games of Solitaire on his computer until well after midnight, when he knew Jo would be asleep.

They slept, or rather didn't sleep, on opposite edges of the bed, their backs turned to one another. In the morning, Lee felt wretched – hungover from lack of sleep and remorseful for his unkindness. He opened one eye and looked at the clock. Seven thirty. Jo was already up. He could hear her downstairs in the kitchen with the kids. He couldn't make out exactly what was being said, but from the pitch and tone of the voices, he could tell Zach was being a right little brat, either refusing to do something, or doing something he shouldn't. The mornings were often a nightmare. The kids, Zach in particular, would be downright awful to Jo. She understood it was because Zach knew she'd be leaving, going to work for the day, and that he would miss her, but it didn't make it any easier. On any other morning, Lee would have been in the kitchen to run interference and be the bad cop, so Jo didn't have to yell at Zach, but this morning, she was doing battle on her own. The selfish, ugly part of him wanted to stay in bed and leave her to deal with the tantrum. After all, he'd be handling the kids and all their nonsense for the next ten hours at least. But he knew he had been vile to her the night before, and also that he had been unfair. He jumped up and made the bed, trying to get the pillows straight and nicely plumped up, the way Jo liked, then headed downstairs.

It was ominously quiet in the kitchen. Imi was in her high chair, and Zach was sitting at the table. His expression hovered somewhere between evil satisfaction and fear. Jo was on her hands and knees. There was a massive splodge of porridge on the floor, and the fragments of a broken bowl, and Jo was trying to clean it up with a wodge of dampened paper towels and a brush and dustpan.

'Zach!' bellowed Lee. 'What did you do? Did you throw your bowl? That's very, very bad. Go and sit on the step.'

'But—' started Zach.

'No buts. If you don't go right now, I'll take your Transformers away for a week.'

Zach burst into tears and ran from the room. Jo sat back on her heels and looked at him.

'Well done, Genghis Kahn. Why don't you beat the soles of his feet with a ruler too?'

'He was naughty . . .'

'I threw the bowl. Not him, okay?'

'What?'

'I made cereal and he refused to eat it, so I poured that away and made porridge, and then he said he didn't want that, so I threw the bowl on the floor. But well done for screaming at a four-year-old before you find out what's actually going on.'

Jo finished cleaning up the mess in silence, then she went to sit beside Zach on the bottom step. Lee could hear the murmur of her voice as she spoke soothingly to him. Then she went upstairs and got ready for work, and left without saying goodbye to Lee.

He had a lot of time to think that day. For Jo to have hurled a bowl of porridge, especially in front of the kids, she had to be stretched to the limit. He'd let her down and he needed to find a way to make it better. He spent the afternoon giving the house a good clean, prepared a roast-chicken dinner and walked down to the flower stall on the high street with the kids. Together, they assembled a giant arrangement. Lee chose white roses that reminded him of the flowers in Jo's wedding bouquet. Zach loved the bright orange gerberas, and Imi was drawn to the pink peonies. It was an unusual combination, but he thought it expressed their love. They took the bouquet home and Lee arranged the flowers in a vase and put it on the table, where Jo would see it as soon as she walked in.

As the clock crept around to five thirty, Lee couldn't shake the niggling feeling that Jo might just not come home. What if she'd snapped? What if she just decided not to come back? Where would that leave him? He knew it was irrational, but it was a measure of how bad things had got that he even considered it as a possibility. But sure enough, at five thirty-two, he heard her key in the door and he let out the breath he didn't even realised he'd been holding.

'Hi,' he said warmly, walking to the door to greet her. He went to kiss her, and she turned her head slightly so he caught the corner of her mouth.

'Mummy! Mummy! Mummy!' Zach yelled, rushing into the hallway and barrelling straight into Jo's arms. 'We got you flowers! Come and see! The orange ones are the best and they're from me!' He dragged her through into the living room. Lee followed. Zach was chattering excitedly, and Jo was standing looking at the flowers, Imi in her arms. He walked up behind her and put a hand in the small of her back. 'I'm sorry, love,' he said softly.

She half turned and glanced at him, and he felt her back straighten and stiffen under his hand. He recognised the look. It said, 'Not now.' He took a step back.

'Come on, Zach,' he said as calmly as he could. 'Mum's hungry. Are you going to help me do the veggies for dinner?'

They barely spoke to one another while they organised dinner and got the kids ready for bed, although they both made a huge effort to be even-tempered and nice to the kids. After a raucous bath game called 'Daddy's hand is a shark, splash him as much as you can', they got both children into their pyjamas and down for the night. Lee stayed upstairs a little longer, reading 'one more story' to Zach. When he came down, Jo was sitting at the table working on her laptop. She had moved the flowers to the kitchen windowsill.

'I'm sorry if you didn't like the flowers,' said Lee. 'I was trying to find a way to say I was sorry.'

Jo looked up at him and took off her glasses. 'When did you last buy me flowers?'

'What? I . . . Where is this going?'

'Seriously, Lee? When did you last buy me flowers?'

'I don't know.'

'Never. You've never bought me flowers.'

'Wow. Okay. Well, I'm sorry for that too.' Lee threw his hands up in the air.

'No, no. That's not what I'm saying. It's the opposite of what I'm saying. You never bought me flowers because you're an amazing husband. You've always been so amazing, so loving, so committed. Flowers always seemed to me to be a cop-out – a way someone less attentive than you says, "I'm thinking about you," or, "I'm sorry." Usually "I'm sorry I fucked up". You never bought me flowers because you didn't need to, and I loved that. But do you know what? If we're entering the phase in our marriage where you have to buy me flowers, I don't know that I want to go there.'

'I was just trying—'

'I know. And I do appreciate the effort, I do.' She stood up and touched his arm. 'It just feels more serious than a bunch of flowers, Lee.'

'I know.'

'I love you, I do, and I love being married to you. Whatever else was going on in the world, it always felt like I had one part of my life completely sorted, being with you. You were my soulmate and my best friend and my lover . . . but now . . .'

'I'm still all those things. I'm just . . . in a bad place right now.'

'I know. I can see. But it's a place you chose, Lee. I didn't make you give up work. You chose to. And if you're feeling lost, I will help you as much as I can. But you have to remember I'm not the enemy.'

'I know,' he said, but he wasn't entirely sure that he did know. 'It's just . . . we're in very different places right now. Things are going so well for you—'

'They are going well, and that's also scary. Very scary. And lonely, when I don't have your support.'

Lee felt a little bubble of anger that he just couldn't quell. 'Here's a thought,' he said, his lip curling, 'why don't you start by not interrupting me? It would be super to form a complete thought into words without you telling me what

I should and shouldn't feel. And secondly, can you cut it out with the condescending "poor little rich girl, poor me" routine?'

Jo's face hardened. 'Okay,' she said, folding her arms. 'Form a thought.'

'I was going to say that things are going so well for you, and that's great, but I feel left out and left behind. You keep making decisions without me.'

'Like what?'

'Like the whole American thing.'

'It wasn't a decision. It was a possibility, which I tried to discuss with you.'

'I hate America!' Lee burst out. 'I hate Americans and their politics and their lifestyle and their consumerism and the way they do business, and I could never, ever live there.'

'That is the most irrational, xenophobic and racist thing I've ever heard you say!' Jo exploded. 'You've never even been to America! You're basing your views on Fox News and *The West Wing*, and a few episodes of *Sex and the City*!'

'I don't care if it's irrational. I don't want my children to be Americans.'

'Here's what I don't want,' Jo said. 'I don't want to be married to someone who supports me up to a point and then decides to withdraw his support because things are going well for me and he's threatened.'

'You don't want to be married to me?'

'That's not what I'm saying.'

'Sounds to me like it is.'

'I want to be married to the Lee I used to know. The Lee who thought anything was possible and had enough drive and ambition for ten people. Who rejoiced in other people's success, instead of trying to put them down.'

'And what if that Lee doesn't exist any more?'

'He does. I know he does.' Jo's eyes begged him to hear and understand her.

Lee, who had been standing in the doorway for the whole conversation, walked over and held out his hand. Jo went to him and he drew her into his arms. She started to cry, big gulping sobs, and he held her tightly. Later they sat on the sofa, watching a terrible sitcom, their hands knotted tightly together, listening to the canned laughter and watching the bright colours. After what seemed like hours of silence, Jo said quietly, 'I booked my flight to New York.'

Lee didn't say anything. He just nodded.

She flew out on a chilly and rainy morning, the first hint that autumn was definitely on its way. Lee and the kids drove her to the airport. They kissed goodbye at the departure gate, but there was no real way to talk, because Zach was jumping up and down, yelling that Lee had promised him they could go to the newsagent's to get a Doctor Who magazine, and Imi was toddling off determinedly towards the Air Singapore check-in.

'We'll talk,' said Jo, looking into his face for reassurance.

'Yes,' said Lee. He wanted to say something meaningful, but he really did have to go after Imi. 'Yes,' he said again. He kissed Jo one last time and set off after the intrepid explorer, Zach in tow.

She rang late that afternoon to say she had arrived and was in her hotel. She sounded tired and lonely, and Lee wished, not for the first time, that he had been less of a bastard and gone with her. But to be honest, they couldn't have afforded it. Jo's trip alone was costing more than she had anticipated.

He found it very draining being a single parent. Even though Jo usually only came home a couple of hours before the kids went to bed, her arrival from work signalled the end of his stint of sole responsibility. Without the relief of her key in the door at five thirty, the days seemed monstrously long and the evenings very lonely. The kids missed Jo and they both played up. Imi stopped sleeping through the night, and Lee very quickly capitulated and put her in the big bed with him, more for the comfort of her small warm form than because it was a good idea. When Zach woke up the next morning and saw Imi had slept with Lee, he demanded to sleep in the big bed too, so by the third night, Lee was lying awkwardly hemmed in by two hot, restless little bodies that seemed to lie perpendicular to him, whichever way he turned.

It rained every day, and it wasn't till the fourth day after Jo's departure, a Friday, that there was a long enough gap between downpours to take the kids to the park. They both ran around like overexcited terriers, releasing days of pent-up energy, and Lee, now a pro, followed them from swing to slide with a muslin cloth, ready to dry the equipment before they used it. After the kids had run themselves ragged, they all sat on a dry bit of bench and shared a snack of digestive biscuits and raisins. Lee kept an eye on the clouds – there were dark grey ones gathering ominously low, and he didn't want to get caught in the rain. The playground was far from the car park and he hadn't brought the pushchair. If they had to make a run for it, they would all get drenched.

Sure enough, as they stood up to go, the first fat drops began to fall. Just a few at first, but very quickly the rain began tumbling down in great sheets. Lee gathered both children close to him and stood under a tree. Zach laughed with delight, but Imi, who hated showers or having her hair washed, began to wail.

'What are we going to do, Dad?' said Zach excitedly. 'Are we going to run to the car? It's far!'

'Maybe we should stay here, try to wait it out,' said Lee.

'Or we could go to Martha's house. It's really close.'

'Brilliant idea!' said Lee. He should have thought of it himself. Martha's house, or rather Miranda's house, was just a few yards from the playground entrance to the park . . . maybe a thirty-second dash from where they were. If she wasn't in, there was an overhanging porch where they could shelter until the rain passed.

She was in, however, and she laughed when she saw the three drowned Hockley rats on her doorstep.

'Come in,' she said. 'We've just been baking muffins. Your timing is perfect.'

Lee hadn't seen Miranda since her mother's funeral, and he had hoped she would be looking and feeling better, but if anything she had lost even more weight. She had soft features and delicate skin, and being thin aged her. He could see some threads of grey in her dark curls too. She looked sad, he thought. Her mum's illness and death had clearly taken it out of her, and the plump, cheery, chatty woman who used to annoy Jo so much in the park had all but dis-appeared. Nevertheless, she was trying her best to be sociable and bubbly.

'I heard from Holly that Jo's off to New York,' she said. 'How exciting!'

'Yes, she's there now.'

'Ah, well, I hope it goes well for her,' said Miranda. 'I'm also a business-trip widow. Paul's in Japan – again.' There was an uncharacteristic sourness in that 'again'. She obvi-ously heard it too, or registered Lee's slightly surprised expression, because she changed tack completely.

'Now,' she said brightly, 'you're all drenched. What can we do about that?'

Lee, veteran of many a playground accident, had a com-plete change of clothes for both children in his bag, and he stripped them off and dressed them in dry trousers and jumpers. They scampered off to the playroom with Martha and Oscar.

'What about you?' Miranda asked.

'Oh, I'm fine,' he said.

'No, you're not, she said, putting a hand on his shoulder. 'You're soaked through. Let me get you something dry.' She dashed upstairs and came back with an expensive-looking grey jumper.

'Paul never wears this,' she said, handing it to him. He was very aware of the odd intimacy of the situation, so he took the jumper into the downstairs bathroom and changed there. Paul was slightly smaller than him so the sleeves were too short. Other than that, the jumper was a good fit and was very comfortable. It was so soft he suspected it was cashmere. He pushed the sleeves up and went looking for Miranda. He found her in the kitchen putting the finishing touches to some delicious-looking home-made cappuccinos.

'I love my new coffee machine,' she smiled, handing him a mug. 'And the muffins are ready, so help yourself.'

They chatted easily about all sorts of things: school places for Zach and Martha, changes that had been made at the nursery, a television documentary that they had both seen. Lee glanced out of the window and saw that the rain clouds had cleared, but that the sun was low. It must be later than he'd thought. He glanced at his watch.

'Damn! It's nearly six o'clock!'

'Time flies when you're having fun!' said Miranda brightly. He had forgotten her habit of resorting to clichés, but he realised now that she generally did it when she was uncomfortable. He stood up to go, and she said suddenly, 'What are your plans for dinner?'

'The best that PizzaExpress has to offer,' said Lee. He had exhausted his limited repertoire of recipes over the past few nights, and he'd decided to treat the kids and himself.

'Stay.' Miranda smiled. 'We're only having macaroni cheese, but there's loads. The kids could watch a film.'

'Well, macaroni cheese is Zach's favourite.' Lee smiled too. 'And, if I'm honest, it's mine too. I don't think my taste buds have ever grown up.'

'Brilliant!' She seemed genuinely pleased, and began bustling around the kitchen. Lee went through to the playroom, where there seemed to have been some kind of tornado or other natural disaster. The floor was carpeted in Lego, wooden bricks and dismembered dolls. He sighed and organised a clean-up team. The older two were helpful, but Oscar followed them around determinedly trying to unpack anything they put away, while Imi sat in a corner chewing on a Barbie leg. Eventually, order won over disorder, and he got them all to sit down for a story.

Miranda came to call them for dinner and they all sat around her big kitchen table eating macaroni cheese and chattering. Lee and Miranda had a glass of wine each, and once the kids had eaten, she ushered them all into the living room to watch a film. They were all tucked in under a fluffy blanket, and Lee took advantage of the moment's respite to jog through the park and fetch his car, which he then parked outside Miranda's house. When he came back in, she put a finger to her lips and they tiptoed into the living room. All four kids were asleep, tumbled against each other. She had muted the film, and now she switched it off and dimmed the living-room lights.

'I should go,' Lee whispered.

'There's no hurry,' said Miranda. 'Tomorrow's Saturday. Have another coffee, and then you can pop your two in the car. They don't have to be up early tomorrow, and neither do you.'

He followed her through to the kitchen. She'd loaded her expensive dishwasher and it was humming quietly. The kitchen was immaculate.

'So how's the book going?' she asked, as she made coffee.

'Okay,' he said. 'I think I've got the outline of the story, and I've been experimenting with styles of illustration. I think when I know what it's going to look like, I'll be able to finalise the words, and then know exactly which illustrations I need to do.'

'You're just so amazing,' Miranda said, handing him his cappuccino. 'I don't understand the creative process at all – how you can make something out of nothing. I admire people like you and Holly so much.'

'Now you're going to make me blush.'

'No, really, it's a mystery. Tell me more. Can you tell me your idea about the story, or is it a secret?'

He gave her a rough outline, and she asked loads of questions – not, he thought disloyally, the sort of penetrating, hypercritical questions Jo would have asked, but naive questions born of genuine curiosity.

It felt different from their easy conversation of the afternoon – much more intimate, now that it was dark and the children were all asleep. They talked softly, and she sat closer to him than she had that afternoon. Close enough that he could catch the occasional whiff of her perfume, which was something very sweet and floral. Wild rose, maybe.

A silence fell, and he looked up to see Miranda staring into her cup. A shadow crossed her face.

'You all right?' he asked.

'Yes.' She managed a small smile. 'It's just . . . every now and again, my mum . . . well, I forget for a moment and then I remember. I know it's supposed to get easier, but at the moment it just seems to be getting worse.'

'I'm sorry,' Lee said. 'It must be hard.'

'It's not even as if we were that close, but she was always there, you know? I felt like I was connected to my family, to my past, to growing up . . .'

'And now . . . ?'

'Well, it's a rite of passage, isn't it? Your last parent dying. It means you're a grown-up.'

'I hate to point this out, but you're a mum with two kids and a house and a husband . . . you're a grown-up.' He smiled gently.

'I know all that,' she said. 'But none of us really believes we are, do we? We all think we're still teenagers, really.'

He laughed at this. 'I suppose we do. Although I was the gawkiest teenager – long, skinny legs like bits of spaghetti . . . and the biggest Afro you ever saw.'

'I bet you were the coolest kid in town,' she said. 'I on the other hand . . .'

'You?'

'Holly was always the cool one in our family. I was just . . . ordinary, you know. The good girl. I went to university and all that, but then I got married, had kids . . . somehow I thought one day I'd wake up and know what my purpose was. That it would all make sense. But now all the signs show that my life . . . is what it is.'

'Is it so bad?'

'No . . . No, of course it isn't. It's just Paul – he's never here, and when he is here, he isn't, if you know what I mean. And the kids are great, but they're going to need me less and less, and then where will I be? I'll be my mum, that's who I'll be. A boring beige woman who's never had a day's excitement or mystery in her life.'

'You don't know that.'

'No, I do. She was the dullest woman ever. Seriously.'

'No, I mean about you. You're not dull. You're warm and

lovely and compassionate. Maybe you haven't found your thing yet, but you will. I know you will.'

Miranda smiled, but then the corners of her mouth turned down, like Imi's did when she was about to howl, and she shook her head. 'Don't be nice to me, unless you want me to cry all over you. Sorry, I'm an emotional mess at the moment. I just wasn't ready . . . to be an orphan.'

The word 'orphan' seemed to tip her over the edge, and the tears started to flow. Lee leaned closer and put his arm around her shoulder, and she turned her face into his neck and cried like a child. She was straining awkwardly, so he stood and so did she, so he could hug her properly. She was much shorter than Jo, and although she felt soft, her bones were light and small, like a bird.

He knew it would happen a moment before it did. She turned her wet face up to his. Her mouth found his and she was kissing him hungrily, and he was kissing her back. For a moment, just a moment, he responded instinctively to the warmth and physical contact, but then the thought came roaring into his head like a foghorn: THIS. IS. WRONG. In that first instant, it wasn't the moral transgression that struck him, but the wrongness of the person in his arms. She wasn't tall and lithe. Her lips didn't have that soft springiness he knew so well. Her hands on his shoulders were soft and small, not strong and capable. She wasn't Jo.

He released her and stepped back quickly. 'No,' he said firmly. 'Miranda, you're a lovely person, but this is just the worst – wrongest – thing I've ever done. I'm so sorry.'

'I'm sorry too. So sorry,' she said, and he could see she

was actually trembling. 'That was a moment of total madness. Please forgive me.'

'Nothing to forgive, but – look, sorry, I have to go.'

He loaded the kids into their car seats while Miranda stood by the door. She gave a small wave as he drove away. He knew it would be a long time before he spoke to her again.

He got home and carefully carried the sleeping kids in one by one. He tipped them both into the big bed, and gently changed Imi's nappy. She barely stirred. He sat on a chair in the dark bedroom and watched them sleep for an hour. What had he done? What had he risked? He had gambled everything he had, all the treasures of his marriage, his family and his home, on a stupid kiss to make his ego feel better. He could have lost everything. He still might, depending on Jo's reaction when he told her. Not telling her was not an option. He knew she was out at meetings all day, and it was still mid-afternoon in New York, so speaking to her immediately wasn't a possibility. Besides, he needed to think, to process what had happened and what it said about him, and make some changes. Some big changes.

31

HOLLY NOW

Eleven rain hats. How could any woman need eleven rain hats? Holly thought with exasperation. She had begun going through her mum's things. In Judith's tidy wardrobe she had a jacket or coat for every season – a calf-length woollen winter coat, a light spring mac, a mustard-coloured hip-length jacket for the autumn and so on. In the right-hand pocket of each, Holly found a plastic rain hat, of the type old ladies wear to preserve their 'hairdo', tightly rolled with an elastic band around it. There was also one in each of Judith's handbags. A total of eleven. Surely, thought Holly, it just didn't rain that much? And it wasn't as if Judith didn't have an umbrella. She had seven of varying types in different locations. She couldn't have got wet since about 1970.

It was no surprise that Judith's affairs were in perfect order – she had made David the executor of her will and he found all the paperwork he needed in a neat folder in her desk. The estate was to be split equally between the three children, with a generous bequest to the church. David, Miranda and Holly had agreed to sell the Ealing house and split the proceeds, and they had also decided to give a bequest to the hospice and the Macmillan nurses who had made such a difference to Judith's last days. Judith had been prudent with her money and the house was completely paid off, so each of them would be getting a substantial sum once it was sold. Holly hadn't thought about this at all, and it came as quite a shock. From being an itinerant, living half in her mum's house and camping in her barely furnished flat in East Finchley, she would soon become a woman of means, with enough money to put down a big deposit on her own home.

She and Miranda threw themselves into clearing the house. There was thirty years' worth of stuff – not junk, but the thousands of things any family accumulates and never gets around to giving away. They started out sorting items one by one, but as they seemed barely to be making a dent in the mammoth task, they decided to go through the house, take the things they wanted to keep and call a charity that did house-clearances to deal with the rest of it. They both wanted surprisingly little – Miranda because she already had a complete household of her own, and Holly because very little of the stuff was to her taste, and it all seemed tainted with the sadness of her mum's loss. David came and took a few paintings and the old football flags from his boyhood bedroom. He had no intention of helping with the actual clearing, but he was more than happy to pay for the clearance people.

The day the van came, Holly and Miranda both came to the house, but they found it very upsetting to watch the history of their childhoods being carried out of the door and chucked into a skip. Holly went and spoke to the foreman. She came back to Miranda. 'He says it'll take them all of today and some of tomorrow. He's happy to carry on without us.'

'Are you sure it's okay to leave them?'

'What do you think they're going to do? Steal something? We're trying to get rid of the stuff.'

'I suppose . . . I just feel bad, letting them empty Mum's house like this.'

'Me too. But she doesn't know it's happening, and there's no point in us upsetting ourselves over it. Tell you what – let's go for coffee on the Broadway. Maybe even get a bit of breakfast. We'll come back in an hour or so and see how they're doing.'

As they walked down the road, Holly thought how her relationship with Miranda had changed. Miranda had always been the big sister, the sensible one, and very bossy. But through Judith's illness, Holly had become the practical one who had made all the decisions. Miranda had not been very much use at all. Over the last few months, Holly had got used to telling her what to do, and on the whole, Miranda took her advice. Even though it was all over, she still looked very anxious and sad.

They found a little patisserie and Holly ordered them cappuccinos, and even though Miranda said she wasn't hungry, she got them each a pain au chocolat. She knew about Miranda's sweet tooth, and sure enough, once the pastry was put in front of her, she bit into it with relish. 'Oh, if I could live on naughty baked goodies, I would,' she said, brushing crumbs from her lips.

'Well, now you're a woman of means, you can,' said Holly. 'You could hire your own pastry chef.'

Miranda shook her head. 'No, I'll need that money, sadly. I can't blow it on frivolities.'

'What for? Are you and Paul planning to buy somewhere bigger?'

'Er, no,' said Miranda. And it was clear she was trying to decide whether or not to say something. Holly resisted the urge to bombard her with questions. She sipped at her coffee and waited.

'The thing is . . .' Miranda said, 'well, I suppose I have to tell you sometime. Paul and I are having a trial separation.'

'What?' said Holly, forgetting her manners. That was the last thing she had expected Miranda to say.

'He came back from his business trip to Japan, and I said to him I thought we had problems, and that maybe we needed to see a counsellor. He said he thought there were no problems and he was perfectly happy. So I packed his bags and threw him out. Now he realises I'm serious.'

Holly had to stop her mouth from falling open with shock. She couldn't imagine a more unlikely scenario.

'Losing Mum, and . . . some other things . . . well, it made me think,' said Miranda. 'I don't want to live my life as a single parent when I'm not one, feeling like my husband doesn't even see me, and he just takes me for granted. I don't know what I want, but I know I want more than this.'

'And so . . . ?'

'Paul's living in a bedsit near us, and we're seeing a counsellor. I don't know if it's too little too late, but I'll see.'

Holly couldn't help noticing that Miranda had said 'I'll

see', not 'we'll see'. It seemed as if she was making a decision just for herself for the first time in a long time.

Miranda wasn't the only one who needed to make some big decisions. Since the night after Judith's death, Holly had spent every night in her flat in East Finchley. She had started to gather more household goods, and it almost looked like a home now, if rather a minimalist one. She loved the sunlit space, and it felt to her like the first proper home she had had in more than a decade. It was her own space, and she liked to be there, quietly and alone, doing her own thing and having the time to figure out exactly what she wanted from life, and what her future might look like.

She tried to throw herself back into work as soon as she could, but she found much had changed at Jungletown. Now things were being run from the premises in Angel, it was an altogether more corporate company. The lines between her responsibilities and those of Gary, the buyer in the main office, weren't always clear, and they had to liaise – and sometimes argue – over everything. The thing was, Jungletown had given her a lifeline at what had been a terrible time for her. It had got her designing again when her confidence was at an all-time low. She'd loved the process of developing the look and feel of the range and getting the first shop up and running, and she was immensely grateful to Jo for cutting her so much slack when her mum was ill. She felt terribly guilty that her heart just wasn't in it any more. She worked as hard as she could, but she kept dreaming of the dresses she would be designing and making if she had the time. She even bought fabric and did some late-night sewing, even though it felt as if she was cheating on Jungletown. She felt so bad about it that she didn't even tell anyone. She knew that the time was coming when she would have to make some big decisions about her future – she needed to decide what she wanted to do and where she wanted to live. She still wasn't entirely convinced that England was the right place for her. Then something happened that complicated the picture even further.

You don't expect to be on the loo when you receive a life-altering phone call. The caller ID said 'unknown', which meant it was more than likely someone ringing from abroad. She didn't feel like having to return an international call, so she answered it.

'Ah, Ms Evans,' said a male voice, and she knew with those three words that it was Detective Tshabalala, the detective from the South African fraud squad. Her heart sank.

'Detective Tshabalala. Haven't heard from you in a while,' she said, trying to be polite. 'I'm afraid I haven't got any news for you.'

'I am calling because I have news for you, Ms Evans,' he said, and she could hear he sounded mightily pleased with himself. 'We have Mr Vermaak in custody.'

'You do? Oh my God. Are you sure it's him? Where did you find him?'

'Well,' said Detective Tshabalala, sounding a little less self-important, 'he actually found us. He walked into the station and said "I'm Damon Vermaak, and I'm here to hand myself in."'

'Wow,' said Holly. Funnily enough, she could imagine Damon doing it. He was probably beautifully dressed and very suave. He would have made it look like he was James Bond. 'So where had he been? What happened to him?'

'I'm not at liberty to give you that information, Ms Evans,' said Detective Tshabalala. 'You see, there will be a trial. And you will certainly be called as a witness, at the very least. We're still taking Mr Vermaak's statement. He is cooperating fully, but I wanted you to know that this thing isn't over. So stay where we can find you.'

Holly didn't like the sound of 'witness, at the very least'. She had assumed that the fact she had been allowed to leave the country meant she was in the clear. But who knew what Damon was saying? Was he lying in order to implicate her in the whole mess? She hated to admit it, but he was more than capable of that, and worse. Whatever happened, it looked as if she would be going back to South Africa, and maybe sooner rather than later.

There was no point in stressing about it, so she tried to keep her mind busy with work, and with her clandestine, late-night dress designing. But then she was 'outed', as it were, because Mel asked her to design and make a dress for Serena. Serena, who, it turned out, was a super-talented singer–songwriter, had got her first paying gig at a little wine bar in West Hampstead and wanted something special to wear. She had only just had her sixteenth birthday, so ironically she could play but not drink there, and none of her school friends could come to the gig. She wanted to look 'sophisticated and classy, in a retro kind of way', Mel told Holly. It was just the kind of inspiration she had been waiting for. She did a few sketches – she'd seen Serena in what Mel called her 'early Madonna' outfits before, so she drew an outfit along those lines, then tried something more like a classical pianist's concert attire – a slim, sleeveless column dress with a low back. But Serena fell in love with the design Holly loved best too: a 1940s dress with three-quarter sleeves, a big collar and full skirt. She made it in a beautiful dusty blue, and they found perfect pointy court shoes in a charity shop to go with it. With Serena's curvy figure, and her dark hair set in old-fashioned waves, she looked like a movie star.

Holly went along to the gig with Mel, who looked as if she might explode with nerves and pride. Jo was in New York, but had sent flowers for Serena. Serena's dad Bruce was there too, a stringy, wrinkled individual with a long grey ponytail and a heavy metal band T-shirt. Mel had also invited a friend of hers called Hamish, who she said was a novelist. He was a big, soft bear of a man. Mel had used the term 'friend', but Holly noticed that when the lights went down for Serena to play, Hamish took Mel's hand and didn't let it go. She liked the way he looked at Mel with such tenderness, and the fact that he clearly adored Serena. The last member of their party was Fraser.

Despite the awfulness of their last encounter, Holly had felt that Fraser deserved an apology, although probably not a detailed explanation. The week after Judith's funeral, she took a deep breath and dialled his number. He didn't answer, unsurprisingly, so she left a message.

'Hi there. Look, I wouldn't be at all surprised if you deleted this message without listening to it, but I just wanted to let you know that my mum died. And I also wanted to say sorry . . . for the other morning.' She laughed a little. 'I think between us, we've pretty much had every embarrassing, awful encounter in the book. You and Daniel . . . me and Lindsay . . . There's nothing I can say to make it better. I just wanted to say, well, sorry again. And if you wanted to talk to me ever again, I'd . . . well, I'd like that.'

He rang back within the minute. 'What do you mean, you and Lindsay?'

'What? I mean, hi, Fraser. And . . . what?'

'In your message, you said you had an encounter with Lindsay. What did you mean?'

'You know . . . when I came to your flat. The day you were late.'

'You were there? And you saw Lindsay? She never said.'

'She didn't?'

'I assumed you got my messages saying we were delayed, and you went home. When you didn't take my calls, I thought you were pissed off that I let you down. I thought it was an overreaction, and I found it a bit odd. That's why I came to your flat.'

'I didn't get your messages that day. I got to your flat and Lindsay let me in. I thought it was you opening the door, so I might have said something rather . . . saucy as I came upstairs. It was very awkward. Anyway, that's when she told me how you're still together.'

'She what?'

'She said she was trying to help you overcome your serial infidelity, but that you were still very much together and still sleeping together.'

'Did she?' said Fraser, and she'd never heard him sound so livid. 'Did she indeed? Listen, Holly, please excuse me, but

I'm going to need to ring you back in a little while, if you don't mind.' And he hung up.

It was a couple of hours before he rang back. 'This is going to sound stupid,' he said. 'It's taken me so long to ring you back, because I know that whatever I say, it's just going to sound like I'm feeding you another line. What Lindsay said was absolutely, totally not true, and it was vindictive in the extreme to say it. I've yelled at her, and she's totally unrepentant. I had this mad idea that I could make her ring you herself and say she was lying, but she's refused point-blank to do that. I'm sorry, Holly. I didn't want to mix you up in the crazy crap from my marriage. It's the last thing I wanted.'

'To be fair,' she said carefully, 'you did catch me in bed with someone else.'

'Someone very young.'

'Don't. I know. I'm mortified every time I think about it. Anyway, I think in the mixing-each-other-up-in-crazy-crap stakes, we're just about even.'

'So . . .'

'So . . . ?'

'Where does that leave us?'

'Maybe . . . having dinner sometime?'

'I'd like that,' said Fraser, sounding profoundly relieved.

They had had a few dates since that phone call, each one slightly more relaxed than the last. They hadn't slept together, or even broached the subject, but Holly was enjoying getting to know him. She was touched that he would come to Serena's gig – she imagined it would be like a school concert – but he was genuinely pleased to be invited, and even brought a good-luck card for Serena.

Holly couldn't have been more wrong. Serena looked beautiful (Holly was proud to have had some part in that), and she had a simply stunning voice. She played the piano well, and the songs she had written were poignant and original. She also did a couple of cover versions, and at the end of her thirty-minute set, the applause nearly brought the roof down. The owner of the bar was thrilled, and immediately said he would like to book her again.

'I have the feeling we'll be telling our grandchildren we were at Serena Grey's first gig,' said Fraser, taking Holly's hand as they walked down the road after leaving the venue.

'I hope so,' said Holly. 'She did so well, and the music thing seems to have helped her relationship with Mel.'

'So . . . what are your plans for the rest of the evening?' said Fraser, looking hopeful.

'I have to go home,' said Holly regretfully. 'I have to get up early for work tomorrow. But I'm free on Sunday night . . . all night.'

'Really?' said Fraser, and he drew her close and kissed her breathless.

On Sunday evening, he invited her over and cooked a beef bourguignon. Luckily, he had made it in a slow cooker, because fifteen minutes and half a glass of wine after she arrived, they were in the bedroom, a trail of clothes strewn in their wake. Sometime after eleven, Holly stood up and wobbled dramatically.

'I've gone weak at the knees,' she laughed.

'Why, thank you.'

'Don't flatter yourself. It's low blood sugar. I didn't have lunch, and dinner should have been hours ago. I'm absolutely starving.'

'Come to think of it, so am I,' said Fraser.

She grabbed a sweatshirt Fraser had dropped next to the bed and pulled it on. 'Feed me,' she demanded.

They sat at the counter in the kitchen, devouring big bowls of the stew with spoons. The rice Fraser had put on to steam had dried out unappealingly, and Holly scoffed at his offer of salad.

'Well, Dr John, said Holly, leaning back in her chair, 'that was worth the wait.'

'Stew is always better when you leave it for a bit,' he said, wiping his plate with a slice of bread.

'I didn't mean the stew.'

He smiled at her wickedly, and her stomach did a little flip. 'To be honest, I never thought we'd get here,' he said.

'We did seem cursed, didn't we?' Holly grinned ruefully.

'Like some kind of excruciating farce.'

'So is this the calm before the storm? Is it all going to go pear-shaped again? Is a long-lost ex going to jump out of a cupboard and assault me?'

'I checked the cupboards before you came over. We're okay.' They sat sipping their wine in companionable silence. 'So, if it doesn't sound too . . . pathetic and needy,' said Fraser, 'where do we go from here?'

'We go . . . slowly? One step at a time?' said Holly, getting up. Fraser's wine rack was on the top of one of the kitchen cupboards and she stretched up to get another bottle.

'Dear God, woman,' he said hoarsely. 'You're not wearing anything under that sweatshirt.'

'Am I not?' said Holly innocently.

'There's only one place you're going right now,' he said, taking her firmly by the hand and leading her back to the bedroom.

A week or so later, the house clearance was finally finished, the will was sorted and it was time for Judith's house to go on the market. David found an estate agent he was happy to deal with, and Holly agreed to meet him and hand over the keys so they could begin showing the property. She was lucky with the traffic and got to the house early. It was odd to walk through the empty rooms. The house looked enormous, and it felt very cold. Without the furniture and pictures, it looked like what it was, a rather out-of-date, albeit well-kept 1930s suburban house. She thought this would be a difficult and nostalgic moment, but she didn't feel overwhelmed with memories at all. The house seemed to have lost its spirit. She would be happy to walk out of the door for the last time. She did a last check of all the rooms to see that the house-clearance people had taken everything. It seemed they'd done an excellent job. She wandered into the kitchen, and saw they had left a stack of post on the draining board. She'd written to the utility companies and everyone she could think of to let them know her mum had died, and she had changed her address, but there was probably someone she had missed. She flipped through the envelopes – mostly junk mail. The last one, however, was not. It was addressed to her, and the envelope was crumpled and grubby. The stamp showed it had been posted in Zimbabwe around a month ago. It had taken its time getting to her. Even if she hadn't recognised the handwriting, she would have known who it was from.

Dear Holly,

I don't know if you'll get this letter. I'm making two copies and sending one to Pierre's house in Johannesburg and one to your mom's house in London, because I don't know where you are. I don't even know if there's any point in telling you how sorry I am.

Now I'm writing it, I don't know what to say. This has been the worst year of my life, and believe me, considering the mess I got into last year, that's saying something. I've been moving from country to country – Botswana, Namibia, Mozambique, Zimbabwe . . . trying to stay ahead of the cops. I've needed new ID wherever I went, so I've got mixed up with some very bad guys. I know if I stick around here, someone will end up killing me.

I'm going to go to the border at Beitbridge, and if I can get across, I'm going to Jo'burg to hand myself in to the cops. I'm not doing it because I'm scared I'm going to die . . . in lots of ways I feel like I deserve to die. I just don't want to die without making it up to you and my mom and the people I hurt. I can't fix what I did. I don't know if I'll ever even be able to give you your money back. But I have to make it right. None of this was your fault, Holly, and you didn't deserve any of it.

I'm sorry and I will always love you.

Damon

She read the letter again. Then she thought for a moment about what it made her feel. Nothing. The answer was nothing. So much had happened since she had left South Africa that Damon and his actions seemed like a distant nightmare. She didn't love him any more, nor did she hate him. All she could think of was that the letter would be evidence in her defence if it came to it. The doorbell rang. That would be Roger, the super-smooth estate agent. She stuffed the letter in her handbag and went to hand over the keys to her past.

32

JO NOW

Everyone in New York looked like an extra in a movie. From the sharp-suited businessmen and women, to the villainous-looking cab driver who took Jo from the airport to her hotel, to the pretty hippy girl who rollerbladed past her as she left the hotel the next morning, everyone looked like they were playing a part, and every street corner could have been the set of every film and television show she had ever seen. There was a Starbucks across the road from the hotel. She would never have visited one in London, but it seemed the right thing to do here and she went in and ordered a coffee 'to go'. She'd checked the night before where Verity's office was on the map, and it was an easy walk from where she was staying. Striding down 57th Street with her coffee in her hand, as the yellow cabs roared by honking their horns, Jo realised she was an extra in the film too. When she turned a corner and saw one of the actors from *The Sopranos* standing by the open door of his Cadillac, her happiness was complete.

Well, almost complete. The shadow of her cool parting from Lee hung over everything she did. And, more crucially, she couldn't help feeling that the whole New York experience would have been a thousand times better if he was here. She would have loved to share her first sight of all the great landmarks with him – the first view of the Chrysler Building, the cab ride through Central Park, but much more than that, she thought how much Lee would have loved the little things – the street scenes and interactions between people, the quirky window displays and iconic diners and delis, the fabulous signwriting and typography and the architectural gems you might miss if you weren't looking carefully. She knew if Lee had been there, he'd be walking around with his camera glued to his eye, snapping picture after picture, sketching and making notes as well.

She arrived at Verity's office building about ten minutes early, so she stood outside people-watching and finishing her coffee. It was a typical New York skyscraper, all steel and glass, and the people hurrying through the door looked harried, as if they were going inside to engage in business transactions of great weight and importance. Jo felt scruffy and provincial – she'd worn a smart navy suit and low heels. But her suit was off the peg from Zara, and her shoes were from M&S. The women walking into the building were more groomed and polished than the average London woman, and as one particularly tall model-type ran past her, she caught the distinctive red flash of the sole of her shoe. If these women wore Louboutins to the office, how could she hope to hold her own?

She gave herself a little pep talk. It's the value of your proposition they're interested in, not your shoes, she told herself sternly. What you've built is amazing and unique, and whatever happens in this building today, you still have it. They want to do business with you. You don't need them. She threw her empty coffee cup into the bin, squared her shoulders and marched up to the revolving door. It wasn't until she was in the foyer of the building that she realised the pep talk in her head had been delivered in Lee's voice.

She was directed to Verity's suite of offices, which occupied two whole floors of the building. She sat in a too-low leather chair in the reception area, keeping her feet flat on the floor so no one would see her non-designer shoe soles. Her appointment was for nine, but Verity kept her waiting until twenty past. She smiled when Verity came barrelling out of her office to greet her. Unbidden, Verity's long-forgotten school nickname came to mind: Staffie. She was short and wide and she tipped slightly forward as she walked, as if she was quite prepared to ram anyone who stood in her way. Her forceful personality and extreme intelligence had seen her graduate top of the class from their Hertfordshire school and go to study at Cambridge, and then on to a postgraduate qualification at the London School of Economics. At thirty, she was being featured in business publications as one to watch, and at thirty-five, she had relocated to New York, where she bought, built and sold companies with eye-watering ferocity and speed. She and Jo had not been especially good friends at school – Verity didn't have close friends. But Jo had followed her impressive trajectory in the press, and when she joined the women's business network, Verity's was one of the first names she had looked up.

'Jo Morris! How the hell are you?' said Verity, grabbing her arm and sweeping her along the corridor at speed. Clearly a reunion after twenty-odd years was not a good enough reason to stand still for a second.

'I'm good,' said Jo, trotting a little to keep up. 'It's Jo Hockley now. And how are you? Acclimatised to New York?'

'Couldn't imagine living anywhere else,' said Verity, opening her office door. 'And I am . . . as you see me. Just the same.'

She ushered Jo through the door into her enormous corner office, which had jaw-dropping views of Manhattan in two directions. Her rugby-pitch sized wooden desk was piled high with papers and folders, and her MacBook was balanced precariously on top of one of the lower piles. There were empty coffee cups dotted between the stacks, and Jo was pretty sure she could see the corner of a pizza box.

Verity gestured to the corner of the room, where there was a sofa, three chairs and a low coffee table, which was also covered in files, paperwork and architect's drawings. They went to sit down.

'Sorry, I forgot to ask,' said Verity. 'Coffee? Pastry?'

'I just had a coffee—' began Jo.

'Well, you'll need another one. And you're going to need some sustenance to get you through today.' Verity went to the door, opened it and bellowed, 'Sven! The usual – times two – and my extra-hot latte had better not be extra luke-warm or I'll fire your pretty Swedish arse . . . again.' She slammed the door and came to sit down beside Jo.

'Yup.' Jo smiled. 'You are just the same.'

They caught up on the intervening years until Sven,

Verity's predictably blond, blue-eyed and gorgeous PA, brought them coffees and Danish pastries. As soon as they had finished eating, Verity brushed the crumbs from her lapels and was all business. 'Right, I've set up a pretty punishing schedule of meetings and site visits. I know we don't have long, so we need to cram in as much as we can. Ready?' And they were off.

By mid-morning, Jo was profoundly grateful she'd gone for sensible shoes, rather than designer loveliness. By lunchtime, she was praying for a pair of trainers. Verity had whisked her out of the building and into a cab, and they began a recce of children's boutiques in Manhattan. She reckoned they must have seen every one on the whole island that day – the individual stores began to merge into a Willy Wonka's Chocolate Factory-type blur of noise and colour. She took notes frantically in cab trips between the visits, and Verity was like a ninja, surreptitiously snapping pictures with her phone of shop fittings and displays wherever they went. They left the last boutique at about six and raced across town to a smart hotel on the park to meet some investment partners of Verity's for drinks. Jo was flagging: jet lag meant that for her it was already eleven o'clock at night, and since the pastries in the office that morning, all she had had was a cereal bar and a Diet Coke. Everyone spoke very quickly and asked a lot of questions, most of which didn't seem to require an answer. She left the meeting dizzy, slightly drunk and not entirely sure whom she had met and what she might have agreed to. She got a cab back to her own rather more modest hotel. On impulse, she popped into an electronics store next to the hotel that was open late, and bought a mid-range digital camera. She got upstairs to her room, kicked off her shoes, ordered an omelette from room service and watched a little TV, and was asleep by nine o'clock.

The jet-lag fairy had her up by 5 a.m. She felt reasonably refreshed and spent half an hour going through her notes from the day before. They were less garbled and incomprehensible than she had expected, and she typed them up into a useful reference document. Verity had already emailed her all the photographs, so she inserted them into her document too. By the time she finished it was only six thirty, so she put on jeans and trainers, took her new camera and hit the streets. She wasn't much of a photographer, but she did her best. She didn't take touristy pictures of the sights: she focused on the little details she had spotted on her walk to Verity's office – a beautiful cornice on a building, a ray of sun hitting the pavement (*sidewalk*, she corrected herself) as a shop owner swept the doorstep of his deli. She found some beautiful, faded painted advertisements on the sides of brick buildings, which she knew Lee would love. Then she strolled down to Central Park and took a few shots of people doing yoga and t'ai chi, and a guy jogging with a great mane of dreadlocks and massive headphones. Over breakfast, she went through the pictures, and was frustrated at how badly framed and lit they were. Although she had thought she was being original, they still looked like clichéd tourist snaps. There were only one or two that she didn't absolutely hate. She'd have to put photography to the back of her mind now, she thought, swallowing the last bite of her pancakes. Today would be, if anything, more strenuous than the day before.

They spent the whole day in Verity's office, meeting with a succession of potential investors, architects, retail-space experts, designers and buyers. Everyone seemed to have an aggressive, very in-your-face style, and Jo finished each meeting rather unsure if she'd been sold to or just bossed around. The phrases 'what you have to do' and 'what needs to happen' seemed to ring in her ears. She was due to go out with Verity and some of her business associates that night, but she grabbed an hour in the early evening to walk around and snap a few more photographs. These ones, more candid, and catching the yellowy evening light, were more successful than her morning efforts. The awful hollow feeling she had had on her arrival, the missing-Lee feeling, seemed somehow to ease a little when she was out taking photographs. She didn't quite understand why that was, or what the pictures were for, but she knew it had to do with him.

The dinner was raucous and late and there was a lot of wine and teasing, and she ended up in a club dancing with two rather gorgeous twenty-something boys, while Verity sat at the bar talking marketing campaigns with their boss. She wasn't sure whether the boys were straight or gay, and whether they were genuinely flirting with her or being friendly for the sake of the potential account. All she knew was that she hadn't danced like that since Lee had last DJ'd, and that was . . . wow . . . at least ten years ago. She got back to her hotel in the early hours, elated, footsore and wide awake. She saw she had missed a Skype call from Lee, and her buoyant mood was punctured. She fell asleep hugging a pillow, wearing an old T-shirt of Lee's she'd dropped into her suitcase at the last minute.

The mad treadmill carried her off early the next morning with a trip to Brooklyn to visit Verity's warehouse and talk to her stock controllers. The sheer size of the operation terrified Jo. It was so far beyond what she had done and what she had envisaged, but Verity seemed quite at home, wandering between the pallets and pallets and rows and rows of garments. She talked at a hundred miles an hour about economies of scale and amortising cost, until Jo's head began to spin.

'What's our next meeting after this?' she asked on the train back to the city.

'We're seeing the lawyers at two, to talk about trans-Atlantic legal issues.'

'I need a few hours to catch up on things,' Jo said. 'I'll meet you there.'

She had her camera in her bag, and she took a long walk down to the Hudson River, snapping things that caught her eye. She ended up gazing up at the Brooklyn Bridge. Something was bothering her – something other than Lee. She took out her phone, and ignoring the cost, she dialled Richard.

'Jo!' he said, surprised, but clearly pleased to hear from her. 'How's it all going?'

'A bit like *The Wizard of Oz*, but I think I'm still caught in the tornado.'

'Ah, Verity Ellis's reputation does precede her. She is something of a force of nature. What's she been showing you?'

Jo ran through a brief outline of the things she'd seen and the people she'd met. When she finished, Richard said,

'Goodness me, she really does seem to be trying to woo you.'

'She seems to see the move to the US as a foregone conclusion. She keeps talking in terms of "when", not "if".'

'Loads of people would be beside themselves to have this opportunity . . . The States is an enormous, lucrative market, and Verity Ellis knows more about breaking into it than anyone.'

'But . . . ?'

'I don't know what you mean.'

'Come on, Richard. I've been working with you for long enough to spot the "but" in your tone of voice.'

'There's no "but".' There was a short silence. 'But—'

Jo burst out laughing. 'I knew it!'

'All I would say is this: go with your gut. I've checked out Verity's proposals six ways, and you'd retain plenty of creative control, and we'd stand to make loads of money. It looks like a win-win. But *you* have to be happy. You have to feel this is the right thing for you.' He laughed softly. 'Listen to me – I'm going soft in my old age. "Go with your gut." They'd kick my arse in the City for saying something like that.'

'Thank you, Richard,' she said. 'If I ever needed proof that you were absolutely the right person to partner with, I just had it.'

The meetings that afternoon were successful, and when the last lawyer had left, Verity turned to Jo.

'It wouldn't be a trip to the Big Apple if I didn't take you to The View,' she said.

'The View?'

'You'll see.'

The View, it transpired, was a revolving restaurant, forty-eight floors above Times Square. If she was in New York, she was going to have the full experience, thought Jo, so she ordered a Cosmopolitan at the bar. She knew it was tacky, but she gave her camera to Verity to take pictures of her sitting on the bar stool sipping her drink, with the breath-taking view over her shoulder.

They were shown to a table, and looked out at the low rays of sun bouncing off the glass canyons below them.

'I love this city,' said Verity, sipping her drink. 'Anything is possible here. Absolutely anything. And Jo . . . it's yours.'

'What is?'

'The city. You can take it. Now we've looked at the com-petition, the set-up costs, the possible premises, I think Jungletown US will be a winner. I feel it in my water, and I'm never wrong. Take a look at those streets, baby, because you're about to own them.'

Jo looked. She imagined being the woman who bought her coffee at Starbucks each day and walked to her office in her trainers with her Louboutins in her bag. She imagined a flagship store in the East Village and new shops springing up all the way across the States. She imagined Zach and Imi in matching duffel coats boarding a yellow school bus and shouting, 'Bye, Mom!'

Verity had gone quiet, so Jo started describing her photog-raphy project. To be honest, because she didn't really know what she had been trying to do, she wasn't able to articulate it very well, but she kept talking. The changing vista and the bar turning, albeit slowly, made the Cosmopolitan do the work of three drinks and she soon felt quite giggly. She was a lightweight. A few years of pregnancy and breastfeeding, followed by a few more years of frequently broken nights, meant she usually drank very little, and felt the effects very quickly.

Verity, on the other hand, who was drinking whisky on the rocks, seemed very sober. Jo remembered from their night out clubbing that Verity seemed to have an enormous capacity for alcohol, without showing any ill effects. She was vaguely conscious that she was talking much more than Verity was. Jet lag, overstimulation and exhaustion were combining to make her drop her guard.

'So, Verity,' she said searchingly, 'are you happy? I mean, really happy?'

Verity regarded her coolly. 'Is this the part where we have a big heart-to-heart?'

'No, no, not at all,' stuttered Jo. 'I just, you know, wanted to know. You've made some difficult choices, and achieved amazingly. But it must have come at a price.'

'Must it?'

'Of course. You can't have everything. No one can.'

'I think I have everything,' said Verity. 'I love my work, and I have as much money as I need for the things I enjoy.'

'But . . .'

'But what? I don't have a husband and two lovely kids and a cute suburban semi and fulfilment?'

'That's not what I meant. But there is more to life than work . . .'

'There is,' said Verity, and Jo could see she was getting a little irritated. 'I'm just not sure why you assume I don't have it. As it happens, I am married. I've been with the same person for ten years, and a couple of years ago, when they changed the law in New York State, she became my wife. We have a great house that we renovated ourselves, we have dogs we adore, loads of good friends, and we're godparents to my brother's kids, whom we see most weekends. We sail, we belong to a book club, we throw parties. Does it sound to you like I don't have it all? And before you jump to conclusions, it's not because I'm gay and childless. I can take you out now and introduce you to fifty successful, married women with children who are at the top of their professions in this city.'

'I'm sorry,' said Jo shamefacedly. She suddenly didn't feel quite so drunk after all.

'This isn't some nineties romcom, Jo, where the woman has to choose between her job and her family. There's a world of difference between what you can have, and what you want to have.'

Verity took a massive gulp of her drink. 'Sorry, I didn't mean to be so harsh.'

'You weren't harsh,' said Jo. 'Just truthful.'

'Was it easier when you could pretend I was a hard-boiled, ball-breaking businesswoman with an empty and meaningless existence?'

'Was what easier?'

'Making the decision not to bring Jungletown to the States.'

As Jo opened her mouth to protest, she realised she had made the decision. She'd made it standing by the Brooklyn Bridge talking to Richard. She'd made it when she realised that taking pictures for Lee was more exciting than going to a meeting with lawyers.

'It's not a no,' said Jo. 'It's a not yet. The timing isn't right for me and my family, and it's not the right time for the brand. I think Jungletown has to do some growing up as a company before we go international.'

'Don't be sorry. I'm glad we went through this process. It's been great spending time with you, and I've learned a lot. It's still hands down the best children's clothing retail idea I've come across. If you change your mind about starting up here and want to just sell a franchise, give me a call.'

Jo nodded. Verity was being very magnanimous, and she had no doubt that as soon as she was on the plane, Verity would try to proceed with her own version of Jungletown. Jo made a note to ring Richard first thing to make sure their brand, their designs and their name were locked down and trademarked. She had no doubt that if Verity got her way, the US stores would be highly commercial, with mass-produced clothing and children's entertainers controlling the action. Jungletown's charm was in the higgledy-piggledy way it was run – part mad magical interior, part Holly's lively designs and Mel's quirky personality, part Jo herself. And that was what she wanted to preserve. That, and to go home to Zach and Imi and Lee.

She wished Verity goodbye and made her way back to her hotel. She downloaded all the pictures from her camera on to her laptop, and spent three hours cropping and adjusting them and deleting some that were no good. When she had twenty shots she liked, she opened some free blogging software, created a page and started to type.

My love,

A while ago, you asked me for help, and I was too busy to listen. I'm sorry I let you down. I know I can't fix that, but I wanted you to know I am there for you, in any way you need me.

I want to give you the gift of inspiration. I walked the streets of this incredible city, and because I missed you so much, I tried to see it with your eyes. I hope something in here lights a little spark in you. I'll be home in less than forty-eight hours, and I hope that together we can fan that spark into life.

I love you,

Jo

She uploaded the pictures one by one, captioning them where they needed explanation, letting some of them speak for themselves. By the time she finished and looked at the time, it was 2 a.m. Lee would just be getting up with the kids, probably sitting on the sofa watching a cartoon with Zach while Imi sprawled on his lap and drank her milk. She wished with all her heart she was on that sofa too. She took out her mobile and texted a web address to him – www.lovelettertolee.com.

She closed down her laptop, rang reception and booked a wake-up call and crawled into bed. She was cold, her body ached from sitting still for so long and she was very, very tired. She had just dozed off when her phone rang. She answered it sleepily.

'Hey.'

'Hey, you.' Lee's voice sounded raw and hoarse.

'You okay?'

'What? Yeah.'

'It sounds very quiet in the background.'

'I'm out in the garden. Mum and Dad are inside, giving the kids breakfast, and they're going to take them to the soft-play centre.'

'That's brave of them.'

'Well, I begged them to. I'm paying.'

'Are you sure you're okay?'

'I got your love letter.'

'Oh.'

'Jo . . . it's the most beautiful thing . . . I think the most beautiful thing anyone's ever made for me. But I don't deserve it. I don't deserve you.'

'Oh, my love, I'm the one who should be saying that. I've been the most self-obsessed, selfish cow for the last few months, and I've let you down, time after time—'

'Jo,' said Lee, and she thought she could hear him crying. 'I need to tell you something.'

She listened while he told her about Miranda. He didn't try to justify his actions, or put any of the blame on her. He just baldly, honestly, told her how he had let a playground friendship get out of hand to satisfy his ego, knowing that Miranda was vulnerable, lonely and grieving. When he told her about the kiss, Jo felt ill. So ill that she thought she might actually have to drop the phone and run to the bathroom to vomit. After a while, she realised he had stopped talking.

'Jo?' he said, obviously terrified of the silence from her end of the line.

'You know, it's funny – when you rang, it reminded me of the last time we spoke on the phone when I was staying in a hotel. Do you remember?'

'The night we said we loved each other. I'll never forget it.'

'Wow. How times change.'

'I still love you, Jo. I love you a thousand times more than I did that night, and I loved you a lot then.'

'Those are good words, but they're just words.'

'They're not just words.'

'Last night, you loved me so much you kissed another woman while our children were asleep in the next room.'

'I'm sorry. I will be sorry every day for the rest of my life. Please. Just come home.'

'I can't talk to you any more now,' said Jo. 'I have to sleep. Bye.' And she cut off the call. She wasn't lying. The urge to sleep overcame her like a powerful sedative and she curled into a ball under the quilt and closed her eyes. It wasn't until the 11 a.m. wake-up call roused her that she saw her pillow was wet and she had been crying in her sleep.

She was leaving on an evening flight, landing in London early the following morning. She spent the day wandering the streets. She took no photographs, but she bought gifts for the kids and for Holly and Mel. Then, on impulse, she walked into the Christian Louboutin store on Madison Avenue and maxed out her credit card on a pair of insanely spectacular sky-high heels. She might not be getting New York, but she could still have the shoes.

She spent a lot of the flight staring at the blackness outside the aeroplane window and trying to wrestle a fraction
of armrest from the garlic-scented obese American who
snored beside her. It wasn't the ideal environment in which
to think through potentially life-altering events, and in the
end she gave up and dozed. What would she do when she
came through the arrivals gate and saw Lee? She didn't
know. All she knew was that if he brought her flowers, she
was going to tell him where to stick them, one by one.
Sideways.

She disembarked and made her way through to the
arrivals hall. As soon as she came through the doors,
she was almost knocked flying by the Zach whirlwind. He
jumped into her arms and started talking so quickly she
could barely hear a word. He was trying to get all his news
out at once, and she laughed and kissed his chubby cheeks,
breathing in the smell of his hair and skin like a drug. Lee
was standing back, holding Imi on his hip. Jo struggled over,
still holding Zach and dragging her case.

'Hi,' she said.

'Hi.'

She couldn't work out who looked more apprehensive –
Lee, who was staring at her face, trying to read her
expression, or Imi, who seemed overwhelmed with shyness
and wouldn't look at her at all. She dropped the handle of
her case and stepped closer, so she could gather up Imi with
her other arm. She hugged both her children as if her life
depended on it, then turned to Lee.

'Let's go home,' she said.

They barely spoke on the drive back to Hendon. Zach had

a million things to say, and he and Imi sang 'Incy Wincy Spider' (or an approximation thereof) about twenty times, so the lack of conversation wasn't awkward. When they got home, Jo opened her suitcase and let the children pull everything out of it in search of presents. She'd hidden small things inside socks, under jumpers and folded flat in the various compartments of her suitcase. By the end of it, the living room was strewn with her underwear, but Zach and Imi were ecstatic.

They all had something to eat, and it was soon clear that both kids were exhausted. Jo took them both upstairs and put them either side of her on the big bed. Within minutes, they were both asleep. She slipped from between them and went back downstairs. Lee was sitting at the table, his iPad in front of him.

'I know we have a lot to talk about,' he said, 'but I wanted to show you something. It's my response to your love letter.' He looked wretched, and his eyes were full of tears. 'Please, Jo, will you look at it?'

She nodded reluctantly. 'Okay,' she said, sitting down at the table.

Lee passed her the iPad. 'Open this,' he said, pointing to an icon on the screen.

Jo tapped on the icon and it opened a blog page, not unlike the one she had sent to Lee. It contained a series of images. The first was the title page of a book – a children's book. In quirky, scribbled script across the top were the words *The Adventures of Flo and Jack and Pimmy*. Below the title, there was a drawing of a little girl, with poker-straight yellow-blonde hair (it looked as if Lee had drawn the hair using a bright yellow highlighter pen), a turned-up nose and a fiercely determined expression. There was something very familiar about her, and with a start, Jo realised she was looking at herself. Lee had re-imagined her as a feisty cartoon six-year-old. The little girl, Flo, was holding a toy lion with a crazy, curly mane and a mischievous expression. At her feet sat a white Persian kitten, her paws tidily together, with wide, bright green eyes. The lion and kitten, Jack and Pimmy, were clearly meant to be Zach and Imi. The drawing style was cartoonish and free, using strong black lines and occasional vivid flashes of colour, like Flo's hair and Pimmy's eyes. The background was a photograph, which Lee had faded and made transparent. She recognised it as a shot of the front of their house, with the twin lemon trees in pots that flanked their front door. The style made the idea of the book clear – little Flo lived a vivid imaginary life, and the real world faded into the background when she went on adventures with her trusty sidekicks.

She clicked on to the next page.

'Today, Flo is a cowgirl.' Flo was standing, legs apart and hands on her hips. She was wearing a cowboy hat that was too small for her, and Jo recognised it as one from Zach's toy box. She thought it had originally belonged to a teddy bear. Flo was also wearing a red-and-white checked gingham dress, which was a remarkably accurate rendition of the dress Jo had worn all those years before in the first performance project she had done with Lee. The background was the outside of a bar, and Lee had hand-drawn a sign that hung jauntily on it. The sign said 'Saloon', but Jo recognised the bar as the Rosie, their student local.

The next page said, 'Then she is a fairy.' This time Lee had drawn Flo in a sparkly white dress, wearing ballet shoes, with small gossamer wings (although the wings were clearly secured with rather frayed elastic). The faded backdrop was Sadler's Wells, and she knew he was drawing her that night at the theatre, just before they had declared their love. Jack the lion and Pimmy the kitten were in the audience, applauding wildly.

On the third page, the background was a bathroom with a shower curtain covered in green palm trees and bright parrots. Jo smiled – she recognised the curtain from Lee's parents' house, and she knew the palm-tree design had been an influence in his designs for Jungletown. Flo was wearing a pith helmet and holding a big magnifying glass, and the lion and the kitten sat either side of her. They were both wearing Monkeyman T-shirts. 'Today, Flo, Jack and Pimmy are exploring the jungle,' read the text. An orange and black striped towel lay on the floor, twisted into a coil, and Lee had added a snake's eyes and forked tongue to one end of it. The cord for the light had bright green leaves growing from it, and a monkey peeked out from behind the shampoo bottles.

The fourth and last page was a cityscape of giant skyscrapers. Jo recognised the photograph as one she had taken in New York. Flo was a tiny figure, alone at the bottom of the page, looking up at the giant buildings. 'When Flo goes to the big city,' said the script at the top of the page, 'Jack and Pimmy miss her very much.'

'When did you . . . ?' she asked, looking up at Lee.

'All night. I haven't slept,' he said. 'You were right. Your photographs were the inspiration I needed. The idea for the book just came together. These are just some rough drafts, and obviously there'd be more text . . .' He seemed to have run out of things to say, or the courage to say them, so he stopped.

'It's good,' said Jo. Lee waited. 'No, it's better than good. It's beautiful. It's just . . .'

'Just what?'

'Very personal. I mean . . . it's us.'

'I know. This book isn't for anyone else. This book will be just for you. And maybe for Zach and Imi, if you wanted to share it with them.'

He continued. 'This isn't all I did yesterday. While the kids were at school in the morning, I logged my details with five freelance agencies. I registered a domain name for my own portfolio website and made a holding page. I made an appointment with the GP to talk about the possibility that I might need anti-depressants, and I definitely want to see a therapist, and I found the names of three possible couples counsellors for us to see together.'

'Wow,' said Jo. She kept touching the screen in front of her, moving around the image of little Flo, alone in the big city. 'You have been busy.'

'I messed up,' said Lee. 'I will do anything to fix it. Anything.'

'No. We messed up. I messed up. A lot. I always thought we had enough love between us to get through anything, but . . . I just let my life fill up. Work, stress, the kids, domestic stuff . . . I ran out of space for you.' Jo took a deep breath. 'Us. You and me together,' she said. 'That's the centre of everything, isn't it? Without that, it's all going to just fly apart and shatter.'

Lee nodded.

She reached out and touched the screen lightly. 'Thank you for everything you've done. I will try, with you, to fix what we have.'

'Thank you,' said Lee quietly.

'You're not in the pictures,' said Jo.

'What?'

'These pictures. I'm in them, Zach and Imi are in them, but you're not.'

'I am in them. I'm in the background. I am the background. You . . . you and the kids . . . you're the magic, and the colour in my world. Without you . . .'

Lee held out his hand, and she looked at it for the longest time. Finally, slowly, she took it.

33

HOLLY NOW

On a blustery autumn day, Holly and Jo met for coffee. Or at least, Holly thought wryly, in the old days it would have been coffee. Under the new, more corporate regime, it was probably a tax-deductible breakfast meeting. She hadn't seen Jo for weeks – Jo had had her whirlwind trip to New York, and Holly had been deep in house clearance when she returned. Then Jo and Lee had gone off for a three-week summer holiday in Cornwall, and had only just got back. Jo was a bit late, and Holly was already spooning the chocolatey foam off her cappuccino when she came rushing through the door. She looked fabulous, with a rich golden tan that defied the grey rainy weather outside, and a simple but very classy chocolate-brown wrap dress. She waved to Holly, placed her order at the counter and came to sit down. As she put her bag on the floor and crossed her legs, Holly noticed her shoes.

'Oh my,' she said reverently. 'Louboutins?'

'Yes,' said Jo. 'I'll be paying for them till Zach goes to university, and I know I shouldn't be wearing them in the rain, but I love them like one of my children.'

Holly laughed. 'Shoes should be worn – they cry if you don't wear them.'

'That's what I tell them. And besides, if some nasty New Yorker had bought them instead of me, the weather's worse there. I told them they got off lightly.'

Holly smiled. It was good to see that despite the sleek new look, and the undeniable corporate success, Jo was still just the same.

'How was Cornwall?'

'Oh, like heaven. We had this scruffy old cottage, and we just poddled about on the beach all day. The weather was wonderful. I read about ten books, and we caught up on the four years of films we've missed by watching loads of DVDs. This last year has been' – Jo searched for the right words – 'amazing and brilliant and insanely stressful and hard. And Lee and I . . . have both taken the strain rather. We needed some time away from everything, just to be together. It was perfect. I feel rested and full of energy. Ready for anything.'

'And Zach started in reception?'

'Yes. He's loving it.'

'Where did he go? It's not the same school as Martha, is it?'

Jo frowned a little. 'No. We got him into a little school in Woodside Park. Very outdoorsy, very small, and with lots of personal attention. It seemed to be the best fit for him.'

'I'm sure Martha will miss him. And Miranda. I know she liked the kids to play together.'

'Yes, well,' said Jo, and her expression hardened. 'Things change. So how are things with you?'

'Well, pretty much as you see me. Mum's house is still on

the market, but we've had an offer. It's from a property developer, which means it'll almost certainly be pulled down and replaced with a block of flats. I don't mind – in fact, I'm quite happy to see it go – but David and Miranda are being a bit sentimental about it. Personally I don't think we can afford to be picky in this market. I think they'll agree to accept the offer in the end though.'

'Wow. And how's your flat?'

'I love it. You must come for a meal. It's nice now, and not so much like student digs. I have a bed and every-thing – not just a mattress on the floor. And real plates too.'

'Wow. Real plates. That's a big step.'

'And while we're doing a catch-up, I never heard about your New York trip?'

'It was very interesting. We're not doing a deal with the Americans in the near future – I suppose you've worked that out. But the trip helped me to think very hard about the business, and how it's grown, and what I want it to be. And what I've decided is that I want to grow it, but here in the UK, and I want to keep alive the principles that we used to start it. If we get so big that we can't have great floor staff who care about the kids, or we're sourcing mass-produced clothes from sweatshops in the Far East, I think we'll have lost our way.'

Holly nodded. Maybe Richard had brought a business mind and a cash injection to Jungletown, but there was no doubt that the heart of the company was still all Jo's.

'Which brings me to you,' said Jo. 'I wanted to meet you today for a catch-up, but also to talk about your future, and what you want to do.'

'Ah, now there's a huge question,' said Holly, laughing. 'How long have you got?'

'I thought about it all a lot when I was on holiday. We started Jungletown as a little neighbourhood shop, and it was all a bit amateurish while we found our way. But it's growing into something different, and I don't want you or Mel to feel left behind, or that you're square pegs in round holes, if you know what I mean.'

'I think so.'

'I spoke to Mel yesterday, and we're offering her a promotion to Head of Staff. She won't work in the shop any more. She'll be based in the offices in Angel, and then she'll go around recruiting and training staff whenever we open a store, and visiting stores to make sure the standards remain high.'

'That sounds perfect for Mel.'

'It means quite a lot more money for her, and she deserves it. She's worked so hard and been so brilliant in making the shop a success.' Jo paused. 'And so have you. I could never, ever have done this without you. You created the look and feel of Jungletown's products, and you set the standard. It's as much your shop as it is mine.'

'It sounds like there's a great big "however" coming.'

'Well, there is and there isn't. I'm here in two capacities today – Jo your boss and Jo your friend. Jo your boss wants to offer you the position of Senior Designer, and the commission to create a new range four times a year. You'd hand over the buying of all outsourced items to Gary. All you'd do is design.'

'That sounds . . . great.'

'And now I'm hearing a "however" from you too. And this is where Jo your friend wants to say something. Holly, you've been to hell and back in the last couple of years . . . first the whole thing with Damon and your company in South Africa, then your mum. I want to hang on to you with both hands, because you're an amazing designer and a precious friend, but I have to ask you – what do you want to do? Do you want to design clothes for kids, or should you be launching your own label? What's the right thing for you? Because that's what you should choose to do.'

'I don't know . . .' Holly stuttered. 'I haven't really thought about it . . .'

'Of course you have. I know you're coming into some money from your mum. And I saw pictures of the dress you designed for Serena. You must miss the creative control and the challenge. You're so talented, Holly, and – I can't believe I'm saying this – you're too good to be designing little smocked dresses and dungarees for kids.'

'Richard would have a coronary if he heard you say that.' Holly smiled.

'Well, he would and he wouldn't. Under the banker exterior, Richard's a real softy. He's all for people following their dreams and being happy.' She took a gulp of her coffee and looked at her watch. 'I don't want an answer from you now. Think about it. Think about what you want to do. You have a place at Jungletown for as long as you want it. But if you choose something different, we'll cheer you all the way . . . and be first in line to be your customers.' She kissed Holly on the cheek and was gone.

It was a very strange position to be in – absolute freedom

to do what she wanted, and the financial wherewithal to do it. Not surprisingly, Holly was paralysed with indecision. But then something happened to make up her mind, at least in the short term – she received a summons to appear as a witness in Damon's fraud trial in South Africa. She went to Jo and explained the situation.

'They say I would be needed for a few days – a week at most,' she explained.

'Seems a long way to go for such a short time,' said Jo. 'Why don't you take a few weeks? See some old friends?'

'I can't take any more time off,' said Holly. 'I was away so much when my mum was ill.'

'Nonsense,' said Jo. 'You did amazing work from home. If it makes you feel better, take it as unpaid leave. See it as a sabbatical.'

A sabbatical, thought Holly. She liked the idea of that. 'I could also meet with some suppliers,' she said. 'Make some contacts for Gary. Right in the beginning, we did talk about sourcing some stuff from South African cooperatives.'

'That would be great,' said Jo.

Once she had decided to go, and tentatively emailed a few South African friends, Holly started to get excited. As the weather got colder and the nights longer in London, she thought about spring in Johannesburg. She imagined lying on a lawn in the sun in the shade of a jacaranda tree. She thought about barbecues by the swimming pool and summer evenings drinking wine. All of the friends she emailed replied enthusiastically, and Pierre, her old housemate, who had bought a house with his husband in an upmarket area called Parkview, invited her to stay. She started thinking about going to see some African designers, getting ideas, maybe shopping for fabric at the Plaza . . . the more she thought about it, the more she couldn't wait. She hadn't realised how much she had missed South Africa. The awfulness with Damon had clouded everything, but before he wrecked things, she had been happy there. She had loved the lifestyle, the sun and the crazy, entrepreneurial spirit of the city.

One evening, as she sat in her flat with her feet on the radiator doing some sketches for the Jungletown spring range, she heard the Skype ringtone on her laptop. It was Pierre, and she clicked to answer the call. He had his webcam on, and she could see he was sitting on the wide veranda of his new house. She could hear the night-time crickets chirping in the background, and Pierre was lounging in shorts and a T-shirt.

'My darling!' he cheered, when he saw her come up on his webcam. 'How's it going?'

'Cold. Cold and wet and miserable. I can't wait to get on a plane and come to you,' she said.

'Everyone is so excited to see you. I've had about a million calls to ask if you're coming back to stay.'

'No. I wish!' Holly laughed.

'Well, why not?' Pierre said. 'You've got a work permit. Once the trial is finished, your name will be clear, and everyone is always talking about how much they miss Doradolla, and how they'd love to be able to buy those dresses again. There was even a retrospective in a magazine the other day . . . "Beautiful things we miss".'

'That's very flattering, but it's not really compelling market research . . .' said Holly.

'Well, come and see for yourself. I think you'd have an amazing time.'

'I'm supposed to be buying a house in London and building a grown-up career . . .'

'So? Come and do it here. God knows, you'll get a much better house for your pounds here than you'd get in London. You could buy a mansion!'

Holly just laughed.

'*Ja, ja,*' said Pierre, 'laugh at me. But we're going to start the propaganda campaign when you get here. Now listen, my *skattie*, I didn't phone you just to chat. We need to make some plans, because right now you've been invited to at least two parties every night of your trip. Have you got your diary?'

Moving back to South Africa. Could she do it? Did she want to? She didn't know. Pierre painted a very tempting picture, and he was right, she would get more for her money there than in the UK. Also, surely it would be much harder to launch a fashion label in huge, design-saturated, jaded London than in Johannesburg? What was holding her back? It wasn't as if her family needed her, and while she had friends, they all had lives of their own. About the only thing that stood in her way was Fraser.

Actually, what stood in her way were her feelings for Fraser. She hadn't bargained on falling for him, but she had. He was warm and funny and easy to be with, and she found him irresistibly sexy, not in the domineering, powerful way Damon was sexy, but in a different way. He was disarming and charming, and would spend hours pleasuring her sexually, making her come and come, and then he'd make her laugh with his terrible jokes, and then cook her a fabulous dinner. Fraser had shown her that a relationship didn't need to be edgy and dramatic and unpredictable to be romantic and fulfilling. It could be safe, and fun, and the other person could be reliable and still keep her interest. She thought it was possible that she might be falling in love with him, but what he felt for her was hard to say.

It was very frustrating. He was always lovely to her. He rang when he said he would, was affectionate and caring and seemed to be very interested, but they were still only seeing each other a few times a week. He hadn't asked her to meet Finlay again, or talked about the future, and he definitely hadn't mentioned the L-word. He seemed happy to keep things on a fairly casual basis, and Holly, afraid of ruining things when they were going so well, resisted the urge to push the issue.

She had to accept that it was a casual relationship, that was all, and as a sensible, adult woman, she couldn't factor it into her decision-making process. She decided that she would go to South Africa with a totally open mind. She'd investigate the possibility of resurrecting Doradolla, look at some houses and generally get a feel for life there. Then she'd be able to weigh it against the options she had here in the UK.

On the day she was due to fly out, she arranged to meet Fraser for a late lunch in a riverside pub in Putney.

'I hate goodbyes,' she told him. 'We'll have a giggle, drink too much wine and then I'll drag my case over Putney Bridge and get on the Tube.'

'You had me at "drink too much wine",' said Fraser. 'I'll leave the car at home.'

He looked very handsome in a nicely tailored shirt in a dark plum. If Holly had done nothing else for him, she thought, she seemed to have improved his dress sense and got him to wear some more adventurous colours. He ordered a bottle of champagne, and they shared a seafood platter. Chat was easy and they laughed and shared a few delicious, garlic-buttery kisses. After Fraser's second glass, he took her hand.

'I want you to have an amazing time,' he said. 'I'm so envious . . . you're going into summer while we head down the long dark road into winter.'

Holly waited for him to say something more, but he smiled, took a big gulp of his wine and said, 'The world is your oyster, my lovely Miss Evans, and you're the pearl.'

'I don't know what that means.'

'It means . . . I know that you're going to have a very enthusiastic welcoming committee in Johannesburg. I know it'll be very tempting to stay, and I want you to know that I support you in doing what's best for you. Because I care about you. And I want you to be happy.'

Holly smiled at him, but she couldn't help feeling gutted. He was saying exactly what she had already decided – that he shouldn't be a factor in her decision – but she wished . . . well, never mind what she wished. He clearly didn't feel the same way. She checked her watch. 'Bloody hell! Look at the time. I need to get going. It's going to take me at least fifteen minutes to get to the station.'

'Do you want me to come along and help with your bags?'

'Nope. No goodbyes, remember? Besides, I only have one pull-along suitcase . . . a suit for court, and then a bunch of bikinis and sundresses. I've learned you should never travel with more baggage than you can carry yourself.'

'And on that very profound note . . .' Fraser smiled. 'Bye, Holly. Travel hopefully.'

He stood to kiss her lightly and hug her, and then she left, without looking back.

She'd expected to feel more elated to be on her way, but she felt deflated as she began to walk across Putney Bridge, dragging her case. So that was it. Fraser had, in a way, sent her on her way a free woman. And he had done it because he was a nice guy. A nice guy that she liked more than she wanted to admit, in fact the very nicest guy she'd met in a long time, probably ever. Was she being stupid? Should she be fighting for him? Or was he genuinely not interested? She stopped in the middle of the bridge. She didn't have time to go back, but did she have time to ring him? Would she be mad to? Did she really want him to reject her over the phone as well? No, best just to go. She started to walk again, a little quicker this time.

She heard someone panting heavily behind her, and she thought it was a rather out-of-shape jogger or a mugger with asthma. Either way, she had better get out of his way. She stepped closer to the railing and drew her suitcase out of the path of the oncoming runner, but the panter didn't run past her. He stopped.

'I lied,' gasped Fraser.

'What?'

'I lied. I said you should go and be happy. I don't want you to. I mean – I do want you to be happy, but I want you to be happy with me. I've been trying to play it all cool and grown-up and sensible, trying to give you as much space as you need, but I bloody can't do it any more. I love you, Holly, I want to be with you, and I very much wish to be a factor in your decisions about your future.' And then he kissed her hard, and for a very long time.

'Now I'm going,' he said. 'No goodbyes. But travel safely, and every mile you go, please remember that I love you.' He walked back along the bridge, turning once to wave and blow her a kiss. Through the whole encounter, which lasted maybe two minutes, she hadn't said a word.

Holly stood, gripping the handle of her suitcase tightly. She turned and looked down the river, towards London. The sun was sinking low, throwing mellow rays on to the water. Love, opportunity, freedom. It wasn't every day you got all three.

THE END

ACKNOWLEDGEMENTS

They say it takes a village to raise a child, and I would argue it takes a small city to write a book. Whether it was correcting dodgy punctuation and geography, offering emotional support or answering the author's dim-witted questions about various subjects, so many people have been part of the journey that ends with my writing this page. As the book has been a year in the making, I am sure I will forget someone. Please forgive me . . . my gratitude is unending even if my memory is not.

As always, first on the list is my agent, Caroline Hardman and her partner in crime Jo Swainson, outgoing editor Charlotte van Wijk and her assistant Nicola Budd, and new editor Jo Dickinson and Kathryn Taussig. Six women who have done so much to support, guide, refine, polish and defend my work throughout this process. It would be a poorer book without them. In fact, one might argue it wouldn't be a book at all without them. If I may be forgiven the cheesy title reference, wonder women indeed.

As is the author's privilege, I took great creative licence with my plans for Jo's shop and how it might run. However, I owe a debt of thanks to Lisa Usiskin of Happy Days Children's Clothes, who met with me and talked through the nuts and bolts of running a children's clothing business. She's on facebook if you're looking for something fabulous for your kids. A big thank you also to my dear friend Debbie Melliard, for her insider's advice on Goldsmith's.

As always, many thanks to the great motley crew of friends and family who enrich my life and give so much, who (face-to-face or online), have offered information, character names (yes you, Tina Vaghela), an ear while I wrestle with a knotty plot problem, tea, distraction and chocolate. My heart is fuller (and my behind is wider) thanks to your contributions.

Special mention must go to Maureen Parrington, who won the right to name a character in this book at an Auction of Promises at St Mary's Church, Hendon. She chose her husband Ian Hope as the beneficiary of this dubious honour. I have stolen rather more than the name, and my fictional Ian is a music teacher too, and has some of the real man's sterling characteristics. I hope he will forgive me a little artistic licence.

It was extremely important to me to write about the care of the ill and dying, as my sister Sandy died of cancer in 2004, and the support we got from hospice nurses in South Africa has always stayed with me. More recently, my mum-in-law Doreen passed away at New Cross Hospital in Wolverhampton, and we were overwhelmed at the care and compassion she received from the nurses, and their boundless patience and kindness to us, her relatives. I have no words for those who are brave enough to guide us through the most difficult and sad times of our lives. These are people of great heart, and they deserve our support. If the issues covered in this book touch you, please donate to Macmillan Cancer Support: www.macmillan.org.uk/Donate.

In memory of Doreen Smithies (1930–2012),
a wonder woman indeed.